LODESTONE

LODESTONE

KATHERINE FORRISTER

GenZ
The Future of Publishing

Supervising Editor: Caitlin Chrismon
Associate Editors: Emily Chamberlain, Jaret Czajkowski

Cover Illustration: Deny_Wika
Cover Design and Internal Formatting: L. Austen Johnson, www.
allaboutbookcovers.com

ISBN (eBook): 978-1-952919-23-7
ISBN (paperback): 978-1-952919-24-4

GenZPublishing.org
Aberdeen, NJ

For Tom, who taught me to play pretend and inspired me to write it all down, and for Lindsay, who adventured with me through my favorite stories and helped me see them through new eyes.

CONTENTS

It was late in the day, and there wasn't much magic left. Melaine struggled to guide the pure magic that originated in the marrow of her bones into her clenched fist. The deep power that nestled in every infinitesimal pocket of her body pulsed with a vibrancy not unlike a beating heart, ready to break through her skin and forge the physical with the metaphysical.

She opened her fist and revealed a dark purple gem that flashed under the sun's glaring light.

"That's good, love," said the rough-hewn voice of Melaine's current customer, a stranger. "Better be a good one, aye? I gots a job to do. A big one."

She avoided looking at the man's pockmarked face and squinty eyes and stared at the stone in her palm, diamond in shape and purple-black like a bruise. Every bird-bone of her wiry body felt petrified. The stone scorched her palm from the dense magic she had poured into its confines, but frost crystallized her veins. She waited to thaw and for her lungs to regain the ability to push outward. She begged her muscles to overcome the inertia it would take to become a living being again instead of a vulnerable statue in the streets of Stakeside.

Finally, her lips drew a breath. Her exhale was icy fog, though it was a fine autumn day. The fresh lodestone in her hand grew cold.

She fell back against a grimy brick wall that formed a seam between two ramshackle tenant buildings, her senses reeling from exhaustion. The early autumn sun, drumming the last beats of summer's heart on the land below, warmed her veins, but the damp chill of the wall pressed through her brown threadbare dress.

Her customer, who stank of rotting teeth, leaned into her. His hot, grubby hand peeled the fresh lodestone from her fingers. He tossed it in the air and caught it with a heavy thump before wrapping his greedy paw around it, hiding his prize from view. He grunted with satisfaction as he felt the magic she had infused inside.

"It'll do the job, won't it, love?" he asked, his squinting eyes meeting hers as he gave her a yellowed smile. "You're the best, they say. You charge enough for it, don't you?"

He grasped a fistful of her lank, black hair. Melaine hissed as the back of her head knocked against the bricks, but she didn't yet have the strength to speak.

"You know what I fink? I fink you charge too much, no matter how bounced your stones are."

Melaine parted her chapped lips, drawing air from her tired lungs.

"A tuppence." Her voice was hoarse. "Like we agreed."

The man laughed, showering her with fetid spittle.

A stamp of boots on wet cobblestones rushed toward

them from down the street. The customer loosened his hold on her hair and sauntered back, though his eyes were alert as he shifted them around the huddled passersby.

Melaine kept her eyes on him. She recognized the cadence of the approaching footfalls. A young boy who roamed the streets, called Gim, had once lifted shoes from the corpse of a man who had a peg-leg. One of the boot's soles had a hole in the center from the wooden peg, causing every other of Gim's steps to sound hollow. That, combined with the flapping sound of shoes that were too big for the wearer, made his run unmistakable.

"Marm!" Gim's little voice called from down the street.

Melaine gathered her strength and pushed herself off the wall, though she swayed on her feet. Her customer bounced on his heels as he eyed the boy who was darting through people and past an empty cart, which no one had bothered moving from the middle of the road. Melaine knew Gim was harmless enough, but her current buyer didn't. Even children in Stakeside could be dangerous, either by their own gumption, or under someone else's tutelage.

The customer grunted in annoyance and flicked a coin at Melaine. It landed on the cobblestones. He gave her a last, leering expression before he shifted away down the street. Melaine braced her hand against the wall and prepared for a bout of dizziness as she stooped over to scrape the coin off the street.

Gim puffed to a halt, his damp, windswept hair falling into his eyes. He wiped a hand across his pink cheek, leaving a smear of mud in the light sheen of sweat.

"Vintor wants to see yah, marm," he said. "In his shop."

Gim's voice was a little hoarse, and his frame was as skinny as anyone's in Stakeside, but he hadn't yet outgrown the brightness of youth in his eyes. Melaine wondered how long it would take.

"He's paid you?" Melaine asked. The boy hesitated. Melaine's mouth slipped a wry curve, knowing she had caught on to his trick. "Aye, he's paid you. Go on."

She nodded down the street, though she didn't really care which way he decided to go. Gim averted his eyes. A flicker of disappointment tinged their hopeful light as he lost the opportunity to trick her into paying him twice over for his delivery. Melaine had no doubts he'd learn his trade in time.

He took off down the street at a more relaxed jog than before. Melaine was probably his last message recipient for the day. He would find some hole to crawl into for the night, most likely one of the little dens that children tended to make for themselves in the tight crawlspaces and sewer entrances where adults couldn't fit. Melaine's one-time haunt had been a half-buried supply crate at the base of the Stakeside wall, right behind the butcher's yard. She'd stayed there till she was six and then moved in with a group of fifteen or so orphaned waifs who lived together in a cistern.

That was before she'd started peddling lodestones, of course.

Melaine looked up the street in the direction the boy had come from. The sun was casting long shadows from the disheveled tenements and tiny shops, all stacked on top of one another without adhering to any real standards of structural integrity. Wooden beams jutted out at odd angles to hang crudely painted signs, most with pictures instead of words; the vast majority of Stakeside's residents couldn't read. The plaster walls were yellow with water stains and black with mildew. The thatch roofs secreted a damp, sickly sweet smell that only added to the thick stink of the streets, cramped with people, animals, excrement, rotten food, and the tang of residual magic that clung to every gutter.

Melaine mustered her strength and started walking up the street. If anyone else had asked to see her at this time of evening, she would have laughed in their face. But Vintor was one of the few people in Stakeside who was actually worth listening to. And Melaine felt a kick of cautious excitement in her breast as she suspected the nature of Vintor's upcoming discussion.

She slid the tuppence into her pocket, and it scraped against a brass key, a glass vial of corrosion potion, a small knife, and a crust of bread, all of which took up far more physical space than the simple dress pocket should allow as a result of a pocket-enlargement spell she learned a few years back.

She found the final object—her other glove—within her pocket and took it out. She pulled the glove on to her hand in a stiff but careful motion. Her fingertips slipped through the holes at the top, and she felt a knot of tension loosen when her bare palm was covered from the elements and the eyes of others. She glared at a hole near her wrist that had widened since the day before. She had already stretched the thin fabric to its limit trying to mend it, yet there it was.

Melaine scowled and covered the hole with her clenched fist.

Another day's work. Another day alive.

She paused in a moment of grim satisfaction as her strength began to return. Soon, she wouldn't have to put up with swill like that customer. Soon, her magic would be hers to keep. That or she would die trying. Melaine had avoided death for all of her twenty-one years, a feat for someone who had grown up as a Stakeside orphan. If she succeeded in her plan, she might get another sixty years. Fail, and she would be a miserable lodestone-peddler for twenty, thirty years at the most.

Even if by some miracle she did live longer, would it be worth it?

It was only recently that she began asking that question. Maybe it was reaching adulthood that had done it, but life had gotten a lot more complicated once the simplicity of childhood was gone. Once her mind had matured enough to think beyond the next meal or the next place to sleep that wouldn't attract thieves or rapists, deadlier thoughts settled in. Her gratitude for survival had altered into the question of *What would make survival worth the effort?*

Not peddling lodestones—that she knew for certain. Her bread and butter would get her nowhere but an early grave.

Melaine's strength continued to grow as she threaded her way down the streets of Stakeside. Children picked pockets, but they didn't go near Melaine. Beggars called for alms, but none bothered asking her anymore. Prostitutes smiled at passersby, their red lips chapped and their faces pockmarked from the poison of their cheap, lead-based makeup. One woman on a street corner sent a curled sneer of disgust toward Melaine's gloved hands, but another met Melaine's eyes and sent her a nod with a small, soft smile. Melaine didn't recognize her, but the newcomer must have already learned of her profession. Flesh-peddling and stone-peddling were one and the same, many people thought. Both sold aspects of their bodies. Both sold pieces of themselves. Melaine twitched a nod in return, a silent acknowledgment of mutual existence that rarely came from anyone outside of their respective lines of work. She then hurried past. The other prostitutes spared her nothing more than a passing glance.

The buildings began to stand a little straighter as Melaine walked farther. Their plastered walls were a little less yellow, and the thatch didn't smell quite so ripe. Fewer people walked along the cobblestones as the street-lamps glowed a little brighter, wearing clothes that weren't as threadbare as Melaine's. But the step-up was minuscule. No matter how much closer these buildings and their tenants were to the wall, they were still a part of Stakeside.

Melaine shivered as a chill breeze rode the evening between the cramped rows of buildings. A warming spell was out of the question in Melaine's weary state, so she dealt with the cold as best she could and tried to pick up the pace, looking forward to the small fire that no doubt burned in Vintor's hearth.

She stopped when she reached a shop whose façade stood out from those around it. It still bore the same dingy, weathered cracks and wrinkles as the rest, but the mud had been scrubbed from its plaster on a regular basis, and its door bore a tarnished, brazen knocker. The sign hanging above the entrance had an actual word stamped below its carved picture of a candlestick, a sewing needle, and a cooking pot. Though Melaine already knew what the sign said, she still focused on the letters of the single word because, as her friend Salma had told her when she began teaching her to read a few months ago, practice was the only way to get better.

The sign read: *Goods*.

Stepping into Vintor's shop was always a gamble. His store sold knickknacks and household items—all of the odds and ends you could need at one point or another in life. But there was never any way of knowing exactly what he'd have in stock at any given time. Melaine had come in once looking for an eating bowl and hadn't found one. She'd soon realized that she could never afford one from Vintor's shop anyway. Yet, as Melaine opened the door and stepped into Vintor's shop now, several stacked wooden bowls sat right by the entrance.

Other shelves and tables held an assortment of goods. Not all of the candlesticks were unused, but they all stood at least six inches tall. Some of the bowls and basins were scratched, but none had cracks or holes to lessen their function. There was a tarnished chamber pot, but it didn't reek of piss, and a couple of waste bins didn't even have a trace of magical refuse in their depths. None of the goods were dusty, and the floor under Melaine's worn boots was swept clean. And, as Melaine had hoped, a few coals burned in the small hearth at one side of the shop's interior.

Melaine smoothed her skirt and winced as crumbled leaves crackled down her dress. A single strand of her long, black hair floated to the floor until it curled up like a tiny worm near her boot. Vintor's shop was the nicest place she had ever stepped into. She felt like she brought the filth of the street in with her each time she came.

"Melaine!" cried an exuberant voice from the front of the shop. She stepped around a protruding shelf and saw Vintor standing behind the wooden counter. His slick-backed brown hair and sculpted beard made him look like a newly shined shoe, his smile the gleaming boot buckle. Yet something was different about his smile today. It was a little too broad.

"Vintor," Melaine greeted with a cautious nod.

"By the fire, please, Melaine," Vintor said. "You look frozen."

Melaine nodded in thanks, though it bothered her that he could see anything weak about her, even if it was as simple as being cold. She tried to hide her exhaustion with a firmer resolve as she approached the fire, though its welcome heat only made her want to fall asleep right then and there.

"I have something for you," Vintor said as he joined her by the hearth. Melaine frowned as he reached into his vest pocket. He wore a blue one today, corduroy for warmth. His shirt underneath was one of the whitest she had ever seen, and though the suit coat he wore over the ensemble was dingy, it was cut from thick, green and gold brocade. Even his trousers didn't have any holes.

He bought the entire outfit used, of course. But he was still one of the finest-dressed men in all of Stakeside. Melaine felt a thrill of pride, knowing she'd had the privilege of working with him for a few months now.

Vintor, who was still smiling, had thin crow's feet around his eyes—the only telling sign of his middle age. He pulled a small item from his pocket and let it fall flat on his palm as he held it out to Melaine with an expectant shine in his green eyes.

Melaine's lips parted. "Is that—?"

She analyzed the object with a closer eye, checking for every small tell she knew that would belie a counterfeit. But the small, flat, wooden coin was flawless. Its grains were smooth, and its gleaming polish didn't bear the slight greenish tint of cheap straw-fly wax. The engraved letter "C" on its center hadn't been burned into the wood with a hot poker. It was too perfect. The "C" had been engraved with magic.

"That's regulation," Melaine said, her eyes widening as she looked back at Vintor. "Where did you get that?"

Vintor chuckled. "From my buyer. It's for you."

Melaine paused. "I don't take handouts," she said, her mind flaring with suspicion. What did Vintor want from her?

Vintor shook his head. "It's not a handout. You earned this."

He reached out to touch her shoulder in a friendly pat like she'd seen him use with others, but he withdrew his hand mid-motion. Good. He still remembered the painful shock she'd given him the last time he'd tried it.

"Melaine," he said, dropping his hand while raising the other that held the wooden coin a little higher for her inspection. He glanced at the empty shop's closed door but still lowered his charismatic voice a small amount. "Your fresh batch of lodestones fetched a higher price than I expected. The buyer was impressed. She threw this in. I already know the spell, and," he eyed her clothes, lingering on the hole in her glove, but his expression wasn't unkind, "I knew you'd appreciate something like this."

Melaine's cheeks flushed under his inspection. "What's in it?"

"A mending spell," he said. "Spinning, specifically. It allows you to spin more fabric from an article you already have. Not a large bolt, mind you, but it's useful for patching holes."

"Really?" Melaine asked. A smile almost made it to her thin lips. "You sure you're not attaching any strings to this little prize?" *Little* was a major understatement, but she couldn't let Vintor know that she thought so.

"Not a one," Vintor said, placing his hand on his heart in a solemn promise.

Melaine eyed him for a moment and then reached out and took the wooden coin from his palm between two fingers. She held it up, twisting it from one side to the other. There were more letters engraved on the back of the wooden disk, so small that Melaine would have had a hard time reading them, even if she could read without her mind stuttering to prevent the flow of words.

There was no doubt about it. This was the real thing. A regulation-quality Insight.

Melaine had only been able to get her hands on a few Insights in her lifetime, and this was only the second officially regulated one she'd ever seen in person. The first had been shown to her by a visitor of the Greasy Goat several years ago. Salma, the owner of the pub, had vouched for its authenticity, and Melaine trusted Salma. She could also recognize the differences from the counterfeited ones she herself had used before, though she'd never been fooled.

Most Insights in Stakeside weren't even attempts at counterfeiting. Though the official term—Insight—stemmed from the elitist Luxian religion's theology, the name had long-since entered day-to-day vernacular, and the actual spell to create them, while difficult, was as common as dirt. Magic was biological in nature, so any material that stemmed from living things retained the qualities necessary to become Insights. In Stakeside, children's lost teeth, dried rat tails, and matted braids of hair were passed around for tuppence. They all contained the most basic spells, and more than a year had passed since Melaine had seen any spells in circulation that she hadn't learned twice over from an Insight.

More advanced spells never made it past the Stakeside wall. No middlemen, not even Vintor, had ever bothered. No one in Stakeside could afford anything beyond basic household spells that lit candles or scrubbed residual magic—the waste byproduct of magic use—from the floors.

Some spells were taught without Insights, of course,

instead passed down through word of mouth. But the only way to *truly* learn a spell, to understand all of its components, all of its applications, and to *feel* the spell in one's bones and never forget it, was to inhale it from an Insight. They were coveted possessions, no matter what part of society one belonged to. The rich hoarded Insights and bragged to one another about how many they had, which ones were embossed with gold or silver, and how many times an object's knowledge could be consumed by different people. Then the owners would lord their Insights over each other, deciding if they would be so benevolent as to *share* the limited use of an Insight with their fellow aristocrats.

The coin in Melaine's hand was a one-timer, no question. She could use it and be done, and not have to worry about anyone trying to steal it from her in the dark.

But she couldn't use it now. She was far too drained, and learning magic from an Insight took magic from the pupil in return. She placed it in her pocket with care.

"I would say that's a taste of what's to come, but uh..." Vintor's mouth twisted in a way that made Melaine's stomach clench with worry. He sighed.

"It's a pity, Melaine," he said. "Your lodestones are better than Stakeside. Buyers from Middun were starting to talk about you, and this newest buyer was, well, *not* from Middun."

Melaine's heart picked up its pace. She had hardly dared to dream that her stones could cross the Stakeside wall into Middun, Stakeside's nickname for the middle-class district of Centara. Vintor's implication that someone from an even higher class—the aristocrats in

Crossing's Square—could want *her* lodestones was unthinkable. But the hesitation in Vintor's voice didn't reflect good news.

"I honestly thought we could give this a go," Vintor continued. "The talent of making lodestones is rare these days, and stones of your caliber are next to impossible to find. As far as I know, your stones are better than Avery Katchmore's up in Crossing's Square. I was drumming up the gossip, preparing for sales. People *were* starting to talk, but...that's not so good a thing anymore. I don't know if the news has reached Stakeside, but the Luxians are acting up again. They're starting to gain influence in certain circles. Unfortunately, those are the circles that matter to us."

"Those loons?" Melaine said. "I thought they were all still slinking underground. The ones the Overlord didn't stamp out after the war, anyway."

"The Overlord may hate them, but his overseers aren't as strict. Some are even sympathizers, I think," Vintor muttered.

Melaine frowned. She didn't much like the corrupt overseers of Dramore, either, a dozen men who controlled the populace with duplicitous smiles and deep pockets. But the true ruler of Dramore, the Overlord, was above all that—a man so great, he cast aside his birth name so no one would ever doubt his power, his reign, or his self-less devotion to his kingdom. He was and would always be known simply as the Overlord.

Vintor clicked his tongue against the roof of his mouth and slipped three fingers into each of his vest pockets. "Look, Melaine. You know how the Luxian

Order feels about lodestones. And people who make them."

"Aye, I think rounding people up and committing mass murder makes their feelings clear," Melaine said.

"You can speak lightly about it, Melaine, but relatively speaking, that wasn't so long ago," Vintor said. He twitched his head with a speck of guilt. "My aunt was a Luxian. Fanatic. The stories she would tell about her childhood, the way she'd speak about those 'cursed' lode-stoners. Melaine, I'm sorry, but I'm out. I've barely stepped into this business. I need to get out before I'm in too deep."

"Vintor, you can't be serious. Those Luxians have no power in Centara. The Overlord made sure of that. You say my stones can fetch a good price. If they're as good as you say, we could get a fortune for them, Vintor. Don't throw that chance away."

"Lodestones aren't my only chance, Melaine," he said, stepping back. He slipped his fingers from his pocket and spread his hands. "I've got other enterprises. Safer ones."

"The Overlord would never allow the Luxians to take hold again," Melaine said, her voice rising. She closed the gap Vintor had made. "Lodestones aren't illegal. They never will be. Tell your buyers—"

"The Overlord doesn't seem to care much what happens down here, does he?" Vintor said. Melaine closed her mouth. Vintor looked aside. He glanced at the door again as if the Shields were going to knock it down and arrest him for treachery right this moment. The name of Centara's law-keeping force had always sounded false to

Melaine. A shield implied protection; Melaine had only seen their blades.

"Vintor," Melaine said.

Vintor threw his hands up as though placing a wall between himself and Melaine.

"I'm done, Melaine," he said. "I paid for that last batch of stones in full. You've got your extra for the sale." He nodded to her pocket, where the Insight was stowed. "We're even."

"You're a coward, Vintor," Melaine said. "I could make you a fortune."

"You could also make me dead if things in the upper side keep going the way they are," he said. He no longer smiled.

Melaine's lip twitched as she almost let another insult fly, but she scowled and looked at the glowing coals in the hearth.

"Keep your ear to the ground, Melaine," Vintor said. His voice was kind again but resolved. "Things could get dangerous in your line of work."

"They won't come down here," she said. Vintor gave her a shrug that wasn't a disagreement. Melaine turned around and walked across the swept floor, no longer caring if she left mud-crusted footprints.

"Stakeside might be the best place for someone like you," Vintor said. Melaine heard him sigh as she reached the door. "I just mean, for a lodestone-peddler. As you said, they might not bother you down here, even if stones do get banned. No one likes coming through that wall."

"Well, you would know, wouldn't you?" Melaine said.

"Coming and going every day?" She looked over her shoulder at him. "Let me tell you something, Vintor. When I go through that gate, I won't ever be coming back."

Vintor gave her a half-smile of pity. She knew what he was thinking.

No one from Stakeside ever made it out. Even middlemen like Vintor were always destined to come back.

⚜

MELAINE NEARED THE GREASY GOAT PUB JUST AS THE streetlamps were being lit. The iron cage of the closest lamp housed no more than a candle stump. By the looks of the skinny lamplighter, with fingers so arthritic they could barely snap a flame into being, she doubted he'd be able to afford a new candle anytime soon. Melaine nearly scoffed aloud as she conjured the far-fetched image of a long-lasting candle, like those in the better parts of Centara, flickering with emerald-green everflame in a Stakeside streetlamp.

Keeping the streetlamp in sight, she crossed the opening of a shadowed alleyway.

She stopped as a man sauntered out of the darkness to stand right in front of her. It was her vile customer from earlier that evening, wearing his same leering smile. But his lips were slack, and his gait was clumsy. His breath stank of mead.

"Look who it is," he said, sucking on his teeth. His words were slurred, his eyes predatory. "I still fink you charged too much for that stone, little doxy. What's say you give me my money's worth? Sweeten the deal, eh?"

He crowded her, making her heel hit a cobblestone with the same force as her heart's next harsh beat. She slipped her hands behind her back. Tiny purple lightning bolts of defensive magic crackled at her fingertips but were far weaker than she would have liked.

"You can't afford what my stones are really worth," she said, keeping her eyes on the man's bleary, reddened stare. "You don't deserve my magic."

"Oh, I fink I deserve a lot more than just your magic, doll."

He lunged for Melaine, but she thrust out one hand and sent a painful shock into his chest. He growled and jumped back, but her magic was still weak after a full day of crafting stones. After a mere flinch, he came at her again.

Melaine ran down the alley, the hem of her dress lifting wet leaves as her boots splashed through puddles. The man's heavy steps pursued her, and her vision of escape flashed with white-hot panic as she realized he was catching up. She tried to force more magic to her fingertips, but it sputtered and went out.

The man crashed into her back and snaked an arm around her waist. She shoved her sharp elbow into his gut and clawed at his arm with dirty fingernails. He grunted but didn't relent. He grabbed her hair and yanked her head back as his other arm pinned her arms to her sides.

He pushed her to the ground. The rough cobblestones burned pain into her knees, shooting fire through her thighs and shins as his weight pressed against her back.

He shoved his chapped lips against her ear as he drove her other against the muddy street, pressing cold on to the entire length of her body. His yellow and black-pocked teeth scraped her earlobe and then bit her neck as his bony fingers tightened in her hair. Melaine gave a weak cry and struggled to pull on her depleted reserves of magic, begging her bones to send the smallest drops into her tendons and muscles. She squeezed the sap from her veins as it trickled toward her hands, but nothing came.

The brute shoved her head back down. She felt the cold of the street seep into her forehead and nose as gravel dug into her chin and grime smeared her lips. She heard the sharp pull of leather laces, and then his hot hand dug through her skirt, his fingernails sharp like the tusks of a rutting boar. She gritted her teeth and dragged her fingertips down the cobblestones as if a smithy's anvil had been pressed on the back of each hand.

The man bunched up her dirt-stained petticoat. Then he stopped.

"Oy, now, what's this?" he said. Melaine tried to glance back but couldn't move. "This is an Insight, this is." The man whistled. She heard the quiet slip of the wooden coin against the coarse cloth of his trouser pocket before his hand ran up her stocking again.

Melaine pushed herself to move with the silent word, *No*, and she slid her right hand down to her side. She finally touched the rumpled fabric of her homespun dress, and she fumbled until her spider-like fingers found her pocket, the other contents ignored by her attacker in his haste to collect the Insight. She wrapped her hand around a hot glass vial just as the man's equally warm skin touched hers.

She thumbed open the vial's protective cork and gave a hoarse, gut-wrenching yell as she slammed the back of her head onto the man's nose. He cursed and raised off of her just enough for her to twist her body, elbow him in the ribs, and hurl the burning vial at his face. A sound of a splash and a high-pitched squeal of pain blistered her ears. She ducked her head away from the spray and rolled aside as the man fell. He landed on the street, quaking and rolling in fetal agony as the frothy, puce potion ate into his flesh.

Only a couple of drops landed on the edge of Melaine's dress, eating more holes into the worn fabric. Her attacker wasn't so lucky. She watched his skin sizzle from inches away and breathed in the acrid smoke. He clutched his potion-spattered face in his hands, but the corrosive liquid burned his palms as well. He jerked them away, still screaming as he stared at his flesh being eaten away, exposing the bone in a few places. She tried to catch his wild, rolling eyes as he shook and wailed. She wanted him to see her fury.

But he rolled away into a filthy puddle in the gutter. He submerged his face and hands into the water underneath the skim of grime and brown leaves. Melaine hoped he would drown. She watched his body twitch and his hands tremble, and then he was still.

Then with a great, gurgling gasp, he raised his head and sputtered to the side. His face bore raw, speckled worm-tracks where the potion had crawled and burned. Not for the first time, Melaine almost regretted that the corrosion potion was not meant to kill. Whether the repugnant man deserved it or not, his face and hands would heal with time.

But she got some satisfaction in knowing that his plundering hands would never regain sensation, and his face would be scarred for life. His survival and those scars would spread the word to any newcomers that Melaine of Stakeside was not to be meddled with.

Melaine breathed in and out against the cobblestones. Her thin bodice and the fingerless glove on her left hand soaked in the wet cold, and her dark brown skirt and dirty white chemise did little to protect the rest of her body. A gust of wind raised goosebumps on her bare legs.

She shivered, closed her black eyes, opened them, and then found the strength to lift herself off the ground.

Her petticoat and skirt fell back down to her worn, black boots as she settled on all fours. She focused her eyes on sharpening the outlines of the mud-bordered cobblestones, pushing dizziness away. Another few breaths and she was on her feet.

She didn't bother lifting her skirt free of the mud and shuffled her feet over to the revolting man lying in the gutter.

She stooped down and plunged her hand into the man's grubby trouser pocket. Finding the Insight he'd stolen was easy; the man didn't have enough possessions to warrant a pocket-space spell. That, or he was too poor to have ever afforded the corresponding Insight. Or he was too stupid to comprehend one.

She snatched the Insight from his pocket. When she

opened her grasp, she saw she'd taken out her lodestone along with it. She paused, eyeing the purple-black stone.

"Y-you can have it back," the man whimpered against the street as his bloodshot eyes took in nothing but Melaine's ratty, laced boots.

Melaine scoffed, a hoarse rattle of a laugh. "What would I do with it?" she asked. "For someone so anxious to get a lodestone, you would think you'd understand how they work. I can't reuse my own magic, pillock."

She shoved the wooden coin back into her pocket, her jaw tight as she fought her outrage. The man's attempt to take her body was wicked, but it wasn't the first time she'd stopped a man from the act. The idea of him taking her precious Insight before she had the chance to use it was unbearable.

"The deal will be exactly what was agreed upon," she said, looking him over in disgust. She tossed the lodestone onto the cobblestones in front of his face. It rattled just like his tuppence had done.

"A pleasure," she said.

She stepped over the man who moaned like a wounded animal and onto the footpath that lined the darkening street. She fought her urge to head straight home, and instead, she walked the long way around through a couple of winding streets. She had to make sure the man wouldn't follow her, though she doubted he'd be getting up any time soon.

The encounter in the dark alley left a disgusted, violated wrench in her stomach, the same as she always felt when anyone tried to touch her. Her body and magic were tied, both inherently *hers*. She gave up one to others on a daily basis. She refused to sacrifice them both. She refused to allow anyone to *steal* her body.

Though selling her body, like so many other women and men in Stakeside did, could have been a lucrative business, she had to keep some part of her for herself. She didn't judge prostitutes for choosing to rent out their bodies; sex was their trade, and like her, everyone had to do what they could to survive these ravaging streets. But flesh-peddlers didn't sell magic as well. They could keep theirs all for themselves.

She took some comfort in knowing that no one could steal her raw magic unless she consented to part with it into a lodestone. She could protect her magic by not making any stones ahead of time and never carrying any on her person. As for her body, well, as she walked the maze of streets, thinking of the most recent brute's potion-eaten face, she took comfort in knowing that her precautions against thieves of either commodity were well-rehearsed by now.

She finally reached the back stairwell of the Greasy Goat pub and lifted her skirt to climb the flight of creaking wooden stairs softened by rot. Jagged splinters littered the bare dirt underneath, insects and worms thriving on the decay.

She had found a luxury in the place with its private entrance, unheard of in Stakeside. Most everyone else lived in cubbies above pawn shops or rank butcheries and tanning yards, those who had homes at all. There were constantly beggars on the streets, but most of them had turned thieves. No one in Stakeside had any money or food to freely give, no matter how charitable their hearts.

Melaine was glad she didn't have to fight her way through the crowded pub every time she came and went. Privacy was a necessity in her business; her riff-raff clients couldn't know where she lived. She didn't want to wake up with a knife or the rare stolen wand at her throat, nor did she want the less violent banging and whining at her door each day and night, begging for handouts.

Melaine did not run a charity. Each lodestone got her no more than a tuppence at most, a few small coins that could buy a half-loaf of bread or a chunk of soap. On a rare day, she could save up enough to buy an Insight, but after her discussion with Vintor, it seemed her only chance to learn from more Insights had been swept away before it had even begun.

The rest, and vast majority, of her earnings went toward her rent, due once a month on Summons Day. While the rich congregated on that day to shower their excessive wealth upon the overseers, done voluntarily to gain favor with the politicians, Melaine scraped up what little she had just to survive.

She reached into her spell-enlarged pocket and summoned a key to her fingers, focusing on the act more than she normally would. Even that minuscule use of magic made her sway. She had made three lodestones that day with only two-hour breaks in between. Days like this were common and necessary, but all she wanted to do now was pass out.

She shoved open the door with her shoulder and caved into her room. Her spotty vision took in the sight of a sleeping pallet, a wooden washbasin, and a dingy chamber pot. All three items were pushed close together, as they wouldn't have fit otherwise. Melaine stooped beneath the diagonal angle of the pub's rough thatched roof and squatted beside the washbasin.

That morning she had filled the basin with well water by hand and used a purifying spell to cleanse it of both disease and residual magic that would inevitably leak into the water. She'd known she would be too sapped of magic to cast the spell by evening and that her exhaustion would make it too difficult to resist the temptation to drink the tepid well water as it was.

She looked down at her hands. Even when she was alone, she felt a biting sense of shame when she had to take off her gloves. She only ever did so in public when she had to make a sale. She despised stripping off her glove in front of a buyer, baring her palm to expose her magic in the humiliating form of a black gem with a purple sheen—her signature color—unique as a fingerprint.

One naïve customer had remarked that her stones were beautiful. They weren't beautiful. They were *pieces* of Melaine. They were her magic. *Her* magic. But she would hold out her palm and offer it to anyone who could pay the price.

As much as she hated it, she couldn't risk making the stones ahead of time, in private. If they were stolen from her pocket on the streets, she would miss a sale. A customer would be angry, and some customers were dangerous when they were angry. Even the rare understanding buyer wouldn't pay for rent or supper.

Melaine tugged at the glove on her left hand and pulled it free. She laid it flat on her pallet, spreading the empty fingers like petals, and started taking off her other glove. She frowned at the hole near her wrist. It was even bigger than before, treading too close to her palm for comfort.

But Melaine felt a small bit of comfort as she remembered the Insight in her pocket. Anger rumbled in her belly as she thought of the man who had tried to steal it. The devastating conversation with Vintor threatened to replay, but she forced herself to focus only on the good aspects of the Insight for now.

Vintor had said it held a mending spell, but a *better* mending spell than any Melaine already knew. It wasn't a simple spell to stitch a tear on its own without a needle. This spell was supposed to spin *more* fabric. That's what Vintor had said.

Her heart gave an excited patter, but she would have to wait to find out if Vintor was right. As much as she wanted to inhale the knowledge, she knew her body, her mind, her abysmally low magic reserves, would never be able to handle it. Not without a night's rest first.

Besides, she desperately needed a wash.

She finished taking off the glove and laid it next to its partner. Then she slipped her hands into the washbasin and splashed water on her face. Its icy bite startled her senses. She reached for a nub of soap and sprinkled it with water, then rubbed it in circles over her bony features—a pointed nose, thin lips, hollowed cheekbones.

She scrubbed hardest on her ears and neck, the places that had been the focus of her revolting assailant's foul lips and breath. Her cheap flannel corset was so frayed and worn that she was able to slip her hands under its cracked bones to wash her torso. She took the extra time to hike up her dress and wash her legs where the man's hand—and worse—had touched her. Who knew what diseases he was carrying?

Melaine splashed water over her skin to rinse, and then she brought the last of it to her lips, not to waste a drop. She tossed the soap to the floor with a thump and slumped back onto her pallet. She stared at the ceiling, looking at each little pinprick of thatch, one by one. She traced the spiraling grains of the wooden beam that sloped over her head. She closed her eyes.

"No," she said, and opened them. She pushed herself up and reached into her pocket. She pulled out the crust of bread, but she wasn't as famished as she should have been. She fished into her pocket again and found the little wooden coin Vintor had given her.

"Why not do it now?" she asked. She made the best lodestones in Centara. Her magic was...*something*. She could push it a little harder. She had to.

Because she couldn't be stuck in Stakeside forever.

Melaine enclosed the coin in her palm and focused on its smooth wooden surface. She felt its fine gloss and then pushed deeper. She felt the tiny spirals of the wood grain, lithe as a thumbprint. She burrowed deeper and almost smelled the sweet wood.

And then she tasted it. The magic within.

She summoned her own magic with care, as if testing out a twisted ankle. She felt the energy in the pockets of her marrow and coaxed it to pass through the hard casing of bone. From there, the dregs seeped through her veins, but she drew on her last reserves. With a dull ache coursing through her arms, she shoved her remaining magic into her hands and entered the wooden Insight. She smiled as her magic began to mingle with the magic that the simple wooden coin contained.

And then its magic pulsed into her. It was a brief flare of foreign power, racing up her veins at an exhilarating pace. Instead of implanting itself in her marrow, it shot straight up her spine and penetrated her brain.

Melaine gasped as the mending spell hit her mind. The Insights she had used before were made by untrained hands in Stakeside, from people who had never had formal education in creating them. The knowledge they passed on was useful and enlightening to anyone like Melaine who hadn't known the spells they contained before. But their level of knowledge and the force with which that knowledge filled Melaine's head was *nothing* compared to the sudden, encompassing force that Melaine now felt from this nation-regulated Insight.

Every minute detail of the new spell wove its way into Melaine's mind. She envisioned a cascade of stacked fabric bolts unfurling across a tailor's shop, and every single type of fabric on display entered her realm of knowledge. Cloths of colors and textures she'd never seen were now under her expertise—not just what they were called but how they were made and how to make more.

She saw silk being woven by tiny worms in a faraway place. She saw cotton and flax being picked and sheep being sheared in a barn. She saw hand-spinners dangling from foreign women's hands, enormous looms standing in large rooms. She saw tiny needles with thread stitching patterns of delicate lace and embroidered pictures and words. She saw enormous vats of dye soaking fabrics with color. She even saw flowers and berries and minerals and tiny shells of creatures being pounded and cured and treated in all manner of ways to procure rich and excellent dyes.

And then she felt her fingers tingle as all of that knowledge flooded down from her brain, through her veins, and into her hands. Then the magic retreated into her spongy marrow, where both magic and knowledge would remain as an integral part of her body. Even if she never used the spell, it would endure, waiting to be tapped into, never to be forgotten.

Melaine let out a breath as the burst of magic faded. She leaned on her hands and stared at the unpolished wood floor to stave off dizziness. When the world stopped spinning, she laughed with happiness, a hoarse sound that was practically foreign to her ears, it happened so rarely. She sat up on her knees and reached for her gloves at the foot of her pallet. She grabbed the one with the hole near its palm.

She could summon a little more magic, surely. Unlike some of the brilliant, rich fabrics she had witnessed in her head, her gloves were made of simple homespun cloth, rough and brown, a color chosen because it would hide the inevitable dirt it would collect. She brushed the hole with her fingertip and brought the spell to the surface of her mind and the tip of her finger. With silent thought, she told the cloth to expand.

A surge of pride and satisfaction shot through her as she watched the coarse weave of the homespun fabric, elongating it thread by thread. The fibers twisted together as if being strung by an invisible spinner. Then the new strands slipped over and under one another through the warp and weft of a tiny, unseen loom. The fibers wove themselves all the way to the other side of the hole, where they began to knit themselves into the existing fabric.

She watched the threads undulate like waves as her mind, and her vision, started to unravel. Her head bobbed as the room turned black, but she smiled as the hole mended within seconds as if it had never been. She lay back on her pallet and inspected the blurry glove through narrowed eyes, pulling it from both ends to stretch the fabric. The newly spun threads didn't split, and their fresh weave didn't loosen.

Melaine clutched the glove to her breast. A new wave of exhaustion swelled stronger than the last, but her sense of power from learning a new spell was far more acute. A satisfied smile was her last conscious act before her spent body finally gave in to sleep.

CHAPTER 2

Melaine grunted as she sat up sooner than she would have liked. The shouts of wives from window to window alerted her that it was morning as they threw the night's piss pots into the gutters. That and the fresh, recharged magic buzzing in her bones and humming in her veins after her night's rest. She snapped her fingers and sparked a purple lightning bolt to the thatch ceiling. A single straw sizzled within seconds and with ease. The bliss of morning magic.

The baker's voice came from around the corner near the Greasy Goat's front entrance. Amond wasn't really a baker—he was only a delivery man who pandered bread he'd nicked from the real baker closer to the Stakeside Wall. But he was good at his nicking, grabbing the previous night's leftovers before they reached the butcher's pigs. The pigs were looking thinner these days.

Every morning, he would stop by the Greasy Goat. Salma was one of his prime customers—one of the *only* customers in Stakeside who could afford to buy bread as fresh as Amond's. The pub Salma ran was the best in lower Stakeside. Her liquors were watered down a little less than the others, and her fires were stoked a little higher in the winter. She was a good cook, too. Salma could turn even nearly rancid meat and overripe vegetables into a decent stew. Melaine suspected the matron had gotten ahold of a valuable Insight at some point in her fifty years to aid her cooking, but she knew Salma would never admit to that.

Salma's voice joined Amond's outside, just like every morning, a signal that it was past time for Melaine to get out of bed. Fortunately, Melaine didn't have any clients lined up until late morning, but that didn't mean she shouldn't try for an unplanned sale around the pub while she waited.

She reached for one glove on her thin blanket but realized the other was crushed under her hand. She lifted it and noticed the glaring hole near its cuff was gone. She glanced at the floor and saw the now-empty wooden Insight resting beside her pallet. She twitched her nose and hurried to put both gloves back on. She snatched a scrap of old newspaper from a little pile by her chamber pot and grabbed the spent Insight through the paper, wrapping up the coin so she wouldn't have to touch the thing.

Even through the newspaper, she could feel the grating gristle of residual magic that clung to the used Insight. People would describe the sensation as a stench, a horrid reek, though it wasn't an olfactory quality, not really. It was more physical, like taking a grinder to teeth or somersaulting a stomach. Residual magic lingered on all spent magical objects after their use, and the effects it had on the human body were acute. Residual magic didn't belong in humans. It was not intended to mix with the fresh magic each person maintained in their bones. Touching, breathing, or magically interacting with residual magic was enough to make a person ill, just as rotten food, blood, excrement, or sex could ruin a person.

Unfortunately, Stakeside was full of all such refuse, and sickness of all kinds ran rampant in the streets. Melaine had always been careful to avoid the obvious risks. The reek of residual magic had never bothered her as much as it seemed to bother other people—not since she'd gotten sick from it once as a child. But she was still careful to properly dispose of any waste.

Last night, she'd been too tired to get rid of the Insight. She'd been breathing the taint of residual magic all night. She grimaced but told herself it would be all right. It had been years since the last and only time she'd gotten the "res," as people called it. Years since she'd stumbled down the street in a vomiting heap, shaking with the sweats, desperate for the sickness to pass. She had recovered, but every fresh year, many weak, old, and young res victims would succumb to its effects that ravaged through their bones.

Melaine stood up from her pallet, newspaper-wrapped Insight in hand. Her boots weren't even unlaced from the night before, which wasn't unusual. It seemed every other night she was too exhausted to bother taking anything off. She was glad she hadn't yet removed them as she hurried to open the door.

The first rays of sunlight pushed away the morning

chill and smoothed the goosebumps on her arms. The alley outside her little room looked different during the day. The mere trickle of the streetlamp's glow had shrouded the lichen-covered stone wall, splattered with old vomit and piss from drunken passersby. The night had hidden the excess trash by the waste crates that Salma tried so carefully to maintain.

A man would come every so often to empty the crates. By the time he came, the last scraps of useful rubbish would have been picked through by beggars. So, he would empty the crates' contents into a basket that he'd pop onto his back with straps. Then he would use his considerable skill to climb up the lichen-crusted wall to dump the trash over the other side.

The wall wasn't the Stakeside wall, of course. Dumping debris onto the well-maintained streets of the higher classes would have resulted in a quick arrest. Rather, this wall was a part of the outer wall that existed behind Melaine's rented room—the wall that surrounded the whole of Centara. The wall was high and thick, with battlements and watchtowers from the old days before the war. No guards patrolled the outer wall now. Why would they? No foreign kingdoms had attacked Dramore, and certainly not Centara, in twenty years. Not since the Overlord conquered all of Dramore from the old ruler, King Malik. Melaine had heard that the Shields still patrolled the wall in the better parts of the city, but that was probably just for show.

The true protection of Dramore, and the Centara palace itself, fell to the Overlord's elite force of battlemages: the renowned Followers.

But no one cared about the population in Stakeside. The poorest residents of the city were, in and of themselves, protection for the rest of the populace. They would be the first slaughtered if an enemy army ever did breach the unmanned section of the wall. And the Stakeside wall would provide a second barrier to protect the rest of the city. The time it would take for an enemy to massacre the poor would be all the time the Centara Shields needed to amass their own force and repel the enemy back.

Melaine looked away from the wall as she tossed the used Insight into the waste crate. There was no point in staring at the wall. To most, it was an unscalable barrier, and even for those who could climb it, what was the purpose of going over when no opportunities lay beyond? Farms and small villages were scattered around Centara, but they were full-up, and crops had been slim lately, so no fresh work for new field hands was likely. Beyond the cultivated lands prowled the Wilds, a vast tangle of dark forest that everyone in Stakeside knew to be cursed. Sordid stories abounded, telling of the creatures and evil forces lurking in those trees. They must be true, everyone said, because why else would all five competing kingdoms avoid it?

Melaine brushed her hands on her dress and stepped away from the wall. She'd considered going over it before, but logic had always stopped her. No, the only way out of Stakeside was to somehow fight her way through the impassible class system.

Her heart plummeted as the previous day's events reentered her memory. Her one viable chance to get past the Stakeside wall was over. Vintor had stripped it from her.

No. The Luxians had stripped it from her.

She knew their teachings. The ones that mattered. They claimed that eons ago, a sleeping entity in the core of the world awoke. The immaterial entity was called Lux, and Lux had awoken to see the first humans of creation in their infancy. He had seen how weak humans were, without the protections of fur or claws or scales or sharp teeth like other animals. He had felt pity for them and decided that humans deserved a trait that would make them not only survivors but conquerors of their world.

So, Lux had given humans a gift. He made them a lodestone containing his own magic—magic that was tapped from the underground marrow of the world's core. When humans inhaled his magic from the lodestone, the marrow of their bones was replaced by the same magic held in the core of the world. Some humans bonded more naturally with the influx of magic than others, and it was from their bloodlines that the strongest of humans descended. The Luxians preferred to teach that the traditional rulers of the five kingdoms and all noble families carried the traits of stronger magic in their bodies. The Overlord was not included in that list.

Per the Luxian teachings, Insights were blessings to share, just as Lux had shared knowledge with humans after he'd infused them with magic. Teaching spells was encouraged in theory, but a human giving away raw magic through lodestones was considered a false imitation of Lux's powerful gift—it was considered blasphemy. Spells were harmless currency. Raw, biological magic was not to be shared.

Worse, the teachings of Lux stated that a lodestone-maker could *steal* another person's magic and store it in a stone for later use. Melaine knew that was a ridiculous notion. Magic could never be stolen. Lodestones had to be freely created by their makers and willingly given to someone else. And lodestone-makers could only infuse their own magic into a stone, not anyone else's.

But the idea of a poor, low-bred person harnessing a nobleman's magic was too dangerous. The incorrect logic of the Luxians hadn't stopped them from using all fear tactics at their disposal to dominate Dramore for years. It hadn't stopped the violent hunt of "accursed" lodestone-makers from happening. The imprisonment of all blasphemers, the mass executions, all approved by King Malik's rule.

But the Overlord had changed all of that. He banned the Luxian religion; he encouraged the secular exploration of magic that had been suppressed by them. He rewrote laws and made sure they were enforced.

Yet he was still vilified by so many. Too many people judged the ethics of the methods he used to conquer the city, and the masses who had supported the Luxians refused to believe the Overlord had changed the kingdom for the better.

Melaine knew she shouldn't dawdle in the day's preparations, but she felt compelled to walk a few more feet along the wall. She passed by the back of the Greasy Goat until she stood in a small space between the pub and the piddling grocer's shop next door. There, plastered on the wall months ago, was a frayed broadsheet. Ones just like it were posted on numerous streetlamp poles and sides of buildings. Twice a year, Shields would come through the Stakeside wall to escort the plasterers through the gritty streets where they would put the broadsheets up. Even Stakeside residents deserved to see—or be reminded of—the Overlord's powerful visage.

If any other posters had been put up in Stakeside, they would have been stripped that very hour to be used as chamber pot paper or stuffing for bedding or tinder. But if the Shields came through again to see pictures of the Overlord missing or desecrated, there would be random beatings in the street for the act of heresy. Melaine had witnessed it before.

That knowledge was the only thing that kept her from removing the broadsheet she looked at now. There had been many times when she'd been tempted to take it down and bring it with hurried steps to her room, where she could look at it for as long as she liked before bed at night and imagine her own face on a broadsheet, reigning over the city, leaving Stakeside far behind.

The Overlord had filled her head ever since she was old enough to comprehend the stories adults told in pubs or on the streets. Melaine had listened with avid anticipation whenever some old-timer would talk about the Overlord's insurgence and the brief Praivalon War that followed, which had neared its end just after Melaine was born. Stories of the young, fierce Overlord charging into the White City with his armies and his mighty Followers to take the kingdom of Dramore for his own. Stories of the powerful magic he used to solidify his reign when the foreign kingdom of Praivalon attacked, their King Vasos trying to take advantage of Dramore's political turmoil. The Overlord had beaten them back swiftly and without fail. Even the tales of the horrific atrocities, fueled by dark magic, that he and his Followers performed made Melaine's heart pound with excitement.

To have fought in that war, to have ridden on horseback at the Overlord's side, to watch him *take* the power he wanted for his own without conscience, without hesitation, everything blocking his way be damned.... Those imaginings had kept Melaine going in her darkest hours. Whenever she was on the verge of giving up on her hopes of escape from the life she led, she envisioned the Overlord in all of his indomitable glory, and she would go on for another day.

She looked at the Overlord's face on the wall, painted by some artist's hand. A replication spell had then copied it onto hundreds of broadsheets to be spread throughout the city. The broadsheets served as a reminder that he was always watching, that his overseers and his Followers were protecting Dramore, Centara, and all who lived within.

The painted image hadn't changed for at least five years now, but Melaine knew the Overlord must still look as strong and magnificent as he did when the painting was rendered. The ruler's black hair framed his pale, statuesque face and touched his shoulders, a few strands wisping out as if he were riding a warhorse in the wind. His every feature was strong, with a noble brow, straight nose, and sharp jawline. His eyes were what had captivated Melaine from the moment she saw his face. They were a fierce, bright blue. Even in the faded colors of the months-old poster, she could see in his eyes how full of life and passion the Overlord was.

He was a constant in her life, as unwavering and expected as the dawn. Yet, the truth was, no one had heard of him before the war. No one knew his birth name or where he came from. Rumors circulated, some spoken in more hushed tones than others. Some people speculated that he wasn't from Dramore at all but hailed from one of the other four kingdoms. They claimed he had seen Dramore's political disease and Luxian-decreed executions from a distance and decided that something had to be done. Others agreed with that origin but viewed him as an avaricious plunderer rather than a savior. A handful of people thought both he and his dark magic came from the Wilds, though that was the most outlandish, to be sure. No one who went into that foreboding forest ever came out. No human could survive the Wilds.

One of the most common viewpoints, and Melaine's personal slant, was that he was once a lesser-known noble who persuaded those who knew him to "forget" his old life. She couldn't imagine him possessing any less wealth and magnificence than he had now, and he'd fought for Dramore with such fervor and invested so much wealth into Centara, it seemed impossible he could have been born anywhere else.

"Melaine," called Salma, startling Melaine from her reverie. She looked back toward the Greasy Goat, where Salma stood halfway out the back door. "Starin' at that ol' thing again? Come get yah breakfast before s'all gone."

Melaine clicked her tongue but nodded. She pulled herself away from the Overlord's visage and walked to the Greasy Goat's back door.

"Someone who didn't know any better might think yah're sweet on him," Salma said with a wink.

"Good thing *you* know better," Melaine said.

Melaine didn't view the Overlord at all like a *man*—he was nothing like the leering brutes in the streets. She had no doubt that the ruler was above the primal urges that kept other men drowning in lust. The Overlord was different.

"Ah yes, Follower Melaine," Salma said with a mock bow. She chuckled as Melaine scowled and ducked through the doorway. "Used ta talk about that when yah were a little thing, do yah remember? Bread's on the counter, love."

Melaine stalked to the pub's serving counter and grabbed the hunk of bread Salma had left for her. All of her meals were included in her rent. Salma might be a friend, but nothing came free in Stakeside.

She grabbed a chair at the closest table and sat down. She took a bite of bread, but it tasted dry in her mouth— and not just because it was stale. Salma's words were eating at her more than her usual teases.

Follower Melaine. Back when she'd had dreams. Back when she hadn't known any better. Back when she'd been foolish enough to think that a nobody-orphan from Stakeside could ever set eyes on the real Overlord. Back when, even as a small child, the Stakeside wall hadn't seemed so high.

Salma followed her into the pub's main room, which

was empty so far, and she slid behind the counter. Her olive-green skirts were cleaner than Melaine's but were still worn and patched. Her hair bounced with curls that were a unique shade of auburn, though graying around the edges. Salma's bosom was much more pronounced than Melaine's, and the pub matron was smart enough in her business to deepen her cleavage for drunken men to lose themselves in.

Salma might have survived Stakeside longer than many, but she still looked good for her age, an even rarer achievement. Good stock, Salma had always said, though as far as Melaine knew, Salma's parents hadn't been anything special. Just another pub owner and his wife. If Salma had gotten anything good from them, it'd been the Greasy Goat.

"Thought yah'd be more chipper this mornin'," Salma remarked as she started stacking scratched, but clean, tin mugs behind the counter. "I heard Vintor was lookin' for yah yesterday. Might want ta find him. See what he says." She sent Melaine a conspiratorial smile.

"I already did," Melaine said, picking at the crust on her bread with one fingernail. "Our business is 'concluded.'"

Salma frowned and leaned on the counter. "What? He's turnin' down *your* stones?"

"Buyers are. The Luxians are scaring them away." Melaine raised her bread to Salma in a wry toast and then took a miserable bite. She swallowed past the lump in her throat and let the bread hit her roiling stomach as she considered the loss of opportunity she'd endured.

"Wise of Vintor," a woman said from the front door of

the pub. Melaine twisted in her chair to see the familiar face of Jianthe. She stepped into the pub and shut the door behind her.

Jianthe was a scrawny woman, even by Stakeside standards. She wore a dress made from spare strips of any colorful fabric she could lay her hands on. She left the garment free at the hems, so strips swayed in a light, mystical way that made her look like a gilded feather-duster.

She was a descendent of immigrants from Zraihya, one of the most distant kingdoms from Dramore. Over sixty years ago, Zraihyans had been invited en masse by King Malik because of their skilled craftsmanship in navigation magic and as cartwrights. His offer of payment was so generous, it seemed no one questioned his reasons for needing their services, and Zraihya had been suffering from a severe drought back then. The number of people who took him up on his offer was enormous.

But when the Overlord conquered Dramore, he had closed all its borders at once. He had offered safe passage for a limited time for Zraihyans to return to their homeland if they wished, but with their travel-related services no longer a commodity, most couldn't afford to travel themselves. Now, the ones who remained were trapped within Dramore's closed borders and had no choice but to enter other, typically less lucrative, lines of work. Resentment against the Overlord was even more pervasive among the Zraihyan people than most Dramorean natives.

Like most Zraihyans, Jianthe had green eyes, dark brown skin, and thick blonde hair. She'd woven her textured locks into braids that also contained feathers, colorful beads, and other sundries that added to her colorful, slinking appearance. She also wore her usual sly smile.

"Those Luxian bastards are causing quite a fuss uptown," Jianthe continued as she slipped between tables on her way to Salma and Melaine. "Even the overseers aren't indulging in their little vices as often."

"Thought I told yah not ta spy on me," Salma said, but her tone was light. She knew as well as anyone that telling Jianthe not to eavesdrop was futile.

Jianthe was a well-known and vital member of Stakeside society. At one fortunate point in her life, she had come into possession of a highly valuable Insight containing a keen-ear spell. She had since made her livelihood as a keeper and divulger of secrets. Whether she did one or the other was a matter of the highest payment that any concerned parties could shell out.

It was a dangerous job. She had stumbled into the Greasy Goat numerous times with injuries inflicted by an angry person wanting to shut her up. But it seemed that there was always an opposing person who would give her enough protection to live another day.

This morning, she was unharmed. She settled herself in a chair opposite Melaine, a smile stretched across her face. Salma poured her usual choice of drink after a long night of eavesdropping and brought it to the table. Jianthe sent her a fliratious wink in thanks. Salma blushed and looked aside, but she shook her auburn locks a little, preening from the attention.

"So, it's like Vintor says?" Melaine asked, her voice down. "No one's buying lodestones anymore?"

"Oh, here, I'm sure they are," Jianthe said, taking a sip of her drink with relish. "People are always in need of a boost for their hard labors, personal exploits..."

Salma snorted, and Jianthe chuckled. Melaine ignored them. She knew why people bought her lodestones. Jianthe was right in saying that some customers only wanted energy to keep them going in honest labors for days straight, but most had more nefarious uses. Pitch fighters used them to gain a cheating edge for their next match. Thieves used them in petty thefts, even a grand heist now and again. Even murderers sometimes paid Melaine for a stone, guaranteeing that their magic would be more powerful than their opponent's, should their victim put up a fight.

Melaine had no qualms with whatever use her magic was put to once it left her body and entered a lodestone. That was the customer's business. She had been asked once before to perform a murder for a client, rather than just selling him a stone. She had refused. On several occasions, she had been asked to join in a heist or a scheme for riches, but she had turned them all down. Though she'd never been invited to compete, she knew, even with her magic, she was too skinny and small to win a fight against a typical trained, muscular pitch fighter.

The acts she had been asked to perform didn't give her pause from a moral standpoint. Everyone did what they had to in order to survive, even Melaine. But as much as she detested selling her magic away, she knew lodestones were the most reliable source of income she could attain. Murders could easily go south. Most of the big heists she'd heard of had failed. And, as degrading as lodestone-peddling was, it made her more money than any honest, laboring job ever could.

Lodestones were consistent. They were in demand, and following the Luxian's past generational purge, she was one of the few people born in Dramore with the ability to make them.

But lately, consistent and safe didn't sound so good anymore.

"Ah, Melaine, cheer up," Jianthe said, raising her glass. "You'll always have a place in Stakeside."

"The overseers have vices," Melaine said as an idea prodded her brain.

"Yah're surprised?" Salma asked.

"No," Melaine said. She looked at Jianthe and lowered her voice. "People can use that against them, though. Right?"

Jianthe raised an eyebrow, and the corner of her red lips matched.

"Of course, they have vices," she said. "Which is why they come here for their very worst."

"Here?" Melaine asked with an incredulous bite of her bread. "To Stakeside?"

Jianthe nodded, leaning forward with delight.

"Then..." Melaine lowered her voice to a barely audible whisper. She knew Jianthe, with her keen-ear spell, would hear it. "They can be blackmailed."

Jianthe's lips quirked in an even curvier smile. Her green eyes flicked in a sneaky affirmation, but then she sidled back in her chair and sipped her drink.

"I'm afraid, though, that no one in Stakeside has that power. Who would listen to us? Well"—she nodded at

Melaine—"to *you*. Everyone knows I, at least, might have something of worth to tell, even the residents of Crossing's Square."

Melaine felt a familiar resentment burn in her chest. It mingled with disappointment and the temptation to resign herself to her fate. But she pushed it all aside and sat straighter in her chair.

"Whatever do you want to blackmail an overseer for?" Jianthe asked. Salma startled behind the counter.

"Do what?" Salma asked. Melaine glared at Jianthe for outing her words at a volume Salma could hear.

"What about bribes?" Melaine asked, ignoring Salma. "You pass on information for payment. It's possible to trade secrets for favors, isn't it?"

"What favor could you possibly want from an overseer?" Jianthe asked.

"Melaine," Salma said, her lips pursed.

"Is it true that the Overlord doesn't accept audiences with the public anymore?" Melaine asked.

"Not for the past five years," Jianthe said, sounding like she was humoring her for now.

"But the overseers still see him."

"They do," she said.

"So...the only way to the Overlord is through an overseer," Melaine said quietly.

"Mela, what an outrageous idea," Salma said. "We shouldn't be talking about this, not a one of us."

Melaine bristled at the childhood nickname.

"The very idea of *meeting* the Overlord," Salma continued, forcing a laugh. She returned to her preparations for the day's business, in this case, watering the hearth-brandy. "I thought yah stopped with that childish prattle years ago. If yah'd been alive when the Overlord—"

Salma stopped and licked her lips in a nervous habit. She focused on corking the hearth-brandy bottle. Then she grabbed the one beside it and started counting each pour of water she added.

"Maybe you could spare me a secret," Melaine whispered to Jianthe. "I'll pay you in installments." Jianthe held up a hand to stop her.

"You couldn't afford me, dear," she said. "Not for a secret involving an overseer. Besides, secrets are my domain. My advice? Stick to lodestones. You're good at it. Everyone uptown thinks so." She gave her another conspiratorial grin. Melaine only frowned in return.

"Thank you, Salma, as always," Jianthe said, tipping her glass. Salma nodded. Jianthe didn't fish in her pocket for coins. Even with Salma, she'd paid for a drink-a-day for life with some secret or another.

"Where do the overseers go?" Melaine hissed, trying not to yell as Jianthe stood and began slipping between tables and chairs to reach the door.

"When in Stakeside?" she asked, her tone innocent. "How should I know?"

Melaine scowled and slumped back in her chair, the legs scraping against the floor.

"Careful, now," Salma chided.

"It's covered in scratches already," Melaine growled. She stood up and headed for the back door.

"'Ey now, don't go insultin' my establishment," Salma called. "Melaine!"

Melaine ignored her. She was not in the mood for Salma's nursemaid games.

"Stick to lodestones," Melaine muttered as she shut the door behind her and stepped out into the street. Maybe the Luxian Order was right. Stones were a fucking curse.

But they were her curse to bear.

She knew she should be grateful for the talent. It had kept her fed and clothed all these years. But what else could lodestones give her? Especially if the Luxians were taking hold, stones were as much of a limitation as they were an opportunity.

But Melaine paused in her slow walk up the stairs to her room. If the religion was truly regaining hold in the upper classes, that meant heretical lodestones would be hard to come by. And if the overseers were growing skittish of coming to Stakeside for their vices, then their abilities to get lodestones from even the lowest sources would dry up. They had reputations to uphold, after all. They couldn't be seen fraternizing with those of less noble bloodlines.

Maybe this was a chance. A slim chance, and one that wouldn't last for long. But if Melaine could find the information she needed and could move fast enough to take action, then maybe, just maybe, her lodestones could fuel one last leap out of Stakeside.

❦

THREE DAYS LATER, MELAINE STOOD IN FRONT OF Vintor's shop.

She'd tried other avenues. She'd tried to eavesdrop on certain circles at the Greasy Goat. Hinted at questions with her clients. Even ventured down a few streets known to be more dangerous than most, trying to glean even a mite of information about the overseers' supposed forays into the slums. But she had turned up nothing, and she knew what a risk it was to probe deeper amongst strangers. Jianthe might be the best purveyor of secrets in Stakeside, but she wasn't the only person to make a living out of paying attention to people who asked too many questions about clandestine topics.

And so, Melaine decided it was time to try the one person she knew, other than Jianthe, who might know a little about the goings-on in and out of Stakeside.

She glared up at the engraved sign freshly painted since she'd seen it last. Vintor must have been right when he spoke of other lucrative "enterprises." Either that or he'd lied about how much Melaine's last batch of lodestones had really gone for. Had the Insight he'd given her been only a scrap from the sum he'd garnered?

Melaine lifted the hem of her dress to free it from the crackling, brown leaves and stepped over the gutter onto Vintor's doorstep. She grabbed the tarnished brass knocker and pushed the door open.

It was morning, and though a slight chill permeated the air, it wasn't enough to warrant a fire in Vintor's hearth. Even Vintor couldn't afford to waste coal. Melaine raised her eyebrows when she saw Vintor speaking with a customer toward the back of the shop. Perhaps he could afford to waste coal if he succeeded in selling the item in his hand.

"You see," Vintor said to a woman with tight, brown hair. She had a cleanliness about her that told Melaine she was a Waller, someone from the tenements closest to the Stakeside wall, just like Vintor. "A simple touch of magic to this lever will set the mechanism into motion. Why don't you try?"

The woman was hesitant, but her eyes shone as she looked at the marvelous item for sale. The delicate contraption consisted of a thin, rectangular, brass base with a narrow, horizontal rod attached a finger's width above. One edge of a slightly wrinkled piece of parchment was tucked inside the narrow space between the base and the rod. A fountain pen was attached to the right side of the rod by a small brass hinge.

The woman summoned a bit of sunrise-pink magic to her fingertip and hummed it against the lever. The lever depressed, and the hinge that connected the pen to the contraption raised. The pen slid across the rod to the left and touched its inked tip to the parchment.

The pen began to write. It slid back to the right, along the rod, scribbling script all the way. When it reached the other side, the parchment slipped farther between the rod and base, just enough to give the pen access to write another line of script.

"You enchant the pen to write whatever you wish," Vintor said, his words speeding up as he watched the sparkle in the woman's eyes. "I set it to write a demonstration letter as soon as I procured it. And after it's finished..."

Vintor pressed the lever with his own little pulse of dark blue magic—his signature color—and the pen stopped. Then he pressed a series of metal tabs on springs, and four thin, brass arms, delicate as a spider's legs, unfolded from the device's base. Two latched onto the parchment with tiny clamps and pulled it from the base. Then all four arms began to fold the parchment. Rather than a simple envelope, they created a flower blossom filled with words. They set it gently on the table and folded back into the device's base as if crossing their arms with pride.

"Oh, how delightful!" the woman said, smiling in genuine admiration.

"It can fold many other artistic shapes," Vintor said. "Whatever your heart desires, even if a simple envelope should suffice. The pen will address the envelope, too. Though I'm afraid you'll still have to send it." He winked at the woman, but his eagerness for a sale vibrated through his attempt at casual conversation.

The sight was truly one of the most wondrous Melaine had ever witnessed. The device was a mechagic; it had to be. Melaine had heard word of all kinds of mechagics starting a few years back. They were a product of the Overlord's secular rule, in which experimentation was encouraged. The Luxians held that magic should maintain its organic roots. Insights, after all, had to be rooted in organic matter of some kind, and magic itself was a biological force. But the Overlord thought differently. And though Melaine had never expected to see a mechagic for herself, she had always admired that, in theory, they could exist under the Overlord's reign.

The Overlord wasn't afraid of progress but rather was a catalyst for change.

The mechagic in Vintor's hands was small, and its task fanciful, but at its essence, it held the same core functionality as any other mechagic. The beauty of mechagics was their ability to automate a magical process that used to require a person's direct, constant attention. Simply setting the mechagic in motion with a touch of magic would make it function all on its own for a set amount of time, while the person went about their daily business. She'd heard by now that the nobles had progressed the technology to the point of mechagical toys, dish scrubbers, music players, even mechagic-assisted carriages. The idea of *that* was a marvel to Melaine. She doubted she'd ever see one.

Unless her plan worked.

Melaine hardened her resolve and walked past the shelves of stacked goods and toward Vintor and his hesitant customer. She was clearly in awe of the mechagic, but Melaine could already see she wasn't going to buy it. What was Vintor thinking, bringing something like that into Stakeside? No one would be able to afford it. More likely, it would be stolen by someone as foolish as Vintor himself, and it would be passed around Stakeside from thief to thief until someone wound up dead.

"Vintor," Melaine said. Vintor did a double take, and then glared with a subtle nod at the woman beside him. Melaine denied his hint that she should leave before ruining his sale. "I need to speak with you."

Vintor's temple twitched in annoyance, but he maintained his cool demeanor. He smiled at his potential customer.

"Mrs. Leisy," he said, with a cordial nod of his head. "If

you excuse me for a small moment, I will be right back to finish explaining this fascinating machine."

Mrs. Leisy nodded, but Melaine caught her inaudible sigh of relief for the opportunity to either politely decline the sale or to escape the shop entirely. It seemed she hadn't decided which yet.

With a nod of his head, Vintor motioned Melaine to the other side of the store, his irritable frown becoming more pronounced.

"What do you want?" he asked in a hushed voice. "I thought I made myself quite clear the other day."

"Oh, you did," Melaine said. "I won't dispute that. But I do need something from you, Vintor."

"Oh?" he said, placing three fingers of each hand in his vest pocket. "I thought you didn't take handouts."

"I don't," Melaine responded. "After leaving our business so abruptly, I figure you owe me a little something."

"Is that so?" he said. "And here I thought that trifling mending spell would do the trick."

"That wasn't even a fraction of the extra money you got from that sale, was it?" she asked. She knew she was fishing, but she was pleasantly rewarded. Vintor glanced aside and clicked his tongue in a telling gesture.

"How much did you get for my stones?" Melaine asked. "Tell me."

"I paid you a fair price for them," he said, avoiding her question. "What do you want from me, Melaine? It had better be good." He glanced at his customer, who stayed for the time being.

"You go outside," Melaine said.

He looked at her expectantly. He knew what she meant by "outside." Beyond the Stakeside wall.

"I need information." She lowered her voice. "I hear the overseers come down to Stakeside now and again. Do you know where they go? When they come?"

"Well, that's pricey information," Vintor said, his fingers delving deeper into his vest pockets as he puffed his chest out like an over-fluffed pigeon.

"As pricey as my lodestones?" Melaine asked, not backing down.

Vintor paused, then scowled. So, he *did* feel a little guilty for swindling Melaine out of her full due.

"I don't know any more than you do," he said. Melaine opened her mouth, but he held up a finger to stop her. "But I can try to find out for you. *If* you promise not to come bursting into my shop like this again. In fact, stay clear entirely." He lowered his voice even more. "You're going to scare off my clientele."

Melaine almost laughed, but she was too close to getting what she wanted.

"Fine," she said. "I won't interfere with your illustrious customers."

"How did you learn such big words growing up where you did?" Vintor said, rolling his eyes, but Melaine felt a little surge of pride. She'd worked hard to find big words, eavesdropping from the few who knew them and learning a bit from Salma, who hadn't been restricted to Stakeside before the war. Salma had been married once to a Waller and was able to walk about the other side the way that Vintor now did. But then her husband had died, and she'd taken over her parents' pub. She hadn't left Stakeside since.

"So, if I swear not to come back, you'll find out where an overseer might be and when they might be there?" she asked.

Her heart picked up speed as Vintor hesitated. But then, Mrs. Leisy started sidling toward the door.

"All right," Vintor said in a rush. "I'll do it."

"How will you tell me if I can't come back?" Melaine asked. Mrs. Leisy crept closer to the door.

"I'll write you a bloody note," Vintor said. "Now, please. Go."

Melaine nodded. "I'll hear from you soon, then."

"Yes, fine," he said. Melaine hoped he was serious, but she had done all she could for now. She turned toward the door just as Mrs. Leisy opened it. A glint of a candlestick peeked out of the woman's skirt. Melaine smiled.

"Good luck with your sale, Vintor," she said. Vintor opened his mouth, then he scowled and turned away, not noticing Mrs. Leisy's theft as she stepped into the sunshine. Melaine decided not to enlighten him.

❧

"CAME FOR YAH TODAY," SALMA SAID, PUSHING A folded scrap of newspaper across the pub counter. Melaine almost choked on her drink and sloshed water on her hands as she lunged for the paper. Salma saved her mug from tumbling with a hard frown.

Melaine started to open the note, but then looked up at Salma. "Did you read it?"

Salma's frown deepened. "No."

Melaine looked down, feeling a little guilty for insulting Salma. Salma's word had always rung true, and she'd never been given a reason to mistrust the woman. Salma's look of disapproval continued, however, as Melaine twisted round in her chair so Salma couldn't read the letter.

Over a week had passed since she'd spoken with Vintor. She had begun to doubt his dedication to her request. Now, her hasty fingers nearly ruined the message as the ink ran black, mixing with the water on her hands. She uttered a curse and scrubbed them both on her dress and then rattled the paper until the words that were scrawled across the faded newsprint reached her gaze.

As Melaine had hoped, the script inside was written in Vintor's fluid handwriting. She narrowed her eyes as she studied the words in silence.

S. wi—will.

She filtered the letters through her brain, forcing them to make the right sound in her head. She had to understand this message. It was too important to misread.

S. will be a.... No, *at, t—the Hol—ee....* No, *Hole.*

Melaine shuddered.

Tomo...rrow nig. T? She crumpled the side of the paper in frustration. *N.I.G.H.T.*

She played with the pronunciation of the letters, moving her lips silently, and then what Salma had taught her popped into her mind—*H hushes G.*

Night!

Melaine smiled at her victory in reading the message,

and then her breath came fast in anticipation of what it meant.

S.

If Vintor *had* managed to find information about an overseer, then there was only one overseer who had S. for an initial. Garvind Scroupe was the Overseer of the Treasury, and from what Melaine had heard, he was as greedy as one might expect from someone in his position. Did his thirst for his vices match his greed for money? It seemed so, if the location in the note was to be believed.

Melaine suppressed her doubts. Tomorrow. Tomorrow night, she would have her chance to take a bold step—a step that could change her life forever.

But her stomach twisted into knots.

Did it have to be at the Hole?

CHAPTER 3

Darkness crept around Melaine like a slithering beast, pressing against her shoulders, crawling down her chest, running its claws through her hair. She resisted the urge to writhe with the fearful discomfort from the nighttime streets of Stakeside, and she straightened her spine. She raised her narrow chin, kept her black eyes up, and exuded as much confidence as she was able.

Melaine did not consider herself a decent person, but even she was disturbed by the Hole. All but the most depraved souls avoided that den of vice and insidious pleasures.

And the Overseer of the Treasury of Centara was as depraved as they came.

Melaine had made no lodestones today, a risk. Her clients didn't like to be rescheduled. If she had been a lesser peddler with lower-quality stones, she might have been beaten for her poor business practice. But she was Melaine of Stakeside, the most magically potent stone peddler in the slums and probably beyond. And she needed all of her magic now if she was to keep her wits. She summoned magic to her fingertips with every breath, charging them until they tingled with warmth.

The alley that housed the Hole was thick with fog. Melaine could hear voices beyond; speaking, crying, groaning, shrieking in deranged laughter. She took cautious steps and paused when the thick fog touched her skin. It was warm and wafted strange scents into her nostrils. Melaine turned her head and took a deep breath of the crisp night air before forcing herself to continue into the haze of potion vapors.

But soon, she felt lightheaded. She hurried through the thickest of the vapors and finally had to take a breath when she reached a thinner mist. Her dizziness was replaced by a fierce quickening of breath and blinding snap of her thoughts. She shook her head and drew upon the magic in her bones to supplant the effects of what she recognized as a head potion called sniker. She had tried the venomous drug once when she was fourteen. After a bad night, she'd never touched it or any other cheap street concoction again.

She continued to weave her way down the dark alley, trying to maintain an air of confidence and act like she'd been there before so the leeches wouldn't rush to corrupt her out of pure, wicked delight. Or perhaps, to drag her down with them and assuage their guilt for their own vices, but Melaine suspected most were too far gone for that.

More than just sniker circulated through the huddled grime of drunken hop heads. Circles of degenerates passed pipes around while others surrounded open fires, lowering their faces over the cauldrons of head potions and inhaling so closely that they would come up with scalded faces. But they were too high to notice the pain.

Humping piles of every gender moaned in the shadowed edges of the alley, pressed up against the dirty brick walls of buildings or ignoring the chill of the cobblestones. Melaine ignored the vague calls her way as she walked past, some crudely asking for her to join the orgies, others offering the "best" potions in Centara for an exhortative price.

She had seen such scenes before, though never in such blatant display. The Shields wouldn't step foot here. Black magic had built up throughout intangible desecrating piles in and around the Hole for decades, since the days before the war. It had resisted the Reconstruction following the Overlord's coup. Now, Melaine suspected that the deep, underground cesspool had been secretly *allowed* to remain in place.

Even government officials and wealthy aristocrats needed a place to wallow.

Melaine stopped before the doorway, separated from the alley by no more than a drawn curtain, allowing the head potion vapors to permeate into the depths. The curtain had ceased to maintain any distinguishable hue and was tattered and stained with secretions Melaine did not wish to consider. Although the barrier looked flimsy, she could still feel a sucking, dank, wet pull of dark magic inviting her in.

She shivered as goosebumps fled up her arms underneath her long, homespun sleeves. Experiences in the Hole were said to change people. The quickest saying was, "the Hole licks your soul." Step in once, and you'll come back for more until it consumes you.

Melaine had a single purpose for entering this place, one that would keep her grounded. She did not come for the Hole's temptations. She came to see the overseer.

She took a breath, squared her shoulders, and grasped the edge of the curtain.

The curtain ripped to the side on its own. The worn-out tread on Melaine's boots slipped on the slick cobblestones, and she nearly fell backward but caught herself and regained her breath.

A creature stood in the doorway, in the rough shape of a man but with a bestial face and black fur that was matted with who knew what. It wore a long overcoat and nothing else. It grinned at her with evil, sapient delight, exposing sharpened teeth. Its curled ears cocked and listened to something. Melaine wondered if it was listening to her pounding heartbeat.

It was a Daksun. Melaine had heard of them but never thought she'd see one, let alone in Centara. They were a rough tribe of *almost* people, said to live at the edge of the Wilds on the western side, just a taste of the even darker creatures who lived within that ominous forest.

Human laughter shrieked around the foreign Daksun. Two women even skinnier than Melaine crawled around the beast who dug his claws into one woman's bare arms and the side of the other one's exposed breast. The woman on the right slipped her tongue like a serpent at Melaine. The mocking trio left the exit, and before she lost all resolve and gave into quaking fear, Melaine slipped through the opening and rushed down a dark slope into the Hole.

Curtained rooms lined the narrow corridor, some eliciting sounds that rattled Melaine's ear bones—shrieks and growls and moans and tortured screams of agony that wordlessly begged for more. Here and there, the curtains were open, exposing sights Melaine knew would be branded upon her memory without mercy.

A hulking man in coarse and torn clothes came out of the darkness and pushed past her, heading for the exit. Melaine hit the wood-planked wall beside her with a grunt and rolled into an open doorway. She righted herself and then clung to the rotting doorframe with a sharp inhalation of fear.

A squirming mound of insects dominated a corner of the small room. Worms and cockroaches, millipedes and spiders. Melaine's skin crawled as if she was immersed in them, and then she made a retching gasp as she saw a hand, a hip, then wide lips open in laughter around a mouthful of insects. The bugs swirled around the *person's* tongue and hid in the pockets between teeth and inner cheek.

Melaine shoved herself off the wall and ran back into the corridor, past the room. She batted at her dress and clawed through her hair frantically as if the pests had followed her, but they had all remained with their willing host who writhed among them in pleasure.

She continued down the hall of horrors, constantly blowing smoke and foul smells out her nostrils, trying not to retch at every sight that accosted her senses.

A glow dazzled her eyes in the darkness. Flickering

orange light cast tattered wings of shadow through a curtain to her left. She dared a peek inside as she passed. A man played with spell-fire, sending little sparks to kneeling beggars whose waiting tongues reveled in the magical high the fire singed into them. They moaned and cried out for more, their black and blistered tongues not allowing them to speak worded pleas.

Melaine continued into the depths but cried out when her feet slid on something wet. She latched onto a rattling chain hanging from the low ceiling. Its large and gritty rusted links were also wet, but Melaine kept her eyes on the huddled mass of people in front of her. They were feeding on a gory mess of blood and flesh—raw muscle and a thumping heart, pale lungs, and oozing brain tissue. Too small and misshapen to be human, but that didn't mean it wasn't some other intelligent creature they were feasting upon.

Melaine gripped the chain to keep herself standing but then caught a sheen of red on her hands in the dim light. She let go and started shaking, wanting to turn around and run, to get out of this seedy den. But she had come this far. The unceasing horror would all be a waste if she didn't press on and make it to the overseer.

Melaine gulped a breath of stifling air to steady her senses and walked over the blood-drenched floor with deliberate steps. She wiped her bloody hands on her dress and kept moving. She had to keep moving.

"What are you doing, drab?" said a gruff voice, stopping Melaine from making more red footprints in the corridor. A scruffy man with fetid breath stood in her way. "No one comes through here."

She spied a wooden door beyond his broad shoulders, not simply a threadbare curtain. It had to be the room she was looking for.

"O-overseer," Melaine coughed out in her struggles to fight the guard's smell of sweat and dried shit. "I was told to come here to see him."

"Were you now?" the man sneered. "You'll have to look somewhere else, whore. No overseer would come to a place like this. Go find yourself a hit and fuck someone. You look like you need it."

Melaine felt anger rumble in her belly. She harnessed that unrest and flooded it as magic into her palms.

"I think you're the one who needs a hit," she hissed. She shoved her offal-smeared hand against the man's filthy black mustache. Maybe her evil surroundings were seeping into her, or maybe it was her desperation to see the overseer, but something inside her snapped. She felt an insidious rush of magic like she never had before. She thought of the disgusting sight she'd witnessed of the feeding frenzy as the man inhaled the scent.

"Go find yourself a meal," she ordered. The guard sighed, and his body shuddered with wanting as her words seemed to provoke a hunger in him. Without a word, he slipped past her to find the source of the blood on her hands. She tried not to envision him feasting with the others.

Melaine rubbed her hands together and pushed the blood away, her magic expelling it all to leave her skin clean. She wasn't sure what spell she had just performed upon the guard, but she didn't have time to dwell on the strange occurrence. She clenched her hands into quick fists of resolve and then pushed open the solid wooden door. Its iron hinges gave a heavy groan as it swung inward.

The wide room beyond was red but not with blood. The walls were covered with red velvet, stained and decrepit. Naked women wandered the space, crushing dirty red carpet beneath their calloused bare feet. Dark purple wine in crystal glasses refracted candlelight. Melaine had to blink a few times to adjust after her dark descent. Music played, but it was rough and raw and scrambled from a clanking brass machine that was clearly a mechagic of some kind, covered in shadows on a table in a far corner. Its presence was a startling contrast to the poverty surrounding it. More women squirmed within a pile of bedclothes, their moans joined by the pleased chuckles and murmurs of approval from an old man who sat watching.

A staggering tremble of relief flooded Melaine when she saw that the overseer's tastes were far tamer than most who visited the Hole. She hadn't known what to expect this far down, after everything she'd seen, but the old man's choice to avoid a typical brothel made sense. No one who wished to slander his good name would dare follow him to the Hole to verify the rumors were true. They would slander their own name in the process just for having it spoken in the same breath as the Hole.

Melaine swallowed and arranged her face into a visage that she hoped would hide at least most of her disgust. She approached the soiled red armchair where the man sat smoking a green-ember cigar.

"Mm, you're skinnier than I like," Overseer Garvind

Scroupe grumbled, his voice hoarse and gravelly from years of smoking and making loud speeches to the masses. His reddened skin sagged from his square cheekbones and settled under his jowls.

"I'm not here for *that*," Melaine spat, ignoring the glares from the prostitutes who'd heard. She didn't recognize any of them. Their glinting eyes and sharp sneers suggested that the dark magic of the Hole had long writhed under their skin. Maybe the earnings were higher in the Hole, but Melaine couldn't imagine crawling so low to get them. Even Melaine had a line, and these women had clearly crossed it. Respect ended at the Hole.

She shuddered and tried to keep all of her focus upon the overseer.

"I'm a peddler," she said.

The overseer raised his bushy, gray eyebrows. "Of what?" he asked and took a drag from his cigar.

"Lodestones," Melaine answered. "The best in Centara."

The old man let out a dry, wheezing laugh, expelling smoke in Melaine's direction. It wreathed her head, and she fought the urge to bat it away.

"There's no difference," said Scroupe. "You sell your body as much as a whore does. Worse, if you ask me."

Melaine set her jaw, gripping the side of her dress, feeling the thin petticoat through a hole in the outer fabric.

"I have a proposition for you," she said, pushing steady strength into her voice.

"If I wanted lodestones, I'd have sought you out myself, Melaine," the overseer drawled.

Melaine blinked.

"You think I don't already know who you are?" he asked, taking another puff. Ash fluttered down onto his dark silk and satin robe. "Jianthe told me you were coming, and I would be foolish not to investigate anyone coming into my presence, would I not?"

Melaine frowned and twitched her head in acknowledgement. Vintor could have warned her that Scroupe would be *expecting* her. Unless Jianthe had passed the information along without Vintor's knowledge.

"One of thousands of orphans from the war, scraping by alone in the streets of Centara for as long as anyone here can remember"—he clicked his tongue and one of his women sauntered over to take his proffered cigar—"who has only survived until now because of her gift with lodestones. Peddling them, as you say, to anyone with enough coin. You're talked about all over Stakeside. Oh, yes, I know all about you, Melaine."

He leaned back into his chair with open arms. "Except for the precise reason you are here. What do you want from me, Stonegirl?"

"I want you to get me an audience with the Overlord," she replied, too annoyed at his prying into her life to follow decorum, though etiquette would have been difficult to follow in as squalid a place as this regardless.

Scroupe laughed. He fell forward, nearly burying his head in his knees as he choked on his bite of hilarity. His women smirked around him, those coherent enough to listen.

"I mean it," Melaine snarled, sparks tingling in her fingertips at her side. The crackle drew up the overseer's head. He eyed her hands with their tiny dots of light, glinting like purple star-flies. A slow smile spread across his heavy jowls.

"Why would the Overlord ever see someone like you?" he asked. "What words of worth could you possibly say to him?"

"That is my business," she said. "I am offering you a trade. Three lodestones in exchange for getting me into his presence. That's all you have to do. I'll give you one stone here and now, and I'll give two more once I've spoken with him."

"There's no guarantee you'll be alive once you've spoken to him," Scroupe mocked. "In any case, the Overlord sees no one. I thought it was common knowledge that he has devoted the past five years to private study."

"He may leave the boring governing to you and your fellow overseers, but he still holds audiences from time to time. *That* is common knowledge, Overseer Scroupe."

The overseer fondled the stem of a wine glass on the small table beside him.

"It is true he *used* to hold audiences with *important* people," he said, taking on a quiet air of superiority. "But for the better part of the past year, he's seen no one. Aside from a very select few." He smiled with satisfaction.

"And you are one of them," Melaine said. "You can get me an audience. Tell him I'll be of value to him." She straightened her posture a little and raised her chin. "I am going to offer myself as a Follower."

The overseer chuckled and shook his head.

"Stonegirl, you seem like a smart child, but your

ignorance is pathetic. The Overlord has not accepted any new Followers into his fold since the war. He is ruler now and has been for two decades. He has no need for such sophisticated and aggressive leaders for his army."

"He can be the one to decide that," Melaine countered, ignoring the scratching of doubt in her head. "Four stones," she offered, hesitating a fraction. "Two now. Two after."

The old man's eyes danced like he was watching a delightful puppet show, but there was a gleam of avarice within them as well.

"Five," he said. "For *trying*. That's all I can do."

"Six," Melaine said. "For *doing*."

Scroupe took a sip of wine, his lips already stained purple like twin bruises. He swirled the liquid around his tongue, never once taking his eyes off her. Melaine maintained his gaze, awful as it was.

"Six," he agreed. "But I want them *all* now."

"I cannot make them all now," Melaine said. "I make the strongest lodestones in the city, but no one has the strength to forge six stones in a row."

"Then you don't have the strength to be a Follower." He was taunting her now. He knew six was an impossible number. And Melaine knew it was impossible for him to guarantee an audience, no matter how hard he tried, and if she gave him all the required lodestones upfront, there was no guarantee he would try at all.

But he was going to refuse her. This was her only chance, the closest she would *ever* get to the Overlord, no doubt even to an overseer. She took a breath, trying to ignore her surroundings and the danger they would pose for any poor weakling caught within the Hole.

"Fine," she said. "Six. Do I have your word?"

Scroupe grinned, revealing his crooked and overlapped teeth, like old books stacked on a shelf, stained purple like his lips.

"Six perfect lodestones, my dear," he said with a bow of his head and a raise of his glass. "And you have my word."

Melaine returned a hardened stare, pressing her resolve into the man so that he wouldn't forget it, and then she stood very still. She pushed her anxiety to the edges of her mind and focused all of her energy on analyzing her body. She listened to the rhythmic hum of power within her, thumping against her eardrums. She felt every subtle tingle of magic in the minute layers of her skin, but she delved deeper. She felt the sleek stretch of it through her muscles, riding along the facets of her bones until she penetrated the marrow where her magic twisted and curled in the gelatinous tissue.

She took deep breaths, flooding air into her lungs. Her heart pumped blood through her veins, veins she then filled with fiery magic, bringing it to the surface of her palms through tiny capillaries.

Melaine had been making lodestones for years. The process was easy by now, but it was always draining. As her veins grew cold and her palms grew hot, she wondered how in the Overlord's name she was going to make six in one sitting.

Purple streaks were visible beneath her pale skin as her magic pulsed through her veins and began to coalesce into a lump beneath the skin of her right palm. A purple-black stone began to dig its way out. She winced at the sharp, prickling sensation, always glad that it hurt less than it looked like it would.

She clenched her hand around the hot stone as it separated from her body. It was a diamond shape, an inch wide from one side to the other. Overseer Scroupe had asked for perfect, and he would get what he wanted.

She held out the stone, trying to hide her exhaustion. Scroupe gave her a vile smile and took the stone. He cocked his eyebrow, waiting for more. He was clearly enjoying her misery.

Melaine refocused her willpower and summoned more magic from her bones, through her muscles, and into her veins. Her nerve endings shot in erratic zips of light, but she focused on the pain in her palm from a freshly emerging stone. She had to keep herself grounded. She held her left hand over her right, pushing more magic down onto the stone as she flooded the magic upward. She gritted her teeth and held out a second glowing purple stone to Scroupe.

She was starting to feel lightheaded, but she had to keep going. If she paused even for a moment, she feared her loss of momentum would make her cave. She dragged more magic from her body, infusing a third stone, which she handed off to the gloating overseer.

He took it, but then Melaine staggered and put her hands on her thighs to brace herself. She breathed deep, trying to stop her head from spinning and to keep herself standing. Three more.

I'll be on the floor, she thought. *In the Hole. I'll be stuck in the Hole.*

She shuddered and yanked more magic from her body and into another stone. She had to keep her head. Who knew what beastly things the predators in the Hole would do to her if she fainted? Worse, if she was conscious but too weak to fight back?

Her breaths came faster as she began to panic, and her heart fluttered like beating wings against her ribcage. She dropped the new stone. Tears sprang into her eyes as she desperately tried to wring more magic from her bones, but there was nothing there.

She felt like she was waiting for sticky sap to dribble through her body and into her hand. A stone began to form, but it was crumbling clay, refusing to stick together.

"No," she whispered. They had to be perfect. Six perfect lodestones. She closed her eyes, squeezing out tears far easier than she could squeeze out magic. Slowly, she forced the stone to form, larger and sharper, solid and firm. She dropped to her knees. The stone rolled toward Scroupe's velvet slippers, which blurred and melded into the red carpet in her vision.

"What do you think, ladies?" echoed Scroupe's voice. "Can she do it?" Muffled laughter rang in Melaine's ears, pulsing in time with the gargling music from the clanking mechagic in the corner.

No, no, Melaine wanted to say. She fell onto all fours, staring at a dark, mottled stain on the carpet.

She groaned in concentration and squeezed her eyes shut again. She slumped onto her forearms as a hard, pea-sized lump rose from the skin of her palm. Her hands shook; she struggled to bring them together to press the tiny stone between them. She cupped it like a glowing coal, breathing magic into it as she would air to a fire.

She felt the stone kindle and grow, and she pictured the images she had seen of the Overlord, his black hair, more luxurious than her own, his sharp, cold blue eyes, his mouth's hard line. He was the epitome of strength and dominance. Oh, if she could be like him. If he would teach her. If he would *talk* to her...

Melaine gave a last, wrenching cry and shoved the stone away. Her chin collided with the floor, and she rolled and saw the bleary, evil grimace of Overseer Scroupe above her head before her senses gave out.

❦

FIRE SPARKED AND SPUTTERED. AN EMBER POPPED AND burrowed its way into Melaine's skin. She winced and rolled over until she was staring at the sloped ceiling of her rented room.

A sharp clatter made her sit up so fast that black spots mottled her vision. The horrors of the past night plunged into her heart and permeated her limbs with icy cold. She took short, sharp breaths and looked around wildly.

"Calm yourself, child," snapped Salma. She drove an iron poker into a floating fire in the corner, spraying Melaine's chamber pot with sparks and ash.

"How did I get back?" Melaine asked in a hoarse voice, assessing her body for damage.

"Yah think I was goin' ta let you go down into that pit

by yahself? When Jianthe told me where yah was goin'..."
Melaine watched Salma's skirts wiggle around her large
backside as she set down the poker and ladled stew into
wooden bowls.

"You followed me?" Melaine grumbled.

"Yah'd better be glad I did," Salma said, turning
around and plunking down a bowl in front of Melaine
without ceremony. "More than one of those buggers had
an eye on yah—a lot more. And let me tell yah, my cousin
went down there alone once, and he didn't come out the
same."

Melaine shuddered and shoved her bowl of stew away.
The dank smells of the Hole seemed to meld with the
steam.

"I knew they'd never let me in wit yah ta see his
majesty, the Overseer of Shit, but I wasn't about ta leave
yah wit the likes of him, and you'd be lucky if he was the
worst yah saw."

Salma sat herself down on the pallet beside
Melaine.

"So?" Salma asked. "Yah still lookin' ta get yahself
killed?"

Melaine scowled and scuffed one boot with the other.
"No one's getting killed," she answered. "I'm going to see
him."

"Ah, I see, and *then* get yahself killed," Salma said.
"Well, it's noble aspirations indeed ta wish ta be killed by
the Overlord himself." She tsked and returned her focus
to her stew.

"I'd rather die at his hands than keep living here,"
Melaine growled.

"Eh, now," Salma said between gulps. "This is my place you're insultin'."

"You know what I mean, Salma."

Salma set down her stew, eaten with the haste of those who are never guaranteed their next meal. She set her face into a stern frown.

"Now look here," she said. "I've known yah since you were a babe, toddlin' round Clide Street, beggin' for sweets cause yah didn't know any better. I've never had the time nor means to care for a babe, but I've looked after yah as best I could."

"I take care of myself," Melaine muttered.

"Aye, and that's my point," Salma said. "I spread the word that no one's ta harm yah. I send customers your way, but that's all I can do, yah know that." Salma rapped the low ceiling that brushed her flyaway auburn curls on top of her head. "This place is one of the priciest in Stakeside, and believe me, I cannot afford to charge yah any less than I would anyone else. I dunnot run a charity, Mela. Yah pay for this all on your own. Yah make them lodestones like yah was born for it. Yah live a good life, child. Rough here and there, aye, but yah live a far better life than most. Yah'd be foolish ta ask for more."

"I'd be foolish to think there was nothing better," Melaine retorted. "Anyway, it's done. Overseer Scroupe's going to get me an audience with the Overlord. Things are going to change."

"And what would yah do if yah met the Overlord?" Salma asked. Melaine stiffened at the sudden harshness in her tone. "Yah weren't there when the Overlord took the city, but I was. I'll never forget him ridin' in wit his army, slaughterin' anyone in his way. He uses dark magic, Melaine, *evil* magic. Black as night, blastin' spells, his Followers raging behind 'im. And the fire in his eyes, Mela..."

Salma stopped, her glare turning to disbelief. "And look at yah, lightin' up at an image like that."

She took Melaine's hands and held on tightly enough to stop Melaine from jerking them back. "Child. Yah're surrounded by thieves and murderers in these streets, and yah've never taken up wit them. The Overlord's worse. *Far* worse. The things he's done."

Melaine pulled her hands away. Salma *knew* she hated people touching them.

"Thieves and murderers in Stakeside only do it to survive," Melaine said. "The Overlord does black magic for a *cause*. He stamped out the Luxian Order. He vanquished the old ways. He's made room for progress—"

"And look where that's gotten us," Salma said, raising her hands wide to the tiny, dark room in the middle of Stakeside. Melaine hesitated.

"He murdered Queen Adelasia in cold blood, Melaine," Salma said. "She was so beautiful. I saw her when I was a child, paradin' through the streets with flowers and dancin'.... And then the Overlord's revolt happened, and the streets burned, and a dagger was sheathed in the queen's breast in her own throne room. Yah're tryin' ta get into things yah know nothin' about, Mela. The old kingdom, the Overlord's conquest, the days of the *terrible* war are gone. This is all that's left. It's time ta stop being a child."

"I'm as grown as you," Melaine argued. "And I've already accomplished more than you ever will."

Melaine clenched her jaw, a speck of guilt hitting her, but she refused to take back her words.

Salma shook her head.

"Child, that overseer took your stones, and yah know as well as I do, yah'll never see him again." She softened, giving Melaine a sympathetic look. "There's no point in false hope, Mela."

Salma grunted and stood, her knees popping. "Eat your stew," she ordered. "Good horsemeat, that is. Didn't come cheap."

She rubbed her hands together as though warming them on a cold night. She then pushed her open palms toward the fire as if it was surrounded by a little wall that she had to topple. The fire sputtered and went out under her spell. She swept her hand in dismissal, and the smoke and ashes disappeared with a soft flurry of sepia magic.

"I'd leave the fire for yah, but it'd be at least nightfall before yah'd have the strength ta put it out. Maybe longer." She eyed Melaine with her hands on her hips. "Yah'll be outta work for a day, maybe two. I'll still expect rent on time. Yah know I dunnot 'ave a choice. The customers expect a stocked bar and hot meals."

Melaine closed her eyes and nodded. "Yes, I know."

"I'll check in on yah tomorrow," Salma offered.

"No," said Melaine. "I'll be fine. I always am."

"Aye," grunted Salma, but she wore a begrudging smile. "Yah always find a way. Resourceful, yah are, even if yah are foolish." She shook her head again and opened the door. Stagnant, cold air seeped into the room. Salma looked out at the cloud-streaked sky and the bleak sun.

"Goin' ta be a cold winter," she murmured. She wrapped her ratty shawl closer around her shoulders and exited the room, closing the door behind her. Melaine pulled the extra blanket Salma had brought and burrowed into it, reveling in the quiet darkness, pushing away the creeping visions and squirming doubts that chilled her far more than the cold.

CHAPTER 4

A full two days passed before Melaine was back to work. Even then, summoning the magic to make a fresh lodestone for a demanding old woman with knotted tree limbs for fingers was trying. She only got a half-pence for it, and she had to admit, anything more would have been cheating the customer.

The morning after, she arose finally feeling more like herself. Magic tingled her toes within her holey stockings and worn boots. Warmth in her chest kept out the chill of the early autumn morning as she left her room and walked down the rotted stairs.

She closed her eyes as she reached the cobblestones. If only she could keep it. Keep all of her magic to herself. Never sell it away again to the greedy hands of those whose magic was nothing compared to hers.

A luxury she could never afford.

She exhaled roughly through her nose and started walking. She despised peddling from a street corner, but she didn't have any planned customers for the day, and rent was due soon. She had no time to waste.

The corner on Thatch Street was usually unoccupied this time of morning. The prostitutes were still in bed with their clients or sleeping off exhaustion from a full night, so there was less of a chance she would be mistaken for one, though it had happened often enough. Then again, it might be better this morning if some were already awake. She sold stones to prostitutes, or their pimps or madams, fairly often. Lodestones could give flesh-peddlers the stamina they needed to keep up with customer after customer or give their varied sex spells a boost of intensity. The best brothel in Stakeside had the most unique Insights at their disposal, numerous pleasure spells that were made all the better when they used Melaine's magic.

She'd been invited to join a brothel on several occasions, but even in the smallest glimpses of consideration, she would shudder with thoughts of wrapping herself around a man, immersed in his filthy skin. No matter how often she saw the slip of a satisfied smile on a prostitute's face following a sale, or how often some would claim that sex could be a better high than sniker with the right person, the idea of exposing her body to the risks of countless diseases other humans carried was repulsive. Worse than the taint of residual magic. At least she didn't have to touch her vile customers. She'd fought tooth, nail, and spell before to keep it that way.

A rise of bitterness rose in Melaine's throat. If it was possible for prostitutes to find pleasure in their trade from time to time, Melaine didn't have even that small, simple luxury. Lodestones held no pleasure. Ever. They were a sickening, seeping drain. She didn't know any other lodestone-peddlers, and the closest catharsis she could attain with flesh-peddlers wasn't quite the same. So, despite an unspoken camaraderie between peddlers of either stone or flesh, Melaine kept her distance aside from business interactions. She couldn't shake the feeling that she was alone. That she was different, even from them.

Yet, she tore off her gloves like a ripped bodice and headed for the street corner all the same. She stuffed them in her pocket, exposing her naked hands to the cold air. She rubbed her palms together in circles and felt them push farther apart as if they were repelling magnets. She summoned deep purple wisps of magic to wreathe her hands, ready for display so people would know what she had to offer. The *only* wares she would consent to sell.

Her boots clicked on the cobblestones. She passed a man with a hacking cough, who folded in on himself against the wall of a carpenter's shack. She recoiled and crossed the street. No matter how many murders in alleyways or falls on icy streets there might be, disease was the highest killer in Stakeside.

A child ran by with pounding steps, a purse in hand. Whoever's it was clearly hadn't realized it was missing yet. Otherwise, it was quiet on the streets. A bad sign for business.

Melaine turned a sharp corner into an alley that served as a shortcut to Thatch Street.

A wall of magic slammed into her body so hard that she tumbled backward onto the ground.

"Hey!" she shouted, wincing as she twisted her wrist to check its range of movement. "What the fuck do you—"

Two men in black leather armor rushed at Melaine. *Shields.*

Down *here?*

Melaine summoned magic to her fingertips and dove her other hand into her pocket for a vial of corrosion potion, but the guards were on her before she could do much with either defense. They each grabbed her arms, and one slapped a hand over her mouth. Her lips closed, and her tongue froze under his spell. The man released her mouth, but she couldn't open it as he and his partner dragged her toward an ominous, black prison cart waiting around the corner of the back alley.

Melaine struggled in greater earnest, but the Shields' bodies were stronger than her own twig frame. Her fingers crackled with magic, but the Shield on her right clapped one of her hands against the other. Her palms stuck together, extinguishing her magic. Melaine panicked as the other Shield opened the heavy black door of the cart. She didn't know how to break a captivity spell.

The large brown workhorse at the front of the cart huffed in protest and twitched its broad flank as the men shoved Melaine into the cart and slammed the door behind her. Melaine tumbled to the floor. There were no seats. Prisoners didn't deserve them.

She heard the Shields climb onto the front of the cart to handle the horses. One chided the horse forward, and the cart began to roll across the jarring cobblestones, crushing stray leaves and broken glass.

Melaine tried to get on her feet, but the cart turned a

corner, and she fell back against the wall. Her head hit something that poked her skull, jutting out from the cart's interior. She looked up and saw the thin outline of sunlight surrounding a small, metal rectangle. A piece of metal on the rectangle's left side was the offender that had hurt her scalp. She reached up with both hands, her palms still clapped together, and shoved the crude handle to the right.

The metal slat shifted open, revealing a tiny window to the outside streets. Melaine braced her shoulder against the wall as the cart continued its bumpy course down the main street of Stakeside. Gawkers lined the gutter, and Melaine avoided their stares and paid attention to where the cart was headed instead. Her view was severely limited, but her heart began to beat faster as she realized where they were going.

The Stakeside wall.

It was drawing closer—that barrier that had penned her in for as long as she could remember. It was gray and dirty and covered in moss and lichen. It wasn't even that tall, but when the cart rumbled to the small, simple gate that was always barred and guarded from the Middun side, Melaine realized that she was about to do the impossible. She was about to pass through the gate and leave Stakeside.

As a prisoner.

Her breaths quickened as she heard one of the Shields at the front of the prison cart speaking to another guard who stood on the outside of the wall. The words were muffled through the cart, but the creaking hinges of the gate were loud. The cart started moving again, and as they passed through the gate, Melaine's black eyes widened at the sight of something she'd never seen before—the inner edge of the Stakeside wall. The wall was thinner than she had expected.

The cart rumbled past, and within seconds, they were through the gate and leaving the wall behind as though it wasn't a momentous occasion at all.

Melaine stood on her tiptoes and strained to see as much of her surroundings as possible while the cart kept moving forward. She had only heard talk of the way of life in Middun. Now she was *seeing* it for herself.

The homes and shops on this side of the wall were of boxy, stacked architecture, not unlike Stakeside, but their signs were all straight and well-painted, and the laundry hanging on lines between them had no noticeable holes. The appearance of the people who stepped out of their homes to greet morning's light matched the presentable nature of their laundry—well-mended clothing, styled hair, and clean faces and hands, albeit calloused from lives of hard work. Hard work that clearly paid them well enough to live such good lives.

Each person the cart passed looked into Melaine's peering eyes with contempt.

Melaine glared and turned her eyes forward. They were approaching another wall, yet this wall's gate was already open. Shields stood at the entrance on both sides, but they barely inspected anyone before waving people through. When the prison cart reached them, Melaine heard more muffled words, and then the guard at the gate nodded the cart through.

The buildings on the other side gradually grew even

cleaner and taller, and the people wore more varied colors. Melaine even spotted a few women wearing jewelry around their necks and fingers. One man had a pocket watch, dangling from a blue vest similar to Vintor's but much newer.

Melaine's mind started to feel a touch of magic as she looked at the new and colorful fabrics that people wore while the prison cart continued through the upper section of Middun. The Insight she'd recently imbibed had shown her hundreds of materials, ready to be magically mended should Melaine ever have a need.

A woman passed by wearing a green silk bodice and poplin skirt with a poufy satin bustle. A matching satin ribbon tied a straw hat upon her head, a big bow fluttering underneath her chin. A little girl walked hand-in-hand with a man whom Melaine assumed was her father; the pair looked so wholesome. The girl's pastel dress flounced with taffeta, and Melaine recognized the father's waistcoat as a fine wool under a broadcloth suit.

The knowledge was a little overwhelming, and as happy as Melaine had been to learn the spell, she now pondered how useless something like that would be in prison.

Prison. Was that where she was going? They had now reached the third wall, and Melaine knew what lay beyond. Crossing's Square. All of the rich gathered there, putting the lesser classes behind walls, out of sight and mind. The richest had their own private walls around large estates, of course. Melaine couldn't even imagine what a rich person's estate might look like. She had heard they had gardens—expansive areas filled with nothing but plants, purely for the luxury of walking through them. She couldn't imagine having time to walk for no reason other than to look at something as trivial as flowers. Though she had heard roses were lovely.

Roses weren't the only thing that hid behind the Crossing's Square wall. The Blackspire Prison lurked there as well. It had been a cathedral of the Luxian Order before that religion had been banned. Supposedly, it held many of the Luxian Order still, the ones responsible for the mass executions of lodestone-makers and other supposed heretics. They shared cells with all the other worst criminals of Centara. From what she'd heard, the prison was close to the palace, but its proximity to the Overlord wasn't a good thing, even to Melaine. No one ever came out of Blackspire, yet somehow, stories did. Horrific stories.

Melaine banged on the side of the cart, again and again, sending reverberations through the walls and floor. No response.

When the cobblestones started to smooth and the rumbling grew quieter, Melaine tried again. Soon, the cart hardly shook at all anymore, but the guards continued to ignore her.

Melaine's gaze settled back on the tiny window, and all of her attention latched onto the new, unbelievable sights. No matter her fear, she couldn't look away from the glittering, gleaming spectacle outside of her moving jail.

After leaving Stakeside, the buildings had grown increasingly taller, but here in Crossing's Square, they were shorter again, no more than three stories at most. Their shorter heights made them classy and elegant, as if a building tall enough to block the view of the trees' autumn leaves and the blue sky above would be offensive. Melaine eyed the trees as she passed by. Even Crossing's Square's leaves seemed more vibrant than Stakeside's.

The leaves were nowhere near as bright as the shimmering colors that enveloped the aristocrats who sauntered by arm-in-arm on a leisurely stroll or rode about in open-air carriages drawn by fine horses. Their elegantly tailored clothing adorned impossibly clean bodies. The fabric was even finer and more varied than in Middun. Some of the women's dresses were lined with fur, and they wore pristine, white, kidskin gloves in the light autumn chill.

A couple, who seemed to enjoy each other's company more than their fine surroundings, passed under a wrought-iron streetlamp that glowed with a green flame, despite it being daylight. Melaine's eyes widened as she saw the green everflame, something she'd only heard about in stories. It was highly expensive, flaring from enchanted powder that guaranteed the fire would burn forever—or so the stories said. Perhaps there was a time limit, but it must be a long one to have allowed the flame to gain its name.

Everflame or not, Melaine couldn't believe people were wasting fuel on the lamps when the sun shone down so brightly that the flames were hardly visible. Yet they glowed not only from streetlamps but from lanterns attached on either side of the fine houses the cart passed by, as well as from other carriages.

Stretches of tall, spotless white walls hid all but the roofs of many houses, no doubt encircling large estates.

Shields were posted along the walls and under everflame streetlamps, wearing glinting metal armor—buffed cuirasses and helmets with the regimented symbol of a shield embossed onto their surfaces. No Shield ever wore fine metal armor into Stakeside. The thugs and thieves weren't as intimidated by the Shields when they were in their territory or in great numbers. Shining armor would only attract unwanted attention. In Stakeside, Shields like the ones who'd taken Melaine wore inconspicuous black leather.

Though the Crossing's Square Shields all stood stiff and tall, they also looked bored. Melaine watched several Shields nod or salute passing civilians in respect and deference. She narrowed her eyes in disbelief. The upper-class citizens of Centara weren't afraid of the guards. The Shields were not the authority, not really. The true authority was money.

Why did the Overlord not intervene? Why did he let his guards get so complacent?

The Followers weren't that way. Melaine knew it. They weren't petty Shields in the street. The Followers guarded the palace itself, direct servants to the Overlord, just as they had served him as right-hand battlemages during the war.

Melaine felt a thrill when she pictured them, as she always did. No doubt their armor was even shinier than the Shields'. Her stomach roiled again. Would she ever see a Follower where she was headed? Was she going to die before she ever met the Overlord?

Where were they taking her?

She chewed the inside of her cheek as the cart turned

another corner. She wanted to shout at her captors, but her lips were still glued shut by the Shield's spell. She could hardly even swallow.

Then Melaine's heart slowed. A view far better than any she had seen so far glimmered through the window.

The Centara Palace.

Its stone pinnacles looked like they aspired to touch the clouds, thin and delicate as black lace but sharp as daggers. Every straight section of the roof's ridges was bedecked with wrought-iron railings, twisted into all sorts of strong and beautiful flourishes and angles. The eaves and windows were all pointed arches set in deep hollows where stained glass dwelled, the colors only glinting in the narrow shafts of sunlight that could reach inside each recess.

It had been the palace of the White City once—under King Malik's rule. Much of it was destroyed during the Overlord's attack, and he had rebuilt the wounded sections in a much more modern style, full of wrought-iron and copper, enchanted to stay lustrous forever, regardless of age or weather. The sharp points and over-hanging arches had a menacing nature, but Melaine thought the architecture reflected the Overlord's might. There were many ways to express one's power—fear was one of them. Fear was something Melaine had learned to live with and something she strove to overcome. Fear was something she could appreciate. Fear was something she could use if given the chance.

Her chances were looking slim, however, and her bright glimpse of the palace was fleeting. The cart turned down a narrow alley, where it was flanked on either side by buildings too tall to keep the palace in view. Melaine grew hot as her legs started to feel wobbly. They really were taking her to Blackspire Prison. Her insolence in approaching an overseer and her knowledge that he visited the Hole on a regular basis had done nothing but earn her a cell in Blackspire. Salma was right. She was a fool to think she would ever lay eyes on the Overlord.

The cart reached the ends of the buildings and slowed to a halt in the back alley. Melaine huffed a wry, silent laugh. Even the alleys of Crossing's Square were spotless.

She jerked as the door on the opposite side of the cart opened. Sunlight streamed in, making her squint and unable to dodge a Shield's firm grasp as one of them dove inside to grab her. She let out a closed-mouth scream and kicked the guard's shin. He grunted but didn't loosen his hold on her arm as he dragged her out of the cart.

"Get in there, you bitch," he ordered gruffly as he shoved her out of the door and straight into another confined space. She fell onto a seat and righted herself just as he slammed the door shut.

Melaine's eyes flew about her new surroundings. She was in a carriage, not a cart. A carriage. A *fancy* carriage. The seat beneath her was soft and bouncy, covered by a thick, black velvet cushion. Another seat faced her, empty. The inside walls of the carriage were plastered with silk paper painted with curling, golden designs. Two caged, wrought-iron candlesticks were bolted to each side by the doors with two dim everflame candles shedding soft, green light. Melaine stared at the nearest flame. It wasn't flickering at all, steadier than she'd ever seen a fire before.

She whipped her neck the other way when the door opposite from the prison cart opened. Her eyes widened as Overseer Scroupe slid into the carriage and snapped the door shut again.

He took the seat opposite from her, leering with his salacious grimace in the light of the sun and the everflame candles. His wrinkles looked even deeper in daylight and his jowls heavier, but he also looked far more respectable. His black overseer uniform, with its single, diagonal white lapel and series of white buttons down the sides of his trousers, squared his figure. His silver cufflinks and buckled shoes glittered. He folded his arms across his chest and eyed Melaine. A silent question gleamed in his eyes, like he was trying to discover a vein of gold that someone claimed lurked in a chunk of quartz.

He snapped his fingers, and her tongue released from the roof of her mouth. Her lips parted, breaking the spell the Shields had used to shut her up.

Melaine took a full breath and met his eyes. Her mouth was so dry she barely managed the word, "Well?"

"My, you are a rude one," Scroupe tsked. "That is no way to speak to an overseer." His eyes glinted dangerously, but they were glazed with age and had lost their edge.

Melaine raised her eyebrows, not saying a word. Waiting.

He laughed. "Oh, what I would do to put you in your place if I had the time. But no such luck. It seems *you* are the one with all the luck today."

Melaine's stomach flipped.

"The Overlord will see me?" she whispered, her voice not cooperating further.

"He'll see you," Scroupe said. "Why he would see you confounds me, but I do not pretend to fathom what goes through our Lord's head. I *do* suspect that he will kill you as soon as you open your mouth if you speak to him as you did me just now."

Melaine swallowed, and her hands began to tremble. "I won't," she said.

Scroupe chuckled. "Changed your tune, now?" He snapped his fingers, and the spell holding her palms together released. She twisted her wrists in circles, working out the tight joints.

"This carriage will see you to him," Scroupe said.

Melaine's eyes widened. "Now?"

She glanced down at her torn dress and dirty hands from her fall before she'd been thrust into the prison cart.

The man let out a biting laugh.

"No amount of soap would clean you up, Stonegirl," he said. "You're lucky I'm letting you dirty my carriage. Though this is far from my finest, of course."

Magic crackled at Melaine's fingertips, but her nerves smothered her anger. She eyed the carriage, trying and failing to imagine one any grander.

"Time to go," Scroupe said as he opened his door. Melaine stiffened, uncertain if she should bolt after him to escape, or remain in the carriage and hope for the best. It was still possible that Scroupe didn't want to risk having a stone-peddler knowing of his activities in the Hole, and this was all a ruse to get her somewhere private and do away with her. But why would he go to the trouble? Melaine might be well-known in Stakeside, but as

Jianthe had said, no nobleman would ever listen to her tales, true or not.

If the Overlord really did want to see her, then all of that could change. She could become important enough to influence the city.

Scroupe stepped out of the carriage with grace befitting his station, but Melaine heard one of his knees pop as he reached the street.

"I thank you for your delicious stones, Melaine," he said with a simpering grin. "Perhaps, if you survive, I'll find you again."

Melaine glared as he stepped away, and the door snapped shut by itself with a twang of springs. She didn't know if Scroupe was mocking her or not, but either way, the thought of his disgusting mouth inhaling her magic from no less than six of her stones affirmed that she never wanted to see him again.

She wrapped her boney knuckles around the silver handle of the paper-lined carriage door, both crafted from finer materials than she'd ever touched. The luxuries bore both a promise and a threat. This carriage would either take her to a powerful, decadent life or sentence her to a swift end.

She didn't turn the handle. She breathed deeply the smothering air. It smelled of expensive cologne and flowery perfume—the real stuff, not the cheap imitation scents used in an attempt to mask the stench that clung to Stakeside's streets. A faint whiff of some woodsy scent also drifted into her nose. It had the faint bite of alcohol, but she had never smelled or tasted any alcohol so smooth before.

She eyed Scroupe through a window of frosted glass with silver gilding curled around the frames. Scroupe hadn't moved from his cocky stance, but now he slid a wand from within his uniform sleeve. Melaine focused on it, jealousy surging in her gut.

Every human could use magic to an extent. It nestled in their bone marrow, waiting to be tapped into from birth, but only the wealthy could afford wands. Wands allowed the owner to channel their magic like ice melting down a mountainside. They shot the magic outward with more power than a person could possess by hand alone.

Wands also had the power to collect and store temporary knowledge as Insights could. Learning from Insights took time and energy and magic, but with wands, a person could cast any of the spells stored in the wand without having learned it themselves. Without the wand, they would lose some magical ability, but with it, they could become immensely powerful in an instant.

Scroupe's wand was ostentatious, coated in silver and gold with a massive emerald embedded in its pommel. He flicked it toward the front of the carriage, where a metal lever rose to the side of the place a driver would normally sit. Two mechanical rods with hinges began to steer the reins of two fine, black horses.

The carriage's navigation was autonomous, metal with cogs and springs and levers, fueled by magic.

Just days ago, she'd thought she would never lay eyes on a mechagic-assisted carriage. Even if the carriage was taking her to her execution, at least she could die knowing she'd witnessed wealth. The thought wasn't as comforting as she'd expected.

"Highstrong Keep," Scroupe directed the carriage, his voice muffled by the glass of the windowpane.

"Wait—we're not going to the palace?" Melaine asked, recognizing the name of the new location. She put a hand on the glass.

"*We're* not going anywhere," Overseer Scroupe replied. "*You* are going to Highstrong Keep. The Overlord no longer stays in Centara."

❦

Highstrong.

Melaine shuddered as the carriage fled the city, trading the cobblestone streets and timber-and-stone buildings for a wide, muddy road and tall, menacing trees with ever-thicker trunks. Tangled briars clawed at their roots, not a flower or berry among them in the early autumn. Their twisted, narrow leaves were turning brown, rattling like dried husks in the wind or the scrabbling claws of rats. Crows cawed and beat their wings among the tree branches, their black bodies hunched like hooded reapers on their perch as they watched the carriage go by.

Highstrong Keep was visible from Stakeside roofs—a small, black spot on a high crag far beyond the south wall. Most people avoided looking at it, as if a single glance would bring a curse upon them.

It had long been said the ancient keep was haunted. It had been nothing but First Era ruins in the old days before the war. Then the Overlord had used it as a foothold for his attack on the White City. New rumors held that he had started using it as experimental ground for his darkest magic in recent years.

Now, it was said to be worse than haunted.

Melaine had never given credence to the rumors about Highstrong Keep. Imaginings of the Overlord's mysterious experiments thrilled her with goosebumps, but she had never thought it likely the Overlord would use Highstrong for anything. Not when he had a magnificent palace at his disposal.

Now, she didn't understand why the Overlord sat back in Highstrong's walls while his overseers ate into the populace like termites, growing fat as they destroyed the city from the inside. Judging from his face in the beautiful illustrations, she *knew* he had to have a good reason for being there. Someone as ingenious as he must have a good reason for every little decision he made.

Melaine hoped one such decision would be to *not* kill her upon arrival.

She rubbed her clammy fingers together while the trees crowded round and the horses sped through them. The nervous beasts ran as if the trees were ghastly predators, reaching out to scratch them with skeletal limbs. Melaine kept her eyes on the windows, trying to maintain sharp awareness of her surroundings at every moment, but the closeness of the trees soon blocked out the sunlight. She was riding in the dark.

She could hear nothing but the pounding beat of the horses' hooves and the rolling clatter of carriage wheels. She held on to the seat beneath her, tightening her grip on the velvet cushion with every jarring bump and clenching her teeth so she wouldn't bite her tongue. The carriage started ascending a steep incline. The metal rods and springs of the navigation mechagic grated and rang with every twist up a narrow trail that deviated from the main road.

The trees finally thinned, giving way to massive, looming boulders that took on monstrous forms of hulking giants. The sun was low in the sky behind Melaine, and the stones cast mountainous shadows over the carriage. As the road continued to wind upward, the boulders started to fuse into one another along the roadsides. They appeared to be actively closing in, stomping along the landscape in silent threat.

Melaine shrank against the silk-papered wall and huddled under the everflame candlestick as the carriage made another sharp turn and rolled along a craggy plateau. Trees took over the land again on the left side of the carriage, and the huge boulders on the right fused into an enormous wall of seamless, gray granite that stretched far ahead. It seemed to be a part of the plateau itself, exposed bones of the cliffs, excavated to provide an impenetrable barrier against any army that dare lay siege to Highstrong Keep.

Melaine watched the natural rock wall with wide eyes as it continued to dominate the plateau. It seemed endless, but after some time, the carriage rolled to a stop with the sharp pop of magic and the twang of springs and hinges. The horses whinnied, their hooves stamping hard at packed dirt.

A gate loomed over Melaine. With her jaw dropped in awe, she twisted her neck into an uncomfortable position to stare as high as she was able.

The giant gate was made from countless columns of pure black, iron bars. They extended from the crags at her feet to the top of the towering wall, arranged like a grand pipe organ. Melaine could feel potent magic pushing through her carriage door like the reverberations of a dirge. The magic emanated from the gate's center—a barrier far stronger than the imposing, impenetrable iron.

Dread filled her heart. A spell—a dark spell—consumed her. It told her to turn back or suffer death. Whispers, whispers in her ears, cold fingers around her throat, claws rending the soles of her feet, goading her to run, run....

But then the gate shuddered. The ground shook and rocked the carriage as the groan of mighty gears rumbled from under the gate's threshold. The horses reared, and Melaine's shoulder hit the door, hard. It sprang open, and she tumbled to the ground, barely rolling out of the way in time as the horses bolted, dragging the rattling carriage behind them.

Melaine lay on her stomach, panting against the dry leaves and heather that covered a bed of granite. She braced her hands against the ground and looked up. The great iron bars were opening vertically, every other bar rising while the interlocking rows lowered into a trench in the ground. The black gate yawned like the maw of a dangerous beast. The harsh squeal of metal tingled Melaine's teeth as if she were crunching on iron shavings. She squinted her eyes shut, but the noise morphed into strange, echoing screams, and bombardments of siege trebuchets battered her senses. It was as if the monster of a gate remembered all of the battles it had seen and was moaning in agony at its forced opening.

Finally, with a last great clang, the shaking ground settled. Everything was quiet.

Melaine opened her eyes. The gate was open, reduced to a thick beam of iron that stretched from the top of the stone wall to a grated iron trench in the ground. The magical barrier, so oppressive moments ago, had lifted as well. Melaine took a freeing breath of cool air and summoned the courage to heave herself off the hard earth.

She dusted her gloved hands on her dress out of habit, then attempted to brush the dust off her dress onto the ground. She huffed through her nostrils. Scroupe was right—nothing she did could make her presentable enough for the *Overlord*. He would have to judge her as she was.

She grabbed handfuls of her dress to keep the ratty hem from collecting dried leaves and thistles and then walked forward. She halted when she reached the iron trench. She entertained the horrible idea that the gate would roar to life and spear her with its iron teeth from above and below, crushing her to a pulp. Perhaps the Overlord had only brought her here for his macabre amusement and watched from some tower, waiting for her to cross the threshold.

Melaine lifted her boot an inch. She had told Salma she would rather die than sell lodestones in Stakeside, and if there was one vice Melaine didn't have, it was lying.

She jumped over the trench and stumbled to the other side. The ground shook again. She spun around as the insidious gate shrieked upward and downward to clasp its iron jaws much faster than its reluctant opening. It locked into place. The only way in or out shut as the high, seamless rock wall dissolved into the fog.

Melaine was used to walls. Walls surrounding Centara. Walls segregating its inhabitants by class. A wall penning her into Stakeside. Walls didn't make Melaine feel trapped nor protected. They were just there, a part of her life like every other obstacle she faced.

Still, Melaine was grateful that no harsh defensive magic crawled toward her from this side of the massive gate. There was no question that she would feel claustrophobia like she never had before if she experienced that dark dread from *inside* the wall. At least at this point, she felt she had a way out if necessary.

"Melaine."

Melaine startled and turned around. A woman stood before her, tall and rigid. She was old but did not hunch or possess arthritic fingers like Melaine was used to seeing in people even younger. Gray wisps from her grand bun floated around her head like bees around a cone-hive, the wrinkles in her face as structured as honeycombs. Her black dress collared her neck, and a neat column of pearl buttons ran down her bosom. The hidden corset underneath was tied to force her perfect posture, and the crepe overlay on her skirt matched the poufy sleeves that billowed around her arms before they were suddenly restricted by tight cuffs around her wrists, more pearl buttons glinting at each side.

The sharp-featured woman did a single visual sweep of

Melaine, her eyes the only part of her that moved, but her disapproval was apparent.

"Come," she said, her voice as firm and austere as her appearance. She turned around as if she had no feet at all, her strides so smooth she could have been hovering over the black, stone flags of the courtyard.

Melaine looked past the woman, and her eyes widened.

Highstrong Keep rose from the stone flags as though it, too, had been excavated from the granite plateau. The ancient building was enormous, with sheer cliffs for walls that looked unscalable. Only slits for windows scratched its edifice, just wide enough for an archer to shoot an arrow or a targeted bolt of magic through. Two tall, hexagonal towers rose into sharp points like stakes. One loomed to Melaine's right, and the other's roof was just visible on the rear side of the keep that overlooked the cliffside.

Parapets protected the long, straight walls of the building's roof. They were lined with wrought-iron spikes that looked like studded maces, modern additions that contrasted with the First Era edifice. Only the towers had real windows. They were all near the rooftops and paned with old, green glaze and were no doubt shielded with magic.

Crows decked the battlements as living gargoyles. Their caws sounded like they were exchanging gargled words of warning.

Melaine was too enamored by the sight to consider following the woman, but then a blast of icy wind stole her breath, and a spike of magic kicked her on the backside. She fled from the compelling gate the same way she used to run from Salma whenever she'd nicked a stale scone from the pub as a child.

There was no center door leading into the massive building, adding to its looming, impenetrable presence. Melaine followed the old woman through the courtyard to the left of the keep. Brown grass and withered weeds crept through the flags at her feet, conjuring images of prisoners' fingers trying to escape from underground dungeons she was sure existed in a place like this. A few weeds were long enough to snatch at her dress, begging her to rescue them from the oppressive stone.

A large stable house was ahead, perpendicular to the keep. Its doors were open, the stalls empty of horses and no carriage in sight. If Melaine planned on leaving at any time, it looked like the only way was on foot.

Lean-tos and temporary barracks clustered around the stable. The drab brick and unpolished timber of the open-ended buildings made it clear they were not original to the ancient stone ruins. Remains of thin mattresses, soiled with blood, were inside, and one structure shadowed an old smithy and forge. Melaine suppressed a thrilled shiver. It was all proof that twenty years ago, the Overlord's soldiers and renowned Followers had prepared for battle against the White City within Highstrong's walls.

The strange woman cleared her throat. Melaine turned and saw she was already standing atop a short flight of stairs that led into a small side entrance of the keep. Melaine shivered her goosebumps away as best she could and climbed the stairs. The woman pushed open a dark, wooden door with iron hinges that reverberated from another magical ward. She disappeared into the shadowed, arched doorway, the ward dispelling behind her.

Melaine stopped at the top of the stairs, fidgeted with her skirt between her fingers, and took a steeling breath. She puffed it out and strode across the threshold into Highstrong Keep.

The short, stone passage was cold. Melaine followed its curve to the right. It opened up into a small, paved courtyard, surrounded by four walls pocketed with more arched doorways. Some were shut off with wooden doors, but others gaped open. Most had wicked cobwebs stretching across them or climbing up the walls from the corners. A couple of short flights of stairs ran up two walls, and the old woman ascended one of these, lifting her skirts a small amount as she approached a door bereft of cobwebs.

Melaine followed, wincing at the dirty bootprints she left behind with each step. Normally, she wouldn't give a damn, but this wasn't Stakeside. Highstrong might not have been kept up like she imagined the palace in the center of Centara was, but it was still a home of the Overlord.

She stamped her feet a few times on the top stair to shed dirt. At least that was better than tracking it inside. She ignored the raised eyebrow of the old woman and followed her through the dim doorway.

Once again, the passage was brief. It was lit by a single torch, set into a sconce in the wall. The torch blazed green with everflame, a sign of the Overlord's wealth, even if it did seem strange that he was holed up in a place as dilapidated as Highstrong. Melaine kept her eyes on it, mesmerized even as she walked away. When she looked back ahead of her, she was surprised to find herself inside a large, open room, one that still bore the trappings of a First Era great hall, including stone columns on either side and rotted tapestries of landscapes. A shadowed throne sat upon a dais at the head of the room. Both features were hewn from solid granite that looked to have been raised by ancient hands from the crags below the keep.

Every breath and every footstep echoed in the grand hall. A few iron candelabras were lit between the stone columns, casting Melaine's scrawny shadow onto the wall. Magic seeped through the cracks in the aged stone, but it was old and tired. Melaine's magic contrasted sharply, leaping and crackling with every heartbeat and every step she took toward the stone dais. She was a living and breathing soul while the castle around her decayed.

The woman paced ahead of her, but then she paused and stepped to the side, leaving Melaine in the center of the room. She watched the woman, unsure if she should remain where she was.

Her fingers twitched against the coarse brown fabric at her sides. She met the woman's eyes. "Is he...?"

The woman clicked her tongue sharply, startling Melaine in the quiet surroundings. The woman nodded at the front of the room.

Melaine froze, her stomach somersaulting like the festival entertainers she'd heard sometimes toured through Centara. She had thought the throne was empty, but when she looked closer, she saw the thin shape of a man, dressed and cloaked in black, masked by the shadows. He sat still upon the eroded granite throne.

The man looked infinitely older and more immovable than the stone. Melaine couldn't even see his face, but her impression was wrought from the way he hunched over his knees as if his own shadow, cast upon the high back of his throne in the eerie green candlelight, was crushing him. His long black hair was a death shroud over his bowed head. His shoulders sagged, and his arms rested limply across his thighs, his pale hands dangling like two hanged men. His body rose and fell with each slow, haggard breath that rattled in the silence.

Melaine's lips parted. Was this...?

"M-my lord?" she whispered, her voice meek and unsure, far from its usual force. There had to be some mistake. It was a trick. She knew she shouldn't have trusted Scroupe, and now she was trapped.

"You're the stonegirl."

Melaine frowned and strained her ears. The voice had been no more than a murmur. Its orator hadn't moved. Yet somehow, he must have sensed her flare of anger.

"You don't like the name," he said. He took another rattling breath. His words were short and forced, as if he had to push against a great weight to speak them, keeping them few to save his strength.

Melaine felt betrayed. This was not the man she had come to see. The Overlord she had heard tales of was powerful and magnificent, a sorcerer-warrior who had conquered a kingdom by the age of twenty. This decrepit figure was *not* that man.

"I am more than a simple stonegirl, my lord," she said, her solid voice returning, rising far above the heavy, strained words of the man upon the throne.

"You are here to prove yourself to me," he replied. He took a breath as if he wanted to say more, but he sighed it out instead.

"Aye, my lord," Melaine responded, but she was beginning to wonder if this weak shadow of a man was worth having to prove herself at all.

"Make me a stone," the Overlord said.

Melaine glowered, furious resentment at the damned overseer sparking the magic in her bones. "My lord," she bit out, "I don't know what Overseer Scroupe may have told you, but I have other talents. It was my hope that—"

"I cannot teach you further if I am not aware of what you can do now," he said with more commanding force in his swift retort than she had yet heard. She shivered as an icy chill drizzled down her spine, but an exciting warmth pulsed in opposition. *That* was a glimpse of the Overlord she was looking for, and he had just said he would *teach* her.

"Aye—yes, my lord," she said, excitement bubbling forth into her hands as she tore off her gloves. She dropped them to the floor. A stone, a stone, she had to make a perfect stone, the best she had ever made, for this was the *Overlord* who requested it of her, and she had but one chance to prove herself, to show him her power.

A deep magic, rooted farther down than she had ever drawn from before, pulsed from the core of her marrow through the minute pores in her bones and into her every muscle. It broke through into her veins and rushed through her blood as breathtaking fire. The skin of her palm blazed, and she held her hand aloft, drawing a brilliant, living crystal from her flesh. She ignored the pain and concentrated on hardening the lodestone into a glinting diamond, sharper than any she'd crafted before. Its clear facets reflected the green candlelight, and then the stone began to pulse from within with the deep purple-black magic that always filled her stones—how people on the street knew they were authentically hers.

Then the stone flashed with a powerful surge of magic, and she averted her eyes from the glaring light.

She glanced back up, and her breath hitched in her chest as she saw two bright blue eyes peering at her through strands of black hair from the shadows of the throne. The lodestone in her hands sparkled with an almost audible ring, and suddenly it brightened to as vivid a sheen as the Overlord's striking eyes.

Melaine exhaled a final breath and stumbled forward, wavering on thin legs to stop herself from falling. She took more breaths, slowing them with each exhale, closing her eyes to stave off dizziness. When her head stopped spinning and the stars and squiggles beneath her eyelids stilled, she opened her eyes and lifted them from the now dormant stone to meet the eyes of the man who watched her with a vibrant intensity that did not match his ragged posture.

He twitched the fingers of his right hand, a single movement that beckoned her toward him. She hesitated, her fear of meeting the most powerful man in all the five kingdoms returning full force, but he was waiting. She took a step, and then another, forcing herself to stay steady. When she was only feet away from the throne, her legs trembled so much from exhaustion and fear that she fell to her knees. She hoped it would come across as reverence.

The Overlord turned his hand palm up but did not move farther. Melaine was terrified to go closer, but it was clear he wanted the stone and clear he was not going to waste the energy to go to *her*. She crawled forward on her knees, clutching the stone in both hands. She reached his elegantly tailored leather boots, hardly used, as if he had not stepped outside in them for a long time. She swallowed and carefully looked up.

She couldn't breathe. He was watching her, his bowed head right over her now. His blue eyes hid in the hollows of his sunken sockets, surrounded by black hair that hung so low it nearly touched Melaine's face. She lifted a shaking hand and placed the precious lodestone into his waiting palm. Her hand darted to her chest as soon as she released it. His skin was cold and clammy, like the sick children Melaine avoided in winter streets. She scrambled back but then stopped and bowed her head with respect, trying to cover her fear that he carried some kind of catching disease.

He ignored her. The Overlord lifted his hand against an invisible, heavy weight and brought the stone to his lips. He whispered something Melaine could not make out, and she raised her eyes as he inhaled against the stone's heated surface.

She always hated watching customers use her stones. She felt violated, used, and envious that they could use her magic, and she could not. She tried to avoid being in their company immediately following a sale, but as she watched the Overlord breathe in her magic, she felt a thrill of power and pride. His shoulders lifted, his back straightened, his head raised, and the stone dissipated into dust in his hand.

"You are powerful," he said, his eyes burning coals over her features. A little color returned to his gaunt cheeks as he rubbed his fingers against his palm, feeling her magic in his bones.

Then, with a sudden thrust of his arm to the side, a door at the back of the room slammed open. Melaine jumped, and she nearly stood but remembered that perhaps she should wait for permission. She stayed on the floor as she watched a man trudge into the room. Iron chains clanked around his wrists and ankles, humming with restraining magic.

Thick black ropes snaked from the Overlord's outstretched fingers and whipped around the man, creating a painful-sounding crack against his skin. Then the Overlord twisted the magical ropes into his fist and yanked the man viciously across the room. The man grunted as he came to a halt not ten feet from where Melaine knelt. Red rivulets poured down his dark skin from each lash, fresh liquid streaming down dried, crusted trenches of blood from who knew how many past tortures.

The Overlord's face twitched with rage. He released the ropes from his grasp and jerked his hand into the shape of a skeletal claw. The ropes ripped away from the man's skin, spinning him with an echoing scream of agony. The magical bindings shot back into the Overlord's fingers and disappeared, diffusing into the magic racing through his veins—Melaine's magic, blended with his, to create the powerful display like she had never seen before.

Melaine stared, mouth agape, marveling at the Overlord's sudden strength and the bloody, gangrenous flesh of the victim before her as he struggled to remain standing. His hair looked like straw tufts from prolonged dehydration, crusted from matted blood. His brown skin had become ashen, his face gaunt, his nails cracked and flimsy with necrotic flesh beneath. The stench was unbearable now that he stood closer, and Melaine nearly retched.

The Overlord's ragged breathing punctured the room again in fast pants as if he had just sprinted across Dramore. His shoulders and spine sagged again beneath some great weight. His flash of power was spent.

Melaine saw his brow furrow through his stringy hair, and when he raised his head, his face was full of a dark but patient fury.

"Knock him down," he said.

Melaine looked at the prisoner with a frown.

"Why?" she asked without thinking. "What has he done?"

"If you are to serve me, you will not question my orders. Do you understand?" The Overlord was seething, and while Melaine could see his hatred was only aimed at the tortured prisoner, she did not wish to be included in the fallout of his rage.

She summoned crackling magic through her frosted veins to her fingertips with a little difficulty. Purple lightning sparked, and she held out her palm toward the swaying victim.

"Having someone else doing the torture for you now?" the prisoner suddenly bit out, his voice hoarse and cracking through split lips that smiled. The smile widened into a laugh, wild and triumphant.

Melaine flinched in disgust. She looked him over again. Tattered clothes hung from his gaunt frame, and there was a symbol on his torn shirt, yellowed and smeared with sweat and blood. It was simple—a circle filled with a pyramid of three Xs, and everyone knew what that symbol meant. Melaine's disdain swirled deeper. This man was a Proxy of the Luxian Order. And though he was too young to have been a part of the pre-war massacres of those who opposed the Luxians—including those who made lodestones like her—he was still liable for their atrocities. His brethren had stopped Vintor from selling Melaine's lodestones outside of Stakeside.

Melaine snarled and pushed her magic against the air, finding a current to ride and shooting a pulse into the man with a force resembling a punch to the gut.

He crumpled with a grunt and fell to the floor. His laughing ceased.

"That'll shut him up," she said with satisfaction. She raised her eyes to the Overlord. "What now, my lord?"

"Now we'll feed the body to the crows, I suspect," the Overlord murmured, rubbing his forehead and dragging his hand down his cheek.

Melaine's stomach turned.

"Body?" she asked. Her eyes flew to the man on the ground. "But he...is he *dead?*" She felt the blood recede from her cheeks. "I didn't—my lord, I didn't intend to—"

"The brush of a fly's wings would have killed him,

Stonegirl," the Overlord said. "You did exactly what I expected of you."

Melaine looked down at her hand, feeling a mingling of horror, disgust, confusion, and...relief. She had expected she would cross the barrier between life and death at some point in her life. She was surprised at times that it hadn't happened already, defending herself against some attacker in the streets. From the moment her aspirations to become a Follower began, she had often reminded herself that killing was something the Followers did. At least during the war. She had prepared herself for this moment for years.

Now that she had crossed that line, the future she had chosen didn't seem so scary anymore, but that didn't stop the bile from bubbling at the base of her throat or keep the guilty weight from dropping into her stomach. It didn't stop insidious regret from worming its way down her spine, coaxing her to wish she could fuse with the floor and bury herself in a pit as she looked back at the crumpled Luxian man on the floor.

"You will stay here, Melaine," the Overlord commanded. "You will make me lodestones whenever I ask, and in return, I will teach you all there is to know." He looked across the hall, behind Melaine. "Karina. Take her."

He waved a tired hand in dismissal and then leaned his forehead upon it, shielding his face from the candlelight.

Melaine snatched up her gloves and stood on shaky legs. She turned around, away from the husk of the Overlord and the crumpled mess of a body on the floor beside him. She followed the old woman, Karina, through the great hall. When they reached the shadowed archway that would take them back to the inner courtyard, she glanced back one last time. The rank body on the ground lay still.

In the throne, the Overlord had not moved a single weary muscle.

CHAPTER 5

From the small inner courtyard, Karina led Melaine up a second flight of stairs. They passed through a longer, wider stone corridor lined with more green everflame torches in sconces. They reached the end of the corridor, where a dark curtain hung. Melaine swallowed, memories of the Hole wafting back into her mind like the head potions that permeated the air within that dank place, the memory of the smells making her nauseous. When Karina drew the curtain aside, Melaine was relieved to see a thin sliver of twilight shining through windows of the next room.

The windows were glazed with thick, slightly green-tinted glass, their frames in the shape of tall pentagons. They only lined one side of the room, and as Melaine stepped inside, she could see a second inner courtyard through them.

The courtyard was larger than the first and was covered in scraggly grass. A stagnant pond languished in the middle, no doubt once stocked with fish, but any underwater creature would suffocate within its current condition. On the far side of the area, broken posts fenced off a little vegetable patch. The patch was haggard, but neat rows of hardy cabbages and turnip sprigs showed it was frequently tended to.

The courtyard was a *garden*. A space for simply walking and enjoying the sunshine, like she'd heard rich people kept behind their estates' high walls.

Thrilled, Melaine returned her inspection to the interior of the room, anticipating more grand sights. Shafts of filtered, lingering sunlight illuminated dust swirls that floated around a sitting area established upon a large, dark red rug. Straight-backed, ornately carved armchairs and a worn fainting couch waited to support idle chatter and tea.

The vaulted, arched ceiling descended into stone columns throughout the room, some lining the walls, others supporting the heavy roof down the center of the space. The ceiling was patched with brick and timber in some places where the Overlord's army had repaired the ancient ruins.

Tables were scattered about, some empty, some covered in stacked books with illegible spines. Others were adorned with dusty silver and gold candelabras, brass bowls, delicate china vases, and other signs of wealth and royalty long abandoned.

What the residents of Stakeside would do if they found this wasted treasure trove. After they'd fought over the spoils, killed over it, the winners would have fettered it away to a middleman for a meager price that was well below each object's worth. He would then sell it at an exorbitant price to the limited middle class, people who desperately wanted to emulate the rich and powerful by filling their homes with such useless trinkets.

Melaine felt indignance rise within her at the barbaric cruelty the sheer existence of such items could create, but another swelling emotion surpassed it—a smug sense of satisfaction that she was here, and the poor wretches of Stakeside were not. She was separate from that miserable population now.

Never again would she be lumped in with *them*.

"Come, girl," Karina said. "Don't gawk at things that needn't be paid any mind."

Melaine frowned at the woman's stark lack of appreciation for the position and home she was lucky to possess.

"How long have you lived here?" Melaine challenged.

Karina kept walking. "As long as the Overlord has."

"So, five years," Melaine said. "Or were you here... before? Before the war?"

"You ask a lot of questions," Karina said.

They passed through the room and into another, which was at a slight angle from the first. A third room beyond was angled farther. Melaine glanced out a window and saw the series of rooms wrapped around the garden in a half-hexagon formation. The end of the hexagon was connected to a large, rectangular structure. Smoke drifted up from the roof on one end, so she assumed the building housed the kitchen and larder, perhaps storerooms or more quarters as well.

A stone passage extended from the farthest end of the kitchen and stretched across the opposite side of the garden beyond the pond and the vegetable patch. No doubt it led to the smaller, paved courtyard pocketed with doors. When Melaine raised her eyes, she saw the tall, parapet-lined roof of the great hall stretching west where it met with one of the two high towers. The second tower loomed to the south of the keep. If the Overlord didn't stay in the living quarters she was being toured through, perhaps he lived within one of those dominant towers.

"Come!" Karina said. Melaine jumped and turned back around. Karina stood near a third open curtain across the room. Melaine crossed another rug, clearly a recent addition, judging by its modern geometric patterns, which differed from the rotting landscapes of the First Era tapestries clinging to the walls. The second room was much like the first, with dusty, expensive items cluttering every flat surface of the chairs and tables.

They crossed the floor to enter a third room, which was centered by a wide, shallow, square pit in the floor. A hole in the ceiling above made it obvious that the pit was once used as a fireplace before actual fireplaces were invented. The hearth was dormant now, but coals and a few stacked logs sat inside, waiting to be lit on a cold night of winter that was swiftly approaching.

Melaine skirted the hearth and followed Karina through a stone archway, devoid of a curtain. It led to a short passage with a solid wooden door at the end. Melaine kept her eyes on Karina, analyzing the woman's bulky hairstyle, trying to decide if something was underneath the strands to create the beehive shape.

Melaine shivered as a sensation like ice water trickled down her spine.

She halted and looked to her left as if a hand guided her cheek. A grotesque stone face stared back.

Dark magic pounded like a belabored heartbeat from a statue of a twisted and gnarled man. A ghastly yawn filled most of his face, his rolling eyes wide with terror. He looked caged and cornered like an animal ready to lash out.

"Child!" snapped Karina. Melaine jolted and hurried away from the statue, which she saw in horror was not the only one. His brothers hunched with crooked postures and made disturbing faces along the entire left side of the passage.

Karina opened the door and ushered Melaine inside. She shut the door with a snap as if the statue would follow them.

"Do not dwell on any object too long in this castle," Karina said. "There will be consequences if you do."

"What kind of consequences?" Melaine asked, unnerved.

Karina eyed her, her lips pressed thin, spreading the wrinkles of her chin tight. "If you care for your life, for your *soul*, you will do as I say. And know that the dungeons are labyrinthian. I recommend you avoid them."

Melaine wasn't sure if that recommendation was a command or not, but she nodded.

"Bathe," Karina then said, gesturing across the room to a far alcove where a clawfoot bathtub sat. "Put your dirty clothes outside the door. You will find fresh ones in the armoire. Don't go anywhere," she finished with a warning look.

"I won't," Melaine agreed, her skin still crawling from

the black energy of the statue. Satisfied, Karina turned away and left the room with a fresh snap of the door.

Melaine let out a breath and felt her tight, wiry muscles vibrate from shoulders to toes. She was here, in the Overlord's castle, and she was still alive.

To continue to survive, she needed to stay alert and know every shadow and object that could pose a threat to her.

She scoured the contents of the room. A wooden four poster bed adorned with red brocade curtains sat in the center. The white and red blanket looked fresh, with a rich winter fox fur draped at its foot. The walls were stone, but they were scrubbed, and a large, golden-framed mirror hung on one, showing half of Melaine's wide-eyed reflection. A tapestry, less moth-eaten than many she'd seen, covered the entirety of the opposite wall. On the fabric, horse-riding hunters chased a deer with massive antlers, shooting glowing arrows and magical daggers at the wild beast.

A large, carved armoire stood in a corner. A small table sat beside it, set neatly with a washbasin, a hairbrush that looked like it had never been used, and, to Melaine's dismay, a jewelry box, filled with small pearls and gems that she was afraid to inspect lest she be accused of stealing. She ignored it for now, even though part of her wanted to leap right in and try every piece on at once.

Above hung an old First Era chandelier made of an iron ring with candles spaced all the way around like the battlements of the roofs outside. They glowed with yellow flames, not everflame, but the wicks were long and the candles fresh. Their glow made the gold of the mirror look like it was melting, and the subtle pattern on the curtains shone like fresh blood.

The dripping rivulets streaming down the prisoner's skin in the great hall oozed into Melaine's mind, followed swiftly by the guilt she had promised herself she wouldn't feel if she ever had to kill someone.

The luxuries around her felt hollow. She had committed murder to earn them.

She deserved it, she told herself. She was intelligent, capable, and her veins ran with powerful magic. Life had cast her aside, either by her parents' purposeful neglect or their deaths. Either way, they had ruined her chances of success. She had no choice but to take a desperate leap like this one, and if she had to kill one man, who was already on death's door, to gain her place in higher society, then so be it.

She shoved the guilt back down and walked toward the alcove that housed the bathtub, passing by a sumptuous blue armchair with a matching footstool on her way. She stroked the back of the chair, reveling in the soft, velvety texture, which was just as nice as the seats in the interior of Overseer Scroupe's carriage.

She glanced back at the fox fur and soft blankets draping the bed. She was tempted to immerse herself in the sensations, but the fur and bed were spotless. No dust coated this room at all like the ones preceding it. It seemed that the Overlord had been anticipating her stay, something that thrilled her with growing confidence. But she couldn't help but wonder, why *was* he letting her stay? She had been so focused on convincing him to teach her.

Now that he had agreed so easily, she had the luxury of doubting his motives.

He was weak, disturbingly so. He needed her lodestones, but why? What had caused him to deteriorate from the glowing, young, handsome conqueror who radiated magic in every tale she'd heard? The man whose eyes had pierced her heart with longing to emulate his life whenever she'd stared at illustrations, streaked by rain and dust? Why would someone so powerful need *her* magic? And...were her lodestones all he cared about? Was he really just like everyone else?

Melaine twitched her shoulder and shook the thought away. Whatever his reasons might be, she had a chance to learn magic she had only dreamed of before. That was her new objective, the only thing she should focus on. All other thoughts were mere distractions.

Her eyes traveled back to the bathtub. The water steamed, and Melaine recognized the sweet smell that emanated from the wealthy who had drifted past her prison cart earlier in the day.

She nibbled the inside of her cheek, a nervous habit she'd never outgrown, as she leaned over the tub's porcelain edge and breathed in the scent. The water was pure and clean, and she discovered the source of the divine smell. Roses. A flower she had only seen in faded illustrations on book pages that Salma stocked as wiping paper in the pub's small lavatory.

These roses were real, blossoming in the water as floating palaces of golden petals that drifted through the steam. Melaine's eyes grew wide, and she stripped layer after layer of worn, dirty clothing off her rail-thin body as fast as she could. The vulnerability that stemmed from being naked in a strange place was overcome by the compelling need to feel that warm, soothing, sweet-smelling water on every inch of her skin. To touch those soft, smooth rose petals with her bare fingertips.

She peeled off her tattered gloves last. She may as well have still been wearing them; her hands retained the outlines of the fabric in crusted dirt. Every line in her palms and knuckles was grimy, and her nails were uneven and ringed with crud. She felt a squirm of mortification as she remembered grazing the Overlord's palm with her fingers as she delivered the lodestone. He hadn't reacted. Whenever he looked at her, the few times he did, he had only met her eyes. If he had noticed her soiled appearance, he didn't seem to care.

Karina certainly did. Melaine frowned and dropped her gloves onto the wrinkled pile of unclean skirt and bodice and bunched up the armful. She strode to the bedroom door, and in one swift motion, pulled the door inward and tossed the clothes into the hall. She squinted her eyes shut against the eerie statue outside and slammed the door closed again.

She pulled a reluctant hand from the doorknob, experiencing a strange fear that the nearest statue might reach for it from the other side. She wished the door had a lock but found none. She frowned and summoned a simple ward spell, pressing her palm against the door to set it in place. It was weak. The stone she had made for the Overlord was the strongest she had ever crafted and left her magic nearly tapped. But the ward would have to do. She backed away and returned to the tub.

She lifted a leg and slipped her foot into the water. Its purity and warmth wrapped around her skin like a pair of elegant stockings. Melaine let out a damn near lustful sigh and climbed into the tub. She lay back, letting the water embrace her worn, tired bones, and closed her eyes. One rose blossom batted her breast, and another tickled her toes. She breathed in the sweet, floral scent and ducked her head under the water.

A nearby ocean sponge and a cake of soap made short work of removing the grime, dust, and sweat Melaine had acquired over an entire lifetime. When she finally rose from the water that swirled with the grime from her body and stood before the tall, gilded mirror on the wall, she was in awe of how truly clean she looked and felt. Her skin was paler and smoother than she had thought possible, her long hair soft and fluffy as it dried. Even her teeth looked brighter after scrubbing the inside of her mouth.

She didn't look like herself at all.

She turned away, rubbing her arms against the chill. A trail of water droplets soaked the red rug behind her. She reached for a linen towel that hung on a peg beside the tub and dried herself, eyeing the armoire, wondering what surprises it might hold.

She cast the towel aside and passed by the fox fur on her way to the armoire. She couldn't resist running her fingers over it. The individual hairs tickled her fingertips in the softest caress she had ever known. She resisted the urge to hop in bed and roll around in the blankets and instead opened the door of the armoire.

Her eyes grew round. For a moment, she just stared at the assortment of fabrics: dark blue, vivid gold, elegant black, sultry red, deep green, lustrous silver. Lace, chiffon, cotton, leather, velvet, silk. It was like she had stepped into a queen's wardrobe. A queen from twenty years ago, perhaps, but still too good to be true. As she pulled the dresses off the hooks, she decided their vintage beauty was stunning in comparison with the latest fashions of the rich she'd seen in passing through Crossing's Square. But their age made her curious about where the gorgeous articles had come from.

Even the spotless white underclothes and corsets looked fancy. She put a set on with a little difficulty, tying the corset tighter than she'd managed to in years with her old one. Then she gravitated toward a sky-blue bodice and skirt that she noted in a tiny thought matched the Overlord's eyes. A gold sash draped across the dress's bustle, giving her a much more substantial-looking buttocks when she looked in the mirror after dressing. The clothes were a perfect fit, but she felt small in such bulky attire. Her eyes were still hollowed, her cheekbones still gaunt, her lips still cracked around the edges from weather and thirst. Her hands were still pale spiders.

She closed her hands into fists. Her wardrobe lacked one thing. She closed her eyes and then opened them again along with her palms. She focused all of her remaining energy on her newfound knowledge that she could finally keep most of her magic for herself, that she was on a swift path to rise above her station and gain the respect and dignity she had yearned for since she began peddling stones thirteen years ago.

She twisted her wrists and held a piece of black lace from a purple dress's trim. She touched it with magic, and the lace extended, weaving itself into the fresh shape of a rose as it spread across her hands. She put forth a little more magic to separate the new lace from the dress's trim. Rose-patterned lace enveloped her hands in a delicate touch until a pair of black, lace gloves shielded her skin from the greedy eyes of the outer world, save for her sensitive fingertips.

Melaine smiled. She had taken a life or death chance in venturing to Highstrong Keep.

She had survived.

She had won.

❈

RASPING,   DERANGED   LAUGHTER   CLAWED   INTO Melaine's sleep-clogged ears. She threw herself into the waking realm, her body scrambling upward until she sat panting in bed. She bunched up the impossibly soft fox fur as if she were strangling the animal it came from. The sight of the dead Luxian man—the man she had killed—faded from her inner sight as shadowed objects came into focus all around.

For a moment, Melaine thought she was outside. The space around her was much larger than her little room above the Greasy Goat pub. Defensive magic crackled at her fingertips, but memories soon flooded into her consciousness, and she knew where she was. The prisoner's nightmarish, triumphant laughter dwindled as she looked around the bedroom she'd been given in Highstrong Keep, lit by the low flame of a candle that sat on a small table at her bedside. The soft, eerie glow of the moon pushed against the single window in the room, and the thick, green-tinted glaze of the panes seemed to push back, their lead dividers barring the light access.

The haunting dream wouldn't recede. She had felt powerful when the Overlord asked her to knock the tortured man to the ground. She had been eager to prove herself and show the Overlord her magical talents, but she had tempered her pulse of violence. It was meant to be a strike only, nothing fatal. She didn't know her blow would kill the man.

The Overlord had used her. She had come to Highstrong with the full intent to let him order her as he wished so long as he taught her to be a Follower and helped her rise above Stakeside. She was only doing as she'd planned. She was only following his orders. She was blameless.

And yet, guilt shadowed her like a stray cat she'd once fed a scrap to as a child. The skeletal creature had followed her with a meow as chafing as the dead man's laugh, and just when she'd decided to give in and toss it another crumb, a cart had barreled down the street and crushed it beneath the wooden wheels, catching its tail in the spokes. She still remembered the strangled meow and the crack of bones. She'd never thrown scraps to a stray again.

Melaine swung her bare feet from under the covers and planted them on the rug. The hem of her white chemise brushed her ankles. No matter how comfortable her surroundings, she couldn't sleep now. She *shouldn't* sleep—not without inspecting her surroundings with greater care. The opulence had distracted her, but one thing she had learned from a life in Stakeside was to always know who and what was around you. Death could come from anywhere—a shoddy roof patched together by someone too poor to afford the proper materials, a rusty tooth extractor from a barber that could infect bleeding gums, the seemingly innocent child in the gutter who was paid pocket change to murder for a purse he would never see.

Who knew what traps and dangers lay dormant in a place like Highstrong Keep, where dark magic permeated the walls and slipped through the cracks in the floor? Some of the magic was old and stale, other tendrils were fresher and twisted in ways Melaine had never felt before. The two forms of magic contrasted with each other in the same way that the modern furniture and clothing in some parts of the keep differed from the First Era relics and architecture of the ruins which surrounded them.

Melaine wrapped her finger around the brass handle of the candlestick on the table. She swept a hand across the weak flame. The wick glowed with purple magic for seconds, and then the flame reared higher before turning orange and ordinary again. She lifted the blazing candle to light her path as she padded to the door.

She paused. Were those whispers on the other side? Or was it the wind whistling across the glazed windows? Melaine swallowed and chastised herself for being so nervous. If she could handle the Hole, she could handle an old empty castle.

She wrapped her hand around the vertical door handle and pulled. The hinges groaned. She raced a hand along the metal joints, assuaging them with smooth oil that dripped from her fingertips as she called upon her magic to hush them.

She pulled the door another inch. The hinges were silent. She crept through the doorway, her candle held high.

The corridor was empty, devoid of anyone who could whisper in the dark. The stone wall on her left was blank, but the row of standing statues lined the wall on her right. They were each dusty and absent of any dark, magical energy. But three statues down stood the one that Melaine knew bore a nasty face of fury and terror, hidden in the darkness. She suppressed her fear and took slow steps forward. She kept her eyes ahead, the warning from Karina ringing through her ears, *"Do not dwell on any object too long in this castle. There will be consequences if you do."*

A sense of dread filled Melaine as she drew closer to the statue, but she kept staring forward. Soon, she would cross its path and be done with it.

She shielded the light of her candle with one hand as if coveting the flame, worried it might be stolen the instant she arrived at the statue. Her heart, which had been racing in her approach, halted as her stomach twisted. She nearly doubled over from the intensity of the black magic that surged from the statue, but she pushed onward, all the while hiding her candle flame, terrified to let any of its light illuminate the ghastly face.

The dark pull of whatever magic the statue held released her as soon as she passed. She swayed a little with the sudden freedom and took a deep breath, but then she pattered away with frantic steps, desperate to leave the chill of the haunting statue behind.

The short corridor soon opened up into the room that held a square fire pit in the center of the floor. She took a few moments to inspect the space, though it was empty of everything except stacked wood and spiderwebs. She passed into the next room, which was scattered with elegant but dusty furniture and trinkets. Moonlight stretched its feeble fingers through the windows, elongating shadows of the tables and chairs, which were then twisted and given chaotic motion by Melaine's candle flame.

There were two doorways connected to this room. The narrow, curtained entrance through which she and Karina had passed earlier that day stood across the room. The other, set into the wall on her left, housed an old wooden door with a rotten section in the upper right corner. A glimpse of the garden peeked through the hole. Melaine approached the door, knowing it might be wiser to inspect the other two rooms that made up the living quarters of the keep. Nevertheless, she was enticed to step foot into a real garden for the first time.

She gripped the iron door handle and pulled. Cold wind assaulted her, but she was used to the elements. Even in her chemise, she only shivered a little as she stepped into the night. Her bare soles touched icy flagstone, but she soon found a broad stretch of grass that warmed her feet a small amount.

Her candle guttered in a fresh breeze. She cupped her hand around the flame to provide shelter and whispered to it to coax it to maintain its strength, a flutter of magic in her breath. She lowered her hand, and the flame stayed straight and tall.

The garden was dark, lit only by the small crescent moon above. The kitchen roof no longer puffed smoke from the two-story, rectangular building to Melaine's left. Directly ahead, the stretch of wall that connected the kitchens to the second paved courtyard was vacant of any signs of life.

She narrowed her eyes. There was a deep, shadowed entryway in the lowest stones of the wall across the garden, only big enough for a person to crouch inside. All was still around it, but some inner urge called her to inspect it, an instinct she had learned to follow throughout her life.

She crossed the garden, eyes darting around her in every direction. Karina had told her not to go anywhere, and Melaine didn't know what would happen if the old lady caught her. Or if the Overlord caught her. The thrill of fear and anticipation shot through her at the reminder that the *Overlord* was within these walls.

She rounded the perimeter of the glassy pond and skirted the ragged picket fence of the garden. She approached the dark pocket in the wall with wary steps and crouched down with her candle held out. The flame illuminated a narrow flight of stairs that plunged into the darkness.

Goosebumps prickled Melaine's skin, making the tiny hairs on her arms rise. The staircase led to the dungeons, it had to.

Should she dare?

After a moment of hesitation, Melaine glanced around the courtyard and up at the windows of the surrounding buildings. All appeared empty and quiet. She turned back to the low, arched doorway. She took a breath and crawled into the blackness. The stone ceiling rose a few feet once she was inside so that she could stand with a bowed head. Her candle flame flickered, making her shadow dance as she descended spiraling stairs deep into the darkness. Finally, the narrow staircase ended, and she found herself facing a wall with a corridor running to her left and right, tall and wide enough for two or three large men to walk abreast.

She raised her candle and saw several empty torch sconces along the walls on both sides. She resisted the urge to light them and looked hard in both directions of the hallway. Each side looked identical. More empty sconces and voids of darkness.

Melaine chose left. Her candle flame stretched its light into the crevices of rock and mortar with each step before the darkness swallowed them again behind her. Then she stopped.

Whispers. Or was it the wind again? No, the entrance to the dungeon was far too high above her to create such an audible sound.

But the susurrus continued. It was ahead—she was sure of it.

She shielded her flame and coaxed it down to a small flicker. She focused on silencing her breaths and smoothing her stride as she crept forward.

The whispers grew louder. There was more than one voice, but no overlapping words or back and forth conversations. No, the voices—there were many, countless—were all a united, increasingly vivid chorus.

Their chant was in a foreign tongue, but the tone was

filled with an unmistakable rise in anticipation. Melaine fought the urge to turn around and run back to the garden. She needed to know what—and who—could threaten her in the keep.

She took another slow step toward the source of the whispers. More voices seemed to join in, bringing new undertones and rhythm to add greater depth to the chorus. As the chanting grew in volume and number, the foreign words became a frenzy. It was a song of screams from a people too petrified and tormented for coherent pleas.

Melaine shuddered, the whispers digging into her bones, rooting around in the magic of her marrow and vibrating within the hard casings. She clenched her teeth and took a few steps more. A glint of metal flickered from the darkness ahead. She drew a breath and pulled her cupped hand away from her candle flame.

An ancient urn rested on a table in a hollowed alcove of a dead end. Its clay was cracked and inlaid with silver veins as if it had once been shattered and remade. The whispers intensified, sounding like hoarse shrieks and guttural groans of dismay. Melaine felt her mouth contort into a dreadful grimace. She felt an urge to smash the vase, to shatter it again into a thousand pieces. Anything to make it stop.

She ground her tingling teeth and gripped the candle-stick tighter.

"Quiet," she said. The whispers amplified and evolved into intense pleas as if a host of people within had heard her speak. A thousand men and women housed within the binding confines of sepulchral clay.

"Quiet, quiet, *quiet!*" she shrieked. She raised the candlestick and sliced her arm toward the urn. The clay smashed on impact, shooting pain through her hand as shards crashed to the floor. The soft powder of ash bloomed all around her. The flame of her candle snuffed out.

The horrific chorus stopped. Her arm trembled, still hovering over the smashed urn.

Goosebumps shot up her flesh through every limb, and she felt an uncontrollable burst of fear. She felt like the breath had been leeched from her body. She gasped for air but choked on a mouthful of ash cloud.

Melaine turned her heel against the stone beneath her and sped down the dungeon corridor. Her bare feet pounded against the cold floor. Pitch-black darkness surrounded her. She thought she heard the awful whispering resume, but she shut it out and kept running.

She didn't know if she had missed the staircase leading up to the garden by the time she stopped. She caught her breath as she forced herself to regain her sense of caution. She lifted her dangling candlestick to her breast and summoned a drop of magic from her palm to relight it. A flame pooled onto the wick and lapped into a small wave of light.

A noise ahead made her shelter the freshly created light, but she didn't dare to snuff it out. It was a grating sound, like the swivel of heavy stone against the floor.

An overwhelming tightness in her chest made her torso cave and her breath stop. Her hand shook, but she fought against the immense dread of something awful coming her way, and she raised her candle high. The sound of grating stone tore at her eardrums. It was coming closer. She wanted to run again, but her feet froze to the icy floor. She closed her eyes for an instant, gathering courage before re-opening them.

A ghastly stone face flashed in the flare of her candle, inches from her. The haunting statue from outside her bedroom was *here*, in the dungeons. Its tall mouth seemed longer in the candlelight, its cheeks gaunter, its brows more twisted into a fierce rage, terror, and sorrow combined. Its sharp eyes flickered with the flame as if it were *alive*.

Melaine screamed.

She spun around and fled down the hall. She stretched out her hand, feeling for the draft of the staircase as if she could grasp it and be pulled to safety. She stumbled as she caught sight of the stairs and surged up the steps, skipping as many as she could until she tumbled out of the low doorway and into the brisk garden.

She didn't stop. She hopped over the garden fence and skirted the pond. She bolted up the stairs to the door that led to her living quarters. She slammed it behind her and ran to the room centered by the dormant hearth, but then she slid to a halt as she looked down the short passage that led to her bedchamber. The row of statues loomed on the left-hand wall, though none filled her with as much black dread as the one that had followed her to the dungeons. They were all still, her guttering candle flame highlighting the nearest figure's grotesque features.

She battled her instincts to run and approached the place she knew the worst statue had resided before her explorations. She wasn't sure what would terrify her more

—if the statue was there waiting, having never moved, or if it *had* somehow walked away from its post.

She gathered what defensive magic she could muster this late in the night and felt it crackle at her palm. She walked past one dormant statue, then another, a third, a fourth, and then—

It was empty. The black hole that had housed the horrific statue was nothing more than a shadow. Goosebumps flew up and down Melaine's limbs. She jumped past the empty space as if the statue might suddenly appear and snatch her. She slammed into her bedroom door and shoved it open with her shoulder. She darted inside and shut it with a reverberating bang of wood and iron hinges. The magical ward she had put into place before she fell asleep felt flimsy compared to the evil of her sentry.

She had left her room to decipher the dangers within Highstrong Keep, and it appeared that one of the worst was stationed right outside her door. She feared that the statue and the whispering, screaming urn barely scraped the surface of what haunted the castle, rife with ancient magic and the rumored dark experiments of its powerful keeper.

CHAPTER 6

A sharp rap on the door startled Melaine from a
groggy daze amidst rumpled bed covers. She sat
up, glancing at her lit candle by her bedside. The wax had
oozed into a useless pool, nothing but a stump left to
support the lowly flame. Wasting a candlestick by letting
it burn all night went against every bone in Melaine's
body, but her terror had stilled her breath from blowing it
out. She kept imagining the vile statue's face, leering
inches from hers.

Besides, there were dozens of candles in the iron
chandelier over her head and in dusty candelabras in the
outer sitting rooms. For the first time in her twenty-one
years, Melaine had candles to spare. The thought filled
her with delight, but a lingering sickness crept inside her
heart at the realization that her excessive surroundings
were already influencing her perspective on waste, and it
had only been one night.

The knock on the door sounded again, even more
impatient this time.

"Yes?" Melaine asked, her voice hoarse from her night of screams, ragged breathing, and fitful sleep.

"It is morning, Miss Melaine," came the critical voice of Karina. "You will eat breakfast and then report to the library."

"Library?" Melaine mumbled.

"Across the garden and up the north staircase. Take the passageway to the left until you reach the northwest tower. The library is there. I trust you know your rights from lefts?"

"Yes," Melaine said, repressing a snarl. She swung her feet to the floor and stood. Karina's clacking footsteps receded down the hall.

Melaine took a deep breath. Despite her lack of sleep, she could feel the strength of recharged magic beneath her skin. Morning was a treasured time, but knowing every day would descend into weakness, stone by stone, often leeched even morning's joy from her, more so with each passing year.

Now, the Overlord was her only customer, and if he would uphold his promise to teach her pathways only the most powerful sorcerers could travel, then he would have to leave her with enough reserves to do so. If he kept his promise, most of the entrancing magic within her would remain hers.

She pulled on some refreshing magic to fill the small basin on the table beside the mirror with clean water. She splashed her face and washed her body beneath her chemise, still marveling at how clean and soft her skin and hair looked and felt.

She marveled at the contents of the armoire again as

soon as she opened it, and she eventually managed to choose a deep purple gown with black, embroidered flowers dancing across the modest bust and encircling the floor-length hemline. It fit well, but she still felt like her narrow hips couldn't live up to the gown's full skirt, and her small breasts were inadequate to support such a charming bodice. She brushed her hair while eyeing the delicate jewelry box on the table. She had been afraid to touch it the day before, and the fear of being accused of stealing the precious jewels lingered. But why would Karina have put them there if she wasn't meant to wear them?

Melaine sifted through the jewels, barely touching each piece as she looked through the collection. There were sapphire rings, pearl necklaces, bracelets, and broaches wrought of silver. The entire box sparkled in the candlelight, the jewelry resembling celestial glimmers.

Melaine chose a simple pearl and gold comb. Most days, she wore her long hair down. Her worn-out pins often broke, and she was unable to afford new ones to hold her hair in a bun or braid. The comb in her hands was so elegant that she couldn't resist pulling her hair back into a bun and slipping the comb into place behind her head. She smiled, peeking at her reflection as if it would catch her staring and chastise her.

Karina had instructed her to eat breakfast but hadn't told her where to get any. Perhaps she would find it in the structure she suspected held the kitchen and larder. She hesitated at the door but then pulled it open. She hastened a peek at the place where she'd seen the fright-

ening statue the first time and where it had been absent
the night before.

The statue was back. Stoic in its place, as lifeless as
the others. Melaine shuddered and scooped up a waiting
breakfast platter and cup from the floor and shut the
door again.

The bread, fruit, and cheese tasted like it could have
descended from the Centara Palace itself. Melaine had
never tasted such rich, fresh food in all her life, and the
sweet mead that filled her cup was better than any Salma
could ever hope to serve. For a few blissful moments,
Melaine let all of her fears and anxious hopes dissipate
into the simple pleasures of scent and taste and the rare,
almost foreign, feeling of a full belly.

Too soon, the day ahead pushed back into her
thoughts. She took a bracing breath, placed her bare
dishes outside her door, and left the safety of her
bedroom. She eyed the statue as she swept past but again
remembered Karina's stern warning not to stare at
anything in the castle for too long. She turned her gaze
ahead and kept it there.

Her palms grew clammy as she left the living
quarters and descended into the garden. She glanced
at the dark, low archway in the wall, which led to
the dungeons where the whispering urn and whatever
else dwelled. She looked away and found the short
staircase that led into the northern section of the
keep. She took a breath of fresh air to clear her head
and admired a tree with bright red leaves that shel-
tered a bed of delicate, white wildflowers in the
corner as she hopped up the stairs. The small garden

was a paradise compared to the dirty streets of Stakeside.

The inner corridor was dim, lit by green everflame torches on the walls. After a few paces straight ahead, Melaine turned down a horizontal passage that led to the northwest tower. Her heart raced faster with every step as she approached the library. Her gut squirmed at the thought of an entire room dedicated to books filled with difficult words, but surely, she wouldn't be expected to read them. The Overlord was going to teach her himself. What use did she have for books?

Her breath caught as she slowed before a tall, wide set of double doors. Their dark-stained wood bore deep carvings of horses and eagles, and they looked as ancient and weathered as the stone of the tower to which they allowed access. Their solemnity and height, twice her size, were imposing, but Melaine stretched out her hand and laid her palm on the wood. It was warm. The longer she held her hand there, the warmer the wood became. The heat was soothing and hummed through her body in a way she imagined a lullaby might sound coming from a mother's lips to a child's ears. She closed her eyes, and a faint, single voice whispered wordless comfort.

"Come in," murmured a different, more concrete voice through the soothing barrier.

Melaine opened her eyes. The Overlord's energy was faint from the other side of the doors, but she felt a tiny brush of his cool magic against her palm, interrupting the warm glow of the wood.

She pushed. The heavy doors swung inward, magic aiding their movement like mechagics, but these doors seemed to hold an inherent power, living within the wood itself. The magic felt ancient, as old as the First Era carvings in the doors' surfaces.

Melaine's black eyes widened as she stood in the doorway. She had thought the library would only reside on the ground floor, but she was *so* wrong. She was also wrong about the library being filled with books.

Shelves soared up the walls to the high ceiling, covering every stone. They held objects of all kinds and sizes like in Vintor's shop, and they were just as free of dust as far as she could see. Glittering figurines and ornate snuff boxes, taxidermies of small creatures, jars with questionable liquids, dried flower bouquets, necklaces strung with beads of teeth and bone, and sundry other items met her eyes, too many to comprehend. Even some sections of the spiral staircase that wrapped around the hexagonal perimeter were cluttered with objects large and small.

A high window, far above her head, let in a shower of crisp autumn sunshine. She could see the edge of a parapet outside. She wondered how far down the drop would be if she were to climb the endless staircase and stand on the balcony.

The ground level where she safely stood was large enough to host rows of concentric, hexagonal shelves, while still leaving room for a collection of desks, tables, chairs, and a large open space with nothing but a deep blue rug in the center.

Melaine was startled when she noticed the Overlord seated in a black, high-backed armchair near the center of the room, watching her. His hands were folded upon an oak, claw-footed table, but he leaned on his elbows with more weight than his poised posture should require. His bright blue eyes analyzed her for a moment, taking in her full appearance with more attention than he had the first time they'd met in the great hall. She was glad she was clean and better dressed this time, but that didn't account for the brief, almost wistful glow in the Overlord's eyes as he looked over the dress she'd chosen.

She dared to take a step forward. The doors closed in a gentle swing behind her.

"Good morning, my lord," she said, not sure if she should kneel or curtsy—she had never curtsied in her life —or if he expected her to stand and wait for instruction. Should she even have spoken first? Even the simple phrase she had used sounded awkward. Deferential, polite niceties were not something people in Stakeside used very often.

The Overlord lifted a single finger off the back of his other hand, motioning at a chair across from him. Melaine hesitated but then strode to the table and settled herself on the chair's cushioned edge. She had chosen a dress with a small bustle this time, but there was still much more material on her rear than she was used to, and she felt off-balance.

The Overlord didn't lurk in shadow as he had in the imposing great hall upon his granite throne. Daylight softened the edges of his hollowed eye sockets and jutting cheekbones, allowing her to see the smooth, handsome cut of his features unadulterated by a guise of skeletal death. He looked less decrepit, closer to his true age of not-quite-forty, but dark circles still pooled under his blue eyes. Chapped fissures marred his shapely lips, and his black hair still hung in strings over his shoulders. He wore no jacket or vest, only a supple black shirt of thin silk as if any heavier material would anchor him to the floor.

"Are you adjusting to your quarters?" he asked. Melaine crinkled her brow a fraction. His concerned tone was subtle but seemed to acknowledge the difficulties she faced being surrounded by such overwhelming luxury all at once.

She gave him a slow nod. "They're...comfortable," she said, her voice still awkward to her ears. "It's difficult to sleep in a new place," she added, hoping that would explain some of her clumsy social behavior.

"I trust you'll rest better tonight," he responded. She thought she heard a trace of envy in his voice.

"Or maybe this castle provokes nightmares," she said, probably with more cheek than she should have. The Overlord had lived here for five years, and he looked as sleepless as she felt.

He expelled a short, dry laugh. "You'll need to learn to live with them, Melaine." His inhale rattled. "You're too young and useful to go mad."

"Then you might call off your stone guard outside my bedchamber," she said. "That might make me rest easier."

The man's blue eyes flashed. "You shouldn't go where you're not expected."

"So that statue is one of your...experiments?" she dared, despite her desire to shrivel from the sudden strength in his chastisement. Though she wasn't sure if knowing the Overlord controlled the haunting statue made her feel any safer than if it were some ancient spell.

When he didn't answer her question, she asked, "Is the urn?" Her voice dropped to a whisper like those that came from the clay before she'd smashed them into silence. She might provoke his wrath if he found out she had broken it, but her curiosity about the urn—and what her shattering of it may have caused—was too compelling to ignore.

"This stronghold is ancient," the Overlord responded. "It holds secrets. I've cracked most of them...and created some of my own. I cannot guarantee your safety, but you seem smart enough to survive."

Melaine quieted. There was no mistaking the warning in his tone. She had crossed a line.

"Aye, my lord," she said, suppressing her fluttering nerves. "I mean, yes. Yes, my lord."

The Overlord leaned back in his chair, bracing his hands on the armrests as if he would fall to the floor if they failed to keep him upright.

"You will read these," he said, nodding at a stack of books piled on the table. They were the only books in sight, despite this tower being called a library. "Do you read First Era Qaebian?"

Melaine looked down. She gripped the folds of her fancy, dark purple dress through her black lace gloves. She shook her head once.

"I thought that might be too much to hope for," he said. "I'll have to teach you the illusory disciplines myself." He cleared his throat and winced as he swallowed. He made teaching her sound like a horrible chore, but then again, his every breath seemed an exceedingly exhausting task.

"You can start with these." He gestured again to the pile of books. "They're in standard Dramorean."

Melaine looked at the books and opened her mouth, then closed it again. She felt her cheeks grow hot and bit the inside of her cheek to try to suppress her blush of shame and frustration. She didn't dare disobey such a simple order, or he might not give her any others. She nodded to the Overlord and reached for the book on top of the stack.

Her heart drummed fast, and her fingers shook. She wanted to ask about the objects filling the spacious library. They tingled with magic, and she was beginning to suspect they held far more knowledge than the books he'd tossed at her.

This book was a slim volume, at least. She skipped reading the title and opened it to the first page. She buried her face behind the cover and tried to focus on the scrawling handwriting.

She stifled the urge to mouth the words with renewed gnawing on her inner cheek as she put the letters together.

The deeper realms of magic are unknown to most...

She nodded in affirmation as she stumbled through the first sentence and moved on to the next.

It is only with devoted study...

Melaine continued to read in silence, but she focused so much on deciphering the words that she couldn't take in the meaning behind them. She had to reread each sentence two or three times to comprehend a simple paragraph.

She finally lifted a hand to turn the first page but

gasped as the Overlord deftly took the book from her and set it down on the table.

Melaine's brow furrowed as her chest flooded with heat that spread up her neck and into her cheeks. She had taken too long. Now, he knew she could barely read.

She wanted to apologize but couldn't make the words come. Her pride strangled them.

"When did you become a stonegirl?" the Overlord asked.

Melaine did her best to keep eye contact.

"I was eight," she muttered. He didn't speak, so she forced more words. "I was too old to get any sympathy when begging and too young to get a job that would pay me enough to scrape by. I was tired of stealing. I didn't want to take what wasn't mine. I wanted to earn it."

"Why lodestones?"

Melaine stiffened under his gaze as if she could physically resist his digging into her past.

"I saw an old woman peddling one day on a corner," she said. "Her stones weren't anything more than pebbles. She was tired and wrinkled and weak. And I thought, if she can do it, so can I. I didn't realize most other people couldn't. I started to make my first stones. People started buying them." Melaine bowed her head. "The old woman died not long after. I didn't put two and two together at the time, that I had stolen her business. I caused her to starve to death."

Melaine's voice had become rough and harsh. She stopped speaking, but then a spark crackled within her, and she kept talking. She looked straight into the Overlord's eyes.

"I was too young and stupid to understand that one day I would become her," she said. "An old stonelady kneeling on a corner, waiting to starve to death when a new stonemaker would inevitably take my place."

The Overlord's eyes flicked from one of hers to the other with sharp interest. Was it approval?

"And when you did understand, you came to me," he said. "Do you understand the risk you took, Melaine Stonegirl?"

"I wanted to be more than a *stonegirl*, my lord," Melaine hissed. She swallowed her temper, soothing her tight jaw. After a pause, she said, "I need to be more than that."

He sighed as if she was trying his patience. "You already are, Melaine." The sincerity in his voice washed Melaine's residual anger away. He spoke with a commanding authority that was effortless after twenty years of ruling Centara and all of Dramore. It felt like he was making an official decree that she was, in truth, more than a stonegirl from the streets—that she could become more under his tutelage.

He leaned forward with effort and rested his weight on his elbows, folding his hands together upon the table.

"Overseer Scroupe said you wish to become a Follower."

Melaine's heart jumped. She sat straighter. "Yes, my lord."

"Do you know where my Followers are now?"

"In your palace," Melaine answered, sounding wistful. "Protecting Centara."

"Guarding halls filled with nothing but vying courtiers

and ambitious overseers," he said, his voice flat. "Standing in doorways listening to vapid discussions of modern politicians. They understand that peace is better than war and are proud of their current duties, but they are far from satisfied. Those who aren't dead or too old to function, that is."

Melaine frowned. To hear the Overlord speak of his own Followers that way, of the politicians and overseers that way, was…she didn't know how she felt about it other than surprised.

"Is that why you left?" she asked. "Is that why you've decided to live here these past five years?"

The Overlord paused as if considering a reply, but he looked aside instead, his face disinterested.

"I have no need for more Followers," he said. "You were a mere child during the war, and you still glorify it like one."

His words stung her pride like a poisonous dart the tribal Daksuns were said to shoot at wanderers of the Wilds in stories. Stories. Was that what she'd been looking up to all this time? Useless fables of exaggerated war heroes?

"Then what am I supposed to do with all that you teach me?" she asked, unable to hide the doubt in her voice that he may have decided not to teach her after all.

He was silent a moment.

"Let's see how much you can learn first," he said, the spark fading from his eyes as his shoulders sagged. He looked at the slim book on the table between them.

"Keep this one." He slid the book back to her resting fingers. "Study it in your free hours. Take your time." He drifted his eyes around the library. "I'll teach you the basics, and then I'll move onward, pass on as much as I can to you."

Melaine frowned as she ran a finger along the bottom edge of the book. It was bound in leather and catgut, frayed a little with age. The Overlord spoke like an old man discussing a will, knowing he had little time left. But the Overlord was still a young man. And Melaine couldn't help but think, *he was supposed to be powerful.*

Maybe he *was* sick. Melaine scooted back a little in her chair, but her bustle inhibited her instinctual attempt to put some distance between her and the man who might harbor some disease.

"I'm going to need my strength for that," he said.

Melaine took a breath, her chest tightening. She understood what he wanted, but that didn't mean she had to like it.

She gave him a nod and closed her eyes. She felt her magic humming beneath her skin. It seemed warmer somehow, like she had soaked up a sunbeam from touching the ancient yet living magic of the library door. A smile kissed the corner of her lips.

It faded as she reluctantly slipped her lace glove from her right hand. She set it neatly in her lap and started massaging her palms, working her magic to the surface. The warmth of her marrow burned through her bones and shot into her veins. She opened her palm, paralleling the high, pointed ceiling of the tower.

The warm, soothing magic abandoned her veins and left them frozen, its energy coalescing into a hard stone that started to rise from the skin of her palm. Her palm

burned and prickled with pain as she pushed the lodestone from her body and cupped it between her hands. It
glowed purple, swirling with magic until it deepened to a
nearly black sheen.

She sighed with minute despair and held the lodestone
in offering to the man across the table.

He reached out and took it in silence. He closed his
eyes as if merely touching the lodestone was intoxicating
and then brought it to his lips. He inhaled Melaine's
forfeited magic and, for a second's time, she hated him
for it.

But her hatred was limited by the knowledge that the
Overlord wasn't some crude buyer on the street who
needed magic to commit a crime or stay awake long
enough to enjoy some hedonistic activity or even a simple
hard day's work.

Her resentment withered further when she saw the
immediate change her magic had upon the Overlord. When the stone dissipated into dust, he sat
straighter, and his eyes gleamed brighter. Color returned
to his cheeks and hands. He was a coiled spring, full of
kinetic energy, waiting for a reason to unleash the
powerful magic running through him.

Melaine immediately regretted her bouts of
outspoken disrespect. She ordered herself to never forget
who this man was and what he was capable of, no matter
how weak he looked.

"True power comes from resourcefulness," he said. His
voice was still hoarse from disuse, but his breaths rattled
less and his tone poured confidence. "If you have that, you
can scrape up any magic around you, even if your bones

are tapped, and find that you have more power than you think—more power than anyone else. You've already proven you're resourceful, or you wouldn't be here."

"Aye, my lord," Melaine agreed, her chin lifting a little with pride.

He chuckled. She couldn't tell if he appreciated her gumption or was mocking her dignity.

"Other than lodestones, do you know any magic beyond household spells?"

Melaine paused. "I've never had time to learn anything else."

"No need to be defensive, Melaine," he said. "The best of us start from the lowest rung."

A crease formed between her eyebrows. Was he implying that he had as lowly a background as she? The *Overlord?* She must have misunderstood.

"You say you are keen on becoming a Follower," he said, either not noticing or ignoring her look of pointed curiosity. "Do you know what kind of spells my Followers used to perform?"

"Yes," she answered with smoldering enthusiasm. "War spells. Dark spells. They helped you overthrow a kingdom."

"You're not shy," the Overlord said with a wry smile. "That's good."

He stood, a firm hand still on his chair. His jaw tightened, highlighting a small, throbbing vein at his temple.

"Dark spells require dark thoughts," he said, a subtle, dangerous edge in his voice. "They require a motive. The more powerful the motive, the more powerful the spell becomes. You have a strong motive overall—the desire to prove yourself and have a life worth living. But you also need to dissect the subtleties of your incentives. Find a specific motive for each spell, whittled down, but still a part of the whole."

He flicked his gaze to a black, tapered candle on the table's edge. "Light the candle."

"That's a household spell," Melaine said with a frown.

"Light it with the intent to use it against someone," he said, a subtle rumble in his voice. "Tell it to burn more than just the wick."

"Near the books?" Melaine said with a raised eyebrow.

"These books are protected," he dismissed with an impatient wave of his hand.

"Oh," Melaine said, quelled. If those books could burn, she wouldn't have to read them, but she accepted that fate and eyed the candlestick. She could light it with a sweep of her hand, but she tried to focus on what the Overlord had instructed. Light it with the intent to burn.

She swam through a river of reasons why she would want to hurt another person before her mind rippled toward certain people. A young girl who had tried to pick-pocket her on one of her best sale days, a man who had tried to rape her at the age of twelve, and then her mind hit Overseer Scroupe. His grotesque, jeering face was galling enough to make a spark jump from Melaine's hand of its own accord.

She felt the Overlord watching her, but she focused on her thoughts of Scroupe, what he had looked like in the Hole—a rotten apple core, in his red room with his yellowed smile.

She took a breath and propelled magic from her palms in one solid push. A bright red flame erupted from her palm like a volcanic spray. It swirled around the candle and snagged onto the wick. The fire stayed red, spewing sparks like angry, bloody spittle from the mouth of a feasting carnivore.

She stared at the flame in awe for a moment and then looked up at the Overlord. His eyes danced in the fire-light, scanning her features with shrewd appraisal.

"You'll do," he said, with a touch of a smile on his lips.

"Yes, my lord," Melaine said.

Lighting the candle was the most exciting thing about the lesson. The rest consisted only of the Overlord speaking and Melaine listening. He lectured more about deciphering motives and how to use them, how to harness a thought and turn it into action. His words were eloquent, and Melaine imagined how beautiful they must have sounded earlier in his life when his voice was smooth and strong and compelling enough to garner a mass of thousands in his uprising against the kingdom of Dramore.

After an hour or two, he became distracted. He lost trails of thought mid-sentence and kept looking at the high window and the shifts in the shelves' shadows as time passed.

"I have work to do," he finally said, interrupting himself at a particularly interesting point of monologue that danced around the edges of blood magic. Melaine tried to hide her disappointment.

The Overlord rubbed his fingers together absently, and Melaine understood. He was itching to use the magic he had imbibed from her stone. For what purpose, she didn't know, but she stayed her curiosity and nodded in obedience. She rose from her chair, hurrying to put on her glove. She'd forgotten to replace it in her excitement.

"Don't forget the book," the Overlord said.

Embarrassment heated Melaine's cheeks, but she picked up the book from the table. She would have to read it. If the Overlord was going to get distracted after two hours of teaching a day, supplemental reading could be vital.

She chanced another look at the shelves filled with countless objects around the tower. She had tried to find a moment to ask the Overlord about them during the entire lesson, but she never found an opportunity that wouldn't have involved insolent interruption.

The longer she'd sat amongst them, the stronger her awareness had grown—powerful magic arose in the air like invisible smoke batted about by conflicting winds, as though each individual object was its own flame.

They couldn't be...

"Should I come back here tomorrow, my lord?" she asked, desperate to learn more.

He nodded, but his thoughts were elsewhere.

Melaine gave a small bow and approached the tall library doors. Their warm magic brushed her skin as they opened under her simple touch. She closed her eyes, reveling in the glow that filled her, and she smiled.

She could keep this magic. The Overlord had his lode-stone for the day, and he hadn't asked for more. For once, she could look forward to an evening in which the rest of her magic was *hers*.

No timepiece ticked in Melaine's bedchamber, but the cool light of the moon and the tingling of her scalp told her it was the wee hours of the morning. Her body always felt different this time of night, lingering drowsiness paired with the edge of nearly recharged magic, along with the question of why she wasn't asleep when she should be. What danger had woken her up?

She sat up in bed. The room was black, but the shroud was not heavy or oppressive. The dim light from the window wasn't a savior but rather a gentle call to other times and places.

She felt comfortable. Safe.

Powerful.

She looked down at her fingers, assessing the potent magic coursing through the minuscule spaces between bone and muscle and veins within her wiry body. She rubbed her fingers together. An arcing spark of purple lightning leapt from her first fingertip to the second.

Melaine's delight flooded into a smile. She hadn't felt this strong since she was a child. Never before had she made so few stones for two full days in a row. Her magic bubbled within her, an ever-rising simmer of magic waiting to be used.

Yet she still didn't know how to make the most of all the magic raging through her bones. Her lesson with the Overlord had remained theoretical and, aside from the candle, well, rather boring. Melaine itched to *use* her magic, not just think about it. She wanted to use it for spells other than lighting candles, purifying water, or mending stockings.

She had been struggling through the book the Overlord had lent her, which now sat on the floor near the bathtub. She'd tried reading it while bathing that evening, but the jumbled words and the warmth of the water had induced her to sleep.

Books. Nothing but paper and ink bound with leather but filled with powerful information that would remain untapped and useless if she couldn't reach it. She hadn't had enough time to practice under Salma's brief reading lessons, which she had only begun a few months ago. The enormous amount of effort it took to read a single page was infuriating.

Why did her journey forward have to depend on a *book*?

Why indeed, when so many Insights sat in the Overlord's library, waiting to be tapped.

Her certainty that the myriad objects on the library shelves were not ordinary trinkets, useless baubles, or exotic oddities had grown with every passing hour following their lesson. Why was he keeping them from her? The lessons contained in Insights were far more thorough than mere words could ever teach. Especially once he'd found out she couldn't read, why had he not done the obvious and let her learn spells from the Insights instead? He looked so tired, why not let Insights do all the work?

Melaine nibbled the inside of her cheek, looking around her room, trying to decide if she should stay awake or lie back down. But then she stiffened. A low voice pushed against the walls of her dark room. It was crooning and plaintive as it trickled through her window, but the volume and pitch thumped against the panes with a manic lilt every few words. The words themselves were indistinguishable, but as she continued to listen, she deciphered a melody. A song tingled with a tiny stroke of magic as if its orator was trying to reach her from a great distance, or perhaps to reach anyone who would listen. That must have been what awoke her at such an early hour.

Her sense of comfort and safety dwindled. The Overlord's ghastly guard statue and the ancient, whispering urn from the night before rushed into her thoughts. She debated rolling back over and going to sleep, safe within her bedroom walls, but the distant, muffled song poked at her ears. She doubted she could sleep if she tried.

Curiosity scrabbled at her mind as she sat in indecision. The song continued, and Melaine focused again on the powerful feeling of magic in her bones. With magic like this, she felt invincible. She could handle Highstrong's secrets now.

She climbed out of bed. She summoned magic into her palms and ignited a small, purple flame. She cupped it in her hands and brought it to the candlestick on her nightstand. She dropped the flame neatly onto the wick. It caught hold with a small singeing sound and flared orange.

She collected her dressing gown—an elegant, brocade tapestry of a thing—and draped it over her chemise, tying it closed below her breasts, so it fit like a fine dress. The pastel, floral-patterned garment seemed such a useless luxury to never wear out of the house, but it was warm, and she couldn't help but yield to the tentative concept of feeling beautiful. Not attractive—not tempting prey for lustful men—but simply beautiful for her own enjoyment. She shook out her soft, clean hair so it cascaded down the small of her back. She took the candlestick in hand and walked to the door.

She opened it a sliver and peered into the hallway. Three statues down the guard line, she could see the tip of the nose and chin of the fourth statue. The one that could move. At least, she hoped it was the only one.

She stilled her shaking hand and stepped into the hall, shutting the door behind her. Magic hummed beneath the surface of her hands, the Overlord's hoarse voice speaking of motives and dark magic echoing between her temples. Her motives to lash out at the statue were strong indeed.

The statue's face was obscured in shadow when she approached, as if it was drawn back, ready to pounce. The mystery of its current features and stance sent shivers down her spine. She averted her eyes, braced herself, and darted past. She skidded into the room with the dormant fire pit, letting out a quiet sigh of relief when the statue didn't follow with its telltale grating noise of stone against stone.

The strange singing sounded louder now, but it was still muffled through walls of stone, drifting toward her on magical currents. She crossed the hearth room and entered the adjoining sitting room, where the song seemed to waft from the garden courtyard. She opened the courtyard door and headed down the outside steps, her feet hitting the shriveled grass as she listened.

The song was clearer now, but the voice was too slurred to make out the words.

She walked farther into the garden, around the edge of the stagnant pond that reflected the waxing moon. She hesitated when she reached the other bank. The song was louder still, and her breath caught when she realized it drifted from the low, small archway in the stone wall ahead. The dungeons.

A warning knell in her chest told her to go back, to ignore the song. Who was to say it wasn't another trick of dark magic, calling to her like the whispering urn had the night before? The dungeon was a labyrinth, Karina had said. The urn might well be the least of the evils those underground halls housed.

The song didn't sound dangerous. The voice wasn't the Overlord's and was certainly not Karina's. Yet it sounded familiar. How could that be? Melaine knew of no one else staying in Highstrong. The halls had been empty aside from herself and its two other occupants.

Melaine gripped her candle and the brocade of her dressing gown. Her instincts vied for control. Curiosity was a dangerous friend, but if another person *did* live in the keep, she couldn't risk a stranger catching her unawares.

She licked her lips and ducked into the archway. She descended the long staircase, her breaths short and her every sense on alert, straining her ears for the haunting whispers of the shattered urn or the solid, grating sound of the swiveling statue. Nothing but the erratic song played through her ears, growing louder with each step. Soon, the magic that the song carried wasn't the only reason for its volume. The source was close, the voice echoing through the dungeon's halls.

She reached the bottom of the staircase, where the horizontal corridor waited for her to choose a path. She knew, with a residual shiver, that the shattered urn lay at a dead-end down the left-hand hall, its ashes scattered, assuming Karina hadn't swept them away.

Melaine swallowed her nerves and turned right. The sconces were bare of torchlight like the last time she had wandered the dungeons. She held her candle high, analyzing every crack and corner and cobweb as she passed. The edge of a corner peeked out of the shadows, indicating a passage branching off to the left. The echoing, wordless song swirled within.

She peered her head around the corner, but her candle only illuminated a few feet ahead before the darkness swallowed its light. She tried to push down her panic from the thought of getting lost in these cold, underground halls, especially if her candle burned too low. Cupping a flame in her palm was only possible for short bursts, an inviable method for navigating the dark for hours on end.

The sudden sound of scraping stone made Melaine jump and her body writhe. She whipped around, candle held aloft, eyes frantically searching the darkness for the silent moan on the guard statue's face. She saw nothing in her little patch of orange light. She held her breath and shielded her candle, listening for the ominous sound.

Stone swiveling on stone came louder and faster from the direction of the only exit she knew. The mysterious singing continued to drift through the air from her left.

Melaine spun to the left and darted down the narrow passage, summoning a bit of magic from the bones of her feet in an attempt to silence her steps.

The stench of mildew flooded her nostrils as the air secreted damp cold. The rustle of rats replaced the sound of grinding stone and provided an erratic, scuttling beat to the song ahead.

Melaine stopped. The voice was clear now. It was a man's baritone, ragged and off-kilter. The song was more of an indecipherable yell with a tune than it was a ballad with lyrics. She raised her candle and saw a short, arched corridor to her right.

She hesitated, her chest tightening. Her heart jumped when the rough scraping of stone sounded again, louder than before and ever faster, as if the statue had gained her scent and was closing in to trap her in a foxhole.

Melaine looked over her shoulder with wide eyes. All was dark, but the noise continued, no longer swiveling stone but instead, the harsh, steady pounding of pursuing footsteps.

Melaine ran. She flew down the passage, toward the singing voice, and nearly fell down an unexpected flight of stone stairs that crumbled with age. She hit the bottom and followed a curve to the right where she saw a solid, wooden door.

She grabbed its heavy iron ring and heaved. The thick door swung open. She plunged inside the new room and wrenched the door shut. She summoned magic to her palms, and her determination to expel the statue pushed a powerful binding spell through her skin and onto the door. The ward snapped into place, freezing the door into an immovable barrier against anyone who should try to enter.

She caught her breath, surprised at the force behind the simple door-locking spell she'd always used for her flat in Stakeside. The Overlord's methodology of honing in on direct motivations *was* effective. She smiled in satisfaction with a small, extra flare of pride that his teachings made her powerful enough to stop *his* guard.

Only then did she realized the singing had stopped.

She turned around. Two everflame torches in sconces illuminated a row of iron-barred cells lining the long room in which she now stood. A large rack with dangling, rusted chains and lifeless ropes loomed on the far wall. A spiked, narrow cage stood in one corner next to a scratched wooden chair with manacles, and various other First Era torture devices glinted sharp, evil threats.

"Not sure this is the kind of place you want to lock yourself into," said a wry, gravelly voice.

Melaine startled. Her eyes darted across the row of iron cages. A hand dangled through the bars of the second cell down.

She glanced once more at the door beside her. The spell held fast, and no sound of the statue rasped on the other side. She turned back to the cells and walked with cautious steps toward the only one with an occupant.

A man sat on the cold, damp floor, leaning against one wall with his hand propped on his knee, so his fingers slipped through the bars. He looked up at her with curious hazel eyes, but a bitter, lopsided smile curved his mouth upward.

Melaine nearly dropped her candle. He looked like the man she had killed.

He eyed her up and down. "You don't look like you have anything to run from here," he said. "What's your name?"

Melaine frowned, self-conscious as he analyzed her wardrobe. For once in her life, she looked better kept than this prisoner. The rich brocade of her dressing gown glinted with gold silk threads in the candlelight. The soft white chemise brushing her sharp, protruding collar bones was more delicate than any coarse homespun that had ever touched her skin.

She felt a flowering superiority as she contrasted herself with the dirty, rough man below her.

"Melaine," she answered, chin held high. "*You* don't look like you have anything to sing about."

The man laughed. It was an echo of the dry, ringing laughter of the prisoner Melaine had silenced forever. But this man's face was rounder than the first, his skin darker, his lips fuller, his scraggly beard and chin-length hair blonder. He was younger as well, around Melaine's age, it seemed.

"Always something to sing about, Melaine," he said when his laughter died.

"Who are you?" she asked. "Why are you here?"

"Serj," he replied. "And if you don't already know why I'm here, I'm not sure it's any of your business. Why are *you* here?"

Melaine stood straighter. "I am the Overlord's apprentice," she said with glowing pride.

Serj laughed again but transitioned into coughs. Melaine stepped back.

"Passing on his wisdom, eh?" he said after a moment of hacking.

"He found me worthy of teaching," she said.

"Or convenient. Not like he'd have to search high and low for someone like you. You don't match your clothes," he explained with a wink. "Scooped you outta Stakeside, did he?"

"You don't look much better," Melaine said with a snarl. "Neither did your brother."

Serj stiffened, and Melaine knew she had guessed the familial connection between this man and the deceased prisoner correctly. Her jibe felt hollow as soon as it left her mouth.

"You know where he is?" Serj said.

The full truth caught in Melaine's throat. But she managed to say the crux of it.

"He's dead."

Serj sat very still.

"What happened?" he finally asked, not looking at her.

"The Overlord punished him," she answered, the half-lie rolling off her tongue with an ease she'd never wanted to achieve before. "Did you commit the same crime as he?"

Maybe learning of Serj's crime would wash away hers.

"How is our dear Overlord?" Serj asked, ignoring her question with a bitter spat. "Still a shining pillar of strength for Centara?"

Melaine's eyes narrowed. "Do you expect him to be

anything else?" she said, maintaining her superior tone so she wouldn't betray what she really thought of the Overlord's condition.

Serj was silent. She saw his eyes flicker with doubt.

"I am sorry, Talem," Serj muttered. He leaned his head back against the grimy stone wall of his cell. "There are worse fates, I suppose."

"Than death?" Melaine asked.

Serj rolled his head to look at her. "Worse ways to die. Even the Overlord can only perform so much torture. There are other forces in this world that can do much worse."

He looked down and swallowed. He then surprised Melaine by grunting to his feet. He swayed a little, grasping the bars to hold himself up.

"Let me out," he said, pressing his forehead to the bars. "I can help you escape what hunts you." He nodded at the closed door behind her.

"I don't need your help," Melaine said. "It's only a guard. And I'm sure the Overlord would do far worse to me than that statue ever could if I let his prisoner go."

"Statue?" Serj repeated blankly. "You haven't—" His shoulders slumped, and his gaze dropped. "Too slow," he whispered to himself.

"What are you going on about?" Melaine asked.

Serj's bloodshot eyes flashed back up to hers. "Find out what he's going to do to me. Please. That can't be too much to ask. I only wish to know what's coming."

Melaine shook her head and backed away. Serj's eyes looked far too much like his deceased brother's. She couldn't stand how much his face twisted her stomach.

She looked back at the door. She didn't want to risk meeting the statue, but that terrifying stone visage was beginning to feel preferable to the wasted face of Serj.

"No," she said. "You won't see me again." She turned and walked to the door.

"No. Wait," Serj said, his cracked voice rising with desperation. "Please. That old bitch Karina doesn't tell me anything. I need answers!"

Melaine shook her head in a fierce jerk. She pushed open the door and unlocked her ward spell in the same motion. Then she slammed the door against the sound of Serj's frustrated yells.

The hall outside was dark and empty. The sounds of grinding stone were gone. Melaine gathered courage and ran up the stairs, candle in one hand and hiked-up dressing gown in the other. She listened hard as she reached the maze of dungeon passageways and turned back the way she had come.

The statue seemed to have given up the hunt. She made it down the hallway until her candle illuminated the long staircase that would take her back to the garden. She ascended the steps and broke free of the smothering darkness into the brisk, open air. The moon was low in the sky, and purple stretches of twilight chased the stars away like Shields scattering a gaggle of homeless children.

Melaine ran across the garden and up the stairs into her living quarters. She walked through the dusty sitting room and opened the curtain that led to the room with the sunken hearth.

She screamed.

A fire roared to life in the pit, spearing flames around

the hulking statue of the rage-driven guard. It was waiting for her, blocking the path to her bedchamber. She froze as the statue slowly raised a sharpened battle-axe from the flames. A sound like crunching gravel came, long and harsh and menacing as the statue crouched with its raised axe, readying to leap onto her and drive the blade into her chest.

Melaine ran—but not back the way she came. So far, her chamber was the only place the terrorizing statue hadn't followed. If she could reach it, she would be safe.

She darted along the wall and raced past the statue, aimlessly casting bursts of simple repelling spells that she'd scraped up from Insights in Stakeside.

She reached the short passage that led to her room and bolted past the row of dormant statues. She wrenched open her bedroom door and ran inside. She slammed the door, begging her magic to punch a powerful ward into place.

The glinting blade of the axe crashed through the door and implanted itself right beside her cheek. She screamed and stumbled back, but the blade didn't move. It stuck in the door, a warning for her to stay inside.

She listened hard and heard the rough stone sliding closer. She jolted as the statue wrenched the axe from the door, bringing a few splintered pieces of wood with it. Through the slim crack, she could see the statue stand with the axe at its side in a posture of rest. The guard slid away from the door and turned its back. It returned to its place among its frozen brethren and backed into the shadows. It was still.

Melaine watched it for an immeasurable amount of

time, waiting for it to move. But it didn't. Her ward remained in place on the door. She was right in thinking that the statue's sole purpose was to keep her confined to her bedchamber. Now that she had returned to where she belonged, the guard was satisfied to leave her alone.

She doubted she would sleep, and the statue's presence wasn't the only reason. The face of the prisoner in the dungeon melded with his brother's in her mind. Serj's eerie, melancholy song had burrowed into her brain and stayed there. His plea for her to let him out replayed over and over, followed by hoarse, deranged laughter that matched the voice of the man she had murdered at the Overlord's behest.

CHAPTER 7

The warmth of the library door poured into Melaine's hands as she rested them on its solid oak skin. Its innate, ancient magic was just as comforting as the first time she'd touched it, almost...parental. Melaine had never known the love of a mother or father, but she imagined this sense of care and protection was similar. It reminded her a little of Salma.

She didn't know why the library of all places would withstand the dark magic seeping through Highstrong's walls. She had sensed black magic from some of the Insights on its shelves, and the stack of books the Overlord had tried to give her exuded snatches of darkness as well. Yet the doors and the walls themselves wrapped around Melaine like an embrace. Maybe the northwest tower had not always been a library.

Maybe one day, the books and Insights within would no longer taunt Melaine with their vast but inaccessible knowledge.

She pushed against the strong doors, and they opened at her touch, propelled by their welcoming magic. She stepped inside, and the doors swung shut with a gentle nudge.

She scanned the first floor. It looked the same as it had the day before, except for one thing—the Overlord wasn't in sight.

"Hello?" Melaine said. "My lord?"

The sound of beating wings made her gasp and stumble back as a shadow soared across her. She looked up into the heights of the tower. A large, black crow landed on the open balcony parapet, casting a giant, distorted shadow onto the shelves below. Melaine scowled and waved her hand at the beast.

"Go away, you rotten pest," she shouted. The crow cocked its head and looked at her with a beady, black eye as if considering her request. She frowned and snatched a quartz paperweight from a nearby table. She hiked her arm back and threw the sparkling rock at the distant bird.

Crows were a menace in Stakeside. Always stealing scraps of food and shitting on beggars in the streets. They even had an eye for shiny things and were known to steal valuable trinkets—or fake ones meant to be priced and sold as authentic.

The rock smacked into the shelf-lined wall several feet below the balcony. The crow fluttered its feathers a little in indignation, but beyond its cawing bluster, it didn't seem fazed by Melaine's attack. The hunk of quartz rattled down the shelves. Melaine winced as it knocked a wooden, gilded sculpture of a horse onto its side and then propelled a glass jar containing some beast's innards right to the edge of a shelf.

The paperweight then bounced off the top of a mahogany curio cabinet and popped open the glass doors. It crashed inside and hit the protruding edge of a gnarled tree root. The quartz finally settled, but the root spun like the hands of a clock and tipped off its shelf. It fell to the floor and rolled to an uneven stop at Melaine's polished black boots.

Her breaths resumed as she darted her eyes around the room, looking again for the Overlord and his imminent chastisement. Fortunately, he was still absent. She looked back down at the twisted root at her feet. It was a little longer than her foot, dry and well-preserved. There was no telling how old it was. It looked like an ordinary cutting, but it was surrounded by a room filled with Insights, so it must be one as well.

Her heart started racing again at that thought. The Overlord hadn't given her permission to touch any of the Insights in his library. Perhaps if she asked him today, he would, but what if he didn't? What if he didn't want her knowing whatever powerful knowledge his Insights hoarded? What if this was her only chance alone with them? The Overlord was late today, but would his tardiness ever happen again?

Melaine nibbled the inside of her cheek as she stared down at the root. At the very least, she had to pick it up off the floor. She told herself that was as far as she would go as she stooped down and lifted the root into her hands.

She frowned. She didn't feel the usual magic she'd

always detected on Insights. She twisted the root in her fingers but stopped when she saw words carved into its side. She concentrated on each letter, sounding out the writing.

Roots of the Craft. It sounded like a book title. It *was* an Insight, one that contained spells of...roots? Something with plants, perhaps. Whatever the spells it held, useful or not, Melaine needed to know them. The idea of an Insight in her hands, free for her use, was too much to withstand.

She traced her finger across the carved lettering. The root seemed to shiver under her touch, but that was all.

It was empty. Why would the Overlord keep an empty Insight?

There had to be more to it. She ran her fingers along the length of the root again. Small tremors of energy shuddered beneath her fingertips, but she recoiled as she recognized the tangible reek of residual magic defiling her skin. She dangled the root between thumb and forefinger, watching it sway.

That was it, then. The root may once have been an Insight, but it was spent now. The Overlord had used it, and probably other people had before him, gleaning all of the knowledge there was to know from its depths. All that remained was waste.

She almost returned the root to the curio cabinet's shelf in disappointment, but as she held it, a deeper, cleaner magic began to pulse beneath the stain of refuse, blooming under her fingertips. Her fear of getting ill from handling the dirty root was overcome by curiosity. Maybe it wasn't empty after all. There was still a little pure magic left. If she could just tap into it, find it, *reach* for it...

The new sensation taunted her like a dream buried too deep to remember when morning came. Tendrils of roots and vines pushed through dense loam, seeking water, seeking light, seeding her mind with snatches of spells that she couldn't catch fast enough to grasp.

She growled in frustration and squeezed the root with clawed fingers. The soil in her mind was hardening into rock; the vines couldn't push through. They were shriveling; they were dying. *No!*

The vines burst through rock, and the root in Melaine's hand pulsed with a thundering wave of magic that knocked her backward.

A table's edge bit her spine through her goldenrod poplin dress. She winced and righted herself, clutching the root against her chest. Her body shuddered, and her eyes widened as thin, sinuous trails of black smoke, as if echoes of the vines she had imagined, began to seep from the root's ends. The stench and grit of residual magic was pungent now. She was swamped by the wrung-out refuse from the casting of the original spell on the root. The build-up from years of repeated use had then thickened the taint until the root was devoid of all sweeping, light sensations of fresh magic.

Black tendrils wrapped around Melaine's arms as the smoke thickened into ropes. She cried out and dropped the root. It fell to the ground with a rattle, but the smoke vines continued to creep from its ends and swirl around Melaine's arms and hands. They yanked her toward the root. A loud chanting rushed at her in indiscernible words, but she somehow understood.

She gasped as the black tendrils ripped her magic to the surface of her skin. Her palms flooded with heat, and she focused on the words in her ears and the magic in her hands and pushed.

Thick, dry vines shot out of her fingertips. They were real and solid, taking the place of the smoky residue. The vines erupted with sharp thorns that twisted along their gnarled lengths. They climbed with violent speed up the tower walls, piercing leather spines of books and shattering glass casings while they splintered the wooden shelves.

The botanical explosion flew straight toward the startled crow, who had never left its post on the open balcony. Its caw reverberated against the tower rafters. It flapped its black wings, but the vines had reached the high window and they encircled the balcony in a thorny cage. The crow beat its wings so fast it lost feathers, lurching toward the thorns but veering away before it impaled itself.

Each vine thickened and crisscrossed with countless others. They smothered the sunlight, narrowing the broad shafts to mere slivers. The bird's wings cast wild shadows in the retreating light. Melaine watched the whole scene like she was apart from it all. Was she the one willing the largest thorn to sharpen and aim right at the pesky crow, ready to strike like a viper? Or had she awoken some other evil?

Firm hands snaked around Melaine's arms and gripped her, hard. She gasped as the dry vines snapped off of her fingers and crumbled to the floor. The thick vines on the balcony stopped twisting, and the spike that was aimed at the desperate crow whipped back and smacked into the thorny cage. The entire binding of vines shattered into countless pieces, littering the balcony with dried twigs and fractured thorns.

The crow darted through the opening and beat its frantic wings out of sight into the autumn air.

"What are you doing?" the Overlord said, his hoarse voice rough and fierce. He spun her around, his grip returning just as hard as he held her in place.

Melaine looked up into his piercing blue eyes. "I-I don't know. I just touched that root, and—"

"You touched it?" the Overlord scoffed. He let go of her arms. Her skin felt hot from his touch and a little bruised.

He stooped and picked up the root.

"You said you know little more than household spells," he said, clearly irritable. But his anger was more like she'd awoken him too early from sleep rather than committed some mysterious magical misdemeanor that had scared her.

"I don't," she insisted. "It was the Insight."

"This Insight is empty," the Overlord said. "It has been for fifteen years."

His scathing tone made Melaine's face grow hot with anger.

"It's not! I found its magic. It...worked."

Melaine fought a shudder as she eyed the root. Had it worked? She'd never experienced an Insight with such an explosion of potency before. Was it supposed to do what it had done?

The Overlord frowned and looked at the Insight, dormant in his hand.

Melaine lifted her fingers, inspecting them. All evidence of vines from beneath her fingernails was gone. She drew her eyebrows together and cupped her palm. She felt a gentle nudge of magic in her mind, and she imagined a blossoming flower. Golden petals flowed from the beds of her fingernails. She looked at them in awe, appearing, for a moment, like a rich lady with painted nails. Then, the petals dropped free. They swirled and coalesced over her open hand until a bright yellow rose blossom rested in her palm.

She raised her wide eyes and looked at the Overlord. He was watching the rose with a look of intense intrigue, dissecting each petal with a flicker of analytical thought in his eyes.

"May I?" he said after a moment. He held out his hand.

Melaine frowned but nodded. The Overlord gently scooped the rose from her hand. Feathery energy hovered over her palm in its wake, carrying the scent of forest loam and grass clippings.

"Repurposed magic," he muttered. He ran lithe fingertips along each petal's edge with the air of a connoisseur identifying a fine wine. He nodded to himself.

"You took the latent magic within the Insight, left there from the sorcerer who crafted it, and repurposed the scraps to infuse you with the knowledge this root contained."

"What?" Melaine asked. "I didn't do that."

"Whether wittingly or not, you did," the Overlord said. "It is extremely rare for anyone to be able to use residual magic. *Especially* unintentionally." His keen eyes inspected her with great interest.

"Residual magic?" Melaine repeated with a crinkled nose and a desire to wipe her palms on her dress. "But that's—"

"As useful as any other kind," said the Overlord. "For those of us who know how to be resourceful."

Melaine raised her eyebrows.

"You are desperate to learn magic, Melaine," he said. She shivered under his penetrating gaze as he drew closer. He held the rose between them, its petals trembling near her beating heart. "You are too anxious to wait for me to teach you, and you couldn't stand the thought of all these Insights here, taunting you because they contain knowledge your limitations of status have always prevented you from gleaning. Yes?"

Melaine didn't deny his statement, marveling at how easily he seemed to understand her thoughts.

"So, you *took* it," he said, his voice lower, almost intimate. His blue eyes deepened. "You did what you had to in order to get ahead. Just like you do with your lodestones. That scrappy resourcefulness is more powerful than you know, Melaine. *That* is something that cannot be taught." He searched her eyes, drinking in her confused expression. "I've never met anyone who possesses it as strongly as I."

"What cause do you have to be resourceful?" she asked

to distract herself from her instinct to back away. "You have everything you could want in excess."

The Overlord smiled. "I didn't always."

Melaine silenced. The way he looked at her dove deeper than the day before, as if he was trying to lay steady foundations for a bridge between them, one that scared her. He spoke as if he understood what it was like to *be* her. He understood who she was. She dropped her gaze.

The Overlord drew away. He walked across the room to an armchair and sat down. His exertion from stopping her drastic display of magic seemed to have drained him of energy. Only when he was gone did she notice the absence of his smooth scent of old parchment, warm candle wax, and sandalwood, all cooled by the sensation of his magic that tasted and smelled of freshly fallen snow.

"I admire what you just did," he said, setting the delicate rose blossom on his lap. "But, as you experienced, learning from an Insight is no simple thing."

Melaine opened her mouth.

"With trifling spells, perhaps," he interrupted with a raised finger to stop her protest. "But you are not standing amongst trifling spells, are you Melaine?" His eyes traveled about the room, making his point clear as he addressed the staggering amount of Insights within his collection.

Melaine's heart beat with excitement and a little trepidation. "No," she agreed.

"You will not touch any Insights in this room without my permission." He eyed her hard. "Especially those from this cabinet." He indicated the curio cabinet from which the root had fallen, which contained three stacked shelves cluttered with objects. "Just because you can scrape their dregs doesn't mean they are spells you need to know. Had I known you could..."

He paused, reining in his words.

"Put it back," he said, holding out the root. She hesitated but came forward and took the root from his hand. She focused on its surface, but no taint of residual magic remained, and the cleaner magic beneath was utterly gone.

"Did I use the last of it?" she asked with a wince, worried she might get in trouble.

The Overlord sighed. "Put it back," he said again, nodding to the shelf. "And close the door."

His words had a finality to them. She *had* used up the root's last dregs, and he wanted to make sure she didn't use up the others, too. Perhaps he kept empty Insights because he thought he was the only person who might still get some use out of them. Could he "repurpose" residual magic too? Was she...*like* him, in that way?

She turned her back and approached the cabinet filled with forbidden objects. She felt special because she could do something the Overlord had never expected, something that he thought perhaps only he could do, but anger flared in her heart from his command to stay away from the knowledge he prized.

"Don't worry, Melaine," he said. "There is much I can teach you. Much that this library can teach you."

Melaine placed the root in its spot and closed the glass doors. She turned around.

"I can learn from others?" she asked, flashing her eyes about the tower.

The Overlord nodded. "Under my tutelage."

"My lord, why do I need your tutelage when I can learn from the Insights?"

"Insights are powerful," he said. "But without a greater context, without the support of a strong foundation built upon the principles behind them, they can be next to useless. Or overwhelming." He eyed the balcony, still scattered with snapped twigs and loose thorns.

"And I am not the only one with limited energy this morning," he said with a small grimace as if he'd swallowed bitter tea. "You won't be able to rush about the tower, learning from Insight after Insight endlessly. Temper your impatience, and let me guide you, Melaine. You did come to me, after all."

"Yes, my lord," Melaine said. He was right. She had come to him. She had an opportunity unlike any other—many people would kill for this chance at power. She *had* killed for this chance. Why was she belittling his teachings?

Because he wasn't what she had expected.

Yet his physical weakness wasn't the only thing that differed from her imaginings. The artist who'd created the broadsheet portraits posted around Centara was a failure as far as Melaine was concerned. The Overlord's eyes weren't cold and hard as ice. They shifted dynamically, each small flick revealing a different facet of his personality or hinting at secrets close to the surface but withheld.

Jianthe had once told her about a natural wonder

known as glaciers, which the woman had seen when she'd visited the northernmost kingdom, Wrimid, when she'd lived and traded out of Zraihya as a child. Jianthe had said that glaciers were made of ice that moved and flowed. The Overlord's eyes moved, prodding and consuming Melaine's perceptions, so that she couldn't keep an even footing.

Jianthe had also said that glacier's hearts held a bright yet deep blue color, just like the Overlord's eyes.

"Where should we start, my lord?" Melaine asked, squaring her shoulders and meeting his gaze. She was surprised to see a slight twinkle in his eyes as he looked at her, but it was quickly doused.

"First," he said with a tight frown. "I'm going to need my strength." He held out his hand but avoided Melaine's gaze.

Melaine swallowed her shame and resentment and nodded. She tried to focus on all of the brilliant knowledge ahead as she summoned a lodestone from her marrow, through her veins, and into her palm. She forced the prickling pain to fade and brought the stone to the Overlord with care. He took it in light fingertips and brought it to his lips.

Melaine turned around before she had to watch him inhale her magic. Her heartbeat quickened as she swept her eyes upward to the massive library. As loath as she was to part with her magic, she had to accept that sacrificing one lodestone was, perhaps, nothing compared to the prize she could earn in return.

No lodestone could ever match the staggering power she could gain from this library of Insights.

❧

WRIGGLING, CREEPING VINES SPRAWLED OUT OF Melaine's wrist as if they were extensions of her veins. They climbed up the lurking guard statue outside her room and encircled its every limb in a binding vice. A thick, thorn-covered vine strangled its neck and wrapped around its horrific face. The statue was blind and immobilized—she hoped.

She kept her wrist aloft as she trod past the statue with caution. It didn't move. Her ensnaring spell was working, and the thought gave Melaine the confidence she needed to press forward. When she reached the end of the hallway, she rolled her wrist and flicked the protruding vine away from her skin. It slithered back toward the statue and joined the rest, encircling the dark gray stone.

Melaine took a breath and nearly smiled as she crossed through the hearth room and entered the sitting room. The furniture loomed amidst golden decor that reflected the light of her candlestick, but the superficial luxuries had no sway over her mission. So far, wandering the castle at night had not been successful, but now Melaine had an itch that could not be scratched alone in her bedroom. She had tasted power in the library. Real power. And despite the Overlord's opinion that she should wait until he was around to peruse the Insights, so much thrilling magic had built up within her over the past three days, it seemed a waste not to use it. She would avoid the glass cabinet, at least.

Her mind lit up with anticipation, thinking about

what kind of knowledge she might find next. Conjuration spells? Tactical battle-magic? Necromancy?

Melaine shuddered, but her heart leapt at the amazing, unlimited possibilities before her. The Overlord wouldn't judge any forms of magic she wished to learn. Even the darkest spells, which cowards liked to call "evil."

Melaine continued through her quarter's string of rooms until she reached the staircase that led to the courtyard where the pond and garden waited in tamed serenity. She walked down the stairs and breathed in the crisp night scent of weeds and water and moonlight.

Then a low crooning reached her ears, drifting from the small entrance to the dungeons. The prisoner she had met, Serj, was singing his plaintive, deranged song.

Suddenly, the thought of necromancy somersaulted her insides. The face of Serj's dead brother, Talem, seeped into her brain. She had only used a propulsion spell to knock him down, but the memory still made her sick. Would any battle-magic spells be as glorious as she'd dreamed? Or would they all give her this twisted feeling inside if she tried them?

She pushed away the guilt bubbling inside her, but the urge to avoid Serj's melancholy song was too great to ignore. She turned to her right and hurried across a patch of grass and up another flight of stairs toward a different paved courtyard that served as a crossroads to the maze that was Highstrong Keep.

She passed through a brief, dark passage and again entered the open air. She could still hear Serj's song. She looked around at each short, narrow doorway and alcove, trying to judge if there was an alternate path to the library that would keep her as far away as possible from the dungeons.

Across the courtyard, the door to the great hall lurked. She knew the library tower was on the other side, but she didn't know if the two sections connected in the interior. One courtyard staircase led to the wall above the great hall's flat roof, and Melaine decided on that route. The night was cold and damp, with clouds that threatened rain, but better to take a straightforward path than to reenter a maze of dark corridors.

She kept every sense vigilant as she crept across the cracked granite flags and up the crumbling stone stairs. She reached the roof, where a walking path ran between two rails of wrought-iron posts, a sign that the ancient wall had been modified in more recent years. Perhaps the Overlord had repaired it five years ago when he'd moved back into Highstrong. Maybe it had been a necessary reinforcement when his army had holed up in the keep before the war.

The light from Melaine's candle danced on the spearheads of each iron post as she padded on silent feet down the path. A chill permeated her dressing gown and chemise, and she paused when she felt a light draft rustle her hair. She smelled rain. A thin mist started to drizzle down.

She shivered but kept walking. She could see the library's tower ahead. Its few windows were dark, and the quickening rain glistened on its stone sides and parapets.

Melaine's candle went out. She paused as harder raindrops fell on her skin and soaked her thin clothing. The iron rails beside her splayed inward, twisted and frayed, as if a heavy cannonball had blown their other halves away.

She looked out over the iron posts and into the night. The rain and mist obscured most of the world, but she could see the massive shadow of the menacing outer wall of Highstrong Keep. She eyed the wall, a brooding cliff of sheer stone that stood as a dark shadow against the eerie, moonlit clouds, which poured rain in dismal patches.

For a moment, she took stock of her brief life within Highstrong's walls. For once, she was in a place she wanted to be. The wall of Highstrong Keep wasn't like the wall of Stakeside, which served as a constant reminder that she was excluded from the higher levels of living in Centara. The wall of Highstrong was a symbol that the rest of the world was excluded from the Overlord's illustrious presence, and only Melaine was good enough for those monstrous walls to let her in.

She lowered her eyes and let them wander the courtyard, enjoying the moment despite the rain that plastered her chemise to her freezing skin. She leaned over the splayed iron posts and peered down to her right, where she saw the abandoned stable house. She then looked left at the hexagonal library tower, not far away.

A blurred figure stood on the tower balcony. Melaine straightened and looked harder through the rain. The pale shape of a woman stood watching her, but Melaine blinked, and the woman disappeared. Fog rose like steam from the balcony, swirling in the increasing rain.

Melaine looked away with a little shake of her head. Clearly, it had been her imagination making shapes from clouds. Then she heard a small whisper that shivered along her skin.

"Down."

Melaine stiffened. The whisper was so soft, it could have been as insubstantial as the woman she'd imagined on the balcony. But she shot her eyes down to the court-yard below the parapet where she stood. Her frown deepened. She may have imagined the woman and whisper, but what she saw leaning against the wall of the building below was far more concrete. She let out a breath when she deciphered what it was.

A body.

Melaine's stomach turned. It was a human body; there was no mistake. Soaked, ragged clothes clung to four limbs, and a sopping head of hair was plastered to a bowed skull. The poor individual was dead, their bones twisted at odd angles. The half-prone position suggested that they had either fallen, jumped, or been tossed from the roof's railed pathway.

Melaine inhaled a sharp breath. Was the body the Overlord's? Surely, not. Karina? She knew it wasn't Serj because she had heard his singing only moments before.

From what she could see through the rain, it appeared that there was too much flesh on the body's bones for it to have been there long. Even with Highstrong's walls, vultures would at least have access to the body's fresh meat. Or those damn crows that flocked everywhere.

She had to find out whose body that was and why they were there. She swallowed and called upon her magic. Once, when she was a young child and all of her magic had still been her own, she had cushioned a fall from a shop roof when running from a person she had just pick-pocketed. She'd never learned the spell from an Insight, nor was it taught to her, but somehow, she had landed safe and sound. Though it had been many years since she had retained enough magic to pull off such a feat, she believed it was time to try.

Despite the grim purpose, she couldn't help but feel a fresh thrill as she prepared to test the potential of her magic. She set down her dormant candle—enough moonlight shone through the clouds to light her way. So, she focused all of her magic on the wind around her. She inhaled the cold air, tiny mist droplets entering her nose. When she exhaled, all the rain around her splashed away as if knocked by an opposing wind. She focused on keeping the rain off her skin so nothing would hinder her careful leap from the high castle roof.

She jumped.

She maintained a cloak of dry air around herself to steady her course as she fell but channeled most of her energy into pushing air down to her feet. The blurry ground rushed at her, but she slowed as the wind under her feet built up resistance. She landed, and wet, frigid mud sucked at the soles of her bare feet. She lifted the hem of her dressing gown and raised one foot from the muck, then the other. Rain continued to bounce off of a dry aura of air around her skin and hair, but the damp cold of the autumn night still infused her bones.

She considered using her magic to agitate the air around her, to make its infinitesimal particles dance so quickly that it would warm. She glanced back up at the roof, high above her head. She still wasn't sure of the extent of her magic. She didn't know a spell to propel herself back up the wall, and there was likely a ward on the keep's door. Better not waste any magic on comforts until she was sure she was as powerful as she *felt*.

So, shivering with an uneasy turn of her stomach, Melaine walked toward the body she had seen from the rooftop. The pouring rain made it difficult to make out anything beyond blurred mud and stone, but after a few paces, she deciphered a mud-spattered shoe lying on its side.

She stopped and followed the line of the shoe up to a shin clothed in tattered rags, then up to a bare knee and froze. The leg was torn clean off from the rest of the body just above the knee. The bone inside was splintered, its jagged edges protruding from the inner flesh like a shattered icicle.

Melaine stepped back with a grimace, but she slowly forced herself to view the body as a whole.

It was in pieces. The body's clothes were shredded, revealing dark, sticky blood that the streaming rain couldn't thin. Most of the flesh had been flayed from the bones but sat in tatters beside the body, uneaten by any animal that Melaine would have suspected could be responsible for this amount of carnage. The bones' surfaces were cracked and split like white birch branches. Their marrow was raw and open in the mud.

Melaine stood still for a moment, staring at the grisly sight. She felt a nauseating flip in her stomach but lifted her eyes to see the body's face.

"No," she whispered, but couldn't hear her own voice over the beating rain.

The gaunt face was frozen in time in an expression of dark triumph, caught mid-laugh in the moment of dying. Melaine recognized that expression, that face. It had haunted her since her first night in Highstrong.

Talem.

Melaine fell to her knees beside the broken body. How had he wound up here? Was the Overlord so callous that he had tossed the body over the wall without thought of burial? But then, had Talem deserved burial? The Overlord must have imprisoned and tortured him for a reason. He must have had Melaine...knock him down...for a reason.

Melaine closed her eyes, almost unable to think past the chill in her bones in the wet night. Talem must have deserved death. He must have done something terrible. If he hadn't, did she bear more guilt than he?

She opened her eyes and again took in the unsightly body. On Talem's emaciated chest, the ragged symbol of the Luxian Order peeked through a smear of blood. His crime must have been related to the harsh religion. Melaine had been afraid that the Overlord wasn't aware of its resurgence in Centara, but it seemed he was still bent on stamping the Luxians out. Their unforgiving, closed-minded, and violent practices held no place in his secular reign.

Though she wasn't sure why, she reached out and laid a hand upon the corpse's shattered arm as if Talem was still around to feel her comfort. Perhaps, her apology.

She jerked her hand back. She looked down at her fingers, and then eyed the body with sudden caution. Something was wrong. Something was very wrong.

She looked closer at Talem's exposed bones. She could see the spongy marrow inside, but some of it was missing, hollowed, as if sucked out by a carnivore. But what animal would only go for the bones and leave the meat?

Even if an animal were to suck every ounce of marrow from a body's bones, magic would still linger on the bones themselves, on the flesh, in the tiny strands of hair, under a corpse's blue fingernails. Magic was always present in a human's body, whether in copious amounts or only a little. It was essential to human life. A corpse retained that magic until it dissolved into the earth forevermore.

Melaine had seen a body like this once before, drained utterly of magic. It had rooted her to the spot in horror when she was a child. It was the reason she was here now, in the Overlord's castle.

The body of the old stone-peddling woman in Stakeside had lacked all magic when Melaine had found her curled up on the street one day, lifeless and still. Her palm had been open, her knotty, wrinkled fingers spread as if offering something, though her hand was empty. Melaine had easily guessed what happened.

The old woman had created her final lodestone. She had emptied all of her magic trying to make a sale. The buyer had obviously grabbed the stone without a thought, leaving the dead woman's body to stiffen in the cold. They were probably glad they didn't have to pay for the weak pebble the woman had offered.

Melaine had realized, then, that her death was going to be the same if she let it. As she had told the Overlord, she had resolved to change her life after the woman died. What she hadn't admitted was that she had taken pity on the woman that day. She had buried the body in an old soil plot behind a tannery. She surrounded the woman with the offal and rancid discards from the skinned carcasses, so no graverobbers would try to dig the woman up. Melaine had forgone eating that day so that she would have the magical strength to lift the soil and cover the body before she was seen by others.

As she'd witnessed that day, the only way a person's body could be completely drained of magic was to offer it freely. It was something so bound to their bones that it could not be torn from them by another, though Melaine was certain that plenty of dark sorcerers had tried to devise methods and failed.

So Talem must have given his magic away freely before he died. But who had he given it to? Serj acted like he didn't know what had happened to Talem, so unless he was lying, Talem hadn't had a chance to bestow his magic onto his brother. And Talem wouldn't have given it to the Overlord. Unless the Overlord had tortured him enough, persuading Talem to hand over his magic to create a lodestone, just as Melaine was doing for the Overlord now.

Or maybe the Overlord's darkest, rumored experiments had included spells to steal magic, and he'd succeeded where all others had failed.

Melaine's mind raced. Was she in danger? Did the Overlord intend to take her lodestones, use her up, and dump her body as he may have done to Talem? Fear started to grow, and a sense of betrayal crept at the edges of her mind. But then logic took over. Why would the Overlord ever persuade her to empty her magic for him? He had no reason to torture or punish her as he had done with Talem. Keeping her alive would allow her to give him unlimited lodestones for years, so long as he continued to only require a few or less per day. Draining her magic and killing her would help no one.

Melaine continued to stare at Talem's body until she could no longer stand the pervasive cold through her bones. She squinted through the beating rain around the courtyard. In one isolated corner, a tangle of wild roses rioted against the wall. Their scrabbling thorns were formidable, but their bowed, petaled heads were yet another beautiful luxury the Overlord possessed but didn't tend to or seem to appreciate.

Melaine summoned magic from within her bones, kept whole and safe within her flesh, and brought it to the surface of her fingertips. She lifted Talem's broken body without touching him, as if by invisible strings. His shattered limbs dangled in the air like a disjointed puppet. She grimaced and tightened her magic's hold, wrapping him as a spider would its prey so that his limbs joined together in a bundle instead.

Her mouth set in a hard line as she walked toward the rose bushes, magically coaxing Talem's body to follow. She looked up at the walls of the keep, eyeing the windows in particular for any watching eyes. The rain made it nearly impossible to see them. She hoped she was obscured in the same manner.

When she reached the thicket of roses, she stopped. Concentrating on keeping Talem aboveground, she swept her hands in an open motion toward the bushes. Tingling magic flowed from her fingers and caught the branches and thorns in its binding grasp. Melaine widened her arms and pulled the branches apart. Then she eased the roots themselves away from a patch of soil, careful not to disturb the plants' abilities to flourish. She would never have paid attention to such details before she had imbibed the Insight on botanical magic, but now it felt like innate knowledge that she had always carried with her.

Rain poured down into a bare patch of soil. She pushed her magic into the earth, feeling every small grain and every living insect and worm creeping within. She made a lifting motion with her hands, and the soil rose in a heap. She set the heap down to the side and then repeated the motion several times. Soon, a hole formed, long enough for a man, deep enough to discourage animals from tampering with the body, though she hoped the thorns would also work toward that end. And, hopefully, they would dissuade any searching human eyes if Karina or the Overlord realized the body of their former prisoner was no longer where one of them had dumped him.

She exhaled through her nostrils against the rotting stench and brought the hovering body of Talem toward the hole. She was surprised that she could keep him aloft so easily while pouring so much magic into the task of digging his grave.

Her shoulders fell, and her enjoyment of enlightened power drained as she watched the broken, magic-less body hover over the hole in the ground. The hole was already filling with rainwater. It seemed like such a cold, dismal place to rest.

The roses would blossom and glimmer in the sunlight, at least. Hopefully, Talem would know peace.

The Overlord *must* have had her kill Talem for a reason, but that thought wasn't as bracing as it had once been.

She let the body of Talem fall into the grave. It crumpled in a pile of bones and matted hair and blood-sticky flesh. The tattered rags and the skin of his face barely covered everything else that was raw death. His death felt so much more final when the body was empty of magic. Even Talem's purest essence had abandoned him. Or been stripped from him.

Tears stung Melaine's eyes. She wiped a hand roughly across them. Crying was *not* something she ever allowed herself to do. It was weak, and it would be seen as weak to any onlookers, anyone who wished to prey on a sad, vulnerable, pretty young woman in Stakeside.

Melaine gathered more magic, and straining a little, lifted the large pile of soil from beside the grave in one heave. She dumped it into the hole, hiding Talem forever from sight. The soil settled into place, churning into mud under the rain. But the hole was filled. The grave was finished. Melaine swept her hand across the scene. The rose bushes' thorns dragged like sharp fingernails across the opening. Melaine sensed the roots infiltrating the grave, though none touched Talem's body—she made sure of that.

Nothing but a large row of wild roses met her sight, the grave forever hidden within the tangled mass. The roses' heads still bowed under the heavy rain, showing respect for the man buried in their midst.

Melaine swallowed and backed away. Now that her task was done, her shivering reached a violent level. She was close to the side entrance of the castle now, so she darted toward the innocuous arched door and pulled the iron handle. It stuck for a moment, but with a burst of magic from Melaine, the door opened.

A wave of dark magic swelled over her, making her stumble into the keep. She braced herself on the cold stone wall and kicked the door closed. The dark magic slammed back into the door and clung to the wood.

She stared at the door. It had been locked and sealed by dark magic, but she had burst through without a thought. Either the Overlord was so confident in the towering, outer walls of Highstrong that he had only installed weak magic to bar the door, or Melaine was more powerful than she thought. She was wary to believe the latter, but the idea was tantalizing. She had used magic to shove rain away from her body and maintain it throughout her evening. She had leapt from a rooftop and magically cushioned her fall. She had lifted a heavy, disjointed body from the ground and held it aloft while she'd used even more magic to shift plants and dig a grave. Then she'd used magic to drive away a locking curse upon a door.

And she wasn't tired at all.

No matter how much magical strength she felt, her spirit felt weary. All her excitement about going to the library was gone. Talem's grotesque remains and the haunting lack of magic in his bones submerged Melaine's mind in anxiety. She didn't understand how all of the pieces fit into a larger puzzle. She didn't understand the

Overlord's motivations in killing Talem—in having Melaine kill him. She didn't understand how Talem's body was devoid of magic, and she wasn't sure if the Overlord was to blame.

Melaine continued to shiver as she wandered down a brief corridor and into the first inner courtyard. She repelled rain from her body as she ran across the stone pavement to the door Karina had used the first time she'd escorted Melaine to her chambers. She climbed a set of stairs, feeling her way in the dark corridor beyond because she'd left her candle behind. She was fairly confident she knew the way.

She could see the glimmer of a green everflame torch in a sconce ahead, and she knew she was close. All she wanted was to get out of her wet clothes and crawl under the blankets and furs she knew waited in her luxurious bed.

The sound of heavy, slow footsteps stopped her trek. She tried to stifle her shivering breaths, her mind leaping to the image of the hulking, terrifying guard statue, but she had restrained it before her venture tonight. Had it broken free?

She turned around. A shadowed form met her eyes, but it stood straighter and was thinner than the menacing statue. Its footsteps weren't caused by grating stone but by the soles of supple leather shoes that she recognized. She stepped to the side to let the green light of the ever-flame torch behind her illuminate the shadow enough to see a familiar face. A face that was pale and gaunt with bright blue eyes that gleamed in the light.

She took a breath of relief, but her heart pattered

faster as she let out a bracing exhale. She had the urge to smile, but she bit her lip and waited with taut muscles. The Overlord stopped ten feet away.

"My lord," she whispered. The man was dressed for bed, wearing a long, black, silken robe embroidered with subtle, shimmering threads along the lapels and cuffs. The garment closed over his black nightshirt with silver frog fasteners. Given his casual attire, she found it odd that he had bothered to put on his shoes rather than slippers or simply going barefoot.

"I-I couldn't sleep," she said. "I didn't mean to disturb you."

The Overlord said nothing. He didn't even move.

"I'll go straight to bed, my lord," Melaine said a little louder. "If you wish?"

The Overlord's eyes flickered over her shoulder toward her quarters. He looked back at her. Then, he tilted his head with a strange glint in his eye as if he was seeing her for the first time. He scanned her body up and down, and the glint turned hungry.

"My lord?" Melaine asked, her voice shaky. Had he seen her burying Talem? Was he about to unleash his powerful wrath?

The Overlord took a step toward her, but then his body shuddered. He looked down at his hand as if he had never seen it before, and then he turned around and started to walk away.

Melaine opened her mouth to question him but stopped herself as he melded into the dark.

Her spooked nerves made her bolt in the other direction. The vines around the menacing statue outside her bedchamber lay broken and shriveled at its feet, but it hadn't moved so far as she could tell. She darted past the statue and into her room. She placed a barricade spell upon the door and curled into her bed, fear and confusion rolling over her in deep waves as her mind replayed everything she'd seen.

She remained awake till morning.

CHAPTER 8

S leepwalking, Melaine decided.

That was the only explanation for the Overlord's strange behavior the night before. When she arrived in the great hall under Karina's instructions mere hours later, he made no mention of their brief encounter. She didn't dare bring it up, but he acted as if nothing had gone amiss.

He did, however, hold out his palm as soon as she sat down at a table that had been placed far from the dais that held the formidable throne.

"Lodestones," he said, his voice scratchy. He had been twisting his neck and shoulders when she'd walked in, and now his hunched body looked like every bone and muscle ached.

"Stones?" she asked.

"Two," he said, curt and bitter as he always sounded when he expressed his need for her magic. Did he hate being vulnerable as much as she did?

If he did, that didn't stop him from making her feel

weak by taking her stones. Melaine frowned deeply but lowered her head so he wouldn't catch all of her displeasure. She slowly peeled off her glove, exposing her bare palm to his eyes.

He had never asked for two stones in one day. She knew she shouldn't resent it—he was training her as she had wished, and she still didn't have to make near as many stones as she used to. But as she pulled the second stone from her body, she couldn't help but feel a familiar hatred for being used.

The Overlord took them both, inhaling one right after the other. He took a moment to catch his breath, to feel her magic flooding his veins, and when a little color crept back into his deathly, pale face, he gestured toward a narrow wooden box resting on the table beside him.

"I have something for you," he murmured. His voice still scratched like sandpaper.

Melaine raised her eyebrows. The Overlord slid the box into her hands with care. She got the impression that lifting it would have been beyond his capabilities.

"Open it," he said.

She raised her hand toward the box but hesitated, the dangers from the night before creeping into her mind. He had just asked her for two stones, more of her magic than usual. What if her suspicions of him stealing Talem's magic held weight? What if the Overlord craved her magic so much that he meant her harm? What if something horrible was in the box?

"It's not a snake," the Overlord commented.

Melaine flushed. She pinched her lips together and

flung the lid open on its hinges. Her eyes grew round. She halted her rebellious speed.

"A wand," she uttered, her voice hardly there.

She had never been this close to one before. But oh, how many times she had ached to touch one, envious of the pretentious thieves who'd managed to get their hands on one after a successful heist in Crossing's Square. As if they even knew how to use a wand. Most only paraded them around for show, just like the previous, rich owners did.

This wand, however, didn't look like it would ever be waved around by a rich person. It was not carved with ornate scrollwork or gilded with gold and jewels. It was instead rough-hewn from dull wood. The shaft wasn't perfectly straight, and there was no distinct handle to ensure a firm grip. A small spike of indignation hit Melaine, making her realize that the Overlord wouldn't waste any of his good wands on someone like her. But that thought was overridden by her awe-filled lust for *any* wand at all.

"Take it," the Overlord said. His voice was tinged with impatience but also carried a hushed excitement.

Melaine took a quick breath and snatched the wand from its box. A shudder ran through her as she held it, and a dirty, strong flood of magical grit grated her skin— the same sensation she'd experienced when touching the root Insight in the library, but worse. She flung the wand away and jerked her hand back. The wand hit the floor, and Melaine scooted her chair back with a twist of disgust on her lips.

She flexed her hand, now coated in residual magic, and glared at the Overlord.

"Why would you give me that?" she said. "Your idea of a joke?"

The Overlord's cold eyes met hers, and fear flashed through her as it dawned on her how she had just spoken to him. But she held her ground and his gaze.

"Not to your liking?" he asked.

She scoffed. "I guess you think even that's too good for me. A stonegirl doesn't deserve better than a wand coated in refuse? If that's your idea of charity, I don't want it."

The Overlord was silent for a moment—calm, his visage unreadable. Then, he flicked his hand toward the wand. A soft, glimmering wisp of crystal blue magic flowed from his hand and wreathed the wand like frost. Melaine's lips parted as she admired his raw magic's beauty, and she watched the wand rise from the ground and into his grasp. He shifted it to lay flat upon his open palm on display. He showed no disgust, which baffled her.

"You gleaned knowledge from the tree root Insight through its residual magic," he said. "Why is this different?"

"There was only a little on that root, and that was bad enough," Melaine countered. "That wand is...filthy."

"It hasn't been used in a very long time," the Overlord said.

"Neither had that old root."

"Wands are different from Insights," the Overlord said in his lecturing tone. "Insights were once living. Wands, in a sense, *are* living. And this one is from my personal collection. Are you going to refuse it?"

Melaine eyed the wand as if it was a cockroach and fought the urge to run and wash her hands. People had gotten ill off of far less residual magic than what tainted that wand. But the Overlord held it with ease, and whatever caused his weakness didn't match the symptoms of the res sickness.

She hadn't gotten sick from residual magic since she was a little girl, despite the filth of Stakeside. After a long moment's hesitation, she gave in and took the wand from the Overlord's proffered hand. She shuddered as she felt the magic scrape her fingers, but she twirled the wand a little, trying to focus on the speck of cleaner magic she felt within, just as she had with the empty root Insight. And that cleaner magic beat strong like a heartbeat. Its cool, breathtaking energy felt like the Overlord's magic.

Then she felt her own magic pouring from her fingers as if reaching for the magic of the wand. As soon as their magic combined, the residual magic started to chaff away like dead skin. It was as if the wand was another person, working *with* her instead of just infusing her with static knowledge as an Insight would. The wand craved to learn and practice magic just as much as she did.

"Do you see?" the Overlord asked, leaning forward.

She nodded slowly. "I think so."

A wry smile curved the corner of the Overlord's mouth. He rested his elbows on the table and linked his fingers together. "Do you know where I got this wand, Melaine?"

She shook her head, still focusing on the flow of magic between herself and the wand.

"I whittled it from the shaft of a broom handle," he said.

"What?" Melaine asked, looking up.

"This was my first wand," the Overlord said. "It took years to make it. Years to collect enough magic to give it any use." His eyes darkened and flicked to the side before returning to Melaine. "Are you telling me that a wand crafted with this much care is not good enough for you, Stonegirl?"

Melaine swallowed and contained her impulsive retort.

"Why did you have to do that?" she asked instead. "Make a wand that way?"

The Overlord chuckled. "I thought you would have caught on by now that I wasn't always rich." He nodded at the wand. "How does it feel?"

A smile touched Melaine's lips. Now that the residual magic had reduced to nearly nothing, the thrill of holding a real wand returned. Residual magic or not, this wand felt powerful. The longer she held it, the more she felt infused with its magic, meeting with her own that pulsed through her veins. It was such a heady feeling that it caused her to sway.

"Good," she answered. She studied the wand with a closer eye, drawn to its every detail, every scratch, every nick, and uneven edge.

"Tell me, Melaine," the Overlord said after a moment, pulling her from her immersion. "Do you have anyone out there?" He inclined his head toward a window. "Anyone who misses you?"

Melaine hmphed. "No."

"You're an orphan," he said. "But surely there is someone?"

Melaine shook her head. "There's only me, my lord."

After the words left her mouth, a delayed warning bell tolled in her consciousness, too slow for comfort. The state in which she had found Talem's body last night crawled into her head. She still didn't know if the Overlord was somehow responsible for Talem's drained magic. Admitting that she had no family and no one who would miss her if she never returned was probably not the wisest idea.

"Have you ever had any desire to find your parents?" the Overlord asked. His voice was reflective. The change in his line of questioning felt less threatening. Perhaps she was overreacting.

"No. Why bother?"

"Perhaps you have relatives somewhere. You might come from a good family, possibly even a wealthy one. Have you never considered it?"

"It doesn't matter. No righteous, upstanding person wants anything to do with a stonegirl. Not even blood. They wouldn't want to lower their status that way."

He eyed her with a subtle, conspiratorial look. His mouth twitched in a hint of a smile. "Ah, but the upstanding never have any real power."

Melaine frowned and looked from the wand to the Overlord. When he smiled like that, she felt compelled to look away and draw into herself, conjuring an image of blinding sunlight that flashed through thin cracks in a stone wall. He seemed less imposing and more honest, more like a real person. More...more than just an Overlord.

"I..." Melaine's cheeks grew hot as she avoided his striking blue eyes. She took a deep breath, and her thoughts slowed and focused. A small ache throbbed in her chest, dull and long-resigned. "I suppose, sometimes, I've thought that my parents may have died...may have been killed by the Luxians in the aftermath of the war. I can make lodestones. Maybe they could, too. Maybe they died before you were able to banish the Order."

She gnawed the inside of her cheek, still not looking at him. She had never talked to anyone about her theories, though she knew Salma had probably guessed the same thing.

She heard him sigh, but otherwise, he was silent.

"People say the Luxians are coming back," she said. "That man...that prisoner I saw my first day here..." She didn't dare name Talem. She couldn't reveal that she'd spoken to Serj about his brother. "He wore the crest of Lux. People say you aren't doing anything about the resurgence of the Order, but..." She finally looked up. "Are you?"

The Overlord was sitting straighter than he had been. His eyes flickered with concern.

"I hoped those were the rantings of a lunatic," he said. "I'll have my overseers look into the Luxians in Centara. They'll root them out."

"People say some of the overseers are part of the Order," Melaine said before she could stop herself.

The Overlord looked aside, his expression pensive, but Melaine couldn't tell what his reaction meant. He swallowed and massaged his throat as if it pained him, an absent gesture while his eyes lurked in shadowed thoughts. The man looked tired. So tired. She'd never imagined that carrying the weight of an entire kingdom on one's shoulders could be so hard.

The fine-lined crow's feet at the corners of his eyes deepened, but then he exhaled, coming out of his reverie.

"I want you to practice using the wand today," he said. He nodded to a small collection of Insights at the end of the long table. "Touch those with your wandering hands and glean what they know. You'll find a wand very helpful with this vein of spell work."

"Yes, my lord," Melaine said. She wanted to press him more, to ask why he was letting his overseers run the city when they were so corrupt while he was holed up in High-strong, claiming he was experimenting with magic when in reality he was too weak to show his face to his people.

His reminder of the lesson ahead, however, persuaded her to push all questions aside. She stood from her chair and walked to the assortment of Insights. As with all Insights, they were odd things, all containing organic matter of one kind or another. Many were coated in silver or plaster, decorated with trappings so that the twig or hair or animal horn inside was hidden from view.

She scanned the lot and then picked up a small statue of a rathmor. She'd seen a street artist draw one of the beasts before, but this depiction of the sinewy carnivore was crafted from porcelain. Its hunched, feline body and long legs looked incredibly lifelike, as if the creature was about to pounce on unsuspecting prey in the eastern deserts. One of its many teeth was larger and sharper than the others, coated in gold. No doubt that was the real rathmor's tooth, in which the deep knowledge of the Insight was contained.

Melaine touched the tip of the sharp tooth. A spike of magic shot through her. Her whole body stiffened, and she heard a fierce snarl as the power of a beast coiled in her muscles. She gasped as the internal beast leapt up her spine and dug its claws into her brain, sinking its teeth into her mind so deeply she would never forget the rathmor's spell. As she held the wand in her tight fist, she understood why the Overlord had summoned her to the great hall rather than the library.

She set the rathmor statue back down and looked up. A series of moth-eaten tapestries lined the wall opposite the table. She smiled fiercely and aimed her wand at a woven man riding horseback.

"May I?" she asked, keeping her gaze fixed on the tapestry with predatory focus.

"Yes."

Melaine raised the wand and thrust her arm toward the man in the tapestry. A burst of yellow magic sprang from the wand like a rathmor's pounce. It hit the tapestry with an enormous bang and split each thread wide. When the magic disappeared, a large, black hole smoldered on the wall where the man's moth-eaten face had been.

Melaine felt a powerful thrill overcome her every sense.

Battle magic.

"Well done," the Overlord murmured. "Do you see

how the wand channels your magic into a more direct, powerful surge? Wands are practically essential in casting any spell that needs precise aim."

Melaine smiled at his praise and looked at him. He still seemed pensive, only half of him within the great hall, the rest of his mind elsewhere. Her smile fell. His mediocre reaction rankled her mood, but she clenched her jaw and ignored him. She scooped up another Insight. This one was a black-and-white striped deraphant horn, nearly as long as her forearm, with a thick base that filled her palm. Like rathmors, she'd never seen a deraphant in person, but the lumbering, hooved herbivores were said to have faces covered in such horns. They used them to shove aside heavy stones and trees blocking their migratory paths through the northern mountains of Wrimid. She'd heard they could toss a boulder up in the air like it was a pebble.

She eyed the rest of the Insights—a dried othyrem blossom that she knew could be poisonous if its fresh sap was touched, an eyeball in a jar that looked distinctly human, though its pupil glowed red, and a vial of ash and fingernails.

Offensive battle spells, the lot of them.

She smiled. *This* magic was why she had come to Highstrong Keep.

❀

MELAINE CRIED OUT AS CRYSTAL DECANTERS AND GLASS baubles exploded around her, shooting shards at the walls and windows of the hearth room adjoining her bedroom.

She shielded her head until all was still. She darted her eyes to the guard statue outside of her room, still within sight. It remained dormant, wreathed in confining vines. Normally, she would have been in her room at this time of night, but she needed more space to work. She hoped, as long as she stayed within the statue's sights, it wouldn't compel her to return to her bedroom should it wake.

She looked away from the statue and cringed at the sparkle of a glass sliver embedded in her finger, punctured capillaries spilling blood through her split skin. Drops hit the glass shards around her, spreading on the surfaces and running along their edges until the red liquid hit the stone floor.

Whispers seeped from the floor in indistinguishable words. Melaine strained her ears as her heart thudded against her chest. The whispers were haunting and many. They pulsed with ancient magic that smelled of decay and buried secrets. Her throat went dry as if she'd inhaled a cloud of smoke or ash. She coughed and tried to clear her throat, rubbing a hand over her mouth.

The whispers.... They were the same as the ones within the ancient urn she had smashed. But she was nowhere near the urn or its ash-covered shards. Had she released something? If so...what?

Melaine took a freeing breath and twitched the sliver of glass free from its invasion of her fingerprint. She raised her other hand, which held the Overlord's wand, to compel the shattered glass to re-form into useless trinkets. She then concentrated on lifting the blood drops from the floor, but it was as if the stone had soaked them in like a sponge to feed the whispers that kept filling the air with an undercurrent of sorrow and fear. She wanted to scream at them to stop.

Something crunched the broken glass in the curtained doorway that connected to the sitting room of her quarters. The magic she had summoned to clean up the blood halted in its tracks through her pathway of veins. She looked up and froze when she saw the shadowed form of the Overlord watching her from the arched doorway.

The whispers collapsed into a collective whimper and ceased.

"My lord," she uttered. She licked her lips and pushed herself off the floor. "I'm sorry if I disturbed you. I was practicing."

Melaine expected a soft taunt in reply or perhaps the hint of a smile, but none came. The Overlord simply watched her, his eyes gleaming from the shadows.

"My lord?" Melaine said. She took a small step toward him. "My lord. Are you...awake?"

The Overlord still said nothing. Perhaps he was sleep-walking again. But the way he stared at her was not with the vague, restless eyes of a dreamer. His eyes were keen. They were hungry.

Melaine's heart picked up speed. "Say something," she said with a wary frown, her sense of danger weighing down her sense of respect.

The Overlord's eyes narrowed. He stepped forward from the shadows. He wore the same black robe as the night before, but one of the silver frog fasteners was loose, parting the satin lapels to expose his wrinkled black nightshirt and pale collarbones. The slice of moonlight from the narrow windows illuminated his gaunt face, but even through his weakness, it highlighted the good aspects of his sculptured features. Melaine had always known he was handsome, ever since she first saw his illustration on the broadsheets in Stakeside. She had long admired how his appearance added to his potent presence and charisma that could enrapture a nation.

His expression was as serious now as on the broadsheets, but she pictured his soft, wry smile that she could bring out of him on occasion. It seemed to happen whenever they reached common ground. Melaine was surprised by how frequent that was becoming.

As the Overlord stalked closer, she felt like she was stuck in a mudhole after a week of rain. His gaze ensnared her senses. Thoughts of his slightly crooked gait and his subtly twitching fingers failed to send off the warning signals she might normally feel. Her lips parted as he drew close, closer than he ever had.

"My lord?" she whispered. She fought to keep her hands still at her sides. Her every muscle was taut and yet ready to give way like an over-beaten drum. She could smell his cool, icy scent of untamed magic rising to the surface, somehow stronger than it had been before.

She stepped one foot back, but the Overlord grabbed her elbow and held her fast. Melaine let out an instinctual hiss at the intimate contact of a man, but when his warm chest touched hers, she felt a melting heat flood her body and stick her to the ground like hot wax.

Melaine was as speechless as the Overlord, but her mind was screaming at her. It ordered her to run—to get away from this man who only wanted to use her and who no doubt wanted a mistress, to take her body like he took her magic every single day. Why else would he draw so close? Why else would he look down at her with such longing?

She didn't obey her urges. She breathed in his scent of sandalwood and parchment along with a raw musk that was purely masculine. She locked eyes with him, afraid to look anywhere else, and her heart fluttered as his mouth brushed hers.

A muffled shout and a loud, distant rumble jolted Melaine back before the Overlord could fully kiss her. His head whipped toward the sound as he jerked back. A sinister, red gleam vanished from his pupils as he looked in the direction the noise had come from.

Melaine recognized the voice of the prisoner, Serj. It sounded like he was railing against his cage, rattling chains and shouting indistinguishable ravings.

The Overlord recoiled from the sound. He ignored Melaine and turned away, his black robe twisting around his thin frame as he strode back through the shadows into the sitting room, leaving Melaine behind.

Serj bellowed and roared from floors below. Melaine was petrified for a moment, her mind trapped in the tension and fire of her body. She blinked and shook her head and then darted for the window and peered outside. The garden was empty.

She listened hard for the Overlord's fading footsteps but heard nothing. She waited a little longer to see if he would descend the steps into the garden. Perhaps from there he would use the small dungeon entrance and see to the raucous prisoner.

But there was no sign of the Overlord. Melaine crept

through the hearth room and peered into the sitting room. It was empty. The Overlord must have passed through and taken the interior hallways toward elsewhere in the castle—to the great hall or his personal quarters, perhaps. For an instant, Melaine wondered what the man would do if she followed him to his bedchamber, but she thrust the thought aside and headed for the windows of the sitting room.

She looked out into the garden again. Serj still rattled his chains and wailed. She tightened her grasp on her wand and opened the door that led outside. She descended the steps and breathed out white puffs of condensation.

Winter was creeping over Dramore. She wondered how Salma was faring, and what the woman would say if she knew where Melaine was or that an unthinkable kiss had nearly happened.

She drew her dressing gown tighter around herself as she crossed the garden, heading directly for the dark pocket of a doorway that led to the dungeons. She ducked inside and felt her way through the route that she remembered would lead her to Serj.

She avoided the direction containing the urn of whispers and passed unscathed by any other dark mysteries that might lurk in the dark. She scuttled down more stairs and reached the thick torture chamber door.

She pulled it open and twitched her head in annoyance as Serj's ravings assaulted her ears. She shut the door and stepped in front of the barred cell, crossing her arms.

Serj was standing and gripping the bars of his cell with white knuckles. His eyes blazed with rage, his face a vicious snarl, but he stopped yelling when he saw Melaine. He started laughing instead, so hard he doubled over into a coughing fit.

"You're going to wake everyone up," Melaine said. "Are you yelling for a reason or simply to be an ass?"

Serj's shoulders stopped shaking with laughter. He smiled wide enough to suggest madness. "Got your attention? I was hoping it would be you, not that old crone. I knew the grand Overlord wouldn't bother to grant me an audience. But you...oh, yes, you. I knew I could count on you."

"What do you want? Stop wasting my time."

Serj chuckled again, but a sharp gleam flashed through his eyes.

"I felt you," he said. He looked up at the ceiling with a grin. "Through the floor. Your magic." He looked back into Melaine's narrowed eyes. "You are powerful, Miss Melaine from Stakeside. Very powerful. I can imagine all sorts of things you could do with that magic of yours."

"I didn't come here to talk about me," Melaine said, but she felt a stirring excitement at the thought of Serj being able to *feel* her magic through the floor several stories up.

Was that why the Overlord had come as well? Had he felt her magic and come to investigate? Or was his goal just to...? She pushed away the intimacy of their almost-kiss and focused on Serj.

"You got your way. I'm here," she said. "But you're going to give me something for my time."

"Am I?"

Melaine ignored his coy tone. "You know something.

Something about the Overlord. I want to know what it is."

"Why would I tell you anything?" Serj asked, pushing himself lightly off the bars, though he swayed on his feet. "I asked you to tell me what he has planned for me. You refused. Someone like you should know that nothing in this world comes for free, Melaine."

Melaine clenched her jaw, but after a pause, she relented. "I don't know what he has planned for you. He hasn't said one word about you. But I can find out if you tell me what I want to know."

Serj scanned her eyes. Then he shrugged and leaned one shoulder against the bars.

"You asked about the Overlord's strength," Melaine began, careful to control her words. "He's the most powerful man in the kingdom, perhaps the world. Why would you doubt him?"

Serj's hazel eyes sparkled. "Because you do."

"No, I don't," Melaine said. "He's my Overlord and my teacher. I respect him."

"But does he respect you?" Serj countered. His lip twisted in a smile. "Ah, you don't think he does."

Melaine opened her mouth to argue, but her words caught.

Serj turned to face her, still leaning his weight on the bars. "The Overlord's power wanes, doesn't it? He grows weaker by the day? Tell me I'm lying."

Melaine stared at Serj's ragged face. His gaunt cheeks and fierce eyes mirrored the Overlord's in some ways, but Serj still had color to his cheeks. He still bore signs of vivid life, whereas the Overlord did not.

"What do you know about it?" Melaine asked. "Did you have something to do with it? Did your brother?"

Serj winced the smallest amount at her mention of his brother, and to Melaine's surprise, she did, too. And Serj noticed.

"See?" he said softly. "I knew you weren't as evil as you believe." He gripped the bars hard again. "You may be the Overlord's apprentice, but you are not like him, Melaine. You watched a man die, and you felt compassion for him. I can see it in your eyes. The Overlord doesn't think twice before he murders someone. He *relishes* it. But you, Melaine, you disdain even watching."

"I killed him," Melaine said. Her heart banged, and her gut twisted. "I killed Talem. It was me." She looked down and twitched her head before meeting Serj's eyes again. His face was slack and his eyes vulnerable, but then he gathered himself.

"How did you do it?" he asked.

Melaine forced a cold expression. "A propulsion spell. He was weak."

"And did you weaken him?" Serj asked. His cocky demeanor was quelled, but the focus in his keen eyes strengthened.

Melaine paused. "No. The Overlord had tortured him. He told me to knock him to the floor. I thought it was just to prove I would follow an order, but..." She swallowed and straightened her shoulders. She stilled her wavering voice. "My spell killed him. I was responsible."

Serj shook his head with a condescending sigh.

"He tricked you, Melaine," he said. "Don't you understand? In killing Talem, you entered into a psychological pact with the Overlord. Killing someone for him? If you had any doubts about your ability to commit evils under his command, he squashed them then and there. And with blood on your hands, there's no going back. No returning to a virtuous, spotless life."

"It was a test, and I passed," Melaine bit out. "Simple as that."

"But you didn't, not really," Serj said. "I see the guilt in your eyes. It haunts you, which makes you a far better person than the Overlord. You have the ability to be good. He's buried his ability so far down it's annihilated. And he's trying to teach you to do the same."

He leaned hard against the bars, his forehead red from the pressure. "Don't let him, Melaine. You are stronger than him now. Your power is growing, not only from his teachings but from within yourself. His power weakens day by day, does it not? You, Melaine, you have the power to supplant him. *You* have the power to rule when he's gone. You have ambition, Melaine. I can see it. Don't waste this opportunity. Life has tossed you out as rubbish for too long. Seize what you are due."

Melaine shook her head. "I'm not a kind person, Serj. I'm a survivor. Even if I could rule, I wouldn't be the benevolent leader you want. It's laughable you'd think so. I killed your *brother*. Besides, the Overlord is fine. With my lodestones, he's regaining power."

"Lodestones?" Serj asked. "You make him lodestones?"

Melaine looked aside, the magic in her bones crawling.

"That's why he's keeping you," Serj continued. "It makes sense now. He doesn't give a fuck about you, Melaine. He only wants your lodestones to replenish his diminishing supply of magic." Serj laughed aloud. "It's futile. Lodestones won't help him, no matter how powerful the source. Don't let him fool you another minute. He is *dying*. Take his throne. The people, like you, have been oppressed by his darkness for far too long. Free us, Melaine. You are the only one now who can do it."

"And you expect me to start with you?" Melaine said. "You think you can trick me with your soapbox words into setting you free?"

Serj shook his head. "It's not about me. I would gladly die just like my brother if it meant I could change Centara for the better."

"Your brother bore the sigil of Lux," Melaine spat. "Is that what you think would better Centara? Letting those lunatics run loose? Slaughtering anyone they find different?"

"No," Serj said, tilting his head in annoyance. He scratched his jaw under his scruffy, blond beard and sighed. "Talem may have thought so, but...there are plenty of people in the rebellion who don't. We aligned with the Luxians in an uneasy truce. Talem assured me that the Order wouldn't be as harsh this time around. The Luxians have learned since the Overlord expelled their old ways. And if *you* help us, they will see that a lodestone-maker can be on our side. You'll lead the revolution for change, Melaine. You'll bring the well-meaning citizens and the religious together in a way that the Overlord never could."

"The Luxians won't change. I don't believe it," Melaine said.

"Just think about it, Melaine," Serj said. "You are his apprentice. You could easily claim that he bestowed the right to rule upon you as his heir before he died. And, *if* you let me out, I could convince the people to follow you. Talem was high up in the Luxian ranks. With Talem gone, the Order will take a hit. The rebels will follow *my* lead."

"And you'll set me upon the throne?" Melaine said. "So selfless? Deferring power to me rather than taking it for yourself, even though so many people already follow you?" She scoffed and turned away.

"Wait!" Serj said. "Melaine. You don't have to believe anything I say yet. But buy time so you can think about it at least. Make him weaker lodestones. Just for a time while you decide."

"Tell me why he's weakening. Then I'll consider it."

Serj released the bars and scowled. "I can't explain everything now. I'll tell you when the time is right, but I can only trust you so much without more proof that you're on my side. I'm sure you can understand that."

"You give nothing; you get nothing," she said. She turned back around and strode past the myriad of torture devices and toward the door.

"Will you willingly kill again, Melaine?" Serj called. "Talem was an accident. But who will be next? If the Overlord orders you to kill someone else in cold blood, will you be able to? What if it's me, Melaine? Would you kill me where I stand?"

Melaine placed her hand on the door and dug her fingernails into the wood. Then she dragged her hand away, leaving shallow claw scratches in its grain. She opened the door, slammed it behind her, and stumbled into the dark.

She waited for Serj to call after her or to start yelling

or singing deranged songs again, but all was silent. All but her pounding heart and her hounding thoughts that pitched loyalty against power.

HE'S DYING.

Serj had to be lying. The Overlord looked weak, to be sure, but dying? He was the *Overlord*. He couldn't die. Not of sickness. He deserved to die in battle and a long time from now.

Melaine felt a stabbing pain to think about him dying at all.

The world as she knew it would be erased, wiped out in an instant. She felt empty and lost at the mere thought of a world in which her idol was gone. She had relied on the man's sheer existence to sustain her through her darkest hours on the streets. He was a light she had never imagined would go out, a light she'd dreamed would always be waiting for her if she could just find a way to reach him. And now that she *had* reached him and learned from him and spoken with him, her ache for him had only grown deeper.

She suppressed her painful longing and forced her thoughts toward a more practical plan. If he died, her place in the castle would disappear. Who knew what would happen? Serj's assurances of Melaine's rise to power sounded far-fetched at best. Most likely, Karina would leave Highstrong and kick Melaine out. The overseers would take over Centara and perhaps work with the Luxians to instigate a new reign of terror for anyone different.

"Different" would include people who tampered with mechagics and other unnatural forms of magic. It would include anyone who dared to imitate the power of Lux to make lodestones. Melaine would either disappear as a Stakeside nobody, or she would be hunted down and executed with any others deemed blasphemers.

Now, standing in the Overlord's vast library filled with Insights, she had an opportunity to save herself. She had to learn as much as possible while she still could. She couldn't handle more than a few Insights at a time without draining her mind to exhaustion, but fortunately, she now possessed something that *could*.

Melaine walked to the nearest shelf, not knowing exactly what the Insights upon it contained. She raised her wand, which she had resolved she would keep, no matter what happened to her position here, even if she had to whisk away and steal it.

She had never filled a wand with knowledge before, but the concept seemed simple. Glean the magic from each Insight as she would with her bare hands, but let it infuse into the wand instead, only passing through her head like a distracting thought.

Then, the wand would remember the spells the Insights contained. The wand's knowledge would be temporary, lasting only as long as the Insight's power ordained. Some might last for only one casting. Others might last for months of use. But none of them would be as permanent as if Melaine were to imbibe them herself.

The wand was a failsafe. She would store as many

spells into the wand as she could and hope that she would be in Highstrong long enough to learn more for herself.

She touched the tip of the wand to a braided leather bracelet upon the shelf. The bracelet looked ordinary and plain, but as soon as she focused on the magic within, a light burst into her head like sunshine through clouds. She laughed with the exhilarating joy. She felt like she was floating from her body upon a swell of euphoria, leaving all of her aches, physical and emotional, behind.

Then the heady sensation faded, and her worries swarmed in like wasps. Her chest spasmed and tightened, her breaths shallow and quick. Sorrow and fear dragged her down with such force, she had to hold onto the shelf. She focused hard on the bracelet's magic again, wanting the happiness to come back, but it didn't. In its place, a whispered spell brushed her mind. Her deep sorrow lifted, her next breath broadened her chest, and she exhaled with a slow flow of soothing calm. She realized that the spell contained in the bracelet was meant to temper emotions across the spectrum from dark to light, pacifying the user.

It wasn't as useful as she would have liked, but the wand accepted it, and she moved on to another object that looked like a gilded horse's tail with a knot at the top, each hair coated in real gold. She brushed the wand through the tail; the long strands rattled like ice-coated willow branches. The wand pulled magic from the tail, and Melaine felt a sudden rush of wind blow past her as if she was in a racing carriage. Her wine-red satin gown fluttered in its wake.

A speed spell. *That* could be very useful.

She was tempted to take the speed spell with her own hands, so it would permanently bind to her mind and body, but she couldn't indulge in the luxury. For now, she had to absorb as much knowledge into the wand as possible. She needed spells that could help her fight or flee, should her life's future provoke either.

Melaine passed by more objects, trailing her wand over them, allowing their knowledge to enter the wand for later use. Just a taste from each, like the lavish and unnecessary dinner feasts she had heard the rich were fond of. But the metaphor dripped away. In truth, she felt more like a beggar scarfing down scraps of bread before someone else came to steal them.

After wandering among the hexagonal ring of shelves for a time, she felt an almost tangible pull from a shadowed shelf ahead. She hadn't even hovered her wand in its direction, yet strange magic twisted through the air and flooded her flesh, seeping into her bones. With her next breath, she felt magical tendrils creeping toward her brain.

She walked toward the dim corner that housed the mysterious shelf. What little light there was shone dark red, different from the crisp yellow sunshine pouring through the library's tall windows and balcony. Melaine took a breath as she stepped into the red light that deepened the crimson fabric of her dress. Magic swept into her every pore, compelling and heady. Invisible strings seemed to latch onto her from every Insight on the shelf, hooking her like a carp in a strong river current.

Some strings pulled harder than others. As she closed the distance, she began to eye the Insights.

She felt called toward several, but one practically yanked her hand toward it. She snatched up a silver locket with words embossed on its oval surface. The chain of the necklace rattled against the edge of the shelf as she squeezed the locket and read the flourish of words.

Keeper of Lust and Seduction.

Melaine shivered, and her body flooded with heat. The locket pulsed, powerful and deep, urging her to open the little silver clasp and learn all of the secrets within. Her mind was overpowered by memories of the Overlord in her quarters during the clandestine night. The heat and intoxicating scent of his body, the unbidden longing she felt in his presence, the mesmerizing brush of his lips on hers before he turned away and disappeared.

Melaine shoved the memories from her head and threw the locket to the ground with a growl. It sprang open, revealing a lock of silky brown hair inside.

A shadow fell over the locket. She gasped and felt foolish when she saw the Overlord standing in the space between two shelves, blocking her way out of the disturbing library corner. He wore a simple black shirt and trousers as she'd come to expect in daylight hours. She couldn't see his collarbones like she had the night before, highlighted by moonlight and softly brushed by his long hair in a pleasing way that made her wonder what the two textures would feel like under her fingers.

Her cheeks flushed as he bent down and retrieved the locket. He inspected the lock of hair, though he eventually set it back and left it alone, curled inside the silver oval casing. He closed the locket with a light click.

When he looked back at her, his eyes glittered, and he wore a subtle smile of dry humor.

"You have a problem with intimacy, Stonegirl?"

Melaine's heart thumped, and her stomach squirmed. Thoughts about intimacy, both physical and emotional, had always been a problem, but that was none of the Overlord's business. She didn't want to think about what he might say if she ever revealed she'd almost been raped several times in Stakeside—that she had nearly been exposed to the filth and disease that could stem from physical contact. That she'd been weak enough at times that she had barely escaped. Or, would he judge her more if he knew she had never partaken in sex, that she was still ignorant of the intricacies?

She bit the inside of her cheek to restrain her frustration, hopefully suppressing the blush she felt burning all the way to her ears. She'd never cared what anyone thought about her choices regarding sex so far, but...after last night, she wasn't sure what she thought or how to respond to his question. He had been so close to her in the dark, so warm, his scent intoxicating. The idea of willingly embracing a man, of welcoming him into her body, into her life, felt different from before. She felt lighter, like a shroud was lifted from her mind. And...not just any man. The Overlord.

Could intimacy be different than she'd always imagined? Salma sometimes spoke of her late husband with great fondness, and Melaine could guess from Salma and Jianthe's flirtations that there might be more between them, whether casual or serious, Melaine didn't know nor ask about. The only women who discussed sex in greater detail around Melaine were the prostitutes to whom she sold lodestones. Sometimes they'd mock their own customers or express bitterness of their lot, which Melaine could identify with. But sometimes, they would describe sex as bliss, that even *love* through intimacy could be achieved, even for people in their position, even for people like Melaine. Consensual intimacy, an equal exchange of equal desires, a partnership rather than a power-ploy, no one taking advantage of the other.... Could that sort of intimacy be possible?

The Overlord raised his hand and sent the closed locket slowly floating through the air on a wisp of bright blue magic. Melaine eyed the Insight until it slipped back into its place on the shelf. When she turned back, the Overlord was leaning against the shelf's edge as if the small act of magic had drained him. His eyes flashed toward hers, and he turned around and walked to the library's center. Melaine forced her unease and embarrassment down and followed.

"Did you know that woman?" she asked. "Whose hair is in the locket?"

The Overlord chuckled. Melaine blushed and wondered what had possessed her to ask that question first when others should have been more urgent.

"No," he said. "An old woman pressed it into my hand when I was young and deemed...eligible. She candidly told me it was the hair of her 'whore daughter', but her daughter was dead from the pox and had no use of it. She said the spell would help me find a wife. I didn't have the heart to tell her that I wasn't interested in such things."

"You weren't?"

"Not when I was seventeen," he said. "I had a kingdom to establish, after all."

Melaine thought "establish" was an odd choice of words, when "conquer" would have been more accurate. She wondered how the glorious and horrific tales she'd heard about the Overlord's revolt would sound coming from his own lips. She almost asked him, but for now, his talk of women and seduction was leading her down an entirely different trail of thought.

He sat down in his favored chair by one of the tables. He took a few labored breaths and gestured with a single finger for Melaine to sit across from him. She circled the table and sat on her chair's edge. The Overlord's humor seemed to have faded fast. His glazed eyes were aimed at the table. Melaine picked at her glove's black lace on the back of her hand. After a moment of silence, she gathered her courage and spoke.

"My lord," she said. "Last night..."

The Overlord didn't respond to her fishing. He didn't respond at all.

"Did you sleep well last night?" Melaine asked.

It took a moment for the Overlord to register her question. Then, he looked up.

"You've never asked me such a trivial question before," he replied. "Why the sudden concern for my wellbeing?"

"I...was just wondering if you felt as restless as I did. I kept waking up at odd hours. Did you sleep all night?"

"I did," he answered. His curt tone signified impatience but not any artifice that Melaine could detect. Had he been sleepwalking again? Did he really not remember their encounter last night? The almost-kiss they had shared in the dark? Or was he toying with her? Melaine glanced at the shelf beyond him where the locket of seduction magic sat. Her nerves fluttered in her breast.

"I was wondering when you would discover that shelf," the Overlord said. "You resisted it longer than most would."

"What do you mean by that?" she asked with a frown.

The corner of the Overlord's mouth twitched in amusement. "The Insights on that shelf have a way of influencing people. The spells they contain involve mind control."

Melaine's eyebrows rose. "Mind control? They...*made* me come to that section?"

"They called to you, yes," the Overlord said. "But they only had the power to do so because for some reason, Melaine, you feel vulnerable today."

"I don't feel vulnerable," Melaine countered.

The Overlord chuckled. "Deny it if you wish, but those Insights don't lie. Their original creators imbued them with so much persuasive magic that their potency extends beyond their physical confines. A side effect of dealing with mind magic. The magic within can sense your desires and seek to control you through them."

For an instant, Melaine was back in the Hole, smearing her blood-covered hand over a guard's mouth, telling him to feed on raw meat with other degenerates so she could gain access to Scroupe. She had felt foreign magic coursing through her in that desperate moment. The guard had done as she ordered.

But that couldn't have been mind magic. How could she have known how to do it?

The Overlord continued, drawing her from her thoughts.

"Insights that hold the most potential for control over you call to you the most. In this case," he eyed the shelf, "seduction and lust seem to be on your mind."

"That's not true," Melaine said. "You don't know anything about me. Neither do those stupid Insights."

The Overlord leaned forward with his elbows on the desk. His eyes were fierce, and his voice turned *too* quiet.

"Know your weaknesses, Melaine," he said. "Deny them, and you are susceptible to failure."

He was so close that she could have lifted her hands from her lap and laid them upon his if she wanted to. But she kept them hidden, clenching her fists tight.

"Was that a test, then?" she whispered. "Last night?"

A flicker of confusion passed through his eyes, which then narrowed with analyzation. Melaine sat still, disconcerted, but she held her ground and tried to read him as much as he tried to read her.

"I don't know what you're talking about," he said in dismissal. "As you said before, this castle provokes nightmares." He sat back, but his attempt to sit straight failed, and he leaned on the back of his chair. "Lodestones," he said, his voice flat with exhaustion.

Melaine dropped her eyes, a disappointed twinge in her heart. "Two, my lord?"

"Yes."

Melaine nodded and kept her hands under the table as she removed her lace gloves. She set them in her lap and concentrated. She gathered magic into her palms.

Weaker lodestones, Serj had suggested. She hadn't yet

decided if she would follow his advice. Now, as she physically felt her treasured magic leaving her, she stopped dredging it from her marrow and lifted it from her pores instead. She infused the forming stones with superficial magic. She clenched her fists and hardened them to purple-black crystal.

She opened her hands and hovered her palms across the table. The Overlord reached out for the first stone and grazed Melaine's palm with his fingertips as he lifted it. Her heart bounced, and she yanked her hand back to clutch at the red satin of her dress beneath the table.

She looked up when the Overlord took the second stone and brought it to his lips. A low, ember's glow burned in her chest and slowed her racing heart as she watched him inhale her magic from the stone. The process had never felt so intimate before. Those same lips had brushed hers, a fleeting sensation, yet so firm and lasting in memory. She could almost taste him, and she wondered what his magic would taste like. For a brief moment, she wished he could make lodestones, too, that they could exchange power, fuse with one another, share, dance.... Fanciful and strange, a reality that could never happen.

The empty stone disintegrated in the air, but the resilience the Overlord usually showed after taking her magic was dampened. She waited for him to notice and call her out on making weaker stones, but he only sat there with his head bowed. Melaine frowned as she watched his shallow breathing, and suddenly, she felt sorry for him.

Her instincts were shouting alarms at her. To feel

sorry for the weak was the fastest way to become weak yourself in Stakeside. Sharing what little food and shelter you had with others could mean your death, ever faster if sickness was involved. Melaine had followed that creed her entire life, and she was alive because of it. She had made her way *here* because of it, and she couldn't let something like...*sympathy* ruin everything.

The longer she watched the Overlord staring at the table, the more her worries grew. Not worries for herself, no, those worries slipped away into the background of her thoughts. She couldn't deny it—she was worried about him.

"My lord?" she asked. He didn't respond. She crinkled her brow. The stones she made were weaker than usual, but they still held more than enough magic to revive him.

Her disapproval started to return. She hadn't suspected it before, but as she watched his shallow inhales and exhales, and saw that even her stones weren't helping alleviate his pain, she started to connect his symptoms with others she'd seen in some of her more frequent clients.

To think the Overlord had weakened *himself* for lack of willpower...

"My lord," she said, remaining cautious as she began to walk along a sheer cliff-line. "I've been making lodestones for a long time. I've seen...I know what happens when people overuse them. They start depending on them. They become addicted. The magic doesn't affect them as strongly as it did at the start. It makes them weaker, my lord."

The Overlord started laughing. It was a harsh, rasping

sound, and he hunched over and leaned his head into his hand to cover his face. His fingers formed claws, and he dragged them back through his stringy hair as his laughter turned bitter at its end. He looked into her eyes, his burning.

"You think I'm weak because of addiction?" he asked. His tone was dangerous, and Melaine's heartbeat quickened.

"I only wish you the best, my lord—"

"You wish the best for yourself!" His face contorted in a livid snarl. "You want to keep all your magic. You don't appreciate what I'm teaching you, how spoiled you are to have a teacher, to have all of these rare Insights at your disposal."

"No," Melaine protested. "I want—My lord, I care about you!" She shut up after that, shocked at what she had just said.

The Overlord slowed his tirade. She wasn't sure if it was because he believed her or because he was too exhausted to continue his strenuous rage. He steadied his breathing and sat still. His eyes were less vibrant than she had ever seen them, and he watched her with a soft, sorrowful frown that became tinged with gentle longing. He parted his cracked lips and spoke in a hoarse voice.

"I'm not addicted, Melaine. Not for the reasons you think." He winced and glanced away, and for the first time, Melaine saw a different kind of weakness in the Overlord. It wasn't physical or magical. It was emotional. His frown deepened into profound despair, and his blood-shot eyes watered. She took a breath to speak.

"I've had enough for one day," he said.

"My lord."

"Go," he responded, but the word was barely audible, and he refused to meet her gaze.

Melaine sat back. Worry for his wellbeing gnawed at her with sharper teeth, claws scratching at the wall she had built years ago to keep the world and everyone in it away.

She felt a strong pull to refuse his command, but she clenched her jaw, then gave a short nod and stood. She felt like she was crawling back into the half-buried supply crate she'd lived in as a young child, someplace just as small and dark. She made her way to the door and placed her hand upon the warm, soothing wood.

It had the same comforting touch she had experienced in a delicate flash when the Overlord's fingers had touched her palm.

CHAPTER 9

The gate was *opening.*

Its heavy groans of iron on iron were enough to awake Melaine from a night of fitful slumber just as the sun rose. The floor vibrated under her feet as she bolted out of her bedroom to the nearest window in the hearth room. She stood, mouth agape, watching the thick iron bars of the gate descend, while others raised, opening like the jaws of an enormous beast.

Melaine had only spent a few days within Highstrong Keep's surrounding walls, but she had grown accustomed to their stability and their protection of her new life. Seeing them open to the outside world was like tearing a hole in her gloves. She wanted it mended.

Melaine squinted as she peered through the window at a small figure of a man standing at the open gate with the reins of a pair of horses in hand. The horses were hitched to a large cart filled with wooden crates and canvas bags. Just inside the gate stood a second, pale figure in the shape of a woman. She wore a long dress whose color seemed to blend with the cold sunlight. The man with the horses paid her no mind, but she must have come with him.

The woman looked up at Melaine, somehow aware she was watching from the high distance. But the man looked past the woman toward the keep. Melaine followed his gaze and saw Karina exit the side door of the castle. Her gray, beehive hair floated over her quick, steady stride across the grounds toward the gate.

Melaine's curiosity propelled her back to her bedroom to throw on some clothes, foregoing the corset for speed's sake as she donned a sapphire velvet dress. She then hurried through her quarters and down the stairs to the inner courtyard. She found the exit through which Karina had left and sprang into the open grounds of the castle. The frigid air nearly took her breath away, but she pressed onward until she stopped ten or so feet away from Karina, who spoke in a voice as stiff as her posture. The swarthy man stood beside the cart. He was dressed like a Midduner in a cheap but unpatched wool suit and a blue coat. A golden tooth glinted with every grimace under his crinkled eyes.

The pale woman who had been with him was nowhere in sight. Melaine frowned and looked around the courtyard and beyond the gate, but the woman wasn't there.

"I trust all is accounted for, Stebbon?" Karina said to the man.

"Yes, m'lady, of course," Stebbon said. "I'd be a loon to try to swindle you, m'lady."

Melaine noticed he didn't mention the Overlord. The delivery man seemed too nervous to speak of where he was. His fear gave Melaine a boost of pride. *She* wasn't afraid to be in Highstrong's walls.

Karina extended a hand and dropped a coin purse into Stebbon's palm, which glistened with sweat despite the cold air. He grinned at the weight of the purse, but his satisfaction was brief. His nervous fidgeting overtook him again, and when his eyes left the purse, he looked at Melaine instead.

Karina spun around. Her eyes held a speck of fright but then switched to cold appraisal. Melaine had no idea what was going through the old bat's head. Karina didn't deign to inform her.

"Don't mind her," Karina said to Stebbon. "She's just a stonegirl. We can't all have powers like the Overlord."

Stebbon responded with a courteous half-smile to Karina's implication that Melaine's stones were for Karina's use rather than the Overlord's. It was clear Karina didn't want her master's condition getting out to the public, and for good reason, Melaine thought.

Still, there was no need for Karina to have called her a stonegirl to belittle her in front of a stranger. Even saying she was a *servant* would have given her a higher standing than a lodestone-peddler, and Karina well knew it. She was degrading Melaine on purpose.

"And the woman who came with you?" Melaine asked Stebbon, hoping Karina would at least spread her disdain around so it wouldn't be centered on her. "Is she an assistant as well?"

Stebbon looked at her with a quizzical expression. "Woman? It's just me and the horses, love." He gave her an awkward smile.

"But I saw someone out here," Melaine said, glancing at Karina. "From the window."

Karina frowned, then pursed her lips with impatience. "Stop this nonsense. Unload the cart."

"I'm not a servant," Melaine spat.

"You will do as I say," Karina said, unwavering in her strict demeanor. Melaine glared. Stebbon shifted his eyes between Karina and Melaine, but it was clear his curiosity was higher than his nervousness about intruding on their conversation. Melaine wondered how much he would twist his observations into rumors upon returning to Centara. Better give him something good to share over a hearth-brandy in some Midden pub.

"Fine," she said, giving Karina a smug smile.

Melaine slipped her wand from inside her dress sleeve. She'd kept it pressed against her skin at all times since the Overlord had given it to her, trying to get used to the grating tingle of residual magic. To her delight, it seemed to have dissipated completely, as if her own, fresh magic had absorbed and transformed it into something beautiful and powerful. Perhaps the Overlord had done the same when he'd first made it. The only reason the wand had felt tainted again was its placement in a box for years.

The idea of the Overlord's magic infusing with hers inside a wand made her feel warm inside, like they were part of a clandestine exchange that no one else could ever understand. It sent flutters through her stomach, and at sudden moments, she would recall the light, tingling brush of his lips, leaving her breathless and uncertain. The intimacy of a union between their magic was alluring, but considering him as a man—not an Overlord, not an idol, but a man like any other—made Melaine's heart buckle and her knees feel weak. She would shiver, and her palms would grow clammy as she willed herself to remember all the vile men she'd had to fend off in the streets.

The Overlord had always been in a separate category in her mind, elevated far above the common swill of men she was used to in Stakeside. Though she'd never before allowed her admiration for him to slip into the realm of attraction, his almost-kiss had forced her to tiptoe along the edge. He was different from other men, but perhaps...perhaps that didn't make him *more* than a man. Perhaps he was just a different *kind* of man. Many prostitutes in Stakeside had talked about this, the notion of different sorts of people in this world, people who could make them feel genuine care, or more, rather than just the act of turning a cheap trick. Melaine had never thought she'd be able to experience that feeling in her line of work, not with lodestones.

Yet, lately, whenever she offered the Overlord a stone, she felt a glimmer of a soothing feeling, like sunlight caressing a gently lapping pool. A sense of care would pull from her heart, a draw to share a part of herself with him and to receive a part of him in return. The line between physical and metaphysical blurred in his presence; she felt at once like they shared an existence, yet were too separate from each other when they sat across the library table, too far away when they stood mere steps apart. She wanted to be closer. Did he feel the same?

But those were thoughts for another time.

For now, Melaine raised the wand and concentrated

on the levitation spell that she had learned from the deraphant's horn Insight in the great hall. The knowledge it had bestowed was so much more intricate and thorough than any of the trifling lifting spells she'd learned in Stakeside.

Karina's eyes were sharp as flint as she watched Melaine focus on the cluster of wooden crates and canvas bags. None were labeled, but Melaine saw a few scattered grains of wheat and dried legumes on the cart. No doubt the supplies were boring foodstuffs and basic supplies that Karina used to keep the castle's four occupants fed and to maintain the keep. Melaine flicked her wrist and scooped all the spilled grains and legumes into a little pile and sent them back to their respective bags.

Stebbon tried to disguise a snigger as a cough, and Karina had a subtle, snide look on her fine-lined face. Melaine fought a flush of shame. She couldn't stand seeing any food go to waste like that, but her actions served to highlight her lowly background, and she couldn't stand for that either.

She lifted her wand higher and pulled a burst of magic from her bones, channeling it into the wand. In one sweep, every crate and bag lifted into the air. She moved her wand to the right, and the entire supply load floated to the ground and settled gently, as if Melaine was tucking in a babe at night.

"Where would you like them?" Melaine asked. Karina glared, her eyes locked on the wand in Melaine's hand. But then she raised her chin and turned back to the delivery man.

"You may go," Karina said. "I'll expect you back next month, Stebbon."

Stebbon bowed his head. "Yes, m'lady. I'll be here." He flicked his eyes to Melaine again, then climbed onto the hard, wooden bench on the cart. He tugged on the reins of his horses and turned the beasts around. Melaine watched as he goaded them through the gate, the empty cart trundling behind them.

As soon as they were over the threshold, the horses whinnied in fright as the metal gears beneath the gate began to turn. The large iron bars emerged from the ground and descended from the looming lintel along the topmost wall. The man tried to calm his horses as they neighed and bucked, but he was tense already, and they sensed it.

Melaine could feel the dark magical ward of the gate reform. The thick, invisible barrier was suffocating but not as suffocating as it had felt when she was outside the walls. As Stebbon disappeared from sight, Melaine turned toward Karina. The old woman's hand was resting on a small lever at the gatehouse as if her simple touch had caused the enormous gate to do her bidding.

"Is that how it opens?" Melaine asked. Karina slipped her hand away as the gates shut with an echoing clang of metal.

"It is," Karina answered. "For those who are worthy to wield that power."

Melaine narrowed her eyes but held her tongue. Karina's gaze had again shifted to the wand in Melaine's grip, as if insinuating that Melaine was nowhere near worthy of neither the gate nor the wand. Not worthy enough to be in the castle at all, more like it.

However, it was also clear that Karina was surprised to see Melaine carrying the Overlord's old wand. She was being forced to reassess Melaine's standing, and she didn't seem to like that notion.

"If you think you're so clever, why don't you take all those crates and bags to the larder?" Karina said. "Surely, a talented young girl like yourself can do that without trouble."

Melaine didn't miss the restrained sneer in Karina's words. She was torn between leaving the Overlord's servant to do all the work or helping so that she could prove her magical prowess.

Karina turned around without waiting to hear Melaine's answer. She headed in her smooth stride toward the side entrance and opened the door. Melaine looked at the largest crates. They would fit but only single file. Melaine pursed her lips and raised her wand again. She had never tried lifting anything in any particular arrangement, but this was a good chance to test her skills.

As she heard Karina's clipped footsteps beyond the door, she felt a sinuous curiosity creeping after her. Melaine knew nothing about Karina other than her service to the Overlord and the keep—and the fact that she despised Melaine. Perhaps now was a good time to discover more about the old woman.

Melaine pushed a flood of magic through her wand and toward the nearest crate. It lifted into the air as she commanded the spell and hovered a foot off the ground. She coaxed it to stay there and then focused on the crate next to it. She imagined a string tying the two crates together and flicked her wand. The second crate lifted into the air and hovered beside the first.

With a pique of satisfaction, Melaine focused on a canvas bag filled with grain next. She lifted it into the air and attached an invisible thread from its drawstring to the second crate. She kept casting magical strings and lifting bags and crates until she had them all lined up in a floating queue, ready to guide them into the keep.

Melaine smiled to herself as she walked to the door, using her wand to pull her chain of supplies behind her.

She followed Karina into the inner courtyard and through a passageway she'd never entered before, one that crossed the small courtyard and the garden and led into the large, rectangular building that she'd guessed housed the kitchen. The hallway was a little wider than others, and fortunately, the supplies made it inside with only a few bumps and scrapes on the stone walls.

They entered the rectangular building. Doors appeared in the corridor in staggered intervals, and peering inside, Melaine suspected the humble rooms may have been servants' quarters at the castle's initial, First Era conception. Like the outer courtyard, however, they held evidence that many people may have lived there at one point in more recent years, some of the occupants being the Overlord's army, preparing for war. Dozens of empty bedrolls were scattered across the floors along with various wooden bowls and tools of daily living.

A few paces down from the servants' quarters, Melaine and Karina passed by a heavy, wooden door with iron reinforcements. A small, barred window was slightly above eye level. It reminded her of the thin, rectangular slit she'd peered through in the prison cart on her way to meet Overseer Scroupe.

A rusty, iron sign was nailed to the door below the window. In archaic, flowery lettering, it read: *Armory*.

Melaine paused. She thought she heard a quiet clanging sound from inside, like two distant swords crossing each other.

"What's in there?" she asked. Karina looked over her shoulder but only tsked.

"Are you in need of a weapon?" she mocked. "Do you have petty schemes against the Overlord or myself that I should know about?"

"I was only curious," Melaine said. Karina expelled an annoyed sigh through her nostrils and turned around to continue her pace. She turned a corner, but Melaine hesitated in following. The clanging of swords was growing louder, and horses' hooves thundered with the rattle of armor and shouts of men.

The sounds were distant, but Melaine had no doubts they were coming from within the armory. Ancient magic seeped through the door like a fog.

She stepped up to the iron bars and peered through the window.

A wide-eyed woman stared back at her from inches away.

Melaine jerked back. The pale woman's eyes were clouded white and sat in sunken sockets. Her veins ran black through the parchment-thin skin stretched tight over her skull. White, straggly hair hung around the woman's forehead like ancient cobwebs.

The woman backed up in slow, jerky steps. Her face was as gaunt and ghostly as her eyes. Her cheeks and lips were riddled with black rot in fractals, and she opened her mouth to reveal a black tongue and rotted teeth.

A clawing scrabble erupted from her throat. The sound grew louder and faster, like a frenzied creature was trying to escape. Black, oozing blood gurgled out of her mouth along with a single, whispered word that echoed in Melaine's head.

"*Walls.*"

Melaine wanted to scream and call for Karina, but she couldn't unclench her jaw, and her feet felt glued to the floor.

Then the horrific woman dropped to the ground. A dark shadow scuttled across the floor to a dim corner of the small armory room.

"*Please,*" a small voice whimpered.

Melaine backed up and pressed her spine against the corridor wall. Every crate and sack lifted by her spell dropped with a heavy bang.

"What are you doing?" Karina asked, storming back around the corner.

"There's a—" Melaine raised a shaking hand to point to the armory door. "There's a woman in there. Something's wrong with her."

"What?" Karina snapped. "Don't be ridiculous. That door hasn't been opened for years."

She strode to the door and looked through the barred window. Melaine waited with bated breath, still pressing her back hard against the wall.

Karina drew back from the door. "There's nothing

there," she said. "Nothing but rusted weapons and cobwebs. Now gather yourself and take those supplies to the larder."

"But—"

"Now."

Karina turned away from the armory and walked at a swifter pace around the corner of the passage.

Melaine let out a short breath.

"It was there," she whispered, trying to get control of her beating heart and trembling body. "She was there."

She struggled to push away from the wall and eyed the armory window with deep, gut-twisting fear. She gathered a breath of courage and approached the door. Karina must have seen something. Melaine couldn't have imagined the imprisoned woman.

But she *had* imagined a pale woman standing on the balcony of the library tower the night she'd discovered Talem's body. She'd imagined a woman standing near the gate mere moments ago when Stebbon first arrived.

This castle provokes nightmares. The Overlord hadn't disagreed with her statement. Nightmares happened when a person was asleep, but this was different. Was she going mad?

Melaine swallowed and stepped up to the door's window.

The woman wasn't there. She looked around, peering hard at the shadows. Karina was right. There was nothing in the room but old weapons and shields of the First Era's regal fashion.

Melaine stepped back again and listened for the clang of metal armor and swords, for the screams of battle, yet she heard nothing. But then, a soft whisper brushed her ear. With it came a familiar comfort—the same warm feeling she got when she laid her hand upon the library door.

"*Walls,*" the whisper said again. The woman's voice was gentle, though no less pressing.

"What do you mean, 'walls'?" Melaine asked, but she got no answer. The warm, soothing magic disappeared, leaving Melaine alone in the dark passageway.

She shuddered and looked down at the crates and bags on the floor, still in a line down the corridor. She pulled on her magic and lifted the string of supplies. She avoided looking at the armory again as she followed the direction Karina had gone. She turned the corner and saw a single open door at the end of the passage. Heat permeated from it, and the thick smell of fire and baking bread filled her nose.

She tugged on the tethered supplies and walked to the door. The room inside was large, with a long table in the center and a wall-sized stone hearth on one side. A large cauldron hung inside the hearth, flickering over a warm fire. Various cooking implements hung in neat rows on the wall, and canisters of dried foods were organized on shelves. The delicious smell of baking bread drifted from a large, cast-iron oven in one corner.

"Where do you want these?" Melaine asked.

"In the larder," Karina replied, nodding to the back corner of the room opposite the oven. Melaine walked around the long table and saw a doorway leading to a large, cool larder.

She raised her wand and directed the crate in the lead

to the larder. The crate obediently floated inside, tugging its fellow crates and bags behind it. When all of the supplies fit snugly in the larder, Melaine lowered her wand and released its magical tie to the supplies.

"All right, I did your chore," she said. Karina walked about the kitchen in clipped strides, taking tools from the wall and removing containers from the shelves.

"Fetch some of that garlic," Karina ordered as she deposited her items on the table. "Make yourself useful."

"I already have use in this castle," Melaine said, not bothering to acknowledge the strings of garlic bulbs hanging from the ceiling behind Karina. "And it's *not* cooking and being ordered around by you."

"Ah, yes," Karina said. "Well, if all you'd like to do is lie about and make lodestones, then by all means."

"That's not all I do, and you know it," Melaine said, her volume rising.

"It's all you should be doing!" Karina said as she slammed a wooden cutting board on the table. Melaine stiffened in surprise.

"You have been allowed into the Overlord's presence," Karina said, her voice taking on a thin quality. "Someone like you should be groveling at his feet. You should be offering him your lodestones without question and without expecting any recompense in return. You are wasting his time."

"I'm not a waste of time," Melaine said.

"You are not worthy of his teachings," Karina hissed.

"And you are?" Melaine asked. "Is that it? You're angry that he's teaching me and not you?"

"Of course not. He shouldn't be wasting his energy

teaching at all. He has far more important things to focus on, and so little time left to—"

Karina stopped. She looked down but not before Melaine caught her eyes watering.

"The Overlord has decided to use his time as he sees fit," Melaine said, soft but stubborn. "If you don't like that, then you must not be the loyal servant he thinks you are."

"Don't you dare question my loyalty," Karina said, her voice low with quiet anger. Her tears were gone when she looked back up. "You are a newcomer. You know nothing of me, of *him*, of what's going on."

"You know what's going on," Melaine said, her narrowed eyes inspecting Karina's. "Don't you? You seem to know an awful lot about the Overlord's condition, whatever it is. And you've been in Highstrong from the start, haven't you?"

"Foolish girl," Karina said, seething. "The Overlord may be able to put up with your insolence, but I will not. Go back to your quarters."

Melaine scoffed. "I thought you wanted help with the garlic."

"I don't want your filthy hands on it," Karina said. She turned aside and tore two bulbs free, their white husks flitting to the floor.

"We'll see what the Overlord has to say about your treatment of me," Melaine said, twirling his wand in her fingers.

Karina eyed the wand again. Then she looked down at Melaine's blue satin sleeve, at her bodice, all the way down her gown and to her fine, tall, buttoned boots. Her cheeks were still flushed red, and more tears watered her eyes before she blinked to clear them. Her expression hardened.

"Don't you dare hurt him," Karina said. "He shouldn't be wasting his energy on anything physically or emotionally strenuous. No matter how tempting the reason. Do you understand?"

Melaine frowned. She glanced down at the Overlord's wand and the dress she wore. When she looked back up, Karina had turned away to retrieve a copper pot.

"He's the Overlord, Karina," Melaine said. "I couldn't hurt him if I tried."

Karina paused but didn't turn around.

"Not all damage is done by magic, Melaine," she said. "Grow up enough and you'll realize that."

✦

MELAINE WANDERED AMONGST THE LIBRARY'S hexagonal shelves, but her mind drifted far from the myriad Insights upon them. Karina's words were a repetitive gnat's bite at her thoughts. She hadn't sated any of her curiosity about Karina after their conversation. It had only brought on more questions. Then there was the *other* woman...the ghostly, horrific woman who looked rife with decay but whose whispered words carried comfort and a sense of warning.

Who was she? Why was Melaine the only person who could see her? Was she a figment of her mind or a vivid taste of the dark magic that wormed through Highstrong Keep?

Melaine fidgeted with the black lace of her gloves as she kept pacing amongst the shelves. The Overlord's wand was pressed against the skin inside her white dress sleeve, contained by the line of pearl buttons all the way to her elbows. The wand had become a comfort when she wasn't with him, but with all that had happened in the nightly corridors the past few days, it was starting to not be enough.

Besides, thoughts of the Overlord were a complicated storm raging in her mind and body, at times swelling with anxious fears, with lulls of pity followed by torrents of longing. Pain and sadness peaked in tall waves before they crashed into bitterness and confusion. It was almost too much for her to take, but no matter how much she would try to banish him from her head, only for a night's sleep or a momentary reprieve, his ghost of a smile would haunt her dreams and waking thoughts.

Melaine tried to focus on the Insights again, desperate for a distraction. None seemed appealing. She *must* be tired if even Insights couldn't excite her, she thought.

But then, she saw a glistening ruby vial on a shelf ahead. Blood.

She approached the vial, a small, innocuous thing except for its contents. She reached out and lifted it from its perch. The flicker of a nearby candelabra glinted off the red, uncoagulated liquid as she tilted the vial. The faint tang of iron hit her nostrils, and when she focused on the scent, it grew stronger. She could taste the sharp flavor of blood, and she could feel its slick, hot texture pouring down her hands. Magic rolled through her body, rising in her stomach like a sickness.

The vial remained intact and unopened in her fist, but the bottle may as well have been a washbasin drenching her in blood. She closed her eyes tight but forced herself to hold on.

This was blood magic. The powerful Insight contained knowledge of ways to overcome another person by turning their own body and essence against them. It was dark and tantalizing—power without parallel if wielded by a strong, dauntless hand.

But Melaine's hand shook as she struggled to maintain her focus. She reminded herself that this was why she had come to Highstrong Keep and presented herself to the Overlord. She had heard countless stories of the Overlord and his Followers using blood magic to fuel their army and overcome the White City's walls. The details were always hazy in the telling. No one wanted to discuss blood magic in the light of day.

Melaine wanted to learn. She needed to learn. This was the power she needed, what would set her apart from the rabble, from the weak and the afraid.

She fell to her knees with another wave of sickness. She clutched her stomach, though the pain was far more than physical. Her fist shook harder around the vial. She squeezed tighter.

It shattered. She cried out and watched blood—her own—mingle with the magical essence trapped within the vial. Both flooded down her palm and between her fingers. Blood ran down her wrist and arm and then spilled onto the stone floor.

Melaine gasped as if she'd been drowning underwater and had finally been rescued. She slammed her palm on the ground, piercing her skin with shards of glass. Then her eyes flew open wide. A familiar gust of whispers assaulted her ears. The whispers of the urn, magnified, seeping out of the floor until they spun around her in a heady wind.

Words were indistinguishable, yet they were telling her all the same things. Death...terrible deaths, slaughters and suicides, forced servitude, and then something greater, something darker, a catastrophic foe that ate through people like a swarm of locusts...

"There's blood in the walls," Melaine whispered. "The *walls*."

A benevolent whisper echoed the word, and a vivid woman's face swam into Melaine's head. She was the woman from the armory, but she was beautiful and whole. She wielded a polished wooden staff, and long, white, First Era robes fluttered around her body as if in a heavy wind. She stood in the center of the library tower with fierce, determined eyes. The library was empty of shelves and Insights. There was nothing inside but stone walls and the gale of whispers rushing around the strange woman in a torrential storm.

"Melaine."

A voice carried through the whispers, low and coarse. The whispers swelled over it like an avenging tidal wave, but their many droplets couldn't break the strength of the single voice. They rose to a clamor but then smashed against the second word by the intruder.

"Melaine."

Melaine opened her eyes, and the vision of the beautiful woman in the empty library vanished. She wrenched her spellbound gaze from the blood-soaked floor and looked up. The whispers dissipated, and only the Overlord's concerned face commanded her senses.

"My lord," Melaine whispered.

The Overlord knelt on one knee and took her wrist. She tensed but allowed him to coax her bloody palm from the floor. He turned her hand over and inspected her wounds. Glass shards poked through her lace glove, now matted with blood.

He hovered his palm over hers and sighed, as if bracing himself for a wearisome task. He then emitted a low pulse of magic. It tickled her skin, tingling each minuscule place around her many, tiny wounds. Every glass shard lifted from the lace to hover and sparkle over her like little rubies and crystals. Then they vanished as if they had never been.

Melaine tried to hold still as he tightened his gentle hold on her hand. He smoothed his thumb over her palm, and she winced.

"May I?" he asked, stroking his finger down the side of her glove where it wouldn't hurt. She parted her lips but didn't speak. She never removed her gloves for anyone unless they had paid to watch her push a lodestone from her body. But the Overlord's expression was earnest and comforting. No one had ever looked at her that way, with deeper care than she'd ever conceived to have for herself. Her shame and vulnerability ebbed away to the edges of her mind, supplanted by the warm glow blooming in her chest. She couldn't control the flush of her cheeks as she focused on his soft touch and smooth skin.

She licked her lips and nodded. The Overlord

twitched a smile and cupped her hand in his while he used his other to coax the lace from her hand. Its tiny threads caught on the torn skin of her small wounds, but she kept quiet as she watched him slowly reveal her bare skin to his eyes.

He took in every little crease of her palm as if he were reading a book and examined every tiny droplet of blood with a tender frown as if he wished he could kiss them all away. Melaine felt a flutter in her chest as he pressed his palm against hers.

With his soothing touch, her cuts began to knit together. The pain was minuscule, but she trembled from the forbidden intimacy of his palm pressed against hers. She felt vulnerable, naked, and exposed yet more flooded with heat and consumed by a deeper ache than she'd felt when he'd almost kissed her lips. When her wounds disappeared altogether, she expected him to withdraw, but instead, he squeezed her hand with both of his, making her gasp. His hands were large enough to nearly hide hers from view, but his long fingers were as emaciated and pale as the rest of him. A knot formed in her throat. How much worse would he get before he...?

The Overlord's cracked lips parted as if there was a word on his tongue, but he refrained. He still didn't let go when he dropped his gaze to the floor. The blood from the vial stained the stones. Its shining red had turned to a deep, black mar. Melaine felt as if she was going to sink into it, and her lips parted when the whispers began to pulse again in her ears.

"Melaine," the Overlord said. "Come away from here."

Melaine met his eyes. His voice had sounded so strong

and loud when it fought through the ominous whispers, but now, it sounded hoarse and weak as always.

"Yes, my lord," she said, allowing him to help her to her feet. But as she found her footing, he swayed, and she gripped his hand tighter and pulled him close to help them keep their balance.

The Overlord looked aside, his jaw tight, trying to maintain a cold mask to hide the shame of his weakness. She wanted to tell him that he shouldn't be ashamed, that whatever was happening to him wasn't his fault. But the silk of his black shirt rose and fell against her bosom with each of his shallow breaths, and she had the unprecedented urge to nestle into him and feel his heartbeat against her cheek. She instead slipped her hand out of his grasp and backed away. Her palm tingled in his absence.

"Those whispers," she said, swallowing. "Did you hear them? Were they a part of the vial or...?"

"This keep has been around for hundreds of years," the Overlord said. His hand hovered between them as if he wanted to draw her close again, but he closed his fist and lowered it to his side. "Rarely have its days been pleasant." He nodded to a place across the library. "Come with me. I want to show you something different."

"Why not help me with that?" She nodded at the blood on the floor, though she felt hesitant at the prospect. "I was learning. I can handle it."

"Please, Melaine," the Overlord said. Melaine frowned. He'd never requested anything of her so politely, as if she was a peer rather than a subject. What was his angle?

He stepped away and tried to feign a slow, thoughtful

pace. Melaine felt a pit of guilt deepen inside, knowing he had used some of his limited strength to heal her hand. She could have handled the pain, too, if he'd let her.

But he hadn't. Seeing what he had sacrificed, Melaine almost offered him a lodestone. But she held her tongue, shocked at herself for considering the idea of freely *giving* him one when he hadn't even asked.

She followed him in silence, and then felt a leap of excitement when his slow walk ended in front of the closed, mahogany and glass curio cabinet that held his collection of empty Insights. Insights that were useless except for those talented few, like Melaine and the Overlord, who were resourceful enough to repurpose magical residue.

Ever since the Overlord had discovered that Melaine possessed that talent, he had forbidden her from touching the Insights within the cabinet. Now, he opened the glass doors and reached inside, pulling out a round sphere of amber.

"I want you to study this," the Overlord said. The amber, golden and deep, looked like the awe-inspiring honey Melaine had found on her breakfast plate her second morning in Highstrong. Inside, she saw the blurred outline of a caterpillar's cocoon.

"What does it hold?" she asked.

"A wealth of healing spells," he answered. "If you can tap into its reserves, it will teach you magic that is crucial for any sorcerer to learn."

"What?" she asked. "You want me to learn *healing* spells? You think I can't handle anything else?"

"If you have any desire to enter conflicts, there is a

risk of injury, correct?" the Overlord said, his voice thinned as his eyes grew cool. "Healing spells may save your life one day."

"Armies have battle-healers," Melaine said, not looking away from his hard stare. "I need to spend my time learning magic that healers won't touch. *That's* why I'm—"

"Melaine!" the Overlord cut her off in a voice much louder and stronger than she could have expected. She tensed and drew back a little. "You came here for me to teach you. Don't question my methods."

"You're sick, aren't you?" Melaine asked, her voice trembling as she struggled for courage and a firmer hold on her swell of anxiety. "You want me to learn healing spells so I can help you."

The Overlord growled in frustration and looked aside. "The spells aren't for me."

"Are they for me, then?" Melaine asked. "Do you think I'm going to catch whatever it is you have?"

"They're for everyone else!" the Overlord said. "There's no need for you to learn dark spells. Don't you understand? I do not need Followers or battles or *war*. I gave Centara a peaceful rule! Didn't I at least do that?"

He gripped the amber sphere tighter and leaned into the wood of the cabinet. His breaths were ragged and fast, but he kept going. "I don't want you to see what I saw, Melaine. There is no need for your corruption, do you understand? I don't want to corrupt you."

His eyes were pleading with her. He clung to the cabinet as if a sword had wounded him deeply, and Melaine was the only one who could help. Her bottom lip trembled as she considered reaching out to hold him, to comfort him as he'd done for her, but her indignation and rising rage stopped her.

"You said I could become a Follower!" she said, her heartbeat railing in panic. All of her expectations of disappointment, of life always breaking its promises, renewed in agonizing force, bringing tears to her eyes. "I want to understand how you got your power—"

"I'm trying to teach you, Melaine," he said, shoving himself off the cabinet and grabbing her hand fast. She tensed, her entire body jolting with the fire of his touch.

"No!" she said. She yanked her hand from his grasp. "You promised me you would teach me everything you know. Instead, I get *this.*"

She snatched the amber out of his hand and threw it to the floor. It hit a table leg and rolled out of reach. She wiped the taint of residual magic on her elaborate white gown, her chiffon and lace now spattered red with blood from the Insight vial.

"All I've done here is degrade myself by whoring out lodestones to you while I learn from your table scraps, your trash!" she said. "I expected more from you."

"And I should have expected less from you," the Overlord said, now glaring into Melaine's eyes. "If this is how you view your life here, then you will never be worthy of my teachings."

"And you will never be the powerful leader I thought you were!" Melaine countered. "The ruler I looked up to since I was a child. *Not* without my lodestones."

The magicless state of Talem's body crawled into her mind, a background threat that had never left her thoughts. She took a step back but lifted her chin in challenge. "Unless you're going to *make* me give them to you."

The Overlord stood still and silent, his breaths heavy with the exertion of a simple argument. Then his hard glare crumbled into a raw expression of unmistakable heartache, but it was gone in a flash. He looked aside.

"You fool," he murmured.

Tears blurred Melaine's vision. Her lip trembled in a pitiful way that she hated. She spun around and ran to the library doors. She shouldered them open with a heave and abandoned the Overlord, leaving him with his insults and pathetic, weak misery.

She strained her ears as she strode with fury through the dark hallway, but the Overlord's voice never followed. Her face contorted with anger and hurt as she picked up speed and bolted through the keep. She slammed into the heavy wooden door that led to the outermost courtyard and pushed it open.

The mighty shadow of the wall loomed ahead. The gray sky looked like dawn had never made way for the afternoon sun. Deep, pervasive mist clouded the grounds, obscuring the wall and the ominous gate that surged into Melaine's heart as if calling to her. She hadn't wanted to step foot outside of the gate since coming to Highstrong, but now, she tripped over the thought. The castle felt oppressive where once it had been freeing.

Then a new thought snagged her. *Could* she even leave? Karina's words about only certain people being worthy enough to open the gate gnawed at her. She had to know if she was worthy enough. She had to know what the Overlord thought of her. Was she just a stonegirl whose only purpose was to serve him? Did he plan on keeping her here for the rest of her days...for his? How brief of a time would that be? How much time did he have left?

Melaine felt the urge to collapse, but she somehow held her feet. Her life had become painful. Highstrong had once promised a life beyond base survival, but now, her heart ached so much that she may as well have been dying.

She forced her feet to walk across the grounds. Her boots, made of much finer leather than she'd ever worn before coming to Highstrong, clicked with perfectly symmetrical heels across flags of stone. The hem of her white chiffon dress brushed the fallen leaves that curled like fetal corpses. The fog closed in around her like a cold hand, and the closer she got to the gate, the tighter its grasp became.

She was suffocating. Every inhale drew in wet condensation that triggered coughs. She paused and caught her breath, looking around her at the heavy fog that seemed to grow thicker with each passing second. It carried oppressive magic within, and its coldness seeped into her bones, plummeting into freezing, paralyzing depths.

Melaine gasped for air but couldn't get the relief her lungs needed. She turned back toward the castle but then stopped with one foot only on its toes.

A ghostly figure stood beside the door that led back inside. It was hard to make out in the fog, but she could see the outline of a head, a neck, a body. The legs descended into the fog so she couldn't see its feet—if it even had feet.

Her first thoughts were of the woman who had been haunting her in waking life and in internal visions. But this figure's presence felt different from the tortured yet benevolent warnings of the woman. This apparition felt angry.

Goosebumps rose on Melaine's skin. She tore her eyes away, but with that one fleeting glance, her heart pumped harder with fear.

There were more of them—more ghostly apparitions scattered throughout the grounds. They all stood still as death in the fog. She couldn't see their faces or eyes. When she looked closer, she deciphered the shapes of helmets on their heads. Battered First Era armor clothed their bodies, and swords trembled at their sides as they began to walk.

"What do you want?" Melaine whispered, her voice too hoarse for a louder sound. Either they didn't hear or didn't care to answer because they all kept striding forward in eerie silence. As they grew closer, their clanking swords and shields and rattling armor became louder with each passing second. The echo of horses' hooves and frightened neighs mixed with the intense clash of swords that would have made sparks fly if the steel was real. The racket of cart wheels rolling violently over the ground sounded, and the bombardment of a trebuchet boomed against the massive, iron gate.

Melaine nearly fell off her feet. The apparitions kept gliding with ghostly slowness toward her, twelve of them, twenty, fifty, all emerging in endless regiments through the mist. She would soon be surrounded by an entire army if she didn't do something. And the whispers...the whispers from the ancient urn. Voices and words she didn't understand kept coming, kept speaking, yelling.

She bolted for the gate. The sounds of an imaginary, perhaps remembered, battle roared around her, assaulting her ears as she tried to focus only on the lever waiting in the gatehouse. The lever she'd seen Karina use to open the mighty gate.

She felt a wind at her back, even colder than the freezing air of winter and filled with more dark, oppressive magic. She pushed herself harder, terrified of the damage that magic might wreak if it caught her. She finally reached the gatehouse and threw all of her weight against the lever. It stuck for a moment but then lurched forward and settled into place with a shudder. Melaine let go and prayed the gate would open for her—quickly.

It didn't move. Panic hit her harder, and she glanced over her shoulder. The entities were closing in. Some of their helmets were shattered in places or dented so far in the skulls beneath must have been dented as well. Through places where the metal had broken off, she could see bone and gristle. Splintered ribs and naked bones peeked through rips in chainmail. Some of the apparitions were missing legs, but they kept walking as if they had them.

The gears buried under the gate started to rumble. As they turned, the gate started grinding its iron teeth. Melaine spun back around and watched its gruesome jaws opening wide.

She didn't wait for the iron bars to sink all the way into the deep trench in the ground. She ran straight to the gate. She didn't feel any dark, warding magic trying to keep her inside, so she jumped over the lowering bars and stumbled on the other side.

Then she gasped as she felt an icy hand grip her wrist from within the castle grounds. She spun around and screamed. A woman's wide, white-clouded eyes looked straight into hers, the familiar apparition's wild white hair wisping around her head. Her skin was rotting on her mottled cheekbones, her veins black and her lips gashed as she hissed, *"It's hungry!"*

Melaine ripped her arm from the spirit's grasp and stumbled back. The spirit dissipated, and the others beyond were camouflaged by the thick fog. The storm of whispers ceased. The dark, nauseating ward of warning that Melaine had felt the last time she stood outside of Highstrong Keep's gate was absent. The gate remained open, but it seemed the apparitions were contained.

All of Highstrong felt like it was its own, encapsulated world of darkness and mystery. Melaine felt like an outsider again, looking into a place in which she did not fit.

She backed away and turned around. The crags and black trees of the surrounding forest were menacing beneath the heavy gray clouds hanging low in the sky. But the fog amongst their trunks wasn't as thick. Cold, meager sunlight shone down brightly enough to light Melaine's path. She didn't know where she was going, but she couldn't stay at Highstrong any longer.

She took off down the winding, rocky path that Overseer Scroupe's carriage had once followed. She didn't have the luxury of a carriage now, only her own two feet. She had her wand still; she'd made sure of that. It carried a speed spell, but she was loath to waste it. What if the spirits came back? What if they could break through Highstrong Keep's thick walls and hunt her with menacing motives?

She ran down the path. Her breaths came hard and fast as her boots pounded the rocky earth. The trees reached down with scratching fingers, and she heard the distant howl of a wolf deep in the forest.

Something big lurked in the path ahead. She slowed her run and tried to make out what it was through her wild senses and the oppressive fog. She let out a breath when she realized it was Stebbon's cart, empty of supplies, with his two workhorses still attached. They stomped and snorted, clearly anxious but not frightened enough to bolt.

Stebbon was nowhere in sight.

Melaine walked with slow steps toward the cart, careful not to scare the horses. This could be her ride home, though her stomach clenched at the thought. *Home*. Stakeside. Where else would she go?

She reached the horses and shushed them. The closest one eyed her with its big, brown eyes. Its flanks were panting as if it had just finished a fast run. It whinnied and bucked its head toward a thicket of bushes off the road. Melaine frowned and looked at the thicket. A scrap of torn, woolen fabric clung to a bramble. It was Stebbon's blue traveling coat.

"What happened?" she asked the horse. She stroked the horse's muzzle. Part of her wanted to hop in the cart, take the reins, and drive back to Centara, but a troublesome thought held her back. Stebbon could be lost or wounded, and Melaine couldn't imagine being out in the thick fog of the menacing forest without hope of returning to civilization. She winced and stroked the horse again.

"Don't leave without me," she said, hoping the animal would obey. She then walked to the thicket to inspect the piece of wool. She didn't see any blood, and a quick look over the thicket revealed no clues as to what had happened to Stebbon. She picked her way around the thicket and trod a few paces into the trees. She saw skid-marks in the fallen leaves mixed with heavy footprints in the exposed mud. It looked like Stebbon had stumbled his way deeper into the forest.

What was he running from?

Melaine shivered and followed the tracks. Her recent encounter with an army of what she could only assume were ghosts or lost souls made her imagination writhe with all sorts of possible dangers. Though she tried to wrangle her rational thoughts, she had to wonder—if it were a wolf pack or some other beast, why would it ignore the horses, who were easy prey when hitched to a cart?

Whatever had chased Stebbon off the road and into the forest could be a threat to anyone who traveled the path, even to Melaine. And the mysterious threat might not stay within the forest. It might go for Highstrong next.

She kept walking, scanning the ground with every step. She saw another scrap of fabric in the leaves a few paces to her right. Then a larger piece of blue lurked through a low thicket of underbrush. She crept toward it with quiet steps, turning her head at various angles to catch more glimpses of blue wool, and then she saw part of Stebbon's brown trousers and black boots.

Her heart thumped as she kicked aside the brush to reach him.

Melaine gasped. Stebbon's shredded clothing was familiar, but the man himself was unrecognizable. His clothes had been torn away, exposing his mutilated body. His flesh and meat were torn clean off his bones and thrown to one side in a bloody, reeking mess. The visible bones were splintered, exposing their insides. The marrow had been sucked out.

Melaine shook all over. Stebbon's body was in the same desecrated state as Talem's when she'd found him within Highstrong's grounds. She wanted to run, but she had to know how deep the similarities went. Her survival might depend on it. She swallowed and crouched beside the body. The smell of piss and blood and offal was consuming, but she fought off her nausea and bolstered her courage. She reached out to touch Stebbon's broken forearm.

She instantly recoiled. The body was utterly devoid of magic. Just like Talem's.

She had assumed Talem had been tossed over the castle wall and that his bones had snapped that way, but she felt foolish for that assumption now. The fractures of Stebbon's bones looked deliberate and methodical, and Talem's bones had been snapped in the exact same places. No fall could have replicated the injuries with such coincidental perfection. Both bodies looked like someone or something had snapped their bones in all the right places to get the most marrow—the most magic—from them as possible.

Melaine's chest concaved. She felt as if it would be impossible to draw her next breath. Her past worries that the Overlord may have been responsible for somehow extracting Talem's magic were extinguished. The Overlord didn't do this. The Overlord hadn't come out all this way to convince Stebbon to give him all of his magic. The Overlord wasn't strong enough—magically or physically— to break a body in this horrific manner. The more Melaine considered it, the more absurd the idea became.

The Overlord wasn't responsible for Stebbon's death. Something else was. Something that could steal magic. Something unheard of.

Melaine stood on wavering legs. If whatever thing had sucked the marrow and magic from both Stebbon's and Talem's bones was still around, then the occupants of Highstrong might be in danger. Karina. Serj. The Overlord.

Melaine could run. She could take one of Stebbon's horses and ride away either back to Centara or a surrounding village, perhaps even to someplace unknown.

But then who would warn Highstrong of the danger outside...even *inside* its walls?

Melaine grimaced at her own idiocy but knew what she had to do. She took out her wand and lifted the heap of Stebbon's bones and flesh and clothing into the air. She pulled it along an invisible, hovering string until she reached the horses and cart. She wrapped Stebbon's body in the canvas that had covered the supplies and laid him inside the cart. Then she slapped the horse's flank.

"Go back to the city," she said. The horses whinnied and took off, seeming glad for an instruction to do *something* other than stand in the dark, scared and unsure.

Melaine knew how they felt.

She watched the cart rattle down the stony path before she turned around and ran in the opposite direction—back to Highstrong Keep.

She didn't stop running when she reached the open gate. She couldn't waste time, and if the soldier apparitions were waiting for her, well, she would just have to face them.

Fortunately, they were gone, and there was no sign of the haunting woman either. The fog wasn't quite as thick as it had been. Melaine crossed the threshold of the massive gate without a hitch and pulled the lever. The gate closed with a heavy, resounding groan.

"Guess I am worthy," she muttered with a wry huff as she caught her breath.

"*What* are you doing?"

Melaine whipped around to see Karina standing stiff and tall at the entrance to the small gatehouse.

"I need to speak with the Overlord," Melaine said. "Right away."

"The Overlord is resting," Karina replied, her frown severe, but she looked paler than usual. "As should you be. Do you know what time it is?"

"I don't care what time it is," Melaine snapped. "I need to see him."

She walked past Karina, but Karina grabbed her arm in a surprisingly firm grip.

"You will *not* disturb him," she said. "You already gave him a trying enough afternoon as it is."

"That—that was not my fault," Melaine said, though she felt a squirm of guilt that she may have exhausted the Overlord during their argument. "When will he be done resting?"

"Tomorrow morning, I expect," Karina said. Melaine scowled.

"Go to your quarters, Melaine. You should be inside this time of evening." Karina glanced around the courtyard. "We both should be. I'm appalled that you would dare open this gate without permission. No matter your motivations."

Melaine felt another chill run through her and looked around the courtyard as well. Did Karina know what her motivations had been?

"Karina," she said, trying to control the trembling overtaking her voice. She might receive nothing but a mocking retort from the woman, but things in High-strong had become too threatening for Melaine to not take this chance. "I've been seeing things. In the castle, in the courtyard. There's some kind of powerful magic happening, and I think it's dangerous. We all, including the Overlord, might be in danger."

"I assure you, the Overlord is quite safe in his quarters," Karina said, though Melaine caught a flicker of uncertainty in her eyes. "As you will be."

"Karina."

"I will escort you to your room," Karina said with a cold expression that offered no room for debate. Melaine clenched her jaw to stop her impending protest. She couldn't tell if Karina knew about the apparitions or not, and her staunch protection of the Overlord was an infuriating obstacle, but arguing now wouldn't do any good when the strict woman was this resolute. Melaine decided that she would find a tactful way to speak with the Overlord about Karina's attitude when she saw him next—which would hopefully be sooner rather than later.

"All right," Melaine said. Karina gave her a clipped nod and turned on her heel. Melaine walked at her side to the castle's entrance, but she didn't feel any safer inside the stone keep than she had in the exposed courtyard.

She would have to stay calm and controlled. Morning would come fast. As soon as the sun was up, she would uncover all of the mysteries of Highstrong Keep, its occupants, and whatever evil hunted them.

CHAPTER 10

The night felt hard and cold around Melaine's body as she tried to sleep. She hadn't felt this on edge since her time on the streets. Her racing heart and sense of dread rivaled the state she had been in when entering the Hole.

She tried to focus on remaining calm. She had to wait until morning to speak to the Overlord. Wandering the nightly corridors didn't sound appealing, but more so, she was afraid for the Overlord's health. He was so frail. Waking him from his much-needed rest might put him in as much danger as any dark magic the keep could possess.

Melaine squeezed her eyes shut as a wave of hurt rolled through her.

She didn't want him to die.

Serj couldn't be right. Karina's restrained grief couldn't be valid. And Melaine had to be misinterpreting the looks of defeat that she'd seen in the Overlord's eyes the past two days. He couldn't be giving up.

Melaine's heart clenched, and she rolled over in bed.

She drew her blankets around her and tucked them under her chin. She focused on taking calming breaths.

Then the cold night felt hot as if the spent coals had leapt from the fireplace and flared beside her bed. She threw off the blankets and exposed her body, glad that her chemise was thin enough to let a bit of air filter through to her skin. But she was still sweltering, and her mind was fraught with frustration. She sighed and then ground her teeth, tugging on a string of her hair. She thumped her head back on the soft pillow and stared at the dark ceiling.

The heat reminded her of the Overlord's touch and how a single glance from him could make her entire body warm. Why couldn't she get his gentle smile and comforting touch out of her head? She had once glorified him as an idol who would uplift her to new heights of power and status. But now, his presence was an anchor in deeper places of her psyche, her heart a sinking ship.

The bedroom door creaked. Was that an imagined step? Melaine frowned and darted her fingers to the nightstand candle. She sparked a bit of magic to light the wick. She pushed herself up on her elbows and gasped.

The Overlord stood at her bedside.

"My lord," she said, her breath resuming. "You scared me."

The Overlord was silent. His shadowed eyes roved over her body, and she was reminded of her nearly undressed state. Goosebumps ran up and down her arms while warmth pooled in her belly and made her quiver.

"My lord," she said again, this time with indignation as she blushed under his forward inspection. He still said nothing, but he raised his pale hand and brushed his finger down her cheek.

Melaine didn't move. She couldn't. Danger warnings flared, but so did a rising sense of yearning. Her lips parted, and her chest ached as she searched the Overlord's face with wide eyes. His gaze was intense and sharp, as if possessed by a hunger only she could satisfy.

Her lack of response seemed to encourage him. He cupped her cheek in his skeletal hand. His cold touch contrasted against the blooming heat in her face with tantalizing sensuality. Her breath caught in her throat as the Overlord leaned over her and brought his lips to hers.

Melaine had been kissed once, before she ever came to Highstrong. It had been a rough, raw kiss by a man she didn't know and didn't want. It hadn't gone further than that—Melaine had made sure it never would, not with him nor any other man in Stakeside.

But this kiss.... The Overlord's lips were firm, but his kiss was soft, and when he slipped his tongue into her mouth, she whimpered in a sound she had never made before. Her heart throbbed, her body coursing with the familiar rush of adrenaline, bringing magic to the surface of her skin. But she didn't use that magic to push him off of her.

She kissed him back.

The Overlord ran his hand through her hair and climbed onto the bed and over her body in one motion.

She allowed him to pour himself into her, dragging her nails down his shoulders as she pulled him closer. Her hips raised before she knew what she was doing, and she startled when she felt something warm and hard railing against her within his trousers.

She snatched a fistful of the Overlord's hair and jerked his face away from hers. She flicked her eyes to his own, trying to understand his motives, fighting against her own scattering thoughts and physical desperation to try to make a conscious decision of what *she* wanted.

The Overlord ran one hand down her waist and squeezed her hip in a fierce grip while his knee pinned one of her hands to her side. He grabbed her other wrist and held her arm down on the pillow above her head.

"Wait," she said.

The Overlord's eyes flashed red in the flaring light of the candle. Then his sallow face cracked in a broad smile. His smile widened farther, as if strings were tied to the corners of his mouth to yank his skin and muscles up. His blue eyes were wholly red now, and they sharpened with a monstrous glint as he tightened his hold over her helpless body.

Melaine screamed as he locked his chapped lips on hers. His kiss was no longer soft and passionate. Now, he pushed his tongue into her mouth to force it open and inhaled the air from her lungs. And then something else emerged from the Overlord's mouth, something far more invasive. It felt like a long snake was trying to shove its way down her throat. Her gag reflex tried to cough it out, but it kept pushing, opening her throat so that she felt the Overlord's next inhale through the long, snake-like tube, stealing more than just her ability to breathe.

Her magic started to crawl from her marrow like insects from a rotting log. It wriggled out and surrounded her bones, then shot through her veins from her toes upward, straight to her throat. The Overlord was inhaling magic from her mouth and into his body as if *she* were a lodestone.

She jerked against his hold on her, but he was stronger than he looked. Her head swirled as her body succumbed to suffocation. But through her muddled mind and draining magic, she focused on the glow of the candle on her bedside table.

Light it with the intent to burn.

Melaine struggled to summon the first spell the Overlord had taught her. She dragged an ounce of magic back from his draining current and shot a pulse at the candlewick. The flame turned red and exploded into sparks that landed on the Overlord's robe. The black silk and silver threads caught fire as fast and violent as if she'd doused him with oil first.

He snarled in an animalistic sound and sucked the long tube from her throat. She coughed and watched in horror as a long, black protrusion slithered back into the Overlord's mouth, like a proboscis of some giant insect. He unclamped his harsh grip, threw his robe to the floor, and fled to the door like the shadow of a stolen carriage. Melaine gasped for air and pushed herself up just in time to see him disappear down the hall as if he'd never been there.

Melaine scrambled to the other side of the bed and grabbed her wand from the drawer of her nightstand. She stood on shaking legs, keeping her wand aimed at the open door. The Overlord's robe burned on the floor, surrounded by stone. It was consumed within a few, tense minutes as Melaine waited for the Overlord to come back.

There was no sign of him. Her entire body trembled, both from fear and weakness. She swallowed with sharp pain and managed to step around the bed. She edged to the door and peered out into the hall.

She threw her gaze to the guard statue, but it was dormant. She walked past and aimed her wand in sharp jerks around the hearth room, casting a beam of purple-white light from its tip that only served to deepen the surrounding shadows. The light dimmed as she paced into the sitting room but not because she wished it. Her magic flickered with her trembling body, depleted as if she'd created a host of lodestones in one sitting.

She hadn't consented to part with her magic as she did when making lodestones. This time, the Overlord had stolen it.

Her thoughts started to weave together. The Overlord had never displayed the degree of strength he had used to pin her into bed. She'd only ever seen him remain silent in such a haunting way when she'd caught him sleepwalking in the halls. He had seemed off, and she remembered a red flash in his eyes that she had assumed she imagined. He'd had no recollection whatsoever of those nightly encounters the following mornings.

His blood-red eyes and wide smile tonight were ghastlier a sight than she had ever seen, and that long, disgusting tube he used to suck out her magic...that wasn't him. It couldn't be.

Melaine felt a stab in her heart as she realized the kiss may not have been real, but her raw disappointment was usurped within seconds by a rush of worry. If that wasn't the Overlord, then where was the real one?

She followed the same direction in which the Overlord had fled the night when Serj's ravings had interrupted their first intimate moment—a moment that might have turned out like tonight's horrors if she had let him kiss her. Melaine shuddered and forced her feet to run faster.

She wasn't sure where she was going, but she let go of reason and followed her gut. She had trusted her instincts countless times growing up in Stakeside. When she'd needed to steal food as a child or escape a threatening client or thief, she'd allowed her feet to lead the way to a safe hiding place. She had often wondered if her innate certainty was a physical sense of direction and subconscious awareness of her surroundings or if her magic was somehow involved in guiding her. Whatever the reason, she trusted it as she turned left and right through the maze of the castle with one thought in mind—reaching the Overlord.

She paused when she passed a narrow slit of a window that overlooked the outer courtyard. She was nearing the tower south from the library. She had guessed that the Overlord's chambers might be in that tower. Now was a good time to find out.

She kept going down the halls, following the hexagonal string of rooms that were a symmetrical reflection of her quarters. But unlike hers, a tower lay at the end of this set. She reached a tall, wooden door and stopped.

A sound infiltrated the pressing silence of the dark stone around her, coming from the opposite side of the solid door. It was a thick, disturbing sound, slick with slurps and clicking teeth and muffled grunts and snarls.

It was an animal gorging on a carcass—she had heard the disgusting noise often enough in the city alleyways. Her stomach turned as she also remembered hearing it in the Hole, where people had been feasting on some kind of raw flesh.

She swallowed down her disgust and took slow steps to the door, holding her wand out straight. The door was as ornate as the library's, carved with soaring eagles and graceful trees, and she could feel similar magic emanating from the wood.

The magic was a protective spell, but the spell was in tatters.

The noise of a devouring creature grew louder. She grimaced and took a final step to reach the door. Though the wood had appeared solid, she now saw a narrow crack scarring its surface. She gathered her courage and peered into the room. Moonlight shone down from a high window. The tower was as large as the library, but instead of shelves, the lowest level was divided into sections by arrangements of furniture. Chairs and tables were littered with loose parchment, scrolls, scattered Insights, and other shadowed objects Melaine couldn't identify. She didn't look around for long. Her eyes were quickly drawn to a bed on one side, half-hidden by a gold-filigree, folding divider.

Her eyes widened, and she nearly gave herself away by gasping, but she clapped a hand over her mouth before she could be heard. A creature scavenged the room as she had suspected, but it was unlike any animal she had ever seen. No fur covered its leathery gray skin, and it hunched over the bed like a hulking gargoyle, its spine protruding in sharp knobs. Its four limbs looked human enough, but one beastly hand with long fingers and knobby knuckles dug wicked claws into the side of the mattress. A long, black tube extended from its throat past glinting, razor-sharp teeth and open jaws. More tubes extended from its sides, latching onto something lying upon the bed. They undulated like swallowing gullets.

Melaine lowered her eyes, forcing herself to look at what the beast was feasting upon with such disgusting relish.

It was the Overlord. He was lying motionless in his bed, pinned beneath the gorging monster. Its black proboscis was invading his mouth and throat while the creature scraped its sharp teeth against his mouth.

"No," she mouthed. She gathered her magic with difficulty then sent a pulse of energy through her veins and into her wand and shot it at the door. Luckily, the protection spell was already weak, and the barrier dissipated like mist. She thrust the door open.

The monster jerked its teeth from the Overlord's mouth. It turned its head and looked at Melaine, but its revolting proboscis stayed inside the Overlord's throat, sucking out his magic in heavy swallows. The edges of the creature's mouth spread in the same ghastly smile that the Overlord had worn in her bedroom. This time, it didn't have the restrictions of the man's human face to contain its evil delight. The smile spread to the beast's ragged, pointed ears, and two rows of sharp teeth glinted in the moonlight.

The creature's proboscis wriggled from the Overlord's throat, and the tubes at its sides detached from his ribs with a sucking sound. It placed one hand on the Overlord's chest and coiled its muscles, ready to leap straight at Melaine.

She sent another burst of magic through her wand and fired the battle spell she'd learned from the rathmor's tooth Insight, aiming it straight at the creature.

Its smile dropped. The spell hit with explosive impact, with such power that Melaine worried she might have hit the Overlord as well. The creature shot off of his body and slammed into the wall. It hissed its way into a ghastly screech and fled. It crawled up the wall with a spider's gait and smashed through a glazed window. It leapt into the night, leaving the room silent and empty except for Melaine and the Overlord.

She rushed to the bed and searched his body for signs of life. Her frantic inspection found that his flesh was intact. His bones hadn't been broken nor the marrow sucked out.

She opened the Overlord's slack mouth and looked down his throat but saw no sign of an invading proboscis. His glazed eyes were blue with no hint of red whatsoever. The creature was gone, but how long had it been feasting on the Overlord's magic? How long had it been weakening him since before Melaine had ever entered his life?

Rage surged through her blood, and a powerful, consuming need to cradle this man and never let him go pierced her heart and brought tears to her eyes. She stared at the Overlord's chest and saw the smallest of movement, the shallow rise and fall of breaths. She pressed her finger on his neck and felt the faint pulse of blood pumping.

"My lord," she said, her throat sore from the creature's invasion. Somehow, it must have usurped the Overlord's appearance, perhaps his very *body*, so it could invade hers with ease.

She placed her hand on his cheek and nudged his arm. "My lord. Wake up. My lord, it's gone. That beast is gone."

The Overlord took a deeper breath, but it rattled dangerously. His lips were so cracked they were bleeding. His skin was tinged yellow, aside from the deep purple hollows beneath his open but dim eyes. His skin was stretched so thin upon his frame that he looked like every bit of muscle and blood he had was drained and only the empty skeletal husk remained.

"My lord," Melaine said louder and with more urgency, her voice returning to its normal strength. "My lord, wake up."

His eyes flickered, and after darting around for a moment with no sense of focus, his gaze fell upon Melaine and stayed there. Consciousness returned.

"What," he started, but paused to take another rattling breath. "What are you doing here?"

"Saving you," Melaine said. "I'm not sure if you noticed, but something was eating you."

His eyes widened. "Melaine," he said and attempted to sit up. She helped lift him so he could lean back against the headboard of his bed. "You left. I heard the gate. You were gone."

"I came back," she said. "And it's a damn good thing I did."

"No, Melaine. You shouldn't have. Leave. Leave Highstrong."

She frowned. "No." Her refusal went against her every instinct for survival, but she had long abandoned that route. "I'm not leaving you like this. I hit that *thing*, but I don't know if I killed it."

"Not gone," he whispered. "You have to leave."

"No," Melaine protested. She released his shoulders and focused her attention on her hands. Her body resisted, but she forced her weakened magic to coalesce in her palm and push through her skin into a hardened stone. The lodestone she forged was small, but she pressed it against the Overlord's lips. With his next ragged breath, he pulled her magic into himself. The stone disappeared into dust. He coughed as if he'd swallowed foul-tasting medicine, but he took a fuller breath and sat straighter. Melaine stroked his hair without thought.

"What was that thing?" she asked.

The Overlord stiffened and clenched his jaw. Then he twitched his head and met Melaine's eyes.

"It's called the Sateless," he said. "A foul creature that wretch, Talem, set loose upon me. It's been feeding on my magic for months."

"What? Why didn't you say something? You didn't tell me that's why you need my lodestones. I would have—"

"I'm sorry," he said. "I stopped wanting to use you after only a day of knowing you. You were so...you weren't what I expected. But I didn't know any other way. It doesn't matter now. It's through with me. One last feeding, and I'll be gone. No lodestone can help me." He raised a single finger to touch the back of her hand, as if any larger movement would kill him. "That's why you have to go, Melaine. Your magic is powerful—*you're* powerful. It will find you next."

"It already has," Melaine muttered. "It used you to get to me tonight. It was like it was *inside* you. Wearing you like a costume, or maybe an illusory spell, a disguise so it could...you...came to my room and..." She looked away but didn't take her hand from the Overlord's touch. She felt him shudder.

"Melaine, please," he said. "You have to leave. Let me die. Don't give the Sateless anything else. Starve it out. It's the only way to stop it."

A creak of the door made both of them jump. Karina stood in the doorway. She frowned like a nursemaid who had caught a sick child out of bed, and then she glared at the thin chemise Melaine was still wearing. Melaine tensed and shifted in front of the Overlord.

Karina ignored Melaine's protective stance and walked to the Overlord's side. Her strict frown softened into dismay.

"Not so soon," she said. She placed a hand on the Overlord's head with a mother's comfort. The soft touch reminded Melaine of Salma, and she felt a pang in her heart.

"I won't stand for it, Actaeon," Karina said.

Melaine looked up at her in surprise, and then back down at the Overlord. *Actaeon.*

The corner of his mouth twitched in a semblance of a smile. "You knew this was coming, Karina."

"What? No," Melaine said. "You can't give up. You can't." She stood and gripped her wand. "Talem did this. His brother must know some way to fix it."

"How do you know about Serj?" Karina snapped. She scowled but didn't waste time pressing further. "You don't think Actaeon's interrogated him already? He detected no lies in that boy's questioning. Not like with Talem."

"Your magic is weaker now," Melaine said to the Overlord, ignoring Karina. "Maybe too weak to know for sure if he was lying. I'm going to try." Her voice softened. "Will you be all right?"

"Leave this place, and I will be," he murmured.

"No," she said. "I'm not going anywhere. Didn't I make that clear already?"

"I am ordering you to leave," he said. "Do not disobey me."

"You can punish me after if you want," she said. "You can kill me." She was shocked that she meant it, but she set her jaw with stubborn resistance. "But I am not abandoning you. I'm going to find out what Serj knows, and I *will* help you."

Melaine turned around before he could protest. She walked to the door and then ran through the dark halls. Eerie green torches of everflame cast dim light and deep shadows, and she couldn't shake the feeling that the shadows were filled with more than simply an absence of light.

But she heard no whispers and saw no apparitions. She saw no sign of the monstrous Sateless. She reached the biting cold air of the garden without harm and descended into the dank dungeons.

She knew the way to Serj's cell by heart now. When she reached the barred door of the ancient torture chamber, she used her lingering magic to unlock the warding spell. The devious devices inside all paled in comparison to the torture she had witnessed the Sateless inflicting on the Overlord.

"Serj," Melaine said, approaching the cell. Serj shot up from the floor, then melted against the bars with overwhelming relief.

"What do you want?" he asked, feigning his casual demeanor and failing.

"What did you do?" she demanded. "What did your brother do?"

His eyes sharpened, and the vein in his neck pulsed faster. She raised her wand at him.

"Tell me," she said.

"We found a way to end him," Serj said, pride surging through his mask of fear. "And not just kill him. We found a way to torture him. Like he's tortured so many. Like he tortured Talem." His voice broke a little when he said his brother's name. "And it's working, isn't it? Why else would you be here?"

"No one deserves that," Melaine said. "No one."

"Why do you defend him?" Serj asked. "Were you too buried in Stakeside garbage to know what was happening in the rest of the city? Do you know what happened, what he *did*, in the war?"

"It's latched onto me now," Melaine hissed, pushing away Serj's words. "That creature. Do I deserve that fate?"

Serj spasmed once as if she'd slapped him in the face.

"No," he said. "You don't." Confusion blighted his usual confidence. "Is the Overlord dead?"

"No," Melaine said. "And he *won't* die. You are going to tell me how to stop it."

"I don't know how to stop it," Serj said. "My brother was the scholar, and he's dead."

"I don't believe you. You know more than you are letting on. I can feel it. I can see it in you."

Serj lifted his chin a little and adopted a taunting, stubborn expression that made her want to punch him in the face.

Instead, she lowered her wand and smiled.

"You know what will happen if you don't tell me," she said. "If this thing is as insatiable as the Overlord says, then it won't stop with him. It won't stop with me. Maybe it will pursue Karina afterward, but between you and me, I think you're more powerful than she is. Besides, she has the freedom to leave Highstrong if she wishes. I doubt she'll stick around because of me. So, what is the Sateless to do? Oh," she said, stroking one of the bars with one finger. "There's a prisoner trapped in the dungeon for its delight. How convenient."

Melaine enjoyed watching the progression of horror in Serj's eyes with her every word. But he blinked it away and caught Melaine's hand fast through the bars.

"Melaine, don't you hear what you're saying?" he said. "Talem said that the Sateless latches onto the most powerful person around. The Overlord had so much magic within him, he was a feast that lasted for months. His body weakens, but the quality of his magic doesn't change in the Sateless's gut. It may not have many meals left in his *lordship*, but each of those meals will be just as divine as the first.

"But your magic is so powerful, Melaine, the Sateless didn't even bother to finish the Overlord before it *had* to taste you. Maybe it will still feed upon him since he's there, but it *wants* you. It's your magic it craves. This proves that you are more powerful than the Overlord. Think of what you could do, especially if you never had to make another lodestone again. You try to be like him, but you're not. You have a conscience. He *never* did. Take his place, Melaine. Rule in his stead."

He pressed his forehead against the bars. "Free me, and the people of Centara will back you as their ruler."

Melaine pried his clammy hand away from hers and stepped back. She was overrun with everything he was saying, but for now, her one goal remained at the forefront. Letting oneself get distracted was yet another way to die in Stakeside. Melaine had come to find that Highstrong Keep was worse.

"The only way I'll free you is if you tell me how to stop the Sateless," she said.

"I don't know how," he said.

Melaine turned toward the door.

"Wait," Serj said. "I...I know that Talem used an Insight to discover how to release it. But I don't know what the Insight was, and he said he destroyed it afterward."

"Destroyed it?" Melaine said, turning halfway back around. "You're sure? Because if it's only empty, I may still be able to learn something from it."

Serj frowned and shook his head against the bars. "He said it was gone. Perhaps he learned how to seal the Sateless back up as well, but clearly, he didn't want anyone else to possess that knowledge. Not even me."

"So, the knowledge died with him," Melaine said, a sinking feeling in her stomach. She looked at the floor. "No, there's got to be something else you can tell me. Even if you don't think it's relevant. Anything at all."

Serj was pensive for a moment. A growing look of quiet anger and grief darkened his features.

"I want to see him before he dies," Serj said, his voice low as he stared through the bars at empty space. "I want to see the Overlord feeble and in agony. I want to look him in the eye and see his hatred for Talem, for me." He looked back at Melaine. "Take me to the Overlord, and I'll tell you what little I know."

Melaine closed her eyes to stop her tears from flowing at Serj's words. In that moment, she hated him, but she needed his help. She nodded and opened her eyes. She lowered the tip of her wand to the heavy iron lock of the cell. Serj stepped back as the lock burst apart, and the cage door swung open.

"Do as I say, or you'll regret it," Melaine warned. Serj held his hands up in defense and nodded. "Move," she said, jerking her wand toward the door. She kept it aimed his way as she walked him to the door and out of the chamber.

"The Sateless is loose," she said as they made their way up the stairs and into the labyrinthine dungeons. "I suggest you stay quiet and on guard."

Serj gave a quick nod and sped up. Melaine kept pace

as she navigated him through the halls, all the while her heart thumping and her wand slick with sweat as she kept her eyes and ears pricked for any signs of the Sateless.

They finally reached the door to the Overlord's—Actaeon's—chambers, and Melaine felt dizzy with relief when she saw Karina still seated at his bedside and heard his voice murmuring from his place on the bed. Karina turned sharply, and her eyes widened as she saw Serj enter the room at Melaine's wand-point.

Karina spread an arm in front of Actaeon.

Serj laughed. "Need your nursemaid to protect you now?"

"Shut up," Melaine hissed.

"Karina," Actaeon said. Karina's mouth thinned in a frown, but she stood at his simple command and stepped to the side. She folded her hands neatly together, her every muscle tight as if she was trying to restrain herself from tearing Serj's throat out in the politest manner possible.

"All right, Serj. You've seen him. Now tell us what you know," Melaine said. She kept her eyes locked on him. She wanted to look at Actaeon, but her brief glance as they entered the room had revealed his condition was worse. She knew, without a doubt, she would break down if she let her fear for his life overtake her.

Serj stared at the Overlord. She had expected cocky satisfaction on his face as he looked over his brother's handiwork, but there was nothing now in his round eyes and slack mouth but quiet horror.

"Serj," she said with a firm tone that made him jump. He looked at her as if he'd emerged from a dark dream.

He swallowed, then rolled his tongue within his dry mouth before he spoke.

"Talem was a Proxy of Lux," he said. "As was my father, Nazir."

Actaeon huffed through his nostrils but said nothing.

"Talem was in deep enough to know certain secrets, secrets that have been concealed by the Luxian Order for centuries. Apparently, some of those secrets had to do with Highstrong. When Talem heard you'd taken up residence here five years ago, not even paying attention to the people you fought a war to rule"—Serj looked Actaeon over with a judgmental curl of his lip—"he started researching as much as he could about the keep. It has quite a history. He wouldn't tell me all of the secrets. Being in the Order prevented him from sharing with... nonbelievers like me. But I was his brother. We shared the same hatred for *you*. He said he knew a way to stop you and that he needed my help. I agreed without question."

"How exactly did you help him?" Melaine asked. "What parts of the secrets could he tell you?"

Serj hesitated, but after another glance at the Overlord's frightful condition—no doubt one that Serj himself wanted to avoid—he continued.

"The biggest thing he told me was that this entire place, Highstrong Keep itself, is an Insight."

"What?" Karina asked in shock. Melaine looked her way, but her attention was captured instead by Actaeon. His eyes were keen as if with sudden understanding, but his brow then knit, and his gaze hollowed. He clutched his stomach, his head and shoulders bowed, and his expression caved into profound guilt. Melaine frowned and looked back at Serj.

"Explain," she said.

Serj licked his cracked lips. "Highstrong Keep was built and occupied by an ancient warlord from the First Era. He was a lovely individual not unlike yourself, my *lord.*"

"Keep talking," Melaine snapped.

"The warlord was called Eylul. He conquered the entire southern lands back then, what was once Dramore and Thillacia. He built this keep as a stronghold for his army and made it his seat of power. And that power, well, he wasn't keen on letting other people take it from him. So, he built Highstrong upon the blood of his enemies. Literally. Countless dead soldiers and slaves drenched this place in their blood, blood that was then used to create the very mortar that seals Highstrong's walls.

"Eylul used the keep as an Insight to store his darkest, most powerful magic. All of the knowledge of his enemies' war tactics and battle spells entered the Insight along with their blood. Eylul fueled his army through the Insight to strengthen them and make them the most ruthless in the land."

"That amount of power is unheard of," Karina said.

"He didn't do it alone," Serj said. "He had help from a sorceress advisor, Desiderata. She was a member of Luxad Obscus, an ancient predecessor to the Luxian religion. That's how Talem found out about all of this. Apparently, she passed down some of her knowledge to people who knew where to look."

Serj shook his head and half-shrugged. "But like I said,

Talem couldn't share most of his secrets with me. He told me he had found an ancient curse buried in the depths of Highstrong Keep. He said the curse involved a creature that would feed on the Overlord's magic. If we unleashed the curse in Highstrong, near the Overlord's presence, he said it would focus solely on him. I...I honestly didn't know it could spread. I thought it would kill you and then leave." Serj's face grew troubled. "Talem never contradicted my assumption, but he didn't tell me the truth either. I trusted him. He was my brother, and I trusted he wouldn't risk anyone else being harmed."

"Sounds like your trust was misplaced," Melaine said. Serj winced but didn't deny her words.

"Did you help him unleash that monster?" Karina asked, her voice quiet but simmering with restrained rage. When he didn't respond, she asked, "How did you do it?"

"Talem needed my help getting him into the keep," Serj said. "He said there was some kind of secret entrance on the cliffside, leading to a hidden chamber beneath Highstrong. Talem was powerful in many scholarly ways, but I have a way of...getting around places. A path of underground rebellion will do that to a person. So, I used my knack for infiltration, found it, and got him inside. The dark wards of the keep didn't extend that far underground. Maybe Desiderata was the only one who knew about the chamber. I don't know. Anyway, Talem didn't let me inside the innermost chamber. But when he came out, he was...triumphant. A little disturbing, too. I...I didn't know he was capable of such a wild..." Serj took a swelling breath and shook away a shudder through one hand as he exhaled.

"I was ready to get out of there, but Talem wanted to see if it worked. He convinced me to try to get inside the keep itself. That's when we must have tripped the wards, and"—he bared his teeth at Actaeon in a vengeful grimace—"he knows the rest."

"So, he caught you," Melaine said. "And Talem."

"And you killed him," Serj said, looking into her eyes.

Melaine didn't speak.

"I killed him," Actaeon said. "Make no mistake about that." Melaine looked back at him. He was speaking only to her, and his dim eyes held compassion and deep remorse. "You were just the tool I used to do it."

Serj chuckled. "See, Melaine? You're just a tool. He admits it."

Melaine frowned, Talem's triumphant laugh and tortured body digging into the conscience that Serj claimed she had. She felt less sorry for Serj's brother the more she heard, but it still made her insides squirm when she thought about her part in Talem's death. No matter what Actaeon said, she felt responsible.

Then, another tortured visage entered her thoughts: a pale, black-veined woman who, nonetheless, seemed to utter words of comfort and warning. When Melaine had spilled the vial of blood magic on the library floor, she had seen a brief vision of the same woman in her beautiful, living prime, wielding a staff. She had looked intense and powerful. Could she have been the ancient sorceress, Desiderata, Serj described? Whoever she was, her whispered words started to compile in Melaine's head and make sense.

Go.

Walls.

It's hungry.

Melaine looked between the three people around her, her searching gaze landing on Actaeon's gaunt face.

"If Highstrong Keep is an Insight, then it might hold knowledge about the Sateless," she said. "Knowledge I can access. Even if Talem thinks he destroyed all traces of knowledge about that monster, there still might be enough residual magic in Highstrong's walls, right?"

"Perhaps," Actaeon said, and for the first time that night, Melaine saw a shred of hope in his eyes.

"Talem made it sound like he used a separate object, not the keep itself, to find out how to unleash the Sateless," Serj said. "I don't know..."

"The walls know something," Melaine said. "They have to. Any clue would be *something* to go on."

"Melaine," Actaeon said, his voice raw. "My study is built over the strongest reserves of residual magic in the keep. I never suspected the castle itself was an Insight, but I've used the residual magic it carries ever since..." He frowned deeply, his clouded look of regret returning. "Ever since my army stayed here before the war. The magic was powerful and potent. I could sense it carried darkness, but I never realized it was steeped in so much blood. I never would have..."

He winced and stopped. Karina placed her gentle hand on the top of his hair in comfort.

"So, my best chance of tapping into Highstrong's knowledge is in your study?" Melaine asked. Actaeon nodded.

"But Melaine," he said between strenuous breaths.

"You must be careful. Learning from residual magic can be dangerous. The knowledge can be fractured, misinterpreted, either consciously or within your very marrow. Sickness isn't the only danger in repurposing magic, Melaine. I haven't had time to teach you all..." He stopped, his chest concaving as if another word would kill him.

"I don't care what the dangers are," Melaine said. "I'll be careful. I'm going to do this."

Actaeon closed his eyes.

"Hurry, Melaine," Karina whispered. Melaine looked at her in surprise. The woman's usual, judgmental disdain was gone. Karina was as desperate for Actaeon's survival as Melaine was.

"Aye," Melaine nodded. She turned to Serj. "You're coming with me."

"What?"

"You think I trust you around him?" she asked with a nod to Actaeon.

"Through the door," Karina said as she pointed to a small door across the room. "Down the stairs."

"No," Actaeon said as if he were only just now able to speak again. "I'm coming with you."

"Actaeon," Karina said.

"Mel...Melaine needs my help. It's dangerous. Please."

"Follow when you can," Melaine said. She knew how awful Actaeon must feel, weak and helpless. For people like her, like him, that was as bad as dying. "Let Karina help you. Serj and I will go first. We can't wait."

Actaeon nodded. Karina frowned but gave Melaine a

grateful nod. Melaine felt a fraction better, knowing Karina at least knew him well enough to understand.

"Come on," Melaine said to Serj.

He looked apprehensive but followed her across the tower. She opened the narrow door and directed him inside before stepping into the dark stairwell herself. She felt a thud in her heart as the door closed behind her. She couldn't stand leaving Actaeon, even for a second. What if he was dead by the time they made it back?

"Hurry up," Melaine said as she followed Serj down the dark staircase.

"Oh, 'hurry up,' she says," he griped. "Never mind that I'm the one going headfirst into the dark when that monster could be anywhere."

"A monster you helped unleash. You don't get to complain."

He scoffed but didn't argue. They kept walking as the staircase spiraled down into the dark. Melaine was reminded distinctly of the Hole, but this was a place Actaeon trod on a daily basis. This was a path to his private study. What awaited her couldn't be bad.

"There's a door here," Serj said.

"Open it."

Serj wiped a sweaty palm on his dirty trousers and then pushed the door open. Either Actaeon had become too weak for a warding spell, or he was still strong enough to have released it from his bedchamber. Melaine hoped for the latter.

She followed Serj into the room.

The Overlord's study was a blend between a workshop, library, and alchemy lab. Melaine marveled over the myriad of puzzling contents in passing. Bottles filled with potions and preserved body parts filled the shelves. Iron and copper contraptions of all kinds stood on tables, looking like sophisticated mechagics of a nature Melaine had never seen. Books with thick, leather bindings were stacked from floor to ceiling against the walls. Some kind of green growth was germinating in a basket, looking like starter for a grotesque variety of sourdough bread. A large cauldron sat in a corner, surrounded by smaller ones like a ring of mushrooms.

In a different corner, a crow cawed at them from within a hanging iron cage. It was thin, as if it hadn't been fed in a long while. Then Melaine noticed it was rotting. Gray skin and dry feathers shed all over the bottom of the cage. Pieces of its skull were visible, and its eyes were cloudy as it stared them down.

"Necromancy," Serj said with a shudder and shake of his head. He picked up a black feather near the empty birdcage with a grimace.

The crow slammed its body against the cage. The door burst open, its warding spell as tattered as the one that had been placed on the tower door.

Serj yelled as the bird flew across the room and out of the door in a torrent of feathers. It flailed and hit the walls of the staircase a few times on its way out.

But Melaine wasn't paying attention to the crow anymore. A yellow rose blossom rested on a table, glowing with glacier-blue magic. It was the rose Melaine had made from repurposed magic after her encounter with the root Insight in the library. Actaeon had kept it, perhaps to study. Yet his magic swaddled each petal with such care that it felt like he viewed it as a treasure to be nurtured and adored.

She reached out to touch a petal but stopped when Serj spoke.

"Melaine," he said. He looked from the crow's feather in his hand to her face with a steadfast gaze. "I know you seem to care for him, Lux knows why. But he is evil." He nodded toward the door where distant cawing echoed through the stairwell. He tossed the ragged feather to the counter. "The world would be better off without him."

"You don't know what you're talking about," Melaine said.

Serj walked forward and leaned close enough for her to feel his breath on her face.

"All you would have to do is knock him down," he whispered.

Melaine startled. She backed away.

"You think you're so noble," she snarled. "Convincing me to murder?"

"No, Melaine, it's different." Serj's voice changed key with desperation. "Talem was innocent. The Overlord has killed hundreds. His Followers have killed thousands."

"He fought for a cause. Just because it's different from yours—"

"*Look* at all of this!" Serj raised his arms to the room around them and all of the evidence of dark experimentation it contained. "How can you defend him?"

Serj swept his arm across the nearest table and knocked all of its contents to the floor. Melaine winced and watched a flurry of parchment and quills and herbal satchels scatter. A heavy mortar and pestle hit the ground with a thunk, and a short pillar candle rolled across the stone.

A large, thick book slammed to the ground with a loud sound of finality. Its black cover opened, a little too delayed to be a result of the fall. The pages flapped fast like crows' wings. Melaine's eyes widened as black scrawls of ink flew from the pages, forming words. They coalesced into paragraphs that inked the walls and coated every object within.

"What did you *do?*" Melaine asked.

"I didn't—! This wasn't me!" Serj said.

Melaine and Serj were the only things in the study unaffected by the crawling black ink. The tables, potion vials, mechagics...all disappeared. Soon, their surroundings didn't even resemble the study anymore. The inked walls expanded into a larger room that was dark and cold. Though words still scrawled on every surface, Melaine began to see solid stone peeking through the gaps of each letter on the walls and floor as if the words were architects with the ability to alter Highstrong at will.

Then more words swirled from the walls in a miniature maelstrom and flew to the center of the room.

They began to form the shape of a *person*.

CHAPTER 11

The ink turned from black into muted colors that highlighted and shadowed the paragraph of a person until a stiff, gruff man stood feet away. More people formed as well, moving clusters of ink that became defined with discernible features. It was as if the illegible words were creating the beings and objects they were enchanted to describe.

Serj looked Melaine's way, but the growing vibrancy of their surroundings soon wrested their attention from each other. The man in the center of the room walked straight toward Melaine. She raised her wand in warning and gasped as he walked *through* her. She spun around and watched him walk over to a row of large, wooden tubs that took up most of the room. Blackened cauldrons of all sizes steeped in the tubs' steaming water.

Several people knelt by the tubs, scrubbing cauldrons with rough wire brushes. There were two middle-aged women and one who looked eighty, an old man, a waif of a teenage girl, and a young boy, who looked no older than five years old. They all scrubbed and polished, washing every cauldron until it was clean and free of grime. Each person was sweaty and dirty and looked like they hadn't eaten a solid meal in ages, if ever. They all had rags tied over their mouths and noses, and Melaine could immediately tell why.

The place reeked of residual magic. Melaine's skin goose-bumped, like insects were crawling all over her. She caught Serj shuddering beside her, sensing it too. Who wouldn't be overwhelmed in a filthy place like this? And where was this? Melaine had only ever heard of having enough sorcerers and alchemists to concoct cauldrons full of potions from tales of the old palace before the war.

"Come on, scrap," said the rough man who had approached the tubs. He headed straight for the little boy and grabbed a fistful of the boy's short black hair. The man had a faded tattoo on his wrist of a black circle filled with a pyramid of three Xs. It was the symbol of Lux, though she doubted he was educated enough to be in the Order itself. She'd heard that the Luxians had plenty of worshipers and sympathizers back before the war, including bigots who only liked to jeer at public executions of so-called blasphemers. A tattoo like that would be hidden these days after Actaeon had tried to eradicate the Luxians. But this man didn't seem to be trying to hide his affiliation at all.

"Scrub harder, or you'll get no supper," the man said.

The boy winced in pain but didn't make a sound. He nodded and squeezed his eyes shut from the extra pull on his scalp. The man sneered and spat into the tub. He let go of the boy and sauntered off to harass one of the women nearby.

Melaine's eyes stayed on the little boy. Tears welled in his eyes, brightening the vivid blue of his irises. He corralled the trembling of his bottom lip and sniffed. He went back to scrubbing a cauldron the size of him. He scrubbed harder, but his cheeks didn't grow pink from exertion. Rather, they turned very pale. Then he coughed. He stumbled back from the cauldron, shaking and then retched on the floor. His symptoms were easy to spot, and the connection was obvious—he was suffering from the res.

The boss laughed. "You'll be cleanin' that mess up as well, boy. I would say you'll get used to it, but that ain't the first time you'll get the shakes in here." He chuckled again and turned back to the other servants.

The little boy finished retching and glared at the boss's back. He wiped the back of his little hand across his chin and heaved himself back up to keep scrubbing the cauldron.

Every scribbled, enchanted word that made up the scene puffed like an octopus's ink and re-formed into a new one. The location was the same, but the people scrubbing the cauldrons were different, save for the teenage girl, who looked to be a full-grown woman who hadn't aged well. Melaine was riled to see the gruff boss of the workers was still there as well, but he was grizzled and slower, holding his chin high in an attempt to hide the hunch of his spine. He walked up and down the line, over-seeing the filthy work as he seemed to have done for years.

"All right, get gone," he said when the last cauldron had been scrubbed and the tubs were empty. "Maybe the servants left you some crumbs."

The workers wiped their hands on their laps and stood in hasty silence, but no wiping or washing would do any good. Their skin had been steeped so long in magical refuse, Melaine doubted it would ever wash off. It was no wonder the servants got to eat before them. Even making lodestones wasn't quite as degrading as the job these poor wretches had. They had signed up to be lepers when they took it, if they had signed up by choice at all.

"There's one left," the boss said as the workers all filed out of a door and disappeared. Melaine looked to the left where the boss had aimed his words. She lifted her eyebrows when she saw a boy she hadn't noticed. He stood up at the boss's words, and Melaine realized he was the same boy from the previous vision, but now he was much taller—he looked to be fifteen or so.

"Get to it, scrap," the boss ordered. He jerked his gray head to a mid-sized cauldron that was drenched in magical refuse. The grit was so thick, Melaine felt nauseous from ten feet away.

The boy gave the boss a single nod, and the boss spat at the boy's feet in return and sauntered back to the door.

"Don't come out until it's done," he said with a half-toothed grin and shut the door behind him.

The boy didn't move until the boss's footsteps were long gone. Then his eyes slipped to the door, and he jerked down the rag covering his mouth and nose as if he'd never needed it at all but just wore it for show.

Melaine had gotten sick from residual magic only

once in her life when she was a young child. Had the same thing happened to him? Did they both possess some quality in their makeup that kept them from coming down with the res twice?

The boy walked with brisk steps to the cauldron and didn't hesitate to grab the foul iron and lift the heavy cauldron from the floor. He carried it with determination to a corner of the room. He set it down and turned his attention to the nearby wall. He ran his fingers along a seam in the stone and pulled a loose brick free. He set it to the side and reached into the hollow space left behind.

Melaine walked closer. She raised her eyebrows when she saw him pull a thin wooden wand from the hole.

She looked down at the rough-hewn wand in her hand. It was the same wand, without question.

"Fuck, it's him," Serj said.

"Shh," Melaine hissed. She took another step closer to the boy. She knelt in front of him, withstanding the overwhelming stink of residual magic to watch the young Overlord's every move.

Actaeon reached into the hole again and pulled out a tangle of twine. When he spread it all out, it resembled three small fishing nets woven together to form a fine mesh. He placed the mesh over the cauldron and secured it into place with three pinpoints of bright blue magic.

Holding the wand in one hand, Actaeon hovered his other palm over the cauldron. Melaine watched as he summoned raw, untamed magic from within himself. It poured easily from his palm, strong and pure with a blue, smoky shimmer just like his eyes.

The magic hovered between his palm and the opening

of the filthy cauldron. He then pushed the magic down so that it mingled with the residual magic beneath the net. Then, without a second thought, he laid his hand on top of the net, pressing slightly down below the lip of the cauldron. Melaine didn't know if she could stomach a pot that filthy, but clearly the Overlord was used to it. He lifted his hand back up, and threads of silver magic passed through the net and clung to his fingers. The magic was pure—filtered directly through the net from the contents of the cauldron. Melaine watched in wonder as the small amounts of clean magic gathered into a glowing silver orb in Actaeon's palm.

He was extracting good magic out of the dregs left behind by lofty palace sorcerers.

Actaeon raised the wand and hovered it over the ball of magic. He slowly turned the wand like a spit roasting meat over a fire. The magic clung to the wand and ran up and down its shaft until it fused with the rough wood. A broom handle—that's what Actaeon had told her in his library. He had whittled the wand from a broom handle.

Now, she knew that Actaeon had not only whittled his own wand, but he had imbued it with magic obtained from the disgusting filth he had been forced to clean his entire life. This was the resourcefulness he had spoken of —the resourcefulness he claimed she possessed as well.

A smile touched young Actaeon's lips. He looked down at the cauldron again. Melaine smiled as well as she realized what must be going through his head. The old boss had thought he was dealing out a horrible punishment when he'd ordered Actaeon to clean the huge cauldron caked in refuse. But in reality, he had given the boy the last load of magic he needed to finish the wand that, as it seemed, he had been working on for months, if not years.

Melaine jumped at the sound of footsteps and voices from the outer door. So did Actaeon. He dismantled the mesh with a single sweep of his hand and stowed both the mesh and the wand back in their hiding place in the wall.

It soon became clear the voices were female, two of them.

"Ugh, I hate comin' down 'ere," one said. "Just passin' by is torture."

"I think I'd kill meself before workin' in a dump like that," the other said.

Actaeon's jaw tightened, but he otherwise made no reaction from his crouch in the corner.

"Let's get it over wit then. Second cellar's that way."

"Always so much work when that fancy King Vasos comes," one said, the voice growing closer as the two women walked in a space which must have been a parallel corridor to the scullery room. "Why's he 'ere this time, yah think?"

"I heard the duke's valet chattin' about cattle land. We need more space, and it ain't like we can use the Wilds. Cows'd die out there. Who knows what might eat 'em?"

"Or they'd just starve," the other woman said.

"Or *maybe* Vasos's just lookin' for some place ta stick his cock," the fellow woman tittered. "Rumor is he's got a lover in this castle. Someone 'e's kept hidden for years."

"The king of Praivalon porkin' someone 'ere? Lucky gal, ain't she?" The woman burst out laughing. "I don't believe it anyway. You're mad if yah believe that horseshit."

The two servant women kept laughing and bickering as their voices faded down the hall. Melaine turned back to Actaeon. He had already stopped paying attention to the women. Seeing that no one was going to invade his experimental lab, he'd retrieved his wand again and was spreading another stretch of magic along its length. When the magic in his palm was spent, a spark lit in his eyes.

He stood, gripping the wand with tense excitement. He aimed it at the cauldron, now filled with useless dregs. He flicked the wand, and Melaine took a step back when the huge cauldron flew across the room and splashed into the largest of the tubs. Two of the hard-bristled brushes started scrubbing the cauldron on their own with the vigor of a Daksun's strength.

Melaine smiled, and so did Actaeon. His eyes were lit with an emotion Melaine was more than familiar with— ambition. Fierce, undaunted ambition.

The scene swirled in a torrent of words and ink, nearly taking Melaine's breath from her lungs as she steadied her feet within a new setting. She glanced at Serj. His eyes were narrowed, his frown deep. Clearly, he was far less impressed with Actaeon's genius than she.

She rolled her shoulder and turned away from him, and then straightened when she saw Actaeon again. He was the same age—this event couldn't have been long after the one they had just seen. But instead of a dark, rank scullery, they now stood outside in bright, white sunshine.

Actaeon lurked at the corner of a back entrance to the grand palace, where Melaine had suspected the visions were taking place. His black hair was still tied in a disheveled knot and tangled down the back of his neck. His clothes were still streaked with stains, and he still reeked of magical refuse, but he raised his wand above his head with confidence. He took a deep breath and pulled some of his inherent magic from his bones, into his skin, and channeled it into the wand. He poured glacier-blue magic from the wand's tip and splashed his body like an overturned bucket of water. The disgusting residual magic washed away.

Like the wand he held, a level of residue still clung to his body, but it was far less and far more manageable. For the young Overlord, the change was so drastic it brought a brilliant, breathtaking smile to his face. Melaine suspected that this was the first time in his life he had been this clean.

Actaeon stowed his wand in his trousers' waistband and hid it under his wrinkled brown shirt. He peered around the corner. The palace courtyard was filled with people. Servants bustled to and fro, arms filled with all sorts of necessities and frivolities alike. It was exactly what one would expect of a king anticipating another king for a royal visit.

It appeared the visiting King Vasos was already here— his soldiers and entourage of servants dominated the courtyard, decked out in their impractical finery.

The palace itself was familiar only in its bone struc-ture. The Overlord's many renovations hadn't yet been installed. No imposing, tall spires reached for the sky, and no wrought-iron railings or deeply arched, stained glass windows adorned the walls and parapets. No modern additions of copper plating gleamed. The old palace's white walls were smooth and straight, with gold-plated domes upon its towers. Round windows were inlaid with clear glass and flanked by ornamental bas-reliefs of gold-gilded flowers. It all looked so innocent, and yet Melaine got an uneasy feeling in her stomach as she took in the sight. She lowered her gaze and focused on the young Overlord instead.

Actaeon's eyes brightened with a sense of adventure. Melaine thought she understood. The world was his for the taking. For once he wouldn't be avoided and treated as the disease-ridden rat he had always been. He could walk among others as somewhat of an equal.

He stepped out into the sunlight and began his exploration of the courtyard. He stayed in the servants' domain, passing behind grocers' carts, walking around people who haggled delivery arrangements, and finally wound up by the stables. Several people shot glances his way during his walk. Some people distanced themselves, but for once, his saturation in residual magic was tolerable enough for no one to vocalize a complaint.

The stables were an obnoxious, grand affair, hosting over twenty of King Malik's finest steeds. Scrolled, golden gilding adorned the eaves and the open doors on either end. The horses inside were glossy, their hair smoother and freer of tangles than Melaine's had ever been.

The air wafting from inside the stables was sweeter than that of any sheep pen or pigsty in Stakeside. Fresh straw was strewn on the floors, sweetening the stink of manure until it was only a background layer in her nostrils.

She followed the curious Actaeon who wandered inside. Serj traipsed behind her in grumpy steps. The light was dimmer upon entry, but Melaine's eyes soon adjusted. A few stable hands milled about far ahead on the opposite end of the long stable, but the area around Actaeon was empty. Then a deep voice and a soft whinny issued from the nearest stall. The stall door was open.

Actaeon stepped closer and peered around the door. His brow furrowed, and then he bit his lip to stop a gasp. He darted back but didn't leave.

Melaine had no chances of getting caught, so she approached the stall without caution and looked inside. A beautiful horse took up most of the space, black as midnight with eyes like stars. A maroon velvet saddle blanket was draped over its back, with the royal seal of Praivalon embroidered on each side in shimmering, golden thread. A man stood next to the steed, speaking to the beast in soft words while brushing its coat.

"That's King Vasos," Serj whispered.

Melaine had never seen a king before, and she was surprised by what she saw. Vasos was relaxed and handsome, though clean and as well-groomed as his fine horse. His black hair was combed back with pomade, and he sported a sculpted mustache and goatee on his strong jaw. He was dressed in a fine riding outfit but wore it in a manner of nonchalance, with his jacket off and his shirt sleeves rolled up to his elbows.

The horse nickered and rolled its head a little. King Vasos laughed and set the brush down on a post. He clapped dust and horsehair from his palms and emerged from the stall.

Melaine glanced back at Actaeon, who still watched from the shadows. He tilted his head a little, and his brow furrowed in confusion. Then he shot his gaze down and yanked up the sleeve of his left arm. He shifted his gaze from his inner forearm to the king and back again.

Melaine craned her neck a little to see Actaeon's arm. A birthmark roughly resembling a small dagger darkened his skin. She looked back at the king. On Vasos's arm, she saw the exact same mark.

Her lips parted as she raced her gaze back to Actaeon. His face showed a rising tide of mixed emotions. What started as a furrowed brow of confusion and blinks of surprise morphed into narrowed, flickering eyes that hinted at dark questions. Blood rushed to his cheeks with indignation, but as he lifted his gaze to look at King Vasos, all conflict receded into innocent hope that sparked in his round, blue eyes.

He swallowed and glanced around the stables behind him. The area was still clear, with all the stable hands at the far end tending to other horses. Actaeon took a quick breath and stepped forward into full view of the king.

King Vasos twitched in surprise. He looked the lad up and down with cold, hard gray eyes. His lip twisted in disgust.

"What are you doing, boy? You reek worse than the stable hands." He flung his hand at the wide-open door. "Go on, before I find your master."

Actaeon froze. His muscles tensed, and the light of hope in his eyes twisted and divided into the emotions of confusion and anger that had threatened to take dominance before. He balled his hands into fists, and when he opened them, he strode forward so fast, Melaine had to dart out of the way.

King Vasos reared back as Actaeon shoved his exposed forearm beneath his gaze.

"Just how many bastards do you have?" Actaeon said.

The king opened his mouth to dismiss the accusation, but his eyes fell on Actaeon's birthmark. His rebuttal disappeared on his lips. After a second of staring, he threw his gaze around the stables. The look of frigid fear in his eyes was acute.

When he saw no one around, he looked back at Actaeon with a ferocity that neither Melaine nor Actaeon expected. Actaeon's eyes widened.

"I hoped it would never come to this," King Vasos hissed. "But you give me no choice, boy."

Actaeon took a step back. His hand hovered over his hidden wand at his side.

"I told your mother she could keep you on the condition that you never knew, but I was right when I knew that secret wouldn't keep."

King Vasos drew a dagger from his belt and lunged. Actaeon dodged and reached for his wand, but the king plunged his dagger into his side and covered Actaeon's mouth to stifle his yell of pain.

King Vasos smiled into the boy's pale face. "Looks like I'll be informing your mother her son had a little accident. If she even remembers you exist."

Actaeon twisted his head away from the king's hand.

"Who is my mother?" he asked in a voice tight with pain. Vasos's smile broadened.

"So sad that you'll only know at the last moment of your young life," he crooned. "Don't worry, boy. Maybe you'll meet Queen Adelasia in whatever poor man's after-life you dream up."

Actaeon's eyes flew wide open. He managed to pull his wand from his belt and shoved its tip into King Vasos's stomach. A fiery burst of magic exploded from the wand and catapulted the king backward. He hit the post of an opposite stall and slid to the floor. Blood ran from the back of his skull, but he was still conscious. He glared at Actaeon and tried to get up, but he fell back with a dizzy swirl of his head.

"Guards!" King Vasos shouted through a wince of pain.

Actaeon jerked away from the wall and raised his wand. Whether or not he had ever intended it to be a weapon, that was its use now. He held his wounded side with his other hand and stumbled out of the stable.

Melaine and Serj ran after him through the castle courtyard. He made his way to a high wall and cringed at the obstacle but then noticed a drainpipe embedded in the stone. It was filthy and barred, but that didn't deter him. He aimed his wand at the bars and peeled them back like a potato's skin. He ducked inside the pipe, but the scene dissolved into scrawls of words and spills of black ink. Melaine stumbled mid-run and barely caught herself against a different wall of familiar black stone.

They were back in Highstrong. Inky words still spun

through the solid fortress, making it clear this was yet another past event in Actaeon's life.

The fortress was filled with people. Together, Melaine and Serj wandered the maze of corridors, passing by rough and lowly groups of men, women, and children who all looked like they could have hailed from Stakeside. They were clean now, their ragged clothes at least laundered, their hair less matted, without the common scratching of lice. Most importantly, they were fed. Even now, many were passing around cups of stew.

Yet, hope commingled with glowers of darkness in their eyes—a malevolence that seemed to seep from the very walls of Highstrong. Melaine had become accustomed to the ancient black magic in the keep's halls. But in this vision, the darkness was amplified as if feeding off of the many people within Highstrong and regurgitating darker versions of them. She passed by a large room filled with a growing mass of farming equipment and bags of seeds, but some of the people inside hefted hoes and pitchforks like experimental weapons. The words on their tongues were muttered with vengeance.

Highstrong was an Insight, created by the First Era warlord, Eylul. Was this a peek into what his ancient blood magic could do? Had the darkness Eylul used to fuel his ancient army influenced Actaeon's recruitments as well?

As if something in the vision were calling her, Melaine followed what felt like a predetermined path through the castle. Finally, she and Serj reached the balcony of the tower now used as Actaeon's chambers, though in the vision, the tower was empty of furniture and trappings, save for two individuals.

One was a big, solid man with the muscles of an ox. He had short, auburn scruff for hair and tattoos covering his exposed back. He'd stowed a wand in a leather holster at his side.

Looking out over the cliffside at the White City glowing in the distance was another man at the balcony's ledge. It was Actaeon.

Melaine walked toward him. He was older now than fifteen, but not by much, possibly nearing twenty. His age and a few years of full meals had filled him out so that he was less gangly. His hair was longer, touching his shoulders. All stains of residual magic were gone from his skin.

He had become the handsome man Melaine recognized—the strong, piercing Overlord of the posters slapped around Stakeside.

"Actaeon," said the muscled, auburn-haired man. "The people are ready. We've got the supplies. They've got their bravery. We're ready to enter the Wilds and find a place of our own. We're ready for the kingdom you promised."

Melaine exchanged a look with Serj. He looked just as confused as she. A kingdom in the Wilds? To not only survive that vast, tangled, dangerous forest, but to tame it? To leave Dramore and the other four kingdoms behind? Had that really once been the Overlord's goal?

"And we will have our place, Yoson," Actaeon said, not turning away from the view. "Soon."

He paused, and Melaine drew close enough to almost feel his warmth and imagine his familiar scent of sandalwood and candle wax that she loved. She peered over the balcony with him and saw the city that she knew as Centara stretched out before them. She could see the southern wall of Stakeside and wondered what her part of town had looked like twenty years ago.

"There's something I need to do first," Actaeon murmured.

The scene dissolved. Night fell, and the White City's palace gates reared to a grand height before Melaine and Serj. They were open but swiftly closing with a heavy groan of chains.

Actaeon stood outside of the gates with Melaine and Serj, sticking to the shadows of the outer wall, alone. He frowned at the gates with confusion and seemed to be stuck in the indecision of whether he should try to slip through the closing gap or not. Melaine guessed that he may have just entered a situation he didn't expect.

Shouts echoed through the gates that had the tone of volleying orders from soldier to soldier. Torches flared to life on the high stone parapets and in the dark palace courtyard beyond the gates. Actaeon backed farther into the shadows.

Then someone new darted around the edge of one gate and slipped into the shadows against the outer wall. Whoever it was wore a black cloak with a hood over their head. They clearly didn't see Actaeon until he had reached out and grabbed their arm, jerking them deeper into the shadows with him.

Melaine gasped when Actaeon yanked the hood off the stranger's head. It was King Vasos.

"You!" King Vasos said, fear wild in his eyes. "You're the one who told them!"

"What happened?" Actaeon asked. His harsh question didn't leave any room for Vasos to doubt that he truly did not know what was going on in the palace.

The king sputtered, "I—King Malik knows. About Adelasia and me. He's got her locked up, and he wants to kill me. You have to let me go."

"Where is she?" Actaeon demanded.

"The East Tower!"

"And you're *running?*" Actaeon grabbed a fistful of the king's shirt.

"No choice!" Vasos said, his voice hoarse with terror. "You should run, too. If they ever find out who you are— what you can do, just like her—the Luxians, Malik...why even come back? I'd have killed you where you stand if... well if the circumstances..."

"I came to say goodbye to my parents," Actaeon said. "I knew you were in the city. I'm going to the Wilds. I may not come back. If I was ever going to see my mother...this might be my last chance. And here you are, running like a coward. And to think, I was going to give you a second chance."

"I—" Vasos started. The voices of the soldiers grew louder. "Please, you have to let me go. They'll kill me. Torture me."

Actaeon stared down into his father's face. Melaine could see it—the darkness of Highstrong boring a hole in Actaeon's eyes. But after a moment, he loosened his hold on his father's shirt and let him go like a piece of rubbish.

"Go," he said. King Vasos nodded and ran without another word.

The gates of the palace closed with a thundering

boom. Actaeon looked at the solid barrier, a glare of hatred overwhelming his handsome features.

The enormous gates erupted in a whirlwind of ink. Words spun around Melaine's head, and Actaeon's voice, speaking the same words, penetrated her mind.

"I tried to stop a war by letting Vasos go," Actaeon said, his voice loud and in the cadence of a speech. "If Malik had killed him, Praivalon would have retaliated without question. But now it seems the unworthy King Malik is bent on revenge. This is an opportunity. Your friends and loved ones who were too afraid to join us in the Wilds will stand with us if they have to choose between a war of kings or a rebellion that brings hope. Together, we can end Malik's reign and stop this impending war. We can bring peace to the White City, and we can create the kingdom we always wanted. A kingdom *here*, not in the Wilds. A kingdom where everyone is fed and clothed and treated with respect. But we have to act now. Will you follow me?"

A roar of voices clattered through Highstrong. Then an explosion of resounding magic, whistling arrows, and clanging swords against pitchforks made Melaine dizzy. The inky words solidified again into coherent surroundings. Melaine and Serj stood once again in the palace courtyard, but this time, it wasn't full of servants preparing for a pleasant royal visit. This time, it was full of fire and screams.

Melaine looked on with exhilaration as she experienced the battle for the White City, the one she'd heard tales of since she was a wide-eyed child. The Overlord's powerful Followers in red cloaks and black hoods swarmed the palace courtyard, blasting enemy soldiers in shining armor with unsurpassable battle spells. Swords clashed while volleys of arrows—their tips dipped in poison and explosive fire magic—rained down from both the palace walls and archers at the gates. Blood splashed from open wounds and sprayed from slashed throats. Red death seeped from bodies like spilled wine. The wails of agony were worse than she'd ever heard from Stakeside brawls or the wretched sick.

Melaine stumbled through the courtyard, her stomach roiling as she clutched her chest and tried to wade through the sickening sights. Salma was right. The glory of battle was a lie. The bright flashes of armor, the majesty of dancing cloaks, and the brilliant luminosity of fiery spells weren't enough to cover up the stench and torture of violent deaths, of lives ended.

A glint of silver armor and a sweeping black cloak tore up the palace steps. Melaine's eyes widened, and she burst into a run after Actaeon. She didn't care if Serj followed.

The palace doors were already open. The Overlord's army—perhaps more of the renowned Followers Melaine had so admired—had penetrated the palace. So, why wasn't he leading them? Why was it only now that he entered his battle-won prize?

Then, she realized. His fierce charge came from the eastern side of the palace. What had he found within the East Tower where his mother was being held prisoner? Was she dead? Had she been there at all or was he still searching?

Melaine surged through the doors and into the entry hall. High ceilings vaulted overhead, but torn banners dangled like hanged men from the rafters. The fine candelabras and silver ornaments placed to welcome the wealthy and powerful were knocked over and scattered. The plush red rug was flattened and covered in the mud of heavy soldiers' boots.

And blood—if one looked closely enough.

She ran farther and stumbled at the sight of a mass of prone bodies—some moving in the wretched twitches of the wounded, some still as the grave they were bound for.

Melaine's stomach lurched. She skirted the wall of the room toward the wide corridor through which she had seen Actaeon disappear. Only a few bodies were strewn within, but there were no living soldiers to be seen aside from Actaeon. He stopped in front of a large, ornate set of white and gold doors. They were closed.

Melaine ran to catch up with him, and she heard Serj's footsteps pound behind her. Actaeon's small hesitation at the door allowed them to catch up. She heard voices from the other side.

"Do it, my liege," someone said from within. "Rid the world of this adulteress, this blasphemous—"

"Malik," a different voice said—a woman's. "You don't have to listen to him. Nazir has trickled poison into your ears for so long."

"The only one poisoning me is *you*, Adelasia," a third person, presumably King Malik, said. "You betrayed me."

"She contains vile power in her bloodline, my liege," said Nazir, his voice a growing, seething hiss with every word. "It was a blessing she never bore you an heir, for she isn't fit to spread her blasphemy. Now, you know she's been intermingling with other kingdoms who hold dangerous, lesser ideals. Kill her, my liege. Wed a new queen who will be faithful to you and won't carry disgusting, heretical magic in her bones that could taint the entire kingdom."

"Father," Serj said. His face was slack with horror and dismay.

"What?" Melaine said, but she jolted as Actaeon aimed his wand at the doors and bombarded them open.

Melaine had never seen a more opulent room. It put every room within Highstrong Keep to shame. The vaulted ceilings were painted with lofty, extravagant murals of heroic deeds from royalty past. Each rib was coated in shining gold, sculpted with golden flourishes and silver leaves. The walls were of white marble, lined with columns that were gilded with silver and gold scrollwork. Arched indentations in the walls housed decadent objects on display—busts of nobility, sculptures of graceful animals, porcelain vases—many of which Melaine suspected contained Insights of immense value.

The floors were gleaming, polished marble, and a lush, purple carpet ran from the door where she stood to a lustrous golden throne sitting upon a dais that anchored the room.

Actaeon lunged inside. She darted after him, followed closely by Serj.

King Malik stood beside the throne with the most beautiful woman Melaine had ever seen, trapped in his arms. Her back pressed against his chest as he held a dagger to her breast. Her brown hair was wavy with half-unraveled braids, her blue eyes watery with tears. But her expression was resolute and held bold courage as she faced her imminent death.

The third man in the room was of dark brown complexion and had his textured blond hair swept back in a ponytail so that all of his confident, sneering features were on display. He looked like an older, sharper version of Talem, and he wore the same Luxian symbol on his blue and white robes. His symbol was freshly embroidered and threaded with lustrous gold, ornate and shining compared with Talem's faded relics.

Both Nazir and King Malik turned with sharp attention to the door as Actaeon ran at them, wand raised.

Malik plunged his dagger into Queen Adelasia's breast.

"No!" Actaeon yelled. He blasted Malik away from the queen with a golden explosion of magic that Melaine recognized as the rathmor tooth Insight's spell she'd learned, but his was far more intense than any she'd been able to perform. Malik hit the back wall and fell to the floor.

Actaeon rushed to Adelasia. She looked up at him with round eyes that matched his own. They were soft in a way that Actaeon's only became when he looked at Melaine.

Adelasia's face paled, and her eyes dimmed as blood leaked from the deep wound in her chest. Actaeon slipped his hand under her head.

"Actaeon," she mouthed, but her voice was no more than a choked sound.

Actaeon's grip on his wand loosened. "Mother," he said.

Adelasia's mouth turned in a small, soft smile. Then she was gone. Her body went limp in Actaeon's hold.

King Malik stirred by the wall, struggling to stand.

"You murdered her," Actaeon whispered. Malik stiffened. The king swallowed and tried to cover his twitching fear with a tall stance of fortitude.

"To keep her from a grisly death at your hands," he countered. "You're the would-be conqueror, are you not? The leader of this messy...this brutal..."

"You murdered her!" Actaeon shouted, raising his wand and pointing it straight at the king's heart.

"So that I could have the satisfaction of ending her before you had the chance! She shamed me," Malik said. "She is my queen, and I can do with her whatever I want. She deserved worse."

He looked down at Adelasia's vacant face. Blood dripped from the dagger in his shaky hand.

Salma was right when she'd spoken of the queen. Adelasia was beautiful, with an innocent yet strong aura that would never again shine or dance down the streets of the White City with flowers and music. Melaine had seen plenty of the Stakeside poor waste away in the streets or get stabbed in the dark. She'd always felt a sympathy that she'd tried to stifle, but she'd never felt it so acutely as she did now. It seemed such a horrible waste for a woman like that to die.

Blood continued to bloom from Adelasia's heart like rose petals. Her dress was light blue satin, embroidered with dainty silk flowers, the color of a sunbeam. The style and rich quality of the bodice and lace-trimmed gown matched many of the dresses Melaine had worn since arriving in Highstrong. She took a shaky breath, feeling like a tiny but strong thread tied her to the perished woman in Actaeon's arms along with a hope that maybe, one day, Melaine could be as strong and self-sacrificing as she.

"Now, *conqueror*, leader of the rabble," King Malik said, dagger raised. "Are you going to kill me and take my throne or not?"

"You don't deserve to be there," Actaeon said. "Just like Vasos doesn't deserve to rule his kingdom. Cowards and murderers, both of you. My mother deserved better. Your people deserve better, Malik." He stood and took a step toward the king, wand still aimed. "You failed them. Just like you failed her." His voice choked up once as he glanced at his mother.

Malik raised his dagger as if its narrow blade could protect him from Actaeon's wand and wrath.

A shout and loud bang erupted from the corridor beyond the throne room. The sounds of battle were growing closer. Actaeon flung a spell at the throne room doors. They slammed shut, and a heavy magical bar appeared to keep them in place.

"You've earned a long, torturous death, Malik," Actaeon said, returning his attention to the king. "But I would rather keep this between us. I hope your blessed Luxian afterlife brings you everything *you* deserve."

Actaeon sent a new powerful blast of magic at the king. This time, an unfamiliar spell hit with an invisible impact. King Malik's high-pitched scream tore at Melaine's eardrums as he writhed in intense agony, but his pain didn't last long. He fell to the ground and rolled off the dais. He lay still, his eyes vacant and his face frozen in a tortured mask.

"They're dead," Nazir said. Melaine and Actaeon looked his way. Melaine had forgotten the Luxian advisor was still in the room. "You killed them both." His voice rose loudly enough to penetrate the doors, so all beyond could hear. "Murderer!"

"No, Father," Serj said, watching his father with soft disbelief. "Lies. You knew the truth."

Actaeon raised his wand, but Nazir cast a speed spell of his own and fled through a side door. The door swayed, un-warded, but Actaeon looked too weary and overcome by grief to follow. He took the few steps necessary to reach his fallen mother again. His shoulders slumped, and then he collapsed to his knees.

He looked like her. He had the black hair and birthmark of his father, but the rest of his features were all from his mother.

"I know you banished me to the scullery to hide me," he murmured. "I know you did it to save me from my father. And from him." He tilted his head at the fallen King Malik. "But I wish you would have told me. Spoken to me. Just once."

He lifted her head off the floor and onto his lap. He stroked her cheek. "I'm sorry I didn't come in time."

Tears watered Melaine's eyes, and one fell as she looked in surprise at a woman who emerged from the shadows of the throne room, where she must have been lurking in secret the entire time.

"Actaeon," she said.

Actaeon startled and looked up, drawing his wand.

The woman held up her hands in defense, showing they were empty. He kept his wand trained upon her but didn't stop her from taking a few steps closer.

"My name is Karina," she said. "I am...was Queen Adelasia's handmaiden."

Melaine's lips parted. The woman spoke true—she was younger, for sure, but there was no mistaking her for Karina.

"I spoke with her not an hour ago," she said, fighting a tremor in her voice. "Before they moved her here from the East Tower. Actaeon, she asked me to tell you how much she loved you and that the only reason she ever parted with you was to protect you—from King Malik, King Vasos, and the Luxian order."

Actaeon frowned deeply, his eyes narrow as he searched Karina's face for truth.

"I saw you the night you allowed King Vasos to live as he escaped the city," she said. "I knew what I was risking, but I told Queen Adelasia what I saw. She told me everything, Actaeon. She told me that you are her son. And I kept her secret. I would never betray her for the world.

"She knew it was you who led the army into the city today. She told me, should she die before she could speak with you, that I was to convey how much she loved you. That I was to beg for your forgiveness on her behalf for never telling you the truth. And that I am to look after you as she never could. Those were her last words, Actaeon, before the king took her from the tower. I thought I could follow her here and stop him, but..." Karina's voice caught in her throat, and she cleared it to keep her composure.

"I should have been here," Actaeon said, seeming too tired to question Karina. He lowered his wand and dropped his hand to his side. He looked back down at his mother's face. "I should have gotten here sooner."

Karina stepped forward and rested a hand on Actaeon's shoulder. He didn't cast her off.

"Actaeon," Karina said. "You did all you could. She would be proud of you. She always was. She believed you were and would always be the rightful heir to the throne. She chose to never bear another child who could challenge your place. In one form or another, this is always what she wanted for you, Actaeon."

Actaeon shuddered and was silent. Karina watched him for a moment and then squeezed his shoulder and stepped back.

"Now," she said, adopting the strict demeanor Melaine was so familiar with. "You have work to do. You've just won a war, Actaeon. You have a throne to sit upon, a city to rebuild and maintain, and people who will follow you. I urge you to remember that you have convinced your people to despise royalty. I am now the sole person in this kingdom who knows who you are—that you come from a royal bloodline and that you did not kill Queen Adelasia. Given the circumstances," she paused, convincing herself as well, it seemed, "I think we ought to keep it that way."

Actaeon looked up at her in confusion, but then a light in his eyes dimmed, and a mask as hard and cold as stone took its place. He nodded once and laid his mother's head gently down to the floor. He stood and looked at the throne.

He stepped over the dead king and onto the second

level of the dais, running his hand along the throne's golden arm. He didn't wear the glorious look of triumph Melaine had always imagined when she'd pictured this moment in his war. He sat down, pressing his wand, coated in residual magic, against the gold under his hand.

"Open the doors," he ordered Karina. She gave a grim nod and obeyed.

The scene blackened with ink, which then sucked Melaine in a strong pull that brought her back to reality and knocked her off her feet. She cried out as she hit hard stone. When she looked up, Karina—the *real* Karina—grabbed her arm and yanked her up with painful force.

Melaine caught a glance of the open book on the floor of Actaeon's study, and she saw Serj crumpled against a wall before all of her attention was forced onto Karina's furious face.

"You prying minx," Karina said. "You're supposed to be finding a way to save Actaeon, and here you are wasting precious time on things that don't concern you. To think, I almost trusted you."

"Karina," Actaeon said with more force than Melaine had heard in quite some time. Karina released Melaine's sleeve, but anger still flared in her eyes.

"It fell off the table," Melaine said. "The book. We didn't open it on purpose."

Karina scoffed. Melaine winced. She knew it did sound like an excuse.

"You dare pry into his personal things—"

"Karina, stop," Actaeon said. His voice was weaker this time. Melaine and Karina both looked at him. He was leaning against a wall, pale and haggard. Karina had laid a warm cloak over his shoulders, but it looked over-sized and heavy as lead as it hung from his skeletal frame.

His eyes were on the book that held his memories, still open like a wound with painful, mangled insides. "There's no point in secrets any longer." He looked at Melaine. "I'm relieved that someone knows. Before..."

He tried to take a step but staggered. He found a wooden chair and sank into it, holding his body upright with both hands on the edge of the seat. His face beaded sweat and his eyelids fluttered with pulsing dizziness.

"No," Melaine said. She darted to him and knelt at his feet. She took his hand and rested her other on his knee.

"Please," she said, tears burning her eyes. "Don't give up. You're the first person I've ever been terrified to lose. The only one I've let in that deep. Dammit, Actaeon, don't make me lose you."

"You can't mean that," he said.

"I do," she said. "It's stupid, I know. But...I've always fought to survive. And now, I...I don't think I can live without you."

Actaeon laughed, harsh and bitter. Melaine's brow pinched, and she reached up and pressed her palm against his cold cheek, digging her fingernails into his stringy hair. He met her eyes, and she didn't budge.

Actaeon silenced. His stone visage was cracked with deathly fractures, worry and exhaustion lines, and shrunken skin shriveled from the Sateless's teeth. But a light in his eyes, once smothered, now sparked.

Melaine nodded and released him. She let out a slow breath through her lips and stood.

"That book," Serj said, shoving himself off the floor. He looked shaken. "That can't be true. You write lies."

"Insights can't hold lies," Karina said, nodding to the book. "Even the simplest of idiots know that. You may not be worthy of the truth, but you have it, I assure you."

Serj leaned against the wall. He stared at the floor.

"I knew my father was...a fanatic. But I never thought he was capable of..." He shuddered and ran a hand through his wild blond hair before looking at Actaeon. "So, you fought against the corruption of King Malik's reign...the Luxians." He cleared his throat as if trying to shake himself into reality. "And then Vasos. Your father. He attacked Centara anyway, didn't he? He couldn't stand seeing you on the throne."

"And he thought I was weak—that my reign was weak," said Actaeon. "Vasos attacked with a massive army, but my Followers and I fought them back, taking on most of the fight so the people wouldn't have to."

"You were outnumbered in soldiers, then," Melaine said. "You had to resort to ruthless tactics to win."

Actaeon nodded, his mouth a grim line.

"Everything you did was to protect your people," she said.

"He didn't have to commit the atrocities he did," Serj said. "He chose that path. That's on him."

Actaeon smiled, a wry lift of the corner of his mouth.

"My only regret is that I didn't get to kill my father myself," he said. "He died outside the city gates. Everything else"—he looked hard at Serj—"*everything* else, I did for the sake of my people. I wanted our city to be perfect—an ideal, peaceful place without the taint of religion or dictatorship. That's why I instigated the overseers so I wouldn't be the sole ruler. I cut us off from other kingdoms, so war wouldn't strike, and their corruption couldn't bleed into Dramore. I fought for our economy to be self-reliant, so we would never have to depend on the evil whims of another tyrant to get resources. I sought to protect everyone."

"By letting your corrupt overseers lead?" Serj said. "You fought so hard, sitting in your study, playing with magic."

Actaeon winced.

"I made a mistake in trusting them," he admitted. "I never...wanted to rule. I wanted to prove myself. I wanted to help the less fortunate. I wanted to weed out corruption. But the everyday tasks of ruling..." He looked up at Melaine.

"I am so sorry," he said, tears watering his eyes. Her heart ached for him, he looked so mournful. "I won a war so children would never have to grow up as you did, so no one would ever know the hunger and squalor you've endured. And I failed. I thought we could be independent, but we don't have the means to feed everyone, to clothe everyone. And the more I realized that my idealistic kingdom might never exist, the further I slipped away—the more I let my overseers manage Dramore. I convinced myself they could do a far better job than I could. Please. Forgive me, Melaine."

"You ask for her forgiveness?" Serj jeered. "And what of my brother? Can you ever ask Talem for forgiveness?"

Actaeon laughed. "I would kill Talem again if given the chance."

"You—"

"Your family," Actaeon said, his voice rising like a crackle of lightning, "is more responsible for the fall of this city than I. Your father urged Malik to murder my mother. And then he ran. Nazir spouted lies about me and rallied a fanatical religion and a rebel force, urging them to lurk in the filth of the sewers instead of benefiting from my reign. Even at the beginning while I was still doing some good."

"He died in those sewers," Serj said, his teeth grinding as he struggled with the words. "You murdered my father as much as you murdered Talem."

"And you've taken your revenge," Actaeon said, lifting an idle hand into the air. "Be at peace, dear, noble rebel. You've succeeded in your quest to foil the evil sorcerer. You've even done the virtuous deed of risking martyrdom, dying for your cause."

Serj's face flickered with fear.

"No one has to be a martyr if you two stop bickering," Melaine said. "It's time to focus on what's happening now."

Serj swallowed. "Yes," he said. He took a breath and pushed himself off the wall. "Let's send this monster back where it came from. Maybe we'll get lucky, and the Sateless will take you with it, my lord."

Melaine sighed in exasperation.

"Melaine," Actaeon said. He nodded toward a stone structure at one end of the room that looked like a well, covered by a thick stone lid. "That's a purifier for residual magic. If it's possible to find what ancient knowledge this castle holds, the magic channeled from below should be the best place to look."

Melaine nodded and walked to the purifier. She braced her weight against the stone lid and shoved it aside. It fell to the floor, propped against the edge of the well.

Inside, a copper contraption took up the entire round opening. It was a much larger and more sophisticated version of the same process that Actaeon had used to filter magic when he'd worked in the palace scullery as a boy. A fine, copper mesh covered the opening, centered by a delicate, pointed spire of copper aimed at the ceiling. She could feel the cool, pure magic filtering through the mesh and channeling through the spire in a swell that exhilarated her senses. But that wasn't what she needed. She needed to reach beneath the purifier to find the refuse the well contained.

She reached into the well and grabbed two copper handles on either side of the circular mesh. She lifted the contraption and placed it with care on the floor.

Residual magic seeped into her skin from the hole. She fought a shudder and gripped the stone lip of the well.

"That's disgusting," Serj said. Melaine ignored him. She closed her eyes and rolled the sharp, residual magic off her skin and felt it shift into a more palatable tingle. She then reached inside the deep, black well and focused all of her energy on gleaning knowledge from its depths.

There had to be something left. If Serj was to be believed and this entire castle was a giant Insight, then it had to hold knowledge of what went on inside its walls over the centuries. If the Sateless had once crawled inside in ancient times, then Highstrong Keep had to remember.

The dry well was so dark, she could barely see the outlines of her outstretched fingers. She tensed as she heard a skittering noise below. It had to be rats living in the walls. They didn't mind residual magic in the least.

She tried to renew her concentration. The filtered magic was *too* clean to hold any lingering knowledge, but for the filter to work at all, there had to be a little useable magic still embedded in the residual waste. She waited and focused and sighed in small relief as she felt little tendrils of power within the well, weak and ancient but cleaner than the surrounding refuse of the pit. She spread her fingers wide, and more tendrils of latent magic laced between them.

A floating image massaged her brain. It was hazy, like a dream, but when she focused on the blurred outlines, dim highlights, and deep shadows, she started to make the image out. Then she stiffened and held onto the solid stone well with one hand as the haze altered into a horrific scene.

The Sateless was gorging itself on a soldier in the courtyard of Highstrong Keep. The soldier wore ancient armor like the spirits that roamed the castle grounds with their horrid whispers. He lay faint and withered on his back, the Sateless's long feeding tube deep in his throat. He was already too far gone to help. Melaine winced when she realized he looked as weak as Actaeon did now. The soldier died before her eyes.

The Sateless extracted its black proboscis from the soldier's throat with slurping speed and jumped to another soldier who screamed, sword raised. The creature knocked the man down with a clatter of armor and latched onto his mouth with its sharp teeth. Its throat undulated as the man's scream was stifled by the feeding tube. The Sateless began to suck out the man's magic with its insatiable swallowing gullet.

Melaine pushed the images away, but then she forced herself to rein them back. She had to know what happened next. She needed to find out how Desiderata had finally banished the Sateless from Highstrong.

The Sateless leapt from soldier to soldier with lustful speed. It fed on them without mercy. Melaine couldn't understand how it was draining them of magic so quickly when it had taken months to feed on Actaeon. Perhaps the beast knew when the castle had been filled with soldiers it could feast without pause. But with only four people in Highstrong now, it didn't know how long its meals would last and meant to stretch them out so it could survive long enough to decide where it would find its next batch of victims.

Or perhaps, in the ancient days, it had fed on enough victims to become more powerful than it was now. Would the Sateless grow stronger if they couldn't stop it?

Melaine shuddered as she watched it continue to feed and kill. The castle grounds were filled with dead soldiers, most drained of magic from the Sateless's greed, but some were drenched in blood, having been killed by others or perhaps themselves in the chaos.

"It's hungry!" a shaky voice said. Melaine recognized it right away as the ghostly voice of the woman who had

tried to warn her of danger throughout her time in Highstrong.

The living soldiers then seized and stared at the sky, as if a puppeteer had yanked on their strings. Their mouths opened as one, and then they screamed and shouted in chaos, speaking a language Melaine didn't know, but it had become familiar by now. It was the sound of fear and sorrow from the urn she had shattered her first night in the keep. She watched in horror as the soldiers crumbled to ash. Billowing clouds blew into the keep in a single, controlled gust.

Yet the ash carried lustrous sweeps of their magic—their essence—with it. Melaine suspected the destination. Now she understood that the living soldiers had been placed in the urn for protection. The caster of such a powerful spell must have been Desiderata. Had she known they would be trapped for centuries? Had Melaine deprived them of peace by releasing them too early, while the Sateless still prowled the keep?

Melaine's questions dissolved as she felt the warmth of the library—the same comforting feeling she got whenever she placed her hand upon its large, wooden doors. A shining golden beam of magic blinded her inner eyes and seemed to shoot into her very marrow, and then she heard the same ghostly woman's voice echo, "*Come to me!*"

Melaine's vision catapulted to the library tower, where the Sateless burst through the doors. The monster stood upright on its two clawed, hind legs. It hunched its knobby shoulders, its gaunt chest a panting cavity. A vicious smile was fixed on its face, and its long, black proboscis writhed between its razor-sharp teeth like a great worm. More of its feeding tubes wriggled from its ribs, all reaching for the tall, lean sorceress from Melaine's visions—the ghost, beautiful and whole—Desiderata, standing in the center of the library.

Desiderata wore a white robe that glistened with fresh blood. The blood flowed down to her feet and seeped into the stone floor. Her hands trembled around the shaft of a long, polished staff that she held upright before her. Her eyes were wide, and her jaw clenched with fear, but she held her ground.

Behind her, a man in full, regal battle armor cowered. He wore a helmet adorned with jewels in the shape of a crown, and Melaine could only assume he was Eylul, the evil warlord. A man who had won countless battles and killed countless enemies was terrified by the monster that pursued him.

"Go!" Desiderata said.

Eylul bolted up the spiral stairs to the library balcony. He leapt from the window. Melaine heard the telltale whoosh of a landing spell to slow his fall so he could escape. She had never seen Eylul's ghost in Highstrong. Perhaps the warlord had—unjustly—survived.

Desiderata gathered magic to perform a second spell. Melaine could *feel* the sorceress dredging magic from her bones to bring it to the surface of her skin as if she were facing down the Sateless in Desiderata's place. Whatever spell the sorceress was about to perform would be incredibly powerful if she needed that much magic. Melaine watched, knowing that this was it—the spell that would seal the Sateless and defeat it.

The Sateless lunged at Desiderata.

A loud scrabbling noise and a vivid echo of the Sate-less's screech punctured Melaine's vision.

She opened her eyes and stared down into the deep, black pit of the well, the vision replaced by reality. She still couldn't see anything but the faint outline of her fingers and the blackness beyond. But the magic within pulsed. Some force pulled at her magic from below, but it couldn't hold on.

Melaine gasped as she saw two gleaming red eyes in the dark, staring up at her.

She screamed and darted back from the well.

"Insight," she said. "Insight!"

"Melaine?" Serj asked.

"Seal the well!" Actaeon said, his voice raspy and horrified.

Melaine scrambled to the stone lid and tried to heave it back onto the well. Serj jumped to help her. Together, they pushed the heavy lid back onto the pit. They heard long, hard scratches scour the inside of the lid. Then they heard a wrenching screech of frustration, and all was quiet.

"Was that *it?*" Serj asked, stammering. "The Sateless?"

"Yes," Actaeon said. "Melaine, you said 'Insight.'"

Melaine nodded, wobbling to her feet. "Desiderata—she was in the library. She sealed the Sateless inside an Insight. I couldn't see which one or what kind of object, but I don't know if that matters."

"It shouldn't," Actaeon said. "Not if the casting is powerful enough."

"So, we need to bait it," Serj said. "We use the Over-lord as bait, and then we seal it inside an Insight."

"We should use *you* as bait," Karina said. "You brought this upon us."

Serj opened his mouth like a caught fish.

"Coward," Karina said.

"We can't waste time," Melaine said. "We have to get to the library. That's where Desiderata sealed it before, and I think...I think she might still be there to help us. I think that's our best chance. Karina? Help him."

Karina didn't protest at Melaine ordering her around. She hurried to Actaeon's side and helped him stand.

"I'll keep it distracted while you get there safely," Melaine said.

"Melaine—" Actaeon started.

"Go!" she ordered. Karina coaxed him to the door.

"Be careful," he said, looking into Melaine's eyes with soft desperation. It didn't match the selfish plea of a beggar in the streets like Melaine was used to seeing. Actaeon looked at her with the same terror she'd often felt when in possession of a hard-won Insight that she feared would be stolen, the terror of losing something deeply cherished. She nodded.

"I will."

She placed her hands on the closed stone purifier and pushed a bit of magic through the lid. She heard another clawing scrape from inside the pit.

"I'll meet you there when it's been enough time," she said. She focused on the lid as the others made their way from the study and walked at Actaeon's slow pace up the stairs.

She listened hard but heard only silence. She pressed her hands down harder and seeped a little more magic through the stone. The Sateless ran its thick, sharp claws along the inside.

Melaine shivered but felt her confidence grow. She may not have seen the final glimpse of Desiderata's ancient spell, but if the castle was an Insight and was filled with other Insights within the library and the Overlord's study, then it proved the Sateless couldn't feed on the magic that Insights housed. So far, she'd only seen evidence that it could feed on the magic of humans or human corpses. If they could succeed in sealing it within an Insight as Desiderata had once done, the foul beast wouldn't be able to gnaw its way out.

CHAPTER 12

The scrabbling of claws stopped. The stone lid was still heavy on the purifier well, but Melaine knew the Sateless wasn't contained in the well alone. The walls were its pathways, the corridors of the keep its roads. It would soon find another way to reach her or the others.

Surely, enough time had passed for Serj, Karina, and Actaeon to reach the library. If Melaine was going to reach the tower as well, now was the wisest time to make her move. She lifted her hands off the stone lid and bolted for the stairwell. She ran up the spiraled stairs into Actaeon's private chamber and then raced down the hallway toward the library.

Her heart hammered as scratching claws and heavy pacing chased after her, but she didn't know where the sounds were coming from. She only knew that she couldn't turn around or slow down. She darted around corners and through shadows, passing under the eerie green torches of everflame. Finally, she reached the warm, comforting doors of the library.

"It's me!" she called when she felt a warding spell in place. "Let me in!"

The doors swung open. She dashed inside and slammed them shut behind her. Karina cast a new warding spell as soon as Melaine was inside.

Melaine caught her breath. "Actaeon?"

"Here," he murmured. He was still alive, though barely able to stay upright in the chair that held his frail body. She rushed to him and took his cold hand.

"What object are we going to use for the Insight?" she asked, not taking her eyes from Actaeon's sallow face as she addressed the others.

Serj stepped forward into her peripheral view, his shoulders hunched in chagrin. He held out a lock of his thick blond hair, which he had twisted together into a little rope.

"I remembered," he said. "Talem told me the spell that once sealed the Sateless took a *part* of the caster. Now that we know we can seal the creature in an Insight, well, I figure this makes sense. And if the Overlord is the bait, and we're worried about the Sateless jumping to you next, Melaine, then both of you will be distractions, so...I suppose I'm the caster. And, uh..." He scowled at the floor. "As much as I hate him"—he twitched his head at Actaeon—"I'm partially responsible for this whole mess. It's the least I can do."

"Damn right it is," Melaine said. She was surprised at Serj's genuine expression of guilt. For all his cocky words and bias, it seemed he had a conscience after all.

"Let's see it done," Actaeon said. Melaine doubted she would have heard his words had she not been so close.

She nodded to Serj. His face was ashen, and his hand shook, but he took a few determined steps back.

"I've made Insights before," he said, feigning confidence with the return of his light smile and a casual shrug. "This can't be that different, eh?"

"Just don't mess this up," Melaine said. She hated knowing that ultimately, the ritual was out of her hands. It was all up to Serj now.

"Do you think it'll know what we're trying going to do?" Serj asked.

"Its only thoughts are on feeding," Actaeon said. A shudder rolled through his body. Melaine wanted to squeeze his hand for comfort, but she feared his brittle bones might break.

"Open the doors, Serj," Melaine said. She took Actaeon's cheeks in her hands. "Stay strong," she whispered. He managed to raise his hand and rested it upon hers, but he didn't answer. His eyes spoke a goodbye.

Melaine couldn't stand it. She pulled away and stepped behind him. She backed up a few paces, ready to leap forward the instant the Sateless attacked. Its draw would be to Actaeon first, but as soon as it realized she was there...

Melaine nodded to Serj, who was braced against the door. He shook less and stood taller as he soaked in the door's warmth, as if the soothing comfort of the ancient wood was infusing him with courage. He clenched his fist around the twist of his hair, grabbed the door handle, and pulled.

The dark hallway was empty. Its depths seemed to stretch on forever as blackness obscured all detail.

Melaine's breaths were tight and shallow as she waited for any sign of the Sateless to appear.

Then she heard a claw drag across stone. It drilled at her ears and drew goosebumps on her skin. She wanted to rush to Actaeon and stand in front of him, but she had to wait.

Another claw scraped the stone floor, and then another, followed by the low, methodical shifting of something heavy. It sounded like the creature was dragging itself toward them. Melaine had interrupted its last feeding on Actaeon. Was it weak with hunger?

The sounds of a dragging body and claws clacking grew louder. Karina slipped a wand from a deep pocket in her dress and held it tight with readiness, but she maintained her composure and her planned position in the farthest corner from all the others. Serj shook like he was standing on a heaving fault line by the open edge of the door.

The claws' scratching grew faster, as if the Sateless had caught a scent it was eager to track. Louder, louder the scratching came until Melaine saw movement in the dark hallway. Then two red, shining eyes glinted at her from the blackness.

The Sateless shrieked and ran to the library with fierce speed. Its lean, gangly limbs made it run with a crooked, unnatural gait. Its gargoyle face distorted in a snarl, baring its rows of sharp, deadly teeth. But it wasn't the teeth Melaine feared; it was the magical sucking ability of that mouth that terrified her. She could see the long, black tube it used curled up in the back of its throat, opening.

Melaine couldn't see Actaeon's face, but his entire

body was stiff as a corpse. Yet he held his head high, as dauntless a warrior as she had always imagined, facing the horrific creature in what he believed was his imminent death.

But she wouldn't let that happen.

She forced herself to hang back behind a shelf. The Sateless ran toward Actaeon and leapt upon him with voracious speed. It knocked over Actaeon's chair and cradled his head with one of its massive hands, stroking his forehead with one sleek, black claw as if the man was a babe. Then it lowered its mouth to Actaeon's, ready to feed.

"No!" Melaine yelled. She bolted out from behind the shelf and planted her feet in a solid stance. "Me. You want me, now."

The Sateless snapped its head up and looked straight at her. Its ragged, pointed ears perked. Its eyes lit up and then sharpened, fierce and predatory with a sinuous smile. It slid its claws away from Actaeon's head, leaving a trail of blood behind. Its every muscle coiled like it was about to pounce.

Melaine's eyes flew to Serj. An aura of jade-green light surrounded him as he clutched his lock of hair in his fist. He approached the Sateless from behind, each step stiff as he pushed through the muck of fear. Clearly, it was taking every ounce of courage he possessed to keep his spell going.

The Sateless sprang off Actaeon. Melaine screamed as the creature pummeled her to the ground. Its weight crushed her, and it snagged her hair in its claws and held her head down just as it had with Actaeon. She wriggled in its grasp, desperate to get away before it latched its fetid mouth on hers, but she could barely move.

Then a bright green light forced her to close her eyes. The Sateless's weight lifted a fraction, and she felt the heat of its face snap away.

Melaine's ears rang from the high, piercing pitch of the beast's scream. She forced her eyes open and saw Serj standing over the Sateless's shoulder, holding his lock of hair as if offering it to the beast.

The Sateless dragged its fierce claws down Melaine's shoulder and chest. She screamed as her skin split. The Sateless shrieked again as it twisted around and snarled at Serj, but it was too late to attack. Serj's jade magic flashed again, and the creature dissolved into a black vapor that spiraled into Serj's lock of hair, twisting ever tighter into the strands. Then Serj stumbled. He winced and doubled over like he'd been punched in the gut. The vapor shivered and bucked within the lock of hair.

The Sateless was fighting the spell.

Melaine's eyes widened as the lock of hair shredded and burst apart, propelling the vapor away. The vapor flew off in multiple directions and thickened and billowed like heavy, black smoke around the library. Each puff split from the others and started darting from one shelf to another as if they were each sentient creatures of their own.

The Sateless's shriek echoed through the tower, but it was a chorus of many screams. The individual swirls of vapor all whooshed toward the balcony window. They fled from the library and into the night in a collective regiment.

"What was that?" Melaine asked. She held her hand pressed against the claw wounds on her shoulder and over her breast. She could feel warm blood on her hand, but she forced her trembling body to sit up. "What happened?"

Serj was staring at his lock of hair. "It didn't work." His face was blank, stunned, and very, very afraid.

"Why? What happened? What did you do?" Melaine tried to stand. She looked at Actaeon, who was still sprawled out on the floor. She stumbled to him and inspected his face. His eyelashes fluttered, but she could barely see his pulse, and his chest wasn't rising and falling as it should.

"Actaeon," she said. "No. No, hold on."

She raised the hand that wasn't staunching her wounds and focused on sending every shred of magic she carried into her palm. "Please." She had to make a lodestone, a powerful one. She couldn't let him fade. She couldn't.

Magic seeped from her marrow and through her veins, pulsing toward her hand. She concentrated hard, despite her mind and heart beating in panic against her. Pain prickled her palm, but she kept pushing. A lodestone formed, glinting and perfect.

She brought it to Actaeon's lips.

"Please, Actaeon," she said. "Here, take it. Take this. Actaeon!"

Actaeon opened his eyes. Melaine pressed the lodestone against his cracked lips. He inhaled, and her magic coursed into his body. The effects were instant. Color flourished in his cheeks, and his eyes cleared.

"Melaine," he said. His voice sounded strong. She grabbed his arm and helped him sit up.

"Actaeon."

"It's gone," he said. "It's gone from the castle. I can feel it, Melaine." Actaeon smiled, full and bright, and he laughed with joy. Melaine had never heard a sweeter sound. "It's gone. For months, I've felt tethered...like a hook driving into my skin, yanking me toward the creature, so it could consume me piece by piece. I don't feel that anymore. I've been released. I'm free."

Happiness bubbled up inside of Melaine with his every word. The strength she had always expected from the mighty Overlord flooded back as if an enormous dam had broken. She could feel his magic growing stronger in his veins, soaking up the air around him. His essence was cool and refreshing and made her toes tingle. A lesser man may have needed more time to recover his magic, but not Actaeon. He possessed so much power, it couldn't be suppressed once his cage was shattered.

He closed his eyes and took a deep breath. His skeletal hands and gaunt cheeks filled out, healthy and renewed. He seemed to be casting a healing spell from the inside of his body outward. The deep circles under his eyes lightened from bruise-purple to his normal healthy complexion, and the cracks on his lips knit back together until they were smooth and formed another refreshing smile as he opened his bright, crystal blue eyes.

He was now every inch as handsome as his visage depicted in the tattered broadsheets in Stakeside. Not only his eyes retained a flicker of ferocity; everything about him was fierce. No matter his strength, his countenance wasn't cold and daunting like on the broadsheets. He was...he was Actaeon, light and joyous and warm.

Melaine threw her arm around his neck and hugged him tightly. He wrapped his strong, warm arms around her and cradled her head under his chin, stroking her long hair and holding her as if he never wanted to let go. But Melaine grunted with pain, and though she didn't want him to release her, he stepped back and searched her face with concern. His eyes landed on her hand, soaked in blood, clutching her chest.

"Oh, Melaine," he said, his brow furrowing. He took her wrist, and with reluctance, she allowed him to remove her hand from her wound. Hot blood stained her chemise, and she swayed a little, feeling woozy.

Actaeon pressed his hand against her chest, making her gasp with pain and quiver at the intimate contact. The blood flow ceased as she felt him heal the deep slices the Sateless's claws had left. He raised his hand to her shoulder, where the skin knit together as well until all signs of the injury disappeared.

Actaeon placed both of his tender hands on her cheeks and looked at her with such devotion and gratitude, she almost wept.

"I, uh, I don't want to interrupt this beautiful moment or anything," Serj said. "But that thing is still out there. *Things.* Did you see it split? How many are there?"

Actaeon frowned and slid his hands down to her shoulders. "What is he talking about, Melaine?"

"The Sateless," Melaine said, "Serj almost trapped it in the Insight, but it didn't work. It split into pieces. It wailed and leapt out the window." She looked up at the balcony, high above their heads. "If you don't sense any of it still in the castle, then...where did it go?"

Actaeon's mouth hardened into a thin line. "I should have known that fool would spoil this." He looked at Serj, who glared back. "Tell us, expert, what would your dear Talem say? Where would the Sateless go?"

"To the largest source of magic it can find," Serj bit out. "Maybe it decided we were too much trouble, but it needs to find prey—and fast. I can't imagine it likes being ripped to pieces. Unless that'll just make it worse. What if it stays that way? What if we have to deal with more than one of those creatures? Seal them each up individually? If we can find them. Oh, gods."

"Calm down," Melaine said. "Spiraling questions aren't going to help us. Let's start with the first part. Where is the closest source of magic that would attract it?"

"The city," Karina said.

Everyone looked her way.

"It's a feast for the taking, Actaeon," she said.

The Overlord stood. He pulled Melaine to her feet with the natural strength of a healthy man.

"Then we'll go immediately," he said.

"Actaeon," Karina said with worry.

Melaine grabbed his arm, feeling a sudden lurch of dread in her belly. "If the Sateless goes straight to the city from here, then it will approach Centara from the south. That's Stakeside. It'll hit Stakeside first."

"Oh, no rush, then," Serj said. Melaine stiffened. "I doubt his lordship cares about that part of town. He hardly cares about the rest of the city's citizens."

Actaeon left Melaine's side and strode to Serj. Serj

tensed and drew back a little at Actaeon's imposing presence.

"Of course, I care," Actaeon said, staring Serj straight in the eyes from mere inches away. "I always have. You think I've failed and oppressed my people—at least I think of all of them as equals. You're satisfied supporting your father and brother's cult. Their oppression wouldn't affect you because you can't make lodestones. People like you aren't the cult's enemy. Therefore, you have no qualms with reinstating them and their atrocities. No, Serj, if you care for your little rebellion as much as you say—if you want to affirm your noble cause and watch out for *all* people of Centara, then you will be at my side on the front lines. Am I correct?"

Serj's eyes were wide, but he took a breath and stood straight.

"I will," he said, to Melaine's surprise. His assertion lacked his usual blasé smile and sarcastic tone.

"If we hurry, we can make it by dawn," Melaine said. "I don't know how fast the Sateless can travel—"

"We can get there much faster than that, Melaine," Actaeon said with grim satisfaction. "Now that I have my strength back."

"A speed spell?" Melaine said. "I saw the Insight in—"

"Better," Actaeon said. "We'll Leap."

"Leap?" Serj said, his eyes widening. "You know how to Leap?"

Actaeon sent him a dry glare.

"You've been holding out on me," Melaine said, her black eyes dancing as she watched Actaeon extend his hands for Serj and Karina. "If I'd known you could teach me to Leap..."

Actaeon chuckled. "If I taught you all of my spells, then what reason would you have to stay?"

"And you needed to keep me for my lodestones," she said, though she didn't speak with resentment.

"I have stronger reasons to want you to stay, Melaine," he said softly. Melaine's heart kicked. His smile was tentative but so tender and full of care that Melaine could have melted to the floor.

"Wild things, all of you," Karina said. "You plan to go somewhere half-way undressed?"

Melaine scoffed, but Karina ignored her. The woman flicked her slim wand in the air at Melaine and Serj. The linen of Melaine's chemise blossomed into two layers, the outer petal thickening as it formed a black silk dress and bodice with silver trim. It was loose enough to fight in. Serj's simple yellowed shirt and dirty brown trousers fluttered clean, the rips well-mended.

"Of course, that's the sort of spell you would know," Melaine said. Actaeon sent Karina a slight eye roll and smile like any son would send his mother. Karina clicked her tongue in a gentle chide and flicked her wand at him.

Actaeon's silk nightclothes billowed and transformed into his regal, black uniform that Melaine had heard tales of in whispers around barrel fires. The ensemble was similar to an overseer uniform, a jacket with square shoulders and a single, diagonal lapel across the chest, though Actaeon's lacked the white trim. His uniform had buttons down the outer sides of his trousers, but they, too, were black, rather than the white buttons of an overseer.

Melaine's favorite part of Actaeon's uniform was the sweeping, black cloak that now adorned his shoulders as a regal mantle. Every morsel of his appearance exuded power, and as he glanced down at himself, a grim smile graced his lips. His next breath was strong, and he raised his chin and stood straighter. It was clear that he finally felt like himself again for the first time in months, perhaps years.

He nodded to Karina in thanks and then extended his arm to Melaine.

"Hold onto me," he said.

Melaine felt a flutter in her heart and wrapped her arms around his waist, leaning into his chest. His heart-beat was a strong drumbeat—a war beat. He was ready to stop the Sateless and save Centara. And she would be fighting at his side.

"You sure you're strong enough for this?" Serj asked as he reluctantly took one of Actaeon's hands. Karina took the other.

"He's strong enough," Karina said. Melaine peeked at her and saw her smile with more warmth than she'd have thought the old woman could possess. Melaine squeezed Actaeon tighter.

"When we get there, no one leaves my side until we understand the situation," Actaeon commanded. Melaine nodded against his chest. *This* was the strong, unwavering voice that had led first an army, then a people. Then again, after seeing his memories, Melaine finally understood that it had once been the other way around. Before Highstrong Keep's darkness had latched onto Actaeon and his people, he had hoped only for peace in the Wilds.

Magic—a pulsing beat followed by a cold, swelling wave—surrounded Melaine. Leaping was one of the hardest forms of magic, one of the rarest known spells. The power to actually perform the feat of starting in one place and suddenly appearing in another was even rarer. And to Leap all the way from Highstrong to Centara—if that wasn't a testament to the Overlord's magnificent powers, then nothing was.

As Melaine felt the pull of Actaeon's magic, she looked beyond his arm to the surrounding library, wondering if it would disappear with a pop or dissipate like dust or wash away with the wave of magic encompassing them.

She froze as she saw the white apparition of Desiderata lying on the library floor, sprawled out on her stomach. She was staring with wide eyes at Melaine, her face a black-veined, rotting grimace of desperation. She reached out for Melaine as if with her last bit of strength. Something small was in her hand, but Melaine couldn't see what it was.

"Stone!" Desiderata rasped.

Melaine cried out, muffled against Actaeon's jacket, as the wave of his Leaping spell crashed. She felt like she was being sucked down into a whirlpool, but Actaeon stayed with her, holding her, providing an anchor to her and Karina and Serj as they flailed between a space that seemed beyond the bounds of the concrete world, beyond time, beyond anything that felt safe and comfortable and *known.*

Melaine screamed as the physical world suddenly rushed back at her. She felt like she would have been smacked five feet into the ground if Actaeon hadn't been holding her.

She heard Serj curse and stumble, but when she raised her eyes from Actaeon's chest, all she saw from Karina was the woman taking deep breaths through her nose, collected as always. The old maid had probably experienced a Leap before, possibly many times.

"It's all right," Actaeon said, peering down at Melaine. She looked up at him with a small nod.

Actaeon tightened his hold on her waist as a scream echoed through the air. They were in Stakeside. The low candles guttered in the streetlamps, and the damp cobblestones at their feet pressed cold through the soles of Melaine's boots. The buildings looked as shambled and off-kilter as always.

The people of Stakeside were running as if every one of them had just nicked a coin purse.

Thick, writhing tendrils of black smoke raced through the street, chasing the fleeing people, amassing around the slow and the weak. An old man wailed as one of the smoky masses consumed him. Melaine could barely see him through the smoke, but glimpses of his face revealed terror as the vaporous Sateless penetrated his every pore and orifice. She could almost see the Sateless's monstrous physical form through its incorporeal smoke, leeching magic from the man's body as he screamed.

"Actaeon," Melaine said, her voice hardly making it out of her throat.

"We have to get these people to safety," he said, loosening his hold on her waist so she could step back. "Serj and Karina, go and help the fallen. But leave him," he looked at the old man, whose body was twitching. "He's gone. Save those who haven't been attacked yet."

Serj's eyes were wide and terrified as he watched the old man's body go still. But then he nodded at Actaeon. He and Karina ran down the street.

"Can those two manage?" Melaine asked.

"Better than these poor souls," Actaeon said. He grabbed Melaine's arm and started running in the direction of the Stakeside Wall. She ran after him, trying to push out the screams that pulled at her to turn back.

"Wait," she said with a sudden drop in her gut. *Salma.* "I have to check on someone. I have a friend. Please."

"If your friend isn't at the wall, Karina and Serj will find them," Actaeon said. "We have the entire city to worry about."

"You may be used to making sacrifices, but I'm not," Melaine said. He stopped and scowled.

"Go, then," he said. "But be careful."

"What will you do?"

"I can feel it again," he said, wincing. "Whatever Talem's spell did...it's still attached. The Sateless craves to finish me. If I head to the palace, at least its most ravenous mass will follow me. I can trap it inside, and we'll try to seal it again. Chances are it's already heading there. Many of the most magically powerful people in Centara are within the palace grounds. These wretches are just an appetizer."

"These 'wretches' have magic, too," Melaine said. "I came from Stakeside, remember?"

"Of course, Melaine," he said with a weary sigh. "But as terrible as it is, most of the malnourished poor don't have the physical strength to make the most of their magic. If we get through this, I'll fix that. But right now, the Sateless is going to be attracted to the palace. Especially if I go there myself."

Melaine turned but stopped with one foot toward the thick of Stakeside. "Will you be all right?"

He placed his hand on her shoulder. "Go and find your friend. Meet me at the palace if you can."

Melaine gnawed the inside of her cheek and twitched her thigh in indecision. But Salma's smile and motherly glares entered her mind, and she knew what she had to do.

"Don't die before I see you again, Actaeon, you hear?"

He gave her a grim smile. "I've survived worse. Now, go."

He released her shoulder and raced for the Stakeside Wall, his majestic cloak billowing in his flight. A tendril of black smoke shot after him.

Melaine didn't have time to make sure he was all right. If he wanted to lead as many vaporous pieces of the Sateless to the palace as he could, then it seemed his plan was already working. She turned around and dashed in the opposite direction.

People were screaming everywhere. The Sateless's black masses of smoke tormented the streets, consuming victims on all sides. Melaine slowed when she saw Serj and Karina helping a crying young girl to her feet.

This was useless. There was no way they could help these people one at a time.

An image swept across her vision. Desiderata shouting an indiscernible word, slamming her staff on the ground, causing a torrent of screams from all over the ancient Highstrong Keep. The screams turned into whispers, so many whispers, sealed into the urn filled with ashes and souls of living soldiers.

Desiderata had saved all the soldiers she could from the Sateless before she'd sealed the creature away. But what kind of life had they led since, trapped in confines of clay? Melaine couldn't cast a spell like that for the citizens of Stakeside. There had to be another way.

Melaine flicked the Insight-infused vision from her mind and ran to Serj and Karina.

"Serj," she said, hoping she wasn't doing something she would regret. "You said you have a rebellion in place in the city."

Serj sent a sideways glance at Karina, whose eyes narrowed as she clutched the hand of the little girl.

"What about them?" he asked.

"Can you gather them? Ask them to help us," Melaine said. "We need more people on our side to stop the Sateless. At the very least to escort people to safety. We can't do this alone."

Serj hesitated.

"Serj!"

"All right," he said. He licked his chapped lips and glanced around. He eyed a sewer grate not far away. "Fine, I'll ask them. But I don't know how they'll respond."

"You have to try," Melaine said. "Karina, can you go with him? Make sure he doesn't sell us out while we're vulnerable?"

Karina gave a grim nod.

"No matter what, they won't hurt the girl," Serj said

with confidence. He lifted the scrawny girl into his arms, heavy tears carving tracks through her dirt-caked face. "She'll come with us."

"Good," Melaine said. "Get as many of these victims to the sewers as you can. Actaeon is drawing the Sateless to the palace, so it should follow him instead of pursuing you, especially if I go, too. Once people are safe, get as many of your group to the palace as you can, Serj, and do it as fast as you can. I'll head there soon."

He nodded and left for the sewer grate he'd been eyeing. The sewer system of Centara was large and interconnected, without the city's dividing walls to separate them. Melaine had never considered living deeper down there than the cisterns closest to the surface, but it was possible Serj and Talem's rebellious following could be huge.

Karina appraised Melaine with a shrewd expression.

"I misjudged you," she said. She turned on her heel and followed Serj to the sewers without hesitation. Serj handed her the girl and told Karina to stay inside while he wrangled survivors.

Melaine hoped her instincts were right—that Serj could be trusted and that she hadn't opened a way to put Actaeon in terrible danger. But it was a risk she had to take. For as the screams continued around her, she knew the four of them could never stop this many incorporeal pieces of the Sateless on their own.

Before she could do anything else, however, she had to make sure Salma was all right.

Salma was a survivor; there was a good chance she was already at the wall, maybe through it by now. But Melaine couldn't leave Stakeside again without knowing Salma was safe.

She barreled through the streets, heading straight for the Greasy Goat. Screams still echoed through the cold night, but they were fewer and weaker. The Sateless had gotten its fill of Lower Stakeside. Melaine hoped that Salma hadn't been one of its meals.

The cracked, painted sign of the Greasy Goat swayed in the breeze. A mass of black smoke beside it didn't wisp with the wind but hovered near the pub door with predatory stillness, as if sniffing for prey inside. Melaine skidded to a halt. The smoke twisted as if cocking its head in her direction.

Melaine darted down the back alley toward her old rented room. It was clear someone new had been renting it from Salma, based on the frayed shirt hanging out to dry and the small, dormant pipe on the steps. Melaine wondered if Salma assumed she was dead. That's what usually happened to people who disappeared from Stakeside. Where else would they be?

Melaine flattened her back against the alley wall, clutching her wand to her breast. She could feel her beating heart pulsing with the magic that coursed through the wood. She tried to quiet her breathing, though she didn't know if that would help. The Sateless might still be able to hear and smell in its current, incorporeal state. It might sense her magic alone, and that, she couldn't hide.

With stomach-turning dread, she saw the mass of black smoke appear at the end of the alleyway. At least she'd pulled it away from the pub. If Salma was inside, she might have a chance to escape. Melaine's heart pummeled her chest harder as she wondered what she would do if the Sateless discovered her. She'd run into this situation without the slightest idea of how to fight the Sateless, a massive oversight. She wished Actaeon were here; maybe he'd know. Then again, if he knew, he probably would have told her. If he knew, he'd have fought it off months ago when it first latched onto him.

That knowledge didn't give her any comfort.

She had delved into Highstrong Keep's walls as deeply as she could to discover how to seal the Sateless. The residual magic had been muddled as it seeped into her mind, but perhaps she could still dive into those murky waters and find some echo of Desiderata's wisdom. If she could just remember...tap into it....

She didn't have the luxury right now to meditate. She stayed frozen against the cold, brick wall, her side-turned eyes watching the Sateless's every move. It wisped in smoky tendrils that prodded the air like feelers of an insect as it hovered on the main street. It shifted a little closer to the alleyway.

Melaine inhaled a gasp through her nostrils and slapped a hand over her heart when a rush of footsteps barreled down the street behind the Sateless. A young man, no older than Melaine, ran straight past the black mass. The creature twisted violently in the air, turning all of its attention to its fresh prey.

"No!" Melaine yelled. She ran toward the street, but the Sateless had already latched onto the man, pursuing with shocking speed. Melaine reached the corner and looked down the street. The man was gone, and she couldn't see the Sateless either. She could only hope he had gotten away.

Melaine dashed around the building to the entrance of the pub. She tried to open the door, but it was locked fast. Melaine was familiar with Salma's locking spells, however. She laid her palm upon the iron lock and concentrated on the empty keyhole. With a stab of crackling, purple magic, she turned the lock from the other side. She pushed open the door.

"Salma!" she yelled. She looked around the empty pub. Overturned tables and chairs on their sides were scattered about. Food was strewn across the floor, weak ale leaking into the floorboards. There were a couple of dead bodies. One was bereft of magic, and Melaine could sense the empty husk from the doorway. A knife stuck out of the other one's chest, his blood pooling on the floor. Perhaps the unlucky chap had been stabbed in the chaos of pub patrons trying to escape.

"Salma," Melaine called again. She entered the pub and shut the door with a locking spell. She stepped over a fallen chair and looked around with caution. Then she paused and shuddered. A swallowing sound issued from behind the bar, a guttural, gorging, animalistic sound. A familiar sound.

She crept toward the bar. She raised her wand and peered behind the counter. Her boots crunched on shattered glass as she froze.

A woman she didn't recognize hunched over another body lying on the floor. She looked emaciated, each knob of her spine poking through her torn dress. Her hands extended like claws, grasping each arm of the prone body beneath. The woman's mouth was locked on the body's lips.

She was sucking magic from the victim the same way Actaeon had done to Melaine when he was possessed by the Sateless.

Melaine raised her wand and aimed it at the woman.

"I'm sorry," she whispered. She summoned a propulsion spell with a queasy feeling in her stomach as memories of Talem swam in her head. Then she fired a burst of magic at the feeding, Sateless-possessed woman. The magic knocked the woman off the body, sending her crashing into the bar.

"Salma!" Melaine cried as she saw who the woman had been feeding upon. She didn't have time to see if she'd killed the possessed woman or not. Salma stared at the ceiling, her face a frozen mask of fear. Then she blinked and drew a long breath, and her wide eyes found Melaine.

"Oh, my dear," she said, her throat scratchy. Melaine hurried to her side and helped her sit up. "I thought yah were a goner."

"Salma, are you all right?" Melaine asked. She glanced back at the possessed woman, but the woman lay still and glassy-eyed. Melaine suppressed her shudder of guilt.

"What is goin' on?" Salma asked. She rubbed her mouth and shivered. "There's somethin' terrorizin' the streets, Melaine. It's—it's—"

"I know," Melaine said. "Salma, come with me. I know what it is and what it wants. Stay with me, and I'll keep you safe."

"What is it then, child?" Salma asked as Melaine

helped her stand. "If yah're so sure of yourself all a sudden?"

"It's a beast that feeds on magic," Melaine said. "And I think it's heading for the palace. We have to go."

"To the palace? Then isn't that the opposite of where we want ta be?"

"I have to help the Overlord, and I'm not leaving you here to get eaten again," Melaine said with a nod at the deceased woman.

"*Help* the Overlord?"

"Yes, Salma," Melaine said. "I'll tell you everything later. But for now, we have to go!"

"I don't run as fast as I used ta, missy," Salma said, "I—"

"Oh, for goodness' sake," Melaine scowled. She grabbed Salma's arm and pulled her past fallen chairs and tables to open the front door. A weak shriek came from behind the bar. Melaine gasped as a billowing black shape rose into sight. The Sateless was leaving its victim's body.

Melaine summoned the speed spell she'd stored in her wand. The magic was a little weaker than before; the wand could only hold so much for so long. But she pushed her own magic through the shaft and cast the spell. Salma gave a disgruntled yelp when Melaine's spell pumped power into both of their legs, and Melaine took off running, yanking Salma behind her.

Buildings flew by as they raced for the Stakeside Wall. They passed by several stray victims trying to make it out alive, but they saw more fallen bodies than people walking, some with magic, some without, all dead.

CHAPTER 13

The Stakeside wall was consumed by people.

"Oh, for mercy," Salma said when she and Melaine stopped.

The wall was too tall for a single person to climb without careful footholds, but the mass of people at the gates was having no trouble—not those on the top of the writhing, wailing heap anyway. The riot's madness was fueled by panic and a thirst for survival that had been brewed and bottled in Stakeside for centuries, all being unleashed by every citizen at once. Melaine could see hands and feet sticking out from beneath the crowd against the cobblestones, their owners smashed by the sheer weight of their fellow men.

The Sateless was feeding on the easy prey. Black smoke writhed in several different spots around the gate, sucking magic from person to person. One patch of smoke, the densest mass of black among them, leapt onto a man who had one foot over the wall. He screamed and fell back onto the vying crowd. People grabbed his limbs and shoved him behind them, discarding him like a piece of garbage. He hit the street below and rolled away from the chaos.

The black smoke devoured him. He screamed until he couldn't, and then his body twitched and convulsed as the incorporeal piece of the Sateless gorged. Then, when the body was still, the Sateless's smoke seeped into his skin and through his pores and orifices. The smoke disappeared, and Melaine felt the urge to vomit when she realized who its victim was.

It was Vintor. His blue corduroy vest, which Melaine had always thought so fancy, was shredded. His white shirt was stained with mud and blood, and his matted hair was no longer sleek with pomade in his attempt to look respectable enough to appeal to his buyers outside of Stakeside.

"Couldn't even get out in death," Salma murmured. She looked back at Melaine. "So, how did yah?"

"I'll explain when this is through," Melaine said. "Assuming we're alive."

Salma nodded. "I'll hold yah ta that, Mela."

She stopped and looked at Vintor's body. His fingers were twitching, but it wasn't the after-death spasms Melaine had seen in occasional corpses on the street. These spasms were controlled, purposeful, and increasing.

"He's alive," Salma said. She started to walk toward him, but Melaine held her back.

"Wait."

Vintor lifted his head and then sat up in a smooth motion, his shoulders hunched and his face twitching as if he couldn't control his movements. As if something else was trying to get behind the reins.

"Salma, we have to go," Melaine said, tugging at the woman's sleeve. "That's not him."

A massive bang made Melaine jump and look to the wall. "Looks like they got the gate open."

"Mela," Salma said. She was pointing at Vintor, her finger shaking. Vintor crawled to his feet and looked straight at them. His eyes were the same red as the Sateless's, and as Melaine watched, his face took on the creature's same wide, ghastly grin.

"Let's go," Melaine said. Salma nodded in agreement. They dashed toward the gate, but Melaine grabbed Salma and led her past the chaotic crowd to run parallel to the wall. She stopped when they reached the butcher's yard.

"There's a way out through here," Melaine said. She scanned the ground along the wall, looking for the half-buried supply crate she'd lived in for a time as a child. "I could never get through before, but I'm strong enough now. I've learned enough."

She stopped when she saw the corner of a piece of wood sticking out of the dirt. The crate was more than halfway buried by now, but no one had bothered digging it out of the earth in the last fifteen or so years. Unnecessary labor, that was.

She squatted beside the crate and tore away scraggly plant roots and weeds that had grown over the opening. She brushed dirt and pebbles aside and peered into the crate. It was an even smaller space than she remembered. Luckily, her time being pampered in the Overlord's castle hadn't been enough to plump her up much beyond her emaciated state. She shimmied inside and looked around in the dim light from a nearby streetlamp and the growing twilight of morning. Scrawny roots pushed through cracks in the stone wall's foundations. A few insects and a massive spider scurried away from the light. Melaine shivered, but she raised her wand and aimed it at the blocked passage.

She summoned a bombardment spell and focused on a small space under a triangle of stones that looked like they would prop each other up, even if the dirt beneath them shifted. She pushed her magic to the surface of her skin and channeled it through the wand. The spell burst from her wand and hit the dirt with an explosion of dust. The dirt funneled away until Melaine saw a flash of lamplight peek through the tunnel ahead.

"All right, Salma," she called. "We can go through." She backed up and hoisted herself from the tunnel. She aimed her wand again and shoved aside more earth and cobblestones to widen the entrance of the crate for Salma's larger frame. "It's stable. I'll be right behind you."

Salma wrung her hands together, but she nodded and ducked into the crate. Melaine kept watch on the surface, breathless as she listened to the continued screams of the citizens of Stakeside. How many were dead by now? How many had fed their magic to the Sateless? How many bodies were possessed?

Was all of this chaos her fault? Hers and Serj's and Actaeon's? Did their ritual only make things worse?

"All right, child," Salma called, her voice faint. "I'm on the other side."

Melaine crawled into the hollow entrance and

squeezed through the tight tunnel. Dirt, roots, and insects pressed around her on all sides, but fortunately, the tunnel was short. She remembered how thin the Stakeside wall had seemed when she'd first passed by in the prison cart, marveling at how such a flimsy barrier presented such an unattainable obstacle to the poor residents of the slums of Centara.

Salma extended her hand when Melaine reached the end of the tunnel. Melaine squeezed it with gratitude and didn't let go when she stood safely on the other side, even though she wasn't wearing her gloves. Not since starting her life as a lodestone-peddler had she ever willingly allowed Salma the warmth of a simple handhold, but now, it felt freeing. She didn't know if it was the threat of imminent death that prompted her well of emotion or if she simply missed Salma, the one person she could rely on from childhood onward, but words came to her mouth like a pot boiling over.

"Thank you, Salma," Melaine said. "For everything."

Salma raised her eyebrows. "Nothin' ta thank me for, Mela." But Salma gave her a warm, motherly smile, and Melaine thought she saw her eyes watering.

Melaine looked down the wall toward the gate. People still vied to go through, but it was so congested by now, hardly anyone was making it out. Fewer and fewer managed to climb over the wall. And as Melaine heard horrific screams ahead, stretching far into Middun, she knew that the Sateless must have moved beyond Stakeside.

"Maybe Actaeon made it to the palace," she said. "We have to help him."

Melaine cast her speed spell, drawing upon what she could feel were the wand's last reserves, and she took off through the streets faster than a galloping horse.

Melaine wasn't used to these streets, but she could see the palace's tall pinnacles against the pink and lavender sky. When people or buildings or the fine estate walls of Crossing's Square got in the way, she would jump over them, using magic she barely knew she had. Somehow, she was also strong enough to bring Salma with her at every leap and turn.

Wisps of black smoke clustered in sporadic masses as Melaine avoided meeting the red eyes and wide, toothy smiles of countless reanimated and possessed bodies. They were all running toward the palace at nearly as fast a pace as Melaine. She didn't know what the creature's aim was—did having a physical body make it easier to feed? Could it get its own monstrous body back with enough magic consumed? Could it make *multiple* bodies? Or was its only motivation to feed, as Actaeon had said? Was taking others' bodies merely an instinctual compulsion? Did it care what form it took so long as it had magic in its belly?

Melaine turned a final street corner. The palace's wood and wrought-iron gates loomed ahead.

"Shite," Salma said over the wind of their race. Melaine felt her sentiment.

The gate was a reflection of the Stakeside wall but larger and more dangerous. A huge amount of the city's population railed at the gates, trying to get inside. Melaine slowed and ducked behind a baker's vending stall. People were crying and shouting—begging for the Overlord's protection, *blaming* the Overlord for the crisis. It was clear that no one understood what was happening, and no one cared, so long as they could get someplace safe.

Melaine scanned the crowd, looking for Serj and Karina. She didn't know if the wretches at the gate were part of Serj's rebellion or not. If they were, they weren't doing anywhere near as well as Melaine had hoped. But she saw no sign of either Serj or Karina in the chaos.

"How do we get through?" Salma asked.

Melaine racked her brain. The limestone walls were far higher than those around Stakeside. She doubted that she could jump over them or dig under them, magic or no magic. She eyed the wrought-iron gate and the elegant spires and stained glass windows of the palace. She had never been this close to the palace before, and yet she felt she knew it.

"Wait," she said. "I think I know a way."

Actaeon's boyhood memories swept into her mind. He had used a drainpipe behind the stables to escape from his father, King Vasos. It had been over twenty years, and Actaeon's modern renovations following the destruction of the war had altered the palace façade considerably, but perhaps the drain was still there.

"Over here," she told Salma as she tugged her hand. They skirted the wall, hiding in what shadows they could find as she looked for the drain. She finally heard a trickle of water, and the edge of a drainpipe came into sight. The tall pipe was blocked by iron bars. But Melaine could handle that.

She summoned the deraphant spell into her wand and

shoved the bars open. They splintered like logs and collapsed around the round perimeter of the pipe.

"I've gotta get me one of those," Salma said, eyeing Melaine's wand. Melaine smiled and ducked inside. Salma followed. They walked with slapping, wet steps. Soon, they reached the other side of the thick palace wall.

There was just as much chaos within the protective palace walls as there was outside. Actaeon's ploy must have worked. Servants darted around the courtyard, trying to get away from the violence around them. Black smoke of the divided Sateless rushed through bodies, devouring everyone in sight. The monster was as fearsome as Melaine had seen in the ancient vision of Highstrong, but this time it was worse because in the vision it had been contained in a single body. Now, at least three pieces of the incorporeal Sateless billowed through the courtyard, and more pieces inhabited corpses that latched their mouths onto those of screaming victims.

The Sateless wasn't terrorizing unchecked. Silver-armored Shields were useless, falling under the Sateless like tossed coins, but several men and women wearing blazing red cloaks with black hoods fought back.

The Overlord's Followers.

The Followers leapt and darted among the chaotic bodies of living and dead alike. Their cloaks flew like cardinals' wings as they shot spells from their wands with deadly aim and force, knocking back corpses and in many cases, blowing them to pieces.

Every walking corpse they destroyed issued a whirl of black smoke that formed an exoskeleton visage of the Sateless's physical, bestial form. One mass tried to leap at a Follower near the front doors of the palace, but he cast a translucent blue shield spell around himself to repel its attack. It kept up its onslaught, sucking the magic from the shield to weaken it. The man held his shield fast, but his true concentration wasn't on the monster but on the doors. He held his palm against one, trying to break a powerful warding spell that coated them.

Melaine recognized him as Yoson, the bulky, auburn-haired man she'd seen at Actaeon's side in Highstrong right before the war. He had fought as a Follower twenty years ago. Now, he was much older, his hair graying and his muscles weaker, but his power was still immense. He kept up the shield while his wand shot dangerous spells at any threats around him, all while still trying to break the doors' ward. Melaine flinched as he hit someone who appeared to be an innocent, caught in the crossfire between himself and a Sateless-possessed corpse.

The vaporous piece of Sateless attacking his shield must have decided it was wasting its efforts on such a difficult target. It jumped into the victim and made the corpse twitch and rise from the blood-soaked ground.

Melaine pulled on Salma's hand and ran full speed to Yoson, wand raised against any attackers, but she and Salma managed to slip through the chaos unharmed.

"Where's Actaeon?" she asked Yoson.

"What?" he said. He shot another spell at a corpse across the grounds.

"He needs me," Melaine said. She grabbed Yoson's arm. He shook her off.

"Get out of here, woman," he said in a gruff, rankled voice.

"I have to see Actaeon," Melaine said. "Is he in there?"

The Follower analyzed her with swift, sharp eyes, finally registering what she was saying. "Who are you?"

"My name is Melaine. I've been apprenticing under Actaeon at Highstrong. I know what this is"—she gestured to the chaos—"and I need to help him, Yoson. Where is he?"

Yoson hesitated a fraction but then seemed to accept her statement. Her use of both his and Actaeon's first names clearly made an impression.

"He's inside," Yoson said. "He tasked all of us with directing people to safety while sending any possessed corpse or smoke creature into the palace after him. But then they came—the fucking Luxians. They're in the palace, barred the doors. Dunno what's happening."

"Luxians?" Melaine said. "Fuck. *Serj*. I have to get in there."

"Don't we all?" Yoson said. Then he spun, his red cloak spiraling as he shot a spell at another corpse barreling toward them. The corpse flew backward and smacked into a horseless carriage that shook upon impact.

"Wait," Melaine said. She caught sight of another corpse looking their way. The Follower saw it too. He raised his wand.

"No, wait!" She grabbed Yoson's arm. "Let it come. It fed on your shield. Maybe it will feed on the warding spell on the doors."

Yoson frowned, but he gave a terse nod. "All right. It's worth a try."

Melaine nodded and pulled the petrified Salma to the side of the doors.

The corpse was facing them now, the man's body wearing the finery of an aristocrat. His smile widened to a painful degree as he took a step back, preparing to charge.

Yoson cast shield spells around all three of them, but Melaine's hopes worked. Now that there was no one blocking a path to the doors, the Sateless's focus changed. The Overlord was within the palace, and according to Actaeon, he and the creature were still attached by some aspect of Talem's spell. Despite Melaine's potent presence and the delectable meals running wild in the courtyard, the creature was desperate to finish him off, especially now that his magic had been restored.

The corpse ran straight for the doors and plowed into them, making them shudder. The corpse inhaled an enormous breath of the magical ward before rearing back again for another punch. The Sateless slammed the corpse into the door again, and Melaine stumbled as a mighty reverberation of magic rang in her bones. The corpse's body was torn and oozing coagulated blood, but it kept battering itself against the doors between deep breaths of magic. The doors shook again, and then their wood and iron buckled.

The Sateless seemed to be getting stronger with every new inhale of magic it claimed from the powerful warding spell. Much stronger. The corpse hit the doors again, and they burst open.

"Yes," Melaine said. The corpse rushed inside. Melaine released Salma's hand and tore after it.

"The throne room!" Yoson called after her from the

threshold. "Straight past the antechamber."

Melaine followed his directions, but he needn't have given them. The Sateless-possessed corpse would lead her right to Actaeon. It was already far ahead, and Melaine's speed spell had long run dry. She followed as fast as she could, running away from the screams and loud hissing from the courtyard behind. She thought she heard some from ahead of her as well.

She could hear Yoson blasting more threatening intruders in the courtyard. She glanced back once to see Salma standing at his side. She was as protected as she could be.

Melaine raced through a wide, extravagant hall that she had seen before, even if she hadn't known the fancy name for it. In Actaeon's memory of the battle for the White City, soldiers had littered the floor, coated in blood. Fine silver and gold trinkets and candelabras had been knocked over. She shuddered at the scene's echo that greeted her eyes now, but she couldn't stop to dwell.

She cried out when a man fell through a side doorway and into the hall right in front of her. He stumbled across the hall and twitched and convulsed against the opposite wall. He wore an overseer's uniform.

He crumpled against the wall, but then his spine rolled back up mid-fall. He stood on wavering legs and then turned around.

Melaine gasped. It was Overseer Scroupe, but his taunting face was no longer the decrepit, greed-filled visage Melaine had last seen. Now, his face was stretched too wide in a smile, and his eyes glowed red.

Melaine summoned her rathmor battle spell and

blasted Scroupe in the chest. Scroupe's possessed corpse shot backward and slammed to the floor. His chest sizzled with embers that clung to his now visible heart and lungs. She watched his heart's last beat as he took his final breath. Then she lifted her wand again and thrust him out of the way.

The black smoke of the Sateless seeped from his pores and through the massive hole in his chest. Melaine took off before it extricated itself, though she doubted she would find any refuge in the throne room ahead.

Four men stood guard outside a pair of dark oak and silver-gilded doors at the end of the antechamber, different from the gold and white doors from Actaeon's memory, one of many renovations more suited to his style than King Malik's. The men wore white and blue robes with the Luxian symbol embroidered across their chests. Their wands were raised against the corpse that had first burst through the palace's front doors.

"Now!" shouted one of the men. All four Luxians hurtled spells at the corpse, but it dodged two of them. One scraped the corpse's arm, and the fourth struck it in the face, smiting its wicked smile. It fell to the floor, but black smoke was already leaking from its pores.

Melaine yelled and summoned a slew of propulsion spells. She sent all four men flying and darted past the black mass of Sateless with more power and speed than she had ever thought possible of herself.

She sent a final burst of magic toward the throne room doors as she shoved her entire body weight against them. They opened, and she slammed them shut behind her.

In Actaeon's memory, the throne room's floor had been carpeted purple and the ceiling painted with lofty images of royalty. Now, Melaine stood upon pale marble, and the blank, vaulted ceiling reflected the simplicity and practicality of a secular reign.

In Actaeon's memory, the blood of his mother had flowed down the dais near the throne. Now, there was no blood, and no one sat upon the throne. Actaeon stood in front of it, a shining black wand in his hand. He faced a room filled with a host of people, all wearing blue and white Luxian robes. Two of the Luxians held Karina in their grasps with wands aimed at her throat. Serj stood freely nearby, though he wore a tense grimace. His arms were folded, and his shoulders hunched.

"What?" said an aged man who stood at the front of the Luxian force as he looked over his shoulder at Melaine. His robes were of finer quality with greater embellishments than the others of his Order, but they were old and faded like the rest, just like Talem's robes had been, and this man looked remarkably like Talem.

He was King Malik's Luxian advisor from Actaeon's memories, who had urged Malik to murder Queen Adelasia right before her son's eyes. Serj and Talem's father, Nazir.

"Melaine, leave!" said Actaeon, not taking his wand's aim from Nazir's chest.

Melaine raised her wand and summoned another propulsion spell, but the closest Luxian clapped a captivity spell around her wrists, one forceful enough to knock her wand out of her hand. A second Luxian picked her wand up off the floor with an evil grin and pointed it straight at her while two more grabbed her arms and held her with such strength she couldn't break free.

"I always knew your rule would come to chaos and ruin," said Nazir, his attention back on Actaeon.

"I should have known you couldn't be eradicated so easily, Nazir," Actaeon said grimly. "Now is not the time for a rebellion. Can't you see that?"

"You said your father was dead!" Melaine yelled at Serj across the room. He had betrayed her, and just when she'd started to trust him.

"Couldn't play all my cards, Melaine," Serj said, though he winced when he eyed his father.

"My son did his duty by leading us here," Nazir said. "A mere shadow compared with what Talem did. My eldest paved the way for *this*. This moment, Actaeon, *bastard* ruler, where I get to watch you die."

"Why only watch?" Actaeon said. "Right, that's what you're good at, isn't it? Standing aside, watching others perform the evil deeds you can't stomach yourself. That's why you sent Talem and Serj. You were too afraid to confront me."

"I'm not afraid, Actaeon," Nazir said. "I have no reason to be. The Sateless has devoured you. What was it you said, Serj?" He eyed his son. "Actaeon and that Stakeside bitch weakened your brother so much that all it took was one spell to knock him down and murder him?" He looked back at Actaeon with an evil grin. "Well, it's my turn to knock you down and seal my reign."

Melaine frowned deeper and flicked her eyes to Serj and Karina. Serj's mouth curved in a small, wry smile, and when Karina sent him a look, her sharp eyes sparked with conspiratorial approval.

"We have bigger things to worry about, Nazir," Actaeon said.

"Nothing is greater than your death," Nazir retorted. He raised his wand, magic glowing from its base to tip.

"No!" Melaine cried.

A shot of bright, white magic flew from Nazir's wand and raced to Actaeon. Actaeon watched it with calm stillness until the last second and then swept his arm out to block it. The magic deflected to the vaulted ceiling and burned a hole into the sculpted stone.

"What?" Nazir said. "But—" He flung a glare at Serj. "You said he was near death. That the Sateless weakened him! You *lied* to me!"

Serj laughed.

"No one in this room is spotless, Father," he said. "But I've realized the Overlord is the lesser of two evils."

Nazir growled. "Foolish boy!" He shot another spell at Actaeon.

The Luxians around Nazir fired more battle spells, but Actaeon deflected them all with a single sweep of his arm. He thrust out his other arm and flung no less than five men into the air. His magic pinned them against a wall and held them there, unharmed.

The remaining Luxians started casting spells in a frenzy. Nazir roared and shot powerful spell after spell. Melaine took advantage of her captors' distraction and shouldered the guards aside. Though her wrists were still bound, she managed to stretch out her fingers far enough to snag her wand from one's grasp before he could react.

She tried to run to Actaeon to help, but he raised his wand and sent her flying out of the way. She hit the ground hard, right near Karina and her guards. Serj was struggling to fight one guard off with nothing but his fists.

Actaeon's spell knocked away the captivity spell that bound Melaine's wrists. She glared at him but took his hint. She rolled over and fired two propulsion spells at each of the guards confronting Serj and Karina. They screamed as they flew backward.

"Thank you," Karina said, prim as always. Melaine found her feet.

"You told them Actaeon was still weak," she said to Serj. "You tricked them."

He nodded. "They wouldn't listen. My father and Talem never could see reason. They were too obsessed with Lux to see the reality of the people in need around them. Now Talem's dead, and my father is too power-hungry to do Centara any good. He abandoned the rest of the rebellion and came straight here. I had to stop him."

"Glad to hear it," Melaine said, but she froze when she heard a rush of pounding footsteps coming from outside the throne room doors. Several Luxians standing by the door backed up with wide eyes. The doors banged inward. The Luxians screamed as a mob of people overwhelmed them. They fell and were crushed beneath the heavy weight of Sateless-possessed corpses flooding into the room.

"Shit," Serj cursed, backing up.

"Actaeon!" Karina said. Actaeon looked her way as he tried to hold off an attacking spell from Nazir. His eyes blazed as he saw the Sateless's barrage.

Melaine started flinging corpses left and right, smacking them with propulsion spells without thought. A woman with a ghastly grin and glowing red eyes ran toward her. Melaine summoned the rathmor battle spell anew. She blasted the woman back, and the corpse fell to the floor in a smoldering heap. Smoke sizzled from her skin and hair, but thick, black smoke surged out as well. The essence of the Sateless rose into the air.

Then a riotous hissing noise overcame all sounds of battle among Luxian fanatics, Sateless-possessed corpses, and Melaine's allies. Every corpse's mouth tightened with aggression and hissed through their teeth with greed. All of their red eyes fixed on Actaeon.

Actaeon and Nazir were locked in a fierce battle. Actaeon was everything Melaine had imagined he would be—powerful and unparalleled in battle magic, firing with expert aim, dodging his opponents' fires in a more graceful dance than Melaine could ever imagine performing. He levitated and threw furniture and trappings of the throne room to shield blasts of Nazir's spells or distract a possessed corpse. But any explosive, body-rending curses he shot were aimed at the reanimated corpses. The spells he used against Nazir were nonlethal paralyzing or stunning spells like he'd used on the other Luxians. Melaine couldn't imagine he had used such restraint before when he overtook the palace from King Malik. It seemed Serj had gotten to him. Perhaps that was a good thing.

But powerful as Actaeon was, there was no way he'd be able to fight both Nazir and the now-unified attack of the Sateless at once. She had to do something.

Melaine closed her eyes, focusing on Desiderata's desperate, rotting face and the vivid but fractured memory of her last day alive when she'd sealed the Sateless away. But why had she died? Why hadn't she survived the ritual?

Stone! Desiderata's last word of warning echoed in Melaine's head.

Melaine opened her eyes. The world seemed to slow as she realized exactly what Desiderata had done, and exactly what Melaine had to do now.

"Karina," she said. "Karina, I need to go someplace secure, away from everyone. Somewhere that can be locked with no distractions. Where could that be?"

Karina's eyes shifted in quick thought. A small look of pain drew down her features. "The East Tower is close. Why?"

"Just take me there," Melaine said. "But wait. Wait till I say."

"What are you going to do?" Serj asked.

"I'm going to finish this," Melaine said. "You stay and help Actaeon."

"Melaine—"

Melaine shook her head. "Karina, which way to the tower?"

"That way," Karina said, nodding to a side door across the room. Melaine ran through the chaos, dodging spells, jumping over fallen bodies. Karina followed, and when they both stood near the exit, Melaine stopped and faced the crowded room.

She closed her eyes and concentrated. She dug deep into her marrow and felt her magic pulse through her veins. She flooded her skin until magic glowed around her as bright, violet energy.

"Karina, stay back," she said. Then she opened her eyes and called to every mass of black smoke and to each reanimated corpse in the room.

"Come to me!"

She put forth a burst of magic so powerful, the Sateless couldn't possibly resist. Its desire for Actaeon was intense, but she knew what it truly wanted. Melaine's power was irresistible, and at this moment, it was far easier to feed upon—she was *offering* it to the creature. Just as Desiderata had once done.

Every corpse dropped to the ground. Writhing black smoke filled the air, and more flew into the throne room from the outer halls. Melaine stood her ground until every tendril of vapor had collected into a single entity that swirled and tangled into the visible husk of the Sateless's grotesque body.

"Take me to the tower, Karina," she said. "It won't hurt you. It only wants me." Karina was speechless for a small moment, but then she nodded and opened the door.

"Melaine, no!" Actaeon shouted. She met his desperate, panicked blue eyes from across the room.

Nazir shot a spell straight for Actaeon's heart.

"Look out!" she cried.

Actaeon reacted just in time. He repelled the spell with one of his own. Nazir ducked out of the way. Melaine tore herself away from the sight. She rushed after Karina through the door.

The Sateless followed close behind.

CHAPTER 14

"I hope you have a sound plan, young lady," Karina shouted as they raced through the palace corridors. They reached the end of a hall and burst through a door into the bright sunlight of dawn. The east courtyard was empty. All of the chaos either thrived at the palace gates or within the palace itself.

"Just get me to the tower," Melaine said. She followed Karina across the polished flagstones until the tower came into sight.

She paused and stared, her lips parting in awe. Vines flourishing with flowers climbed up the East Tower's stone walls, shining with an enchanted luster. They encircled a large, round window paned with magnificent stained glass that depicted more flowers and birds of all colors. Crystals adorned the spired roof, sparkling and casting rainbows in the sun.

"This was where Queen Adelasia was imprisoned before she died," Karina said as they reached the door.

"Actaeon had it preserved as a memorial. Only he and I knew the reason."

Melaine's heart softened, but they didn't have time to waste admiring the tower's tranquil beauty. Karina pressed her hand against the door and pulsed magic into the wood. It opened.

"Stay out here," Melaine said. She pushed out a bracing breath and ran a hand back through her disheveled hair. She pulled hard enough to hurt her scalp before she let go. "Don't open this door, do you hear me?"

"Understood," Karina said. She stepped back and then gasped and pressed herself against the tower as the black smoke of the Sateless swarmed toward them. Melaine ran inside and stopped in the center of the tower's first floor. The Sateless flooded through the door. Its loud hiss shot like steam through her ears.

"Shut the door, Karina!" she yelled. The door slammed shut.

Sunlight shone brilliant colors all over the floor in a puzzle-piece array from the stained glass high above her head. Her black silk dress was overlaid with fractures of rainbows, the silver trim shining like dew drops. All around the circular tower, even spiraling up the staircase, tall and short candles glimmered with soft flames that banished all shadows. She had never seen anything as beautiful as this tower. She wondered if it would be the last beautiful thing she would ever see.

She forced her eyes to the horrific, writhing Sateless instead, a mass so thick, none of the light could penetrate its darkness.

"It's just you and me now," Melaine said as she stared

at the formless creature. She threw her wand to the floor, and it rattled away into a stained glass rainbow. "My magic is what you want. Are you ready?"

The Sateless's eerie hiss grew violent. The mass of black smoke coiled back as if ready to strike.

Melaine closed her eyes, pictured Desiderata in all her living, vibrant glory, and waited.

Black smoke pummeled her body with powerful, physical force as if the Sateless still retained all the muscular strength of its lost body. She gasped as a smoky echo of its claws prized her mouth open, but she overcame her instinctual resistance and squeezed tears from her eyes as she let it in. The smoke ensnared her body, and she screamed in agony as it tore through every pore of her skin and penetrated her bones, leeching her magic. She pictured Talem and Stebbon's bodies, their broken bones sucked dry of magic and marrow, their flesh cast aside because all this creature wanted was magic—pure, raw magic—and now it was taking hers.

Whether the torturous pain was physical or only magical, she let herself scream it out so she could pour all her remaining focus into what she had to do. Instead of fighting to survive the onslaught, she shoved her magic through her veins and down her wrists, ready to feed the beast from the palm of her hand. The scraping claws of the Sateless inside her body dragged along her veins as it chased the stream of magic with untamed lust.

She fell to her knees but kept pushing magic into her palms. She cupped her hands together and screamed louder as harsh, jagged crystals ripped through her skin. The Sateless shrieked, scrabbling its claws in panic through her body, but it was too late. The creature had latched onto her magic with full force, and it couldn't extricate itself from the relentless stream. She *felt* the Sateless's horror as her outpour of magic sucked it into the crystallized lodestone in her hands.

Melaine felt weaker with each passing second, but she had to finish. Desiderata had performed the spell and succeeded, so she would as well. She had to—because if she didn't, Actaeon was next, and then Karina and Serj and Salma and everyone she had come to care about. Everyone in Stakeside, in Centara...every fellow woman, man, and child in her city would succumb to the creature's endless thirst, just as the ancient warlord's army had fallen within Highstrong's walls.

Melaine bored into her marrow, to the very core from which her magic stemmed. She had never pried so deeply before, but the act felt instinctual. Desiderata had embedded the knowledge to perform the spell within the Insight that was Highstrong. Desiderata had taught Melaine what to do.

Serj's attempts to seal the Sateless inside a typical Insight hadn't worked. He'd cast an external spell upon his lock of hair to entice the creature inside, but superficial magic was not what the Sateless craved. The creature had overpowered the spell and split into pieces to hunt its true prey—raw, unfiltered magic. For a sealing ritual to work, raw magic could be the only bait, and the magic had to come from a sole source and offer no alternatives.

Melaine was now the sole source. Her raw magic would bait the creature, and her lodestone, filled with pure, biological magic, would be the Insight that held the monster imprisoned. But to completely seal the creature away, she had to pour all of her magic into the trap.

More of the sharp, jutting crystals tore through her skin as the lodestone grew larger and more powerful with the Sateless's evil presence, influencing the stone to take on a different quality than anything Melaine had ever crafted. She heard a violent hiss and suffered pain like scalding steam rushing through her body. The Sateless clawed and fought. It understood what was happening— what had happened before.

Tears burned her eyes as she pushed harder, yanking the last of the Sateless into the stone. She could feel its furious presence railing against the crystal confines. She gathered her last dregs of energy to perform one final spell.

She brought every small detail she could remember about the Sateless to the forefront of her mind—how its monstrous body had looked, how it ran crooked through the halls, how invasive it had felt to have its long feeding tube deep in her throat, how unnatural and deceptive Actaeon had appeared when possessed, how weak he became by the end. Then she sent a burst of magic and vengeful fury into the lodestone. She sealed all of her knowledge of the Sateless, including how to defeat it, into the fresh Insight.

Now no one could unleash the Sateless unless they imbibed her magic from the stone, just as Talem had found and imbibed the ancient lodestone of Desiderata. She had faith that Actaeon, Serj, and Karina would make sure that no one would ever release the Sateless again.

Melaine dropped the stone to the floor. It was over.

The Sateless was gone, wholly encased by the jagged blood-red crystal. But all of her magic was locked inside as well. Just like the old stonelady from her childhood, Melaine had given up her final lodestone.

She collapsed onto the floor. The stones were warm and colorful from the sun shining through the stained glass window overhead, painting her body with the shapes of bluebirds and cardinals and yellow roses. Melaine smiled as she closed her eyes.

The door slammed open.

"Melaine?" Actaeon said. "No. Melaine!"

She heard his footsteps rush to her, but she couldn't open her eyes. She couldn't move. Everything was fading.

"Melaine." His voice was soft, distant.

All grew silent.

Something pressed against her lips. It was hard and glossy, and she felt cool, refreshing power shining through. Then she felt a different, yet familiar warmth—a brush of her own magic.

She breathed in deep. Magic—Actaeon's exhilarating, snow-crisp magic—flooded her. With it came a burst of her own. Her hot, crackling magic spread through her lungs and pumped through her heart, sweeping through her veins like a flood. It saturated the marrow in her bones and blossomed there.

She opened her eyes. Actaeon was holding her close, watching her with anxious, pleading eyes.

"Melaine," he said.

Melaine frowned. "You...you made me a lodestone."

"Of course, I did," he said. He swept the hair from her eyes. "I still had some of your magic in me, Melaine. From all the stones you made me. The least I can do is repay you."

A wry smile touched the corner of his mouth, but his eyes were busy inspecting her for harm. Since his expression lacked disgust and horror, she assumed the torture the Sateless had wreaked upon her body had only been a magical sensation rather than a physical rending of flesh and bone.

"I never thought you would degrade yourself like that," she said, her voice shaking between shallow breaths. "Before I met you. I never imagined you could make lodestones." She glanced about the beautiful tower, the Sateless's evil presence no longer desecrating Queen Adelasia's memorial. "That's why Serj's father wanted your mother dead, isn't it? She could make lodestones, too. She wanted to protect you because she knew you might be able to make them as well. The Luxians would have killed you had they known."

Sadness weighed upon Actaeon's face. He looked up at the stained glass window.

"She died needlessly," he said. "But the Luxians will never persecute anyone again. I swear it. People like you and I don't need to fear." He squeezed her hand, sending warmth through her heart. "And thanks to you, we needn't fear the Sateless."

"It's gone? Did it work?"

Actaeon nodded. "It worked. It's gone. You saved us, Melaine. Though I might execute you for trying to sacrifice yourself."

Melaine huffed a laugh as she tried to sit up. Actaeon

helped her but kept his arm around her back and shoulders.

"Nazir?" Melaine asked.

"Under custody. Turns out a few of my Followers still have a little spark left in them. They came to help so I could find you. They're managing the chaos as well, making sure everyone at the gates is safe."

Melaine smiled. "So, you do still need Followers."

He laughed. "I'm still not letting you be one, Melaine."

"Why is that?"

"You deserve a much higher role."

Melaine's cheeks flushed as she looked into his joyful and vibrant blue eyes. She searched his face, her lips parting as her long-restrained yearning for him flooded into an uncontrollable downpour of need. She reached up and caressed his cheek with a trembling hand. He leaned into her touch, and there was no fighting it anymore. She took a chance and kissed him.

Actaeon inhaled in surprise but then deepened the kiss with fierce passion as if he had long restrained himself from embracing her as his own. She felt wanted and cherished in his strong arms, which, even when no longer frail, still possessed a gentleness she'd never known.

He ended their kiss sooner than she would have liked and looked into her eyes with tender care and shining hope.

"Come," he said, squeezing her hand. "You need rest, and then we'll discuss the future."

"Our future?" she asked, feeling breathless.

He smiled. "That, and much more."

🜚

"NEVER THOUGHT I'D SEE THE DAY," SALMA SAID AS SHE positioned her wide backside into the deep cushion of an armchair in a lush common area of the palace. Her face sagged with exhaustion, but her eyes glowed with wonder as she looked about.

Melaine slumped down in an opposite chair. She and Salma had spent the past day and night assisting the public. People needed comfort from the chaos, and others needed food, shelter, healing, and pine boxes for their loved ones.

Melaine had never been filled with such purpose. Her care for Actaeon, Serj, Karina, and of course, Salma, seemed to be overflowing into the entire population of Centara. Now that she didn't have to worry about pure survival, she had the luxury of being kind and generous. She felt like an inherent, inner kindness had always been inside of her and could finally breathe.

"So, it's really true, Mela?" Salma said. "The Overlord didn't kill Queen Adelasia all those years ago?"

Melaine nodded. "He was trying to save her. High-strong Keep influenced him and his army before he took the White City. It was an Insight, filled with ancient, dark magic. Its influence on him and his people caused them to become more ruthless than they otherwise would have been. But Actaeon's intentions were always for good."

"Yah've gotten close ta him," Salma said, with a

knowing gleam in her eye. "I suppose yah won't be comin' back ta Stakeside."

"Neither will you," Melaine said, not taking Salma's bait for information on her relationship to Actaeon. Melaine wasn't even sure what their relationship was. She hadn't seen him since they had defeated the Sateless. Since their one kiss.

"What makes yah say that?" Salma asked. "I've got a pub ta run."

"You can get a better one," Melaine said. "I can make sure you get the best location there is."

"Yah insultin' my place again?" Salma said.

"I just thought—"

"I belong at the Greasy Goat, Mela," Salma said. "It's my home, and I plan ta stay."

Melaine sighed. "Fine. Then we'll make Stakeside better. People deserve better."

"I thought only *you* deserved better," Salma said. "Gettin' outta Stakeside no matter the cost, eh?"

"No one should have to pay so high a cost, Salma," Melaine said. "That was Actaeon's first goal, and it's one I want to see through. I wanted to be a Follower for all the wrong reasons. Now I know I can be one for all the right ones."

"Ah, and there's the woman I always thought yah could be," Salma said. She rested her interlocked hands on her belly and leaned back in her chair with a content smile.

Melaine looked up as footsteps turned the corner into the room.

"Melaine," said Serj as he approached. She still wasn't used to seeing him so well-groomed. Not only were his clothes fresh and clean, with a fine maroon jacket and vest with gold buttons, but his face was shaven, and his hair was less matted and blonder, now that it wasn't caked in dirt. "Actaeon wants to see us."

Melaine stood at once and smoothed her violet, poplin gown. "I'll see you soon, Salma."

"Oh, yes. Far be it from me ta interfere wit your meeting wit the mighty Overlord," Salma said with a cheeky wink. Melaine rolled her eyes and followed Serj toward the eastern wing of the palace.

"How did your talks with the rebels go?" Melaine asked. "Do they believe you about the Overlord not being the true villain they thought?"

"They're coming around, I think," he answered. "It helps that I'm not one to sing his praises. Makes me more believable if I speak of his faults as well as his redeemable traits."

"And what does Actaeon think of that approach?"

"Dunno yet," Serj said with a one-shouldered shrug. "Haven't seen him."

Serj stopped their walk at a single wooden door carved with elegant scrollwork. He opened it a crack.

"You did all you could, Actaeon," Karina said from within. She and Actaeon stood side by side on a balcony that overlooked Centara.

"With the Sateless, perhaps," Actaeon said. "But it was my inadequacy as a ruler...as a man...that led to its release. Serj was right. Even Talem was, in his twisted, religious way. I've caused so much misery. I never accomplished what I set out to do."

"Don't be so hard on yourself," Karina said, placing a

maternal hand on his cheek. "You've accomplished more in your mere thirty-eight years than most men do in a lifetime, and you're growing wiser with all this. I believe you're making the right decision. Your mother would have been proud, Actaeon."

Serj cleared his throat. Melaine caught a flicker of residual anguish on Actaeon's face as he turned around, but he smoothed his features in an instant.

"I'm glad you're here," Actaeon said. "We have much to discuss before I address the people."

"Where have you been?" Melaine asked.

"I've been spending time with my overseers," he said darkly. "It seems there are a select few who have not been tainted, either by power or the Luxian Order. They'll continue to function in the reform in some capacity."

"And the rest?" Melaine asked.

"Imprisoned," Actaeon said. "As to their final sentencing...I leave that up to you."

"What?" Melaine said.

"As has been proven, my strengths lie in the study of magic and, unfortunately, war," Actaeon said. "Not in governing. But, Serj knows about the needs and the current organization of people who are ready to make an active change. And you, Melaine, you know what life is like for the poorest citizens. If we can improve their lives, then I'll feel like my reign has been worth something. But the people's trust in me is broken. They need someone new to lead them. I trust you, Melaine. I give it to you. If you want it."

Serj huffed a laugh. Melaine shot him a quick glare,

almost out of habit as she tried to process what Actaeon had said.

Actaeon stepped forward and took her hands. She wasn't wearing her gloves, and his hands felt warm and smooth.

"You are resourceful, courageous, and caring," he said. His eyes were soft, and his voice held unwavering assurance. "You have all the traits to be an excellent leader. Centara needs a change. I had the charisma to rally an army, but I lack the diplomatic skills necessary to lead or to reopen trade with other kingdoms to repair our economy. You have skills as a negotiator, do you not?"

"What, from selling lodestones?" Melaine asked with a critical frown.

"Of course. You put everything you had into your business. A necessity, yes, but so is our trading with other kingdoms now. I closed us off for fear of corruption. I was afraid. You aren't."

"What do you plan to do?" Melaine asked. "If I accept this mad proposition?"

"Anything you ask," Actaeon said, giving both of her hands a firm squeeze. "I can offer my aid, or I can stand aside, whichever you deem necessary for the welfare of Dramore. I am at your disposal, Melaine."

"I told you I could convince the people to follow you," Serj said. "Time to live up to my word, eh?"

Melaine frowned and looked at the floor, past the warm sight of Actaeon's hands locked with hers. She had wanted nothing but power and status her entire life, but now that the ultimate form of power was offered to her, she suddenly felt inadequate. All of her flaws crept into her head—her past willingness to ignore others' pain to better herself, her naiveté about the true horrors of battle and war. But Highstrong, Desiderata, the Sateless, Actaeon, they had all changed her. Actaeon's observations were right, to a degree. Perhaps she could lead others to understand the truths she had found.

Actaeon's deep remorse for his actions and care for his people showed that he still held the wisdom to lead, despite his self-deprecation. And Serj, who could be too idealistic about peace, was now accepting the realities of the past and present with determination and courage to face them head-on. He had spurned what his father and brother had done for the Luxian Order and wanted no part of their beliefs.

And Karina, strict and critical of Melaine and overly protective of Actaeon, held genuine warmth and love for him. She had sacrificed what could have been a normal, peaceful life to dedicate herself to his cause. She had been his surrogate mother; that was clear.

Melaine lifted her gaze to the three of them.

"Serj was right before, what he told Nazir," she said. "None of us are spotless. But we do each have something to offer our kingdom. Even Karina balances us out." She sent the woman a smirk that nonetheless held genuine gratitude. Karina pursed her lips but looked pleased. "We'll do it together. All four of us. We'll rule Centara, all of Dramore, together. If we could tackle the Sateless and handle an ancient curse, then we can handle this, right?"

"I should hope so," Actaeon said. There was soft admiration in his eyes.

"Right then," Melaine said, nodding to herself to

solidify the unbelievable idea of ruling a kingdom in her head. But then came another troubling thought, one that hadn't left her mind nor her pocket since the day before.

She released Actaeon's hands and fished in her pocket for the lodestone she had made—the lodestone that contained the Sateless. She could still feel the creature railing inside the crystal walls, furiously scrabbling to get out.

"First, we should discuss this," she said. She started to hold out the stone to the group but pulled back at the last second, holding it close to her breast instead.

"Can't we destroy it?" Serj asked as he took a step back.

"Not without releasing it," Melaine said. "The only way to destroy a lodestone is for the magic to be used. Talem had used Desiderata's lodestone to release the Sateless."

A low hiss issued from the jagged, red crystal.

"I've heard rumors about a way to destroy lodestones," Actaeon said. "Rumors about the Wilds. I took the initiative to research those lands heavily before the war. I was planning on leading my people there to establish a kingdom, after all."

"Are you suggesting we go into the Wilds?" Serj asked with a tone of incredulity.

"Perhaps," Actaeon said. "Until then, we'll lock the stone away. Now that I know it exists, I can place stronger wards around Highstrong Keep. Between my spells and Desiderata's lingering enchantments, we should be able to keep it secure."

"And if it ever escapes again?" Serj asked.

"Let us hope that day never comes," Actaeon said, clenching his fists at his sides and stiffening as if fighting a shudder.

Melaine closed her fist around the stone. The low hiss of the Sateless sounded again from within its prison, but the others didn't react. Had she been the only one to hear it? She shouldn't be tied to her magic inside the stone, but somehow, she felt a lingering connection to it in a way she had never felt with any lodestone before.

She placed the lodestone in her pocket. One of its jagged edges pierced her palm, but she continued to squeeze it despite the hot blood she felt oozing from her skin.

She looked at Centara from her place on the palace balcony. She approached the intricate, wrought-iron railing and extended her gaze farther, beyond the city walls, beyond the farmlands, and beyond the tangled forest. She raised her eyes to see the shadowed spot on a cliff that was Highstrong Keep.

"No," she said. "We'll keep it here. Perhaps Desiderata and Eylul's army can finally rest, knowing the Sateless is sealed once more, far away from them. And so can we."

"Not if we're running Centara and Dramore," Actaeon said. "I intend to stay very occupied with governing this time around."

Melaine smiled. "I suppose that's true." The people's protection and safety fell to the four of them now.

The lodestone bit into her palm again with another hiss that seemed to sizzle into her skin and simmer underneath. The stone would serve as a reminder of the dangers in the world. It would be a reminder of what Melaine had faced and overcome.

They couldn't destroy it. She had to keep it safe.

She dropped her eyes from Highstrong and gazed out at the city again. Her city. Her people.

She squeezed the sharp, piercing, scrabbling lodestone in one hand and took Actaeon's in her other.

"Ours," she whispered.

THE END

THANK YOU FOR READING

Please consider leaving a review so other readers like you can find this title.

ABOUT THE AUTHOR

Katherine Forrister is an author of speculative fiction who loves to explore the realms of fantasy, horror, science, history, and romance. *Lodestone* is her debut novel.

She lives near Kansas City with her family, where she enjoys local festivals and conventions, hiking, gaming, and curling up on the sofa to read on cold winter nights.

ABOUT THE PUBLISHER

GenZ Publishing is on a mission to bring new authors to the world. We emphasize new, emerging, young and underrepresented authors. We're a traditional, indie publisher that focuses on mentoring authors through each step of the publishing process and beyond: editing, writing sequels, cover design, marketing, PR, and even getting agented for future works. We love to see our authors succeed both with the books they publish with us and with their other publications. That's why we call it the "GenZ Family."

For more information, visit Genzpublishing.org or contact us at info@genzpublishing.org. Connect with us on Instagram, Facebook, Twitter, and LinkedIn for our latest news and releases.